The Adventures of Elizabeth Stanton
Series

Volume 11 The Second Crusade

Vic Broquard

Published by:
Broquard eBooks
http://Broquard-eBooks.com
author@Broquard-eBooks.com
103 Timberlane
East Peoria, IL 61611

Artwork by Crooked Willow Studios

For Morgan and L. Ron Hubbard

Table of Contents

Chapter 1 Prelude

It's June 1, 780. For twenty-three years now, peace has prevailed across Tarra. Honestly, I have truly enjoyed life this past score of years. It has been wonderful, but now I may regret my non-constant vigilance, my forgetting the affairs of other countries and peoples. I hope the price that I must pay will not be too steep this time. As usual, I am getting ahead of myself once more. Let me begin by bringing you up to date with our lives.

My name is Elizabeth Lilly Bartiana now; my friends call me Bethany. I am thirty-four with light brown hair that falls to my waist. Everyone says my light blue eyes are charming, particularly my loving husband, Renzo. Yes, Renzo, who used to be Dita, and I have been happily married for twenty years. We have been blessed with three wonderful children, now nearly grown up. Since they are going to play a role in the coming events, I should fully brief you. Our three children are Rosa, seventeen and married two years, Marco, fifteen and married one year, and Nico, fourteen and just married.

So many are playing a pivotal role, I should introduce you to all them. Our closest friends are Kallisto Ann and Len Bartiana, who are thirty-four. In their most recent past lives, Kallisto was Kali and Len was Ilenakova. Those two are properly and happily married for twenty years as well. Their children are Natale, who is seventeen and married two years, and the twins, Rosina and Pietro, fifteen. Rosina married our son Marco.

Enyo and Alex Angela are with us as well, but they still are running two bodies at the same time. Their older bodies are Dianna Anka West Po and Ania Anka; they are married too. Here it gets a bit confusing. Since Enyo and Dianna are the same beings as is Alex and Ania, they have a double marriage. That is, Dianna and Ania are a couple, while Enyo and Alex are too. It gets stranger, since Alex-Ania answered the desires of Dianna and Ania to have some children. Dianna has a son Dante, now seventeen and married to Kallisto's Natale. Ania has a daughter, Enrica, who is seventeen and married as well to the son of Ania's adopted daughter, Elena, who married Herbert Smythe. They had two sons, Phillipe, who is seventeen and married to Enrica, and Nicolo, who is fifteen. Enyo and Alex have three children of their own. Gavina is seventeen and married to our Rosa, Luigi, who is fifteen, and Isabella, who is fourteen and married to our Nico. The three young bachelors of ours, Nicolo, Pietro, and Luigi, are known as the three mischief-makers around our estate, 42 Hampton Way, Velona, Velona Sea Princes.

Yes, our children have been smitten by cupid close to home. Our parents and the children's grandparents are still living with us as well. Luisa and Enrico Angela and Sandra and Arturo Bartiana are in their mid-fifties.

Yes, they are still our four Forze Segrete members, who are charged with protecting our disparate group. Yet this is not all of us.

Renzo-Dita's adopted daughter, Lady Bianca, is now thirty-nine and married to Louis d'Grange, monarch of Fortress d'Grange, Sea Prince. Yes, he has ascended to the throne of his father and Bianca is now Lady Bianca. They have also built a wonderful ranch home in the extreme northeastern part of Velona, north of Alta and some fifty miles east of Fortress d'Grange. They have two children, Leroy, who is sixteen and dating, and Celeste, who is fourteen. They frequently spend time at their ranch and so do we all as well.

My little girl from last lifetime, my adopted daughter, Alessa has married her inventor beau, Arsenio Bartolo. Both are thirty-eight now and have three children. Danielle is sixteen and is dating; Emile is fifteen; and Juliane is fourteen and also dating. Dianna's adopted daughter is Cosima, who is now forty and married to Gerardo West Po. They have two children, Adrien, who is sixteen and recently married, and Justine, who is fifteen and dating.

Don't worry; it gets even more confusing. Bale West Po, who used to be the monarch of Velona and his wife have passed away. His eldest son, Adolfo West Po is now our monarch and is forty-seven. He and his wife, Marion, have three children. Felix is sixteen and dating Justine — that's Cosima's daughter, and twins Jules and Adriana, both fifteen. Adriana is dating Leroy d'Grange, Bianca's son. Jules is dating Danielle, Alessa's daughter.

Wait. There's more. Lona Benz West Po, Velona's High Priestess and co-monarch, has retired. She's sixty-eight and her husband has already passed away. They have three children: Daria, Luciana, and Marchella. Daria is forty-six and is now Velona's High Priestess, married to Fredio Bola. They have two children, Elaina, who is sixteen and married to Adrian, Cosima's son, and Gervaise, who is fifteen and dating Juliane, Alessa's youngest daughter. While there are other children of the West Po extended clan about, they do not figure into this incredible mixture of relationships. It's hard enough to keep track of all of us as it is!

To summarize the vital facts: Louis d'Grange is the monarch of Fortress d'Grange with Lady Bianca at his side. Adolfo West Po is the monarch of Velona, while Daria Bola West Po is Velona's High Priestess. Gerardo and Cosima also are vital in the running of Velona. Gerardo is their Elder Secretary of State, while Cosima is Chief Detective Inspector of Velona. Alessa, her constant bodyguard, is a Detective Inspector now. Only Chief Inspector Basilio West Po, Bale's youngest son, has more authority that Cosima, as well as Adolfo, of course.

There simply are not enough words to describe the incredible role that the DAE Enterprises is playing in Velona. Dianna, Arsenio, and Enyo formed this engineering and invention company back in 758. They are responsible for the fantastic new inventions and modernizations that have so revolutionized and mechanized our world these past twenty years! Yes, Enyo and Dianna are the same spiritual being, as is Alex and Ania. Both have worked out their ideal way of running and controlling two bodies at the same time. Dianna and Ania work days, while they use their Enyo and Alex bodies all night long. This literally doubled Dianna's productivity! Between Dianna and Arsenio, many incredible advancements have been made. Ania handles the company's security, public relations, and negotiations, of which the latter are now taking all of her daytime hours!

First, the steam-powered trains that she developed have become the norm. The Med Express has just made its inaugural run between Fortress d'Grange all the way across the Sea Princes to Zargarb! This passenger train covers the entire distance in three days! Normally, the single rail line is used by six-wheeled engines pulling vast loads of cargo, both raw materials, such as coal and various ores, as well as finished goods. The line also extends into Calgary, Greenway, from where huge loads of grain are shipped each fall. This ever-expanding rail line is the talk of the world and has brought a great prosperity to all.

Arsenio's clock invention plus his use of the Holy Rose Church as the origin point for longitude has revolutionized ocean-going navigation. Now any navigator can tell their precise position at sea, well precise within say twenty miles or so. Incredible. His invention of the metal steamship has also worked out. Velona has four of these new steam powered metal ships on line. Already they have repaid their exorbitant construction costs, because they have shortened sailing times between ports by as much as fifty percent! Many countries are now negotiating with Ania for rights to build such ships. The royalties from this invention alone may net the company millions!

Yet, Arsenio has gone even further. He's adapted Dianna's steam engines to drive generators to create electricity! It seems every day he comes up with a new use for this new source of power. Right now, Velona, the city, has replaced all its streetlights with new electrical lights, darn amazing in itself. However, he also has his electrical signaling system operational. It is called the LDCS, the long distance communication system, which sends electrical pulses down a wire beside the rail lines. Communication is via his Arsenio Code, a series of long and short pulses of sound. Now we can send a wire message to Zargarb in minutes. Suddenly, the world is shrinking! Again, many countries are negotiating with Ania for rights to make use of Arsenio's invention.

Dianna, on the other hand, put her stream engine principle to use in the manufacturing industry. She's adapted it for mass production of cloth. Velona now produces more cotton bolts and linen bolts than all the rest of the world combined! Now, she's trying to see if it can be applied to the mass production of steel, something that is now in tremendous demand. The waiting time for a new train engine is well over two years and a metal ship is more like five. She has also created a variation of her engine that enables rapid printing of books. Now all kinds of books are being mass-produced and distributed worldwide.

The result of all this is that Velona and neighboring Barcella and d'Grange are now the three most modernized, mechanized countries in the world. Velona's population has swelled to three million while Barcella's is at one million and d'Grange has two hundred thousand. Actually, d'Grange is mostly a mountainous country and very small at that. Their big industry is coal and ores, especially gold.

The geography of Tarra plays an important role in these coming events. Here in the northern hemisphere, the continent is shaped like an enormous dog bone. The center narrow area is the Desert of Desolation, where no living thing can be found. On either side of this enormous desert are two impassable mountain ranges. The Med Sea divides the western lobe. Along the northern coast of the Med are the Eight Sea Prince Sectors or countries. All across the northern part of the Sea Princes is the Appian Way, a tall mountain range. Velona sits at the mouth of the Med Sea. Fortress d'Grange lies immediately north of Velona. Going eastward from Velona are the sectors of Barcella, Vito, Bonito, Pieta, Solamina, and Zargarb. To the east of Zargarb here at the eastern end of the Med Sea is the desert region known as Juda Arad. Above the Appian Way are the fertile farmlands of the Greenway and its twelve kingdoms. East of them is the Northern Steppes, where nomadic horsemen live. A range of mountains separates them from the cold lands of the Axemen of Volksholm.

The entire southern half is called the Southlands. Right below the Desert of Desolation is the giant island of Megalos. The eastern lobe of the dog bone continent is Tashien, a land of yellow-skinned people, very densely populated. Further east across miles of ocean is the island nation of Dorota. Here is where the Guardian now dwells and where he is working on freeing spiritual beings.

In the southern hemisphere lies a long oval continent. Demokritos occupies the western third. Vladimir lies in the middle, home of warlike horsemen. The highly civilized country of Annelise occupies the eastern third of that continent. A pair of impassible mountain ranges separates these three countries. Yet another continent lies far to the west and is largely unexplored.

Finally, just a few miles off shore of d'Grange and a bit north, or just west of Calgary, is the large island of West Reach or Cymry as the locals call their island. This story begins on West Reach. Frankly, it had me baffled at first.

We were just sitting down to lunch with our extended families, when someone knocked on our front door. "I'll get it mom," Nico said, jumping up and growing excited. "It's probably Isabella." She was his fiancé and the fourteen year old daughter of Enyo and Alex. She'd gone to the DAE

Enterprises earlier this morning to help her mom with something.

Nico returned solemn faced, leading a messenger from the Holy Rose Church. "Excuse me, I've a message for Bethany Bartiana," the young woman said. I didn't know her name. I'd only seen her around our church, where I often went just to hear my organi play. Yes, I donated my fancy pipe instrument from Tashien to the Church of the Holy Rose so everyone could hear its incredible sounds. In that vast holy chamber, the low resonating notes were more like felt than heard, but I digress.

"I'm Bethany. What can I do for you?"

"Lady Bethany, High Priestess Daria requests your presence as soon as you can come. She says that it is most mysterious and that you may be able to shed some light on it."

"On what?"

"I'm sorry, I don't know. She only told me to give you this message," the young woman looked slightly perplexed and ill at ease. I could understand why. Why didn't Daria just didn't tell me what she wanted?

"Okay, tell her that I'll be along as soon as I eat lunch." She smiled, nodded, and left. Nico politely followed her to the door and was rewarded with a kiss from Isabella, who arrived just as the young woman left.

"Who's that?" she asked, tossing her purse on the hall desk along with her light cloak. She had her mom's eyes and curly brown hair. Yet, there was always a tinge of mischief in her greenish eyes as well. Isabella wore the now traditional day dress seen nearly everywhere in Velona among the fashionable women. Indeed, here in 780, the latest fashion dictated that one wear traditional Annelise outfits: tight, restricting corsets, many undergarments, an enormous hoop skirt, and an elegant overskirt that billowed out some six feet before one's feet. Topping it off, we had to wear the extremely high heels of the Annelise as well! Yes, women now compared their waist sizes to one and other, either overtly or covertly. Isabella was quite proud of her fifteen-inch waist. She took Nico's arm for support and slowly glided into the dining room.

"Hi all," Isabella gaily said as she entered. "What was that all about?"

"Just a goofy message from Daria," Pietro teased her in his boyish manner. His compatriots in mischief, Nicolo and Luigi, snickered, amused with Pietro's rendering of the message. Pietro is Kallisto and Len's boy, Luigi is Enyo and Alex's boy, and Nicolo is Elena and Herbert's boy, who is nearly always to be found hanging around our place and not his home.

Isabella wrinkled her nose up as though she'd just smelled something awful. "Honestly, Pietro, you three ought to grow up!" She sat down, as Nico slid her chair politely up for her. She gave him a loving smile in return. Nico was a year younger than the other three boys were, but he acted far more mature; he was married to a beautiful woman now and the other three were not. This, he thought, made him far more mature and important.

A frowning Kallisto said, "Pietro, for the last time, behave yourself or you three can take your meals in the kitchen with our cook!" She was intolerant of her son's behavior of late and wished that he'd get some sense and settle down as Natale and Rosina had.

Once lunch was over, I rose to leave. As usual, I wore my yellow day dress. After having three children, I discovered a fine use for these tight corsets. I still retained my youthful shape, well mostly. While many others continued to wear tighter and tighter corsets to gain smaller waists as was the fashion now, I kept mine at a comfortable twenty inches, refusing all attempts by my friends to wear tighter ones. I was uncomfortable enough as it is.

I will give Alex some credit. As Alexia, she had made copies of the Grey Creatures fabulous high-heeled boots; Alexia Heels, they were called. Now that the even higher heels of the Annelise had become popular, she had gone ahead and invented a more practical copy. These were widely popular in Velona, replacing the more fragile ones imported from Annelise. Hers were built with a metal shank and heel, all in one unit. Since the balls of our feet now took the beating, her Alexia Boots had very heavy padding, making hers wearable without too much foot discomfort and pain. Of course, this ensured her already long lasting and popular shoe company even greater longevity.

Still, we women wearing them greatly appreciated an arm for support while we walked. Renzo took my arm, as I got up to go to the Church of the Holy Rose. "Mom, can we come too?" asked Nico. I shook my head no.

He smiled and whisked Isabella off to the living room, while I slowly headed for the door. Len and Kallisto, however, followed us. "We're coming too. Never know when you are going to need protection," Len commented. Indeed, Len continued right where Ilenakova had left off last lifetime. She-he was a Protector and still heavily into the combat arts.

"Yes, but I drive," Renzo teased him. Len made a crushed look with his face and Kallisto and I chuckled. Our heels clicking in unison, we walked across our paved walk to the stables. While she, in her billowing green dress, and I watched, the two men hitched up our carriage. Soon, we were moving through the crowded streets of Velona.

Within a few minutes, the huge gothic cathedral complex known as the Church of the Holy Rose could be seen out of our window. Not too far from it the Church of Jehosanity rose, attempting to outdo in grandeur our Holy Rose complex. Yes, I admit that they had spent at least three times the amount of money in its construction than we had in our church. Still, we all loved our church and wanted nothing to do with the despicable Church of Jehosanity.

Our heels tapped in unison once more, as we traversed the long hallway to Daria's Office. After knocking, Daria herself opened the door. The relief on her face told me at once that she was very glad to see us. "Oh thank you, Bethany, for coming on such short notice! Please come in. I want you to meet Father Amos Pitt. Father, this is Mrs. Bethany Bartiana, Mr. Renzo Bartiana, Mrs. Kallisto Bartiana, and Mr. Len Bartiana. They are the ones that I've been telling you about. Gang, this is Father Amos Pitt of the Church of the Blessed Holy Mother of Nuadilan, West Reach. He's come all this way to tell us about the strangest thing and to ask our assistance. Father, why don't you tell them all that you've told me?"

We sat down and got a good look at this priest. He was fifty-five, streaks of grey added to his fiery red hair. His countenance was exceedingly serious. Actually, I was a little taken aback by the very mention of the name of that church and its location. I'd forgotten all about those lifetimes on that island — that was almost two hundred years ago!

"Well, yes, I suppose I must. Honestly, this is incredibly strange. We just don't know what to make of it at all. I suppose none of this will make any real sense unless I begin at the beginning. It all began over two centuries ago in Juda Arad, where the Son of God, of Lord Jehosa, Jes Amir was born. He was the Great Messiah and possessed great godly powers, as the Son of God on Tarra ought. His wife, Bethany Madelyn Amir, was also a great healer in her own right. When the Centurions slew our Lord on their cross, she fled the Arad, bringing her family here to Cymry, that is West Reach. She settled in Nuadilan and spent time also in the neighboring towns of Amathon, Bedwyn, and Brea."

"There, she worked great healing on the sick and injured and was revered by all her people. When she died, many began to worship her as the Blessed Holy Mother. Over the years, worship of the Blessed Holy Mother spread far and wide. Why, there are even her churches in Velona, d'Grange, and Calgary as well. Yet, the Church of Jehosanity has ever sought to condemn her as a prostitute. Despite all their attempts to wipe us out, we are still here, though admittedly, ours has now become a minority religion. It is with a sad heart that I must say that the Pope's Church of Jehosanity now dominates in West Reach."

All this brought back memories I'd long forgotten! Since I was Bethany Madelyn Amir, from the beginning I disliked them for both worshiping me and building churches in my name and spirit. I thought that incredibly foolish.

He continued, "Now a month ago, the Church of the Blessed Holy Mother in Nuadilan was broken into and the bones of our Holy Mother, Bethany Madelyn Amir, were stolen!"

"What?" I exclaimed. Memories of that lifetime returned to me solidly. I had fled my home in Nuadilan because a Grey Creature was after me. He eventually caught up to me and blasted my body. I died in the ocean. My body was lost there. I had no bones to be buried that I knew of anyway. What was he talking about?

"Yes, her Blessed Sarcophagus was pried open and her bones stolen. This happened a month ago now."

"But I thought that she vanished mysteriously," I protested, though not wanting to come straight out and tell him those bones could not have been mine.

"Oh yes, she did vanish very mysteriously. Yet, the priests back in those days continued to search for her remains relentlessly. Some took a Holy Vow to spend their lives searching for her! This was in 603. Several years later, King Diget I came to West Reach on his own Holy Quest for the remains of our Blessed Holy Mother. It is said that he found her body in the seas off Tewdwr, near a village called Cuch Glyn. It was he who brought them back to Nuadilan and had our Holy Blessed Sarcophagus built with her effigy carved upon its lid. With a great ceremony, her bones were finally laid to rest in the church that she helped found, among her own people, those whom she befriended all her life."

"Now, they are gone, stolen! Please, we must have them back! Can you help us?" he pleaded with us. I was not exactly sure why he'd come to us. That made no sense to me at all. There had to be more to all this. There was.

"Have you no clues at all?" I asked lamely. "Was anyone, any strangers, around before the time of the theft asking about the bones?" I wished that Cosima were here and for a fleeting moment thought of taking a break and sending for her. She was the Chief Detective Inspector.

"Well, actually there was. About a week before, two strangers came to our church asking about her and our long history. He was definitely from Juda Arad — you can tell by the full beard and his accent. He called himself Messiah Bani el Marina and his wife, Tamina. They claimed to be researching their ancient family roots, which they claimed might have come from Jes and Bethany Madelyn Amir. Foolishly, we told them much and took them to visit the Holy Sarcophagus, where they spent an hour worshiping her. Yet, they seemed so reverend, so honored, and so innocent. Now they cannot be found. We fear that they may have stolen the Holy Bones and fled West Reach."

"So that's why you've come here? Velona is close to West Reach, as is d'Grange, and Calgary. You think that they have come here on their return to Juda Arad?" I asked directly, seeing no other reason why he would come here.

"Well, no, not exactly. They seemed such a nice young, reverend couple. No, I came for a different reason. Before I continue, I must ask that what I am about to reveal to you now you all will hold in the strictest confidence, a total secret." He lowered his voice and became exceedingly serious! What was going on? Naturally, we promised to keep his secret.

"You see, Jes Amir and his line were ordained to be Kings and Queens of Tarra. While that has not happened in his day, it has happened with his children and his line. Also, his brother, Josh Amir, was so ordained to become King. His line as well has succeeded in becoming kings and queens, as far as we can tell anyway. Before he was crucified, he had our Blessed Holy Mother swear to him that a continuous record of their lineage would be kept to prove to the world who was the rightful, designated kings and queens of Tarra. Unto this day, she and her children and children's children have dutifully maintained this Holy Ledger."

"Originally, the Holy Ledger was kept at the founding church. However, when the present modern stone Church of the Blessed Holy Mother was built, the secret Holy Ledger was moved into a new secret hiding place. Until two weeks ago, it has been dutifully kept by the many of those two lines, Jes and Josh. Well, I must admit, in these times, it was kept up to date by those who reside on Cymry. While I have never personally seen this Holy Ledger, I know of its use and existence. It has been stolen. Sister Fiana, who was the only member our order who knew of the secret location, was tortured and killed. She must have told her torturers its location before she died. We all saw the empty secret hiding place. It contained only one scrap of paper. I brought it with me."

He showed us the yellowed parchment. The writing said: G. M. S. B. Nothing more. The initials had no meaning to me at all. "We do not know what this means. The lineage documents are gone, stolen." Still, I did not see any connection to us here in Velona.

"Now we of the Church know for a fact that many of the heirs of Jes and Josh moved to the mainland. Some settled in the Greenway, some here in the western Sea Princes. For days, we searched for clues, but found none. We know that a century ago, the Church of Jehosanity sent out its assassins, the Mano del Dio, to kill all living descendants of those two lines. Thus, we fear greatly for the safety of those of that lineage who live here in the Sea Princes and the Greenway. If the Church of Jehosanity stole these documents, it may be that they are once more after the destruction of their lines. Hence, we decided that we must break our vow of secrecy and warn you and those in the Greenway."

"While we do not know who in Velona can trace their lineage back to these two Holy families of Jes and Josh Amir, perhaps someone here might. If indeed the Church of Jehosanity is behind this, their lives may be threatened. They should be warned. Please, if you know anything of this, you must spread the word to their kin, please." He ended up literally begging us.

High Priestess Daria nodded to me, deferring this to me. I reached two decisions. "Yes, you were very wise in bringing this to us. All of us in this room are descendants of Jes and Bethany, Josh and Mila Amir." His eyes opened wide. Awe illuminated his face. He bowed to all of us.

"Second, I wish to send our very best detective back to Cymry and see if she can find any clues that your people may have overlooked. These two crimes may be dis-related or they may be related. We must find out more, if possible. When can you return to Cymry?" I asked.

"I am entirely at your service, most Holy People. Anytime. It is rare that mainlanders call our island by its true name." He smiled. Well, I used to live there and always called it Cymry then, so why change now?

"Okay, let me make some arrangements. We will return to Nuadilan as soon as we possibly can," I replied. After receiving his heartfelt thanks, repeatedly, Daria had her assistant led Father Amos off for some tea. She wanted time to discuss this with us.

"Do you really think that the Church of Jehosanity is back at their assassinations of the descendants of Jes and Josh Amir again? Should we be very worried, increase security?" she asked, plainly worried about this revelation.

"Honestly, Daria, I don't know. I admit that I have not been following much of what that Church of Jehosanity has been doing in recent years. I am slipping. I promise to get on to that at once. Still, we've heard of no assassination attempts. Cosima would have told us all about any if they had occurred. However, I think that it might be prudent to keep a guard on your Church at night. We don't want the thieves, whoever they are, to steal our records that we keep here as well. Meantime, let all your extended family know about the potential threat. Honestly, there are a whole many of us now that can trace our lineage back to those four." She agreed; almost all the extended West Po clan could, as well as most of our group. If this were a serious threat, many, many lives would be at risk.

She agreed and we left to find Cosima. As we rode along, Alex drove, while Renzo chatted with me. "You think the Mano del Dio are up to their old assassinations again? Sure smells like it might be. After all, they have a vested interest in getting rid of anyone who can prove that Jes Amir had a fleshly body and had children. They've turned him into some kind of god spirit instead of just a human man."

"Yes, if we could prove to the world just how twisted and distorted their Church has been with their religious leader, it would likely destroy them. That's plenty of motive for doing it. Yet, we haven't done anything like that. We've not threatened the Pope Christos with this. Why now? It doesn't all make much sense yet."

"Well, maybe it has to do with those Arad people," Renzo suggested. Alex halted at the large police station building just at the start of the wealthy district and at the edge of the warehouse district. Inside, we found Cosima at her desk along with Alessa. Our girls looked their best, even though they were now forty and thirty-eight years old, respectively. They both wore their usual satin billowing dresses, but had shunned high fashion while on the job. That is, they still wore their Alexis shoes with the lower heels.

"Hi Bethany," Cosima looked up.

"Hi mom," Alessa added. Though they were over ten years older than we were, they still called us mom. Alessa was my adopted daughter last lifetime, while Cosima was Dianna's.

"Kids, can we have a bit of your time?" I asked. Cosima closed the door and I relayed what we had just heard. "I proposed to him that you and I go to Nuadilan and see if any clues have been overlooked. Can you get away for a couple weeks?"

"Sure thing, Bethany. This sounds like an intriguing mystery. Besides, we need to determine positively if the Mano del Dio are once more after us. After all, Gerardo and my children are direct descendants, and their lives could be at stake here. When do we leave?" Cosima replied.

"Hey, I'm going too," Alessa added. "You don't go anywhere without your trusty bodyguard." Cosima smiled. We all knew that more than once, Alessa had saved Cosima from dangerous situations. It came with her job, that of Velona's Chief Detective Inspector.

"Let's hold a family meeting first. We need to alert everyone about the threat first," I replied.

"I'd like to see that document with the letters on it before I go," Cosima added, already deep in thought on the mystery. The two joined us and we headed first for her son's office. Adrien West Po was in charge of Velona Caravel Scheduling. I needed to see just how soon we could all hitch a ride over to Cymry. Travel by caravel was preferable to fishing trawler in many ways.

Adrien was able to obtain passage for us in two days. Then, we returned to the Holy Rose Church, where Cosima examined the parchment. I smiled as I watched her. She still wore her nails long, always two inches and always painted bright red. She still claimed that her talons worked well as evidence picker-uppers. Of course, this was a ruse. All women wore their nails long these days, if they wanted to be seen as fashionable. Unlike those in Tashien, here most were two to three inches long, never more. I kept mine shorter, much more convenient for me.

She carefully examined every bit of the document with her magnifying glass, before she spoke. "Well?" Father Amos asked when she finally put the lens down.

"Well, Father. This is an authentic document. No signs of forgery. No signs of any other concealed writing or invisible writing for that matter. However, there are some additional tests that could be run on the paper and ink, but those likely would not reveal any more information, and they are destructive of the document. So I will not conduct those tests. I can say that this document is old, at least one hundred fifty years old, maybe more."

She went on, "It was penned by a left handed person, who quite possibly was originally right handed. You can tell from the shape of the letters. It appears to have been torn from the bottom of a page. This is more like a signature at the end. However, the letters G. M. S. B. mean nothing to me. However, I believe that a safe hypothesis is that they are the initials of a group or organization or company and not those of an individual. While some of us have a number of surnames, having three plus a first name is exceedingly rare. It is more likely the abbreviation of a group or organization. You say it was found in the secret hiding place where the Holy Ledger was kept?"

"Yes Chief Detective Inspector, it was. That was all that was there. The many other documents kept there were gone, or so I've been told," Father Amos answered her.

"Okay. Tell me, do you know of any of their descendants who still live in Nuadilan now? I'd like to chat with someone who updated those documents. For example, my husband, Gerardo, is a descendant. When we had our children, he and I updated the ledger that is kept here in Velona. I'd like to chat with someone in Nuadilan who actually saw those Holy Ledgers," Cosima explained.

"Sister Fiana knew all them, I mean those who used to come to our church and update the Holy Ledger. However, she's been murdered. When we get back, I will make some inquiries and see if anyone will step forward," Father Amos volunteered. That satisfied Cosima. While I remembered the documents that were there about two centuries ago when I updated them with Caitlyn and my children, volumes must have been added since then. If nothing turned up, I decided to tell Cosima what little I remembered about them.

After returning Cosima and Alessa to their office, we went home, and I dashed off a series of messages to our far-flung extended group. Essentially, I wanted everyone to come by at six so that I could discuss this potential threat once with everyone involved. Because of all the interrelationships between us and the West Po clan, nearly all of us and our children were potential victims! Besides, this was the only time of day when Dianna and Ania were awake and present with their second bodies, Enyo and Alex.

Because our mom, that is Kallisto's, Alex's, and my mother, Luisa Angela, could trace her lineage all the way back to Jes Amir and Bethany Madelyn, that meant all our children were at risk as well as their children. Intermarriage into the West Po clan only added more who could trace their lineage back to Jes. On Josh's side, because of all the assassinations, most all his descendants came from the d'Aine family of the Highlands of Ruadan, Cymry.

Of course, the conversation became quite lively, with many expressing all manner of opinions. However, I was besieged with requests to outline our lineage, since many knew that I had been Bethany Madelyn back then. "You see, most of us go back to Jes and Bethany's daughter Sarah Elizabeth, who married Sir Percival Penton, back in the late 590's. On the other hand, the West Po's primarily go back up the West Po line to Ellaina Elizabet and Felix Deitz. She was the daughter of Emil Amir, who was the son of Justice Amir, who was the son of Emil Amir, Jes' youngest son. Here in the present, some of you are a blend of both those lines."

"Josh Amir's line has been carried forward by King Fergus d'Aine, son of Ros, who was the daughter of Josh and Milla. I'm sorry but I've no idea of the descendants from Fergus and Fianna," I admitted.

"Say, Bethany," Renzo asked, "whatever happened to Caitlyn and Ket's sons, Tegid and Taliesin? They married and had children, didn't they? She was assassinated just after giving birth to those twins." Golly, he brought back old, fond memories nearly two centuries old.

I smiled as I remembered Taliesin's wedding to Lia Inez, the armless woman victim of the mantis creatures. She was the most remarkable dancer and singer I'd ever known. "I honestly don't know about them either. Taliesin became the famous traveling bard, as you all know from your history books. Now what you don't know is that Tegid actually went on to become a king. He ruled what is now called the kingdom of Mont Blanc. He was known as King Diget I. Silly boy, spelled his first name backwards. I guess the ruse worked; no one ever knew his true lineage back then."

"Now that is interesting," Cosima commented in her usual thoughtful way. Of course, everyone quieted down. When she spoke like this, everyone had to listen! Everyone knew her deductive and observational skills well. She looked up at the staring, silent faces and giggled. "What's interesting is that there is a King Diget III, who rules the kingdom of Brownsville, Greenway. Quite possibly the Taliesin and Tegid lineage may be found over in the Greenway. Say, Bethany, wasn't Tegid one-handed?"

"Yes, kids pay attention. Tegid was full of youthful silliness, like many of you." I glanced quickly at our trio of mischief-makers. "He dashed off to fight in the first battle he could find and lost his sword hand as payment. After that, he got more common sense, though he had to relearn how to fight with his left hand. He became king later on. So no foolishness, kids." I admonished them all.

"Now, isn't that curious, Bethany," Cosima said thoughtfully. "The writer of that scrap of paper was left handed, but in my opinion was originally right handed. Curious, isn't it? I wonder if Tegid actually wrote that document. If so, what was it about?" Everyone chatted about her theory for a bit.

I then explained that we were heading for Cymry in two days. "While we're gone and from now on, until we get to the bottom of this, please, everyone, take absolutely no chances. If you see anything unusual or remotely threatening, get to a place of safety. I don't want to come back and find half of you assassinated while I'm gone. Understood?" Solemn faces nodded, though some seemed wholly unaffected by this business, especially the trio of mischief-makers. At this point, different groups chatted among themselves, exchanging ideas and safe houses if trouble came.

After everyone left, Renzo's mom came up to me. Sandra offered, "Bethany, while you are away, your daughter Rosa and I will go over all the banking records of the Church of Jehosanity for say the last score years and see if we can come up with anything useful." I thanked her and gave my pregnant daughter a loving hug. Sandra was grooming Rosa to completely take over her job at the Banca del Dio so that she could retire at last.

Sandra then asked, "So who all will be going over to West Reach?"

"Renzo, Cosima, Alessa, and myself," I replied.

"As your Forze Segrete, you should take some additional males along for protection and assistance. If there are assassins about, we cannot afford to have anything happen to you or Cosima," Sandra explained her concerns. Luisa seconded her, while Arturo and Enrico just smiled. I knew that they agreed with their wives.

"Hey, Bethany, why not take us three along?" Pietro suddenly burst out. Kallisto Ann's son and one of the three mischief-makers, Pietro, was the last person I would have chosen, along with his two companions, Nicolo, Elena's boy, and Luigi, Enyo's son.

Luigi jumped off the couch where he was teasing his sister Isabella and Nico. "Yes, take us. We're free," he added getting into the spirit of travel.

"Yes, we want to see the world," Nicolo added, knocking over the house of cards he had built just to annoy his brother, Phillipe, and his wife, Enrica. Nicolo saw my frown and added hastily, "Besides, we three are crack shots with the long-guns. Who better to protect you ladies than us?"

Len cringed at the mention of the long-guns! "What's this world coming too anyway? In my day, when we had a beef with someone, we fought them hand to hand with knives and swords. Nowadays, you can kill someone from nearly a mile away. You can't even see their face at that distance!"

"I understand, Len," I answered him. "Two centuries ago, the average person was far higher in emotional tones. When we had conflicts with another, we were overt enough to settle it with fists or swords, up close and personal. Today, the average emotion is much lower. These new long-guns allow cowards to settle scores from extreme distances against people they would not dare confront up close. These new long-guns make the weak as strong as our best fighters of old, Len." He wasn't mollified, however, but agreed with my analysis.

Dianna spoke up, "Men have always been developing better killing weapons. When those one-shot guns were invented, I went to work inventing my ball stopping vests. While they will prevent a single shot ball from causing more than a bruise if it hits the vest, they can't stop those balls from shattering one's arm or leg. They still work on these new multi-shot handguns; eight-shooters, they're called. However, my vests are useless against these new long barreled long-guns, whose bullets go right through them."

"It's not your fault, Dianna," Len consoled her. "Your vests cannot stop those cannonae shots either. Men just keep on inventing more and better ways to annihilate each other!"

"Yes, dad, we know all about that," Pietro sympathized with his father. He'd seen Len in such a mood many times and knew that he had to get the subject changed rapidly. "That's why we three have spent so many hours practicing to be a good shot with these long-guns. We aim to protect everyone from the bad guys. Bethany, we three are crack shots. You can't get better protection than us on this trip to West Reach."

"Yes, that's true, Pietro," I replied. "But you three don't know the first thing about this island and its culture, people, and language. You've no idea of its geography."

"Well, neither does Cosima nor Alessa. Besides, when was the last time that you were on West Reach?" Pietro retorted. I admit he had me now. "Okay, Pietro, you three boys can come along as our protectors. Mind you, no mischief. You will have to escort Cosima and Alessa. You give us any trouble and I promise you that I'll put you on the next boat for home." Pietro grinned and gave me a hug. So did Nicolo and Luigi. After that, they dashed off to begin packing for the trip, before I or their parents could change my mind.

"Silly boys," Cosima giggled and Alessa smiled. "Seriously, will language be a problem?" she inquired.

"Not where we are going," I guessed. "We'll dock in the southern port of Bregia, where many languages are spoken, of necessity. We'll take a coach northwest from there to Nuadilan, two days perhaps. While they have their own language, many will speak Sea Prince dialect, so we ought to be able to get along fine. If we were going further north or to the western coast, then it's a different story. The Tewdwr dialect is terribly difficult to understand and the speech of the Highlanders is a bit strange." She seemed relieved to hear this and our giant family meeting ended.

Later in our bedroom, Renzo said, "Wise move, Bethany. Taking those three boys along — might just do them wonders. They have a lot of growing up to do." I smiled and kissed him.

As we were doing our final packing, Bianca d'Grange made telepathic contact with Renzo and me. *Hi dad, Bethany. Say, I hear that you two are off on a small adventure again.*

Yes, we are going to West Reach to check on some stolen bones, Renzo replied.

Well, I want you both to take one of the Grey Creature's blasters with you. Keep them on the shield setting at all times. I don't want anything bad to happen to you this time. After all, dad, you have had an awful track record your last lifetime. She was referring to our mutilations in Dorota, Demokritos, and then in Tashien. *Besides, you don't have any more spare bodies lying around.*

Okay dear, but honestly, we don't expect trouble this trip. It's just some stolen ancient bones that we're investigating, Renzo attempted to lessen her fears.

I know, dad. If you do get into trouble, let me know right away and Louis and I will ride to your rescue again.

Renzo chuckled, remembering how they had done just that before. *Okay dear. How's the grandchildren?* He changed the subject and the two chatted a bit longer. I packed us each a blaster. Cosima and Alessa always carried another pair on their person. We all had long ago insisted on that. Their job demanded that kind of ultimate protection. More than once now, criminals attempted to shoot them while the duo was arresting them. Enyo carried one of the other three blasters; we kept two in reserve. Often, Dianna wished that we had found more than the seven Grey Creature blasters.

While we expected to be gone perhaps a week at most, we three women carried along two large boxes of clothing each! Cosima and Alessa insisted that they wear their fashionable dresses and I went along with this as well. All three of us compromised and wore our Alexa boots with the lower heels. We expected to have to do some walking and the Annelise style Alexa boots with their high heels made walking treacherous and more difficult on such an outing. In contrast, Renzo traveled light, one large duffle bag. While the three boys also carried a duffle bag, they also carried their long-guns on straps over their shoulders along with a hefty amount of ammunition. They came prepared for a small battle!

"My, how times have changed," Renzo commented to me. "Last time we headed off to Tashien, I took along an assortment of swords, daggers, and knives. Now the boys carry those long-guns and no swords. Sometimes, my love, I regret all these modern weapon inventions. I guess I am now an old fuddy-duddy, along with Len and Alex. Can you imagine what a real war would be like in these times? I still remember the slaughters that we saw during the First Crusade for Religious Freedom over in the Arad. I thought that was utterly inhumane. Then, we both saw the battlefield devastation caused by the cannonae on the Emperor of Demokritos' legions approaching Zargarb, total annihilation."

"I know, dear, a war with all these new modern weapons will be devastating beyond words. I just hope we never have another war again," I said honestly. Neither he nor I actually believed that. We'd seen too much hatred in the world to believe that peace could uniformly be achieved readily — certainly not with all these new killing weapons being developed.

Chapter 2 Cymry

The morning of June 4, our carriages pulled up at Velona's massive docks, Arturo and Enrico driving us. The men helped us older women out and proceeded to hold our arms, escorting us to the waiting caravel. All three of us wore similar satin gowns, made by Alessandra of Alessandra's Fine Dresses. We all loved her exquisite work.

I wore a bright red gown, Renzo's favorite color, but brought along my canary yellow satin dress — my favorite color. Cosima wore her emerald green dress; she nearly always wore green. Alessa's gown was light blue and her second gown was slightly darker. All three of us wore our tight-laced corsets, which kept our waists at some twenty inches. None of us was in to having a tiny waist as was the current fashion in Velona. After having our children, all three of us were quite happy still to have a twenty- inch waist!

Yes, we needed escorting; our dresses formed a circle some twelve feet in diameter near the ground. Our three mischief boys were on their very best behavior now, playing their roles as our escorts. Renzo chuckled and led the way. It must have been a bit strange to see three elegantly dressed older women being escorted by three fifteen year old boys. Yet, we most definitely needed their hands going up the gangplank in our dresses. We were not given any cabins this trip, because we'd make Bregia before nightfall. Consequently, we stood on deck and watched our six large trunks being hoisted aboard ship.

As we watched our caravel slowly slide out of the docks, Renzo and I realized why Adolfo, our monarch, had assigned his son the dock expansion project! Our commerce had so grown, due in large part to Dianna's trains, that our huge docks were now overly cramped! I counted thirty ships actually tied up, but there were forty more just off shore, waiting their turn to dock! No sooner had our caravel moved out than another caravel came sliding into its berth!

"I don't see how these docks can handle any more traffic," Renzo commented. "Already, they are using all of the bay here."

"I guess that's why Felix West Po is off trying to find another dock site," I replied, suddenly realizing the enormity of the problem Adolfo was facing. Velona had outgrown all possible dock expansion here. Did this mean that Felix was planning a new city and docks? I made a mental note to visit with Felix when we returned.

Several hours later, as we slid past Fortress d'Grange, I saw that Louis and Bianca were also facing growth problems. Their land was mostly mountainous, though by careful planning and labor, they had made usable cropland in a series of terraces going up the mountainsides. Still, their only possible bay was filled to capacity and they simply had no room to grow, unless they went to war and conquered part of the neighboring kingdom of Calgary. Indeed, Louis had already set a maximum allowable population at three hundred thousand. They simply had no more room to accommodate more people.

The three boys got slightly sea sick as we finally hit the open waters, heading towards the large island. We sailed into Bregia around four that afternoon. This international port city lay at the extreme southern edge of the large island. My, how the town had grown since I had last been here over a century ago! I made a rough guess that close to a half million lived here now, incredible.

Once docked, Father Amos took us to the best inn in Bregia, Shannon's Place. Claiming this was the very least his church could do for us, he paid for our night's stay, ten gold. The next day, we rented a large open coach for the two-day trip up the northwest road to Nuadilan. It was springtime and the green hills of Layamon were spectacular! We passed neatly tilled farmer's fields with their low stone fences made from stones removed from their fields. Occasional stands of forest dotted the horizon. It was a perfect day in June!

The three mischief boys were all nursing a hangover. They had spent time at the bar at Shannon's and discovered the local dark stout, Ennis Stout. The strong taste was addictive and all three had consumed far more than they ought to have and now were paying for their foolishness.

Pietro moaned, "Oh that Ennis was unbelievable. We need to get that exported to Velona!" He held his head in his hands. The other three echoed his sentiments. Cosima merely raised her nose, silly boys.

I was amazed to see all the new towns and villages that had sprung up since I was last here. Originally, Jes and I had founded our four new towns out in the uninhabited wilderness northwest of Bregia. Two centuries later, Layamon looked as densely populated as Velona. Yet, I was taken totally by surprise with how Nuadilan looked when we arrived the next day.

Originally, Jes and I had founded the village on a large hilltop, building a wooden palisade around it. Over the years that I was there, the town continued to grow and I added more concentric circles until the town boasted seven concentric walls. Now two centuries later, I was amazed to see that they had continued with my original design. The city was home to some two hundred thousand now and consisted of twenty concentric circles of stone protection walls! The huge valley battlefield before the original outer wall was entirely covered with homes, businesses, and factories!

Towering above all was the Church of Jehosanity, with its gothic spires dwarfing all other buildings. The evil church was within the Seventh Circle, Father Amos explained. His Church of the Blessed Holy Mother lay within the Sixth Circle close to that of Jehosanity, just beyond the stone wall. While vast sums of gold went into the architectural marvel of the Church of Jehosanity, when we pulled up before the relatively plain Church of the Blessed Holy Mother, we sensed a deep reverence and love emanating from this much smaller stone church. Ivy crawled up the brown granite walls, adding to its quaintness. We drove past the teakwood entrance doors, ornately carved with an unusual symbol. A giant circle was inscribed in the dense black wood, with a six pointed star made from two triangles, each upside down to the other. The symbol brought back old memories for me.

Father Amos put us up at the Bray Inn, one block from the church. Once our boxes were taken to our rooms, he led us down to his church complex. We paused before the ornate teakwood doors. "What an unusual symbol. I wonder what it means?" Nicolo asked.

"The triangle with its point upwards represents man, while the inverted one represents woman. The circle is the holy union of the two," I replied. Nicolo blushed as he grasped the significance of the two triangles.

"Well, I'll be!" Father Amos replied, very surprised that I knew about their holy symbol. Few outsiders did. "Yes that is precisely right, Mrs. Bartiana." He opened the doors and we entered the main chapel area. Behind the distant High Altar was a huge statue of Bethany Madelyn Amir, well a reasonable facsimile of what my body looked like, slightly stylized. Off to one side was a smaller stature of Jes Amir, while one of his brother Josh lay to the other side. Clearly, in this church the Blessed Holy Mother was the focus of their worship.

Our dresses rustling and heels clicking on the stone floor, we followed Father Amos as he led the way through the stillness of the chapel to a side stairs. Down we went, arriving at a long hallway. A number of rooms connected to this hall; some were used by Father Amos. We walked the length of the hall to the last room, a private Holy Altar room used only by the Fathers. Behind another statue of their Blessed Holy Mother, a tapestry hid a secret door. Cosima noted that it was locked, but that the locking mechanism was very ancient and crude. Any thief could easily open the lock. So much for security, she thought.

The door led to a spiral staircase that went down some thirty feet, ending in another room carved from bedrock. Father Amos went ahead of us, lighting the numerous lanterns that hung on the walls. The room was twenty feet square, but had numerous side burial chambers carved into the walls. Here they buried their honored church fathers. However, what commanded our full attention was the large sarcophagus that lay prominently in the center of the room.

Its lid held a relief of the Blessed Holy Mother, carved into the brown limestone. The lid had been slid part way off. "We left it as we found it," Father Amos whispered, barely able to keep his tears at bay.

"Okay, everyone, stand back. Let me investigate and look for clues first," Cosima ordered. She put down her black evidence bag, while Alessa retrieved a lantern for her and held it where Cosima needed the light. I marveled at how well Alessa anticipated where Cosima would next look, moving the light to the precise location without a word from Cosima. Well, they had been doing this since they were fifteen, so I guess Alessa really knew her sister well.

After an hour examination, Cosima finally straightened up and reported to us. "Well, the sarcophagus is genuine and looks to be at least two centuries old. This room has been well used. There are traces of many footprints on the floor. Father Amos, does any of your flock who come here to worship wear moccasins or leather pads instead of boots?"

"Moccasins? Why no. We wear shoes like mine. Why?" he replied.

"Well, someone wearing them was here and definitely was right up close to the crypt. Curious. In moccasins, they could move through your church very quietly. That's why I asked. Now then, the contents of the crypt are most intriguing."

"Why so? They held the bones of our Blessed Holy Mother," Father Amos asked, wondering what Velona's Chief Detective Inspector could have seen that they had not.

Cosima smiled and replied, "Well, this then is indeed the strangest thing yet. I hate to be the bearer of bad news, Father Amos, but this sarcophagus has always been empty!"

Father Amos nearly fainted! Only the fast reaction of Renzo kept the old man from collapsing. "What? What?" he finally gushed, holding tightly to Renzo.

"Come close and have a look through my magnifying lens. Alessa, hold the light so that he can get a good look. The rest of you — have a look too. I call your attention to the thin layer of exceedingly fine dust that covers the bottom of the crypt. Look at it closely, please."

One by one, we all took a turn with her lens, bending over and looking at the fine dust. After each of us had a look, she then said, "First, did anyone see any tiny bits of bone or disintegrated burial cloths?" No one had. "Second, if bones had been lying on that crypt's floor all these years, would not the dust have settled around them? When the bones were removed, would not you be able to see an absence of dust where they had been? Would not you have seen some disturbances in the dust when someone removed the bones, scraping the dust slightly as they lifted them out?"

"Yes, but. . ." Father Amos staggered to ask a question, but was unable to formulate words.

"That's precisely the point. The dust is uniform over the entire floor of the crypt! Did any of you see the slightest disturbance in the dust?" None had, but we all wanted a second look.

"Incredible, Cosima," I said. "You are right. The dust is uniform over the whole bottom."

"Precisely. That has only one possible explanation: this sarcophagus has never held anything. The bones of your Blessed Holy Mother have never been inside this stone sarcophagus," Cosima declared flatly.

Father Amos fainted. This was all too much for the old man. As Rezno and the boys grabbed him, I turned around and found myself staring at a burial hole in the wall. The plaque over the remains read: Caitlyn Amir. My eyes dropped down to the remains and saw her desiccated body covered in white linen. I nearly fainted myself as I recognized my young wife from two centuries ago! Alessa caught me as I nearly fell down.

"What is it, mom?" she exclaimed.

My voice sounded hollow and distant, "It's Caitlyn." She understood and whispered it to the others, who looked relieved. The men carried the priest up the stairs, while we followed them, Alessa making very sure that I didn't stumble.

I remember burying dear Caitlyn, but obviously, in subsequent years, someone had moved her here to this Holy Place. Still, it was quite a shock seeing her body after such a long time.

When we reached the private High Altar room, several younger priests were present along with three Sisters. They were on their way down to join us and quickly had Renzo and the boys carry the unconscious Father into the next room, their private meeting room. The Sisters ran off to fetch some tea and soon returned with smelling salts, tea, biscuits, and honey. Soon Father Amos recovered, resting firmly in his large, soft chair.

Over tea, Cosima related her findings. "So you see this crime has just taken on new dimensions. We have a thief who has recently broken in to steal the bones which were in fact never here, probably stolen two centuries ago," she summarized at last.

"But that's not possible," one of the other fathers spoke up. "It was King Diget I himself who came here with the remains of our Blessed Holy Mother! He was the one who found them, and he had the sarcophagus made. He placed her remains in there. All this is documented in our church's records. I can show you them. There must be some mistake."

Oh, how these men and women wanted this to be a horrible mistake, but Cosima led them down to see for themselves the unmistakable dust clue. Three white faced men returned to the meeting room a while later. "But we have the written records. . ." one Father lamely suggested.

"Could we possibly examine them and read what King Diget I had to say?" asked Cosima, her curiosity was now definitely aroused. This had become a very interesting case.

The next room held stacks and stacks of their records. "Please, exercise extreme caution, these pages are very fragile," Father Amos extolled us as he presented the ancient volume to Cosima. While Alessa held the lantern for her, Cosima began to examine the book, using only the tips of her long nails. Once again, she put her talons to good use, not adding her own finger oils to these ancient pages. She did her best not to cause further deterioration of these relics.

"Yes, the paper and ink are indicative of being two centuries old.

Probably authentic. Let's see what he has to say." She read aloud the word written so long ago by my own son, Tegid.

"In 640, I was contacted by the Blessed Holy Mother, Bethany Madelyn Amir, who told me where her body maybe found. I took upon myself this Holy Quest to find the Holy Graal, this Blessed Holy Mother." She read off a description of where he found her remains in the ocean off Cuch Glyn. Cosima read to us how King Diget I then ordered a special sarcophagus and read to us about the burial ceremony he subsequently conducted for her.

"Yes, that all is backed up by our records," Father Amos added. He produced records that showed that King Diget I had indeed ordered and paid for the sarcophagus. Even his words spoken at her burial had been written down and preserved. There were pages of monetary dealings kept as well. These, Cosima examined closely.

"No doubt about it, King Diget I was left handed, but was originally right handed. I wonder if that scrap of paper with the initials is his handwriting. Father Amos, may we compare the two?"

A half hour of intense study later, Cosima looked up, "Yes, this scrap note was written by the same hand as these records. If the author was indeed King Diget I, he also left those letters on the scrap that you found, Father Amos."

"Now that is interesting, but what does it mean?" he asked, baffled. So were we all.

"Don't know yet, but there is more in these old records," Cosima added. "Most strange. Why did King Diget I order two sarcophaguses?" This took us all by surprise. Cosima carefully pointed out the notations in the records. The second one was ordered a week after he ordered the first. With the first order, he sent along a sketch, which was used to carve the top cover in the likeness of the Blessed Holy Mother.

"Perhaps he was ordering his own burial crypt," suggested Father Amos, trying to fit this fact into some reality.

"I considered that, but why would he not send along a sketch for its top? He wrote, 'Same as before.' This leads me to speculate that he ordered two identical sarcophaguses. Why would he do that?"

None of us had any idea. However, later that night when we were alone in our inn rooms, she explained her theory. "I think that he never had any intention of burying her bones at that church. I think he changed his mind after he ordered the original sarcophagus. He then ordered a second and only pretended to place her bones in the church's sarcophagus. I suspect that he took them with him when he left and has buried her in an identical sarcophagus somewhere else. Of course, the where is a complete mystery." I began to believe that she was right. What was old Tegid telling me?

"Now I would like to see the secret hiding place that was also robbed," Cosima asked, having finished her examination of the crypt and documents. We returned to the main chapel. Before the High Altar on the floor was a secret tile, which when lifted revealed their secret hiding place. The space was entirely empty. The only clue that Cosima was able to glean here was some dried blood from the Sister who had died here, after being tortured into disclosing the location of the secret place. While they had cleaned up most of the blood, she found sight traces in the cracks between the stones on the floor nearby this tile. During the past month, the site had been too thoroughly disturbed, to say nothing of cleaned up. Just as she rose from her examination, the teakwood doors were thrown open and a tall man entered.

He bellowed, "Where is my sister's body? Why hasn't she received a proper burial?" The man spoke in a thick Highlander accent. The three mischievous boys did a double take at the unusual sound of his accent and voice.

Poor Father Amos was definitely having a very bad day. He rose and replied, "I am Father Amos. Can I help you? Oh! It's you, King Argus d'Aine. I'm terribly sorry for the loss of our Sister Kelsi. Forgive me, but we thought that you knew of her wishes."

"What wishes? Who are these people? Why are you showing them our secret place?" He instinctively drew his sword. Two of his men came inside the church the moment they heard him draw his sword.

"These are friends from Velona, who have come to assist us in our desperate hour of need. They are also of direct lineage to Jes and the Blessed Holy Mother," Father Amos quickly defused the situation. Come, let us return to our meeting room, and discuss these mysterious events."

"Excuse me, I am Mrs. Bethany Bartiana, my husband, Renzo," I began introducing us all to the king. Poor Father Amos was so shaken up that he failed to introduce us. The king put his sword away and the tensions dropped.

I added, "I'm sorry that I've lost track of the d'Aine line over the years. I assume that you can trace yours back to Fergus and Fianna?"

"Yes," he said with a curious look in his eyes. "Argus, their son, was my father. And you?"

"We go back to Sarah Elizabeth, Jes and Bethany's daughter. We keep our records in the Holy Rose Church in Velona," I answered him, giving him a bit of data not widely known, but probably suspected by many — where our records were kept that is.

He smiled. "Be careful to whom you divulge that information, lassie. In times like these, evil lurks in all corners. Come, I want to hear about my sister Kelsi d'Aine. She joined the church here as one of their nuns, their Holy Sisters, against my better advice. Now she's dead and I've just heard about it and that she has not yet been given the burial befitting one of such noble birth."

"I am sorry for the delay in notifying you, King Argus. So much has happened, so confusing, so terrible. Sister Kelsi was tortured into divulging the location of our secret Holy Ledgers. I am afraid that all those records have been stolen. They are gone, all gone."

"What?" King Argus fumed, anger seethed up, his veins pulsed. "Who did this?" he bellowed.

"That, I am afraid, we do not know. In part, that is why I went to Velona to ask their aid. This is their most famous Chief Detective Inspector, famous for solving the most unsolvable cases there. Already she has shown some light on this matter, making it even more disturbing. As far as Sister Kelsi is concerned, her last will requested that her body be donated to Saint Sarah's Hospital to be used in the training of our doctors."

"What?" he bellowed as loudly as before.

"Yes, we now have a real hospital where the injured and sick can be treated. Yet, the new doctors must be trained to know how to operate on the wounded. She wanted them to use her body in such a manner that more lives in the future may be spared. Sister Kelsi always thought so much for the well-being of others, you know. No one had a kinder, gentler soul than she. She was always doing everything possible for the sick and injured. You should take great pride in all that Sister Kelsi accomplished here in Nuadilan, King Argus," Father Amos replied, finally recovering his shock and donning his priest's hat once more.

"Can I see what's left of her body? That I may say my farewell?" King Argus asked, his anger giving way to his unrequited grief.

"Certainly, our carriage can take you to our pride and joy, Saint Sarah's Hospital. It is not far," Father Amos answered. Quickly, we headed outside where Father Amos had a carriage for us. The king had his own carriage and followed us to the hospital. We said little as we rode along the streets.

The hospital was a single story, stone building in the shape of a huge U. Once inside and recognized, Doctor Cardonagh came to meet us. After brief introductions, he gave us a tour of the facilities, as he led us to their practice operation room. "Saint Sarah's Hospital is divided into three wings. This entrance wing is where we perform our work on the sick and injured. Those with critical needs are then housed in the north wing, while the others are kept in the south wing, where sunlight more readily enters their rooms."

"We are so very fortunate that Sister Kelsi has donated her body to us. We have so many new doctors who want to learn how to treat the sick and injured. They need bodies to study and to practice upon. Sister Kelsi's remains are still helping the injured long after her premature death. Around here, Sister Kelsi is almost a legend. She spent so much of her time here helping others recover."

As we passed a room filled with books, he added, "Here is our priceless library. I must say that the acquisition of the complete works of

Doctor Yi of Tashien is perhaps our most prized set of books! That man has totally revolutionized surgery of arms and legs! He was a genius. Following his very detailed and extensive directions, we have already been able to save three lives!"

Renzo and I nearly fainted! Doc Yi was the sadistic man who cut off our arms and legs, which ultimately led to our deaths! He turned us into his surgical specimens! We and a whole lot more unwilling women had various arms and legs removed. He was a beast, and yet his man was praising him for his works! I didn't know it now, but Doc Yi's works had now been republished in Velona, the Greenway, on Megalos, and even down in Demokritos! Doctors everywhere were hailing him as the century's greatest surgeon! The sadist!

"Ah, here we are at last. You will find that Sister Kelsi's body has been well preserved for our use. Preservatives have been pumped into her body, replacing her blood. Thus, you will see her as she last appeared just before her untimely death." He opened a cabinet door and pulled out a long, narrow shelf on which her covered body lay. King Argus broke down and cried; his grief was too great to suppress. I put my arm around his shoulders, comforting the older man.

After a time, he recovered. "May I see the rest of her body?" he asked. The doctor removed the linen covering, revealing her complete body, though he respectfully kept her lower half completely covered out of respect for her brother.

"Dear God! Kelsi, what happened to you?" King Argus cried out.

"Oh my!" Cosima added her exclamation to his. "May I?" she asked and the doctor nodded. "Both of her hands — incredible." We all stared at her hands. Each of Kelsi's fingers now lay back across the top of her hands; they had each been forcibly broken into that position. I recognized the torture style that had been used by the Mano del Dio on Kali down in Tashien! There was no doubt in my mind who had done this to Sister Kelsi.

"Yes, she was tortured, these are the signature marks of the Mano del Dio," Cosima concluded. "But look further. She was shot with a gun, probably at close range. See the powder burns on her skin by the hole? Yet, in the lower abdomen, that wound probably wasn't fatal. Look at her neck; see this thin line? She was then strangled. Cause of death: strangulation, probably after the gun wound failed. Father Amos, no one heard a gun firing in the Chapel?"

"No, no one heard it," he replied, mystified once more. Clearly, he had not known that she had been shot first.

"Well, perhaps he fired with the gun pressed to her chest, muffling the sound," Cosima concluded. "Because her body has been so thoroughly cleaned, I cannot tell more. Say, I forgot to ask a vital question, Father Amos. Was Sister Kelsi killed at the same time as the bones were stolen?"

"Why no, she was killed a week later. We were all so unnerved and upset over the theft of the Holy Blessed Mother's bones. Then, a week later, she was discovered in the morning as when we opened for morning services," he explained.

"Interesting and curious," she replied. "At first glance, the two crimes do not seem to be related. You see the Mano del Dio do not wear moccasins. Further, we did not see any small drops of blood on the floor beside the sarcophagus. Had a Mano del Dio assassin been the one opening that crypt, we should have seen telltale blood drops from their own self-mutilations. Unfortunately, the crime scene of Sister Kelsi has been thoroughly cleaned, so we cannot look for such signs there. So it does appear that we are dealing with two unrelated crimes. Yet, they may be related. Why should anyone want to kill Sister Kelsi?"

Cosima didn't wait for a reply. "She was beloved of her people. No, she was killed solely and only because of what she knew and guarded: the secret chamber where the Holy Ledgers were kept. Based on her torture, it had to be the Mano del Dio. But why would they be so interested in these records just now? Centuries ago, they went on a rampage assassinating everyone who could trace their lineage back to the Holy Family. But that was then, not now. It doesn't make any sense yet, just as the non-theft of the bones."

King Angus requested that Kelsi's remains be sent to him when they were no longer of use to the hospital. We all then headed back to the church.

In our carriage, Cosima asked, "Say, before the theft of the bones, who knew that they were kept in your church?" she asked.

"Only the most devout — our priests knew and a very few others. We kept it a secret all these years out of fear of what just happened — their theft. After the many assassinations by the Church of Jehosanity, we kept the location of the Blessed Holy Mother's remains a total secret," Father Amos explained as we headed back to his church. "Not even King d'Aine knew that we had her remains."

"Curious. Obviously, the Church of Jehosanity didn't know. Had they known, your church would have been raided centuries ago. So we can rule out them from attempted theft of the bones. Yet, someone knew the precise location where they were hidden."

"Oh!" Father Amos exclaimed suddenly. "Those holy visitors from Juda Arad that were here a week before the theft. He's one of their holy messiahs, just like Jes Amir was. I mentioned to him that we had the Holy Mother's remains here. You see, he explained that for centuries the wicked Church of Jehosanity had scoured every inch of Juda Arad, seeking Holy Relics. Never were they able to find the actual body of Jes Amir, which only adds credence to their ridiculous notions that Jes was not flesh and blood. I just couldn't help myself. I told him of our most Holy of Holies. I even showed him and his wife the sarcophagus. Oh my! Do you suppose that it was they who broke in and attempted to steal the bones?"

"Well, well, well," Cosima said with a big grin. "Now we are getting someplace. Yes, Father Amos, the theory that these two from Juda Arad broke in and attempted to steal the bones is the most plausible thus far, considering how few knew about it. After that theft, did you widely announce the theft?"

"Well of course we did!"

"So after the theft, the Church of Jehosanity discovered that all these years you had the remains of Bethany Madelyn Amir and that now someone had stolen them. Ah, this casts a while new light on motivations! Discovering this, they once more felt threatened with exposure and had to recover the lineage documents so that they would know who could trace their lineage back to Jes. Oh my, then perhaps we are all in danger of assassinations once more!"

We arrived back at the church and headed down the meeting room once more. Quickly, Cosima outlined her deductions about the theft to King Argus, who was astounded to learn that all these years this church had been the resting place for the Blessed Holy Mother. "So the remains were then never here?" he said when she finished her outline and summary.

"Yes, that is my conclusion. I suspect that King Diget I's first intention was to have them lain to rest here in the very church that she founded and in which she preached. Something subsequently changed his mind, and he ordered a duplicate sarcophagus a week later. I believe that he took her remains and buried them in this duplicate sarcophagus at some other location, as yet wholly unknown to us," Cosima replied.

"So close and yet so far," King Argus sighed. "Well, what are we to do about the lost records and the new updates that must be done? Surely we cannot stop keeping our records."

"This location is no longer safe. I believe that prudence dictates that a new location be created. Of course, the difficult task will be to notify all those descendants here on Cymry where this location now is so that they can keep the records up to date," I suggested.

"I will create a new location in the church in my capital," King Argus decided. "Father Amos, you send any who come here to add to the ledger up to me personally, and I'll see that they are taken to the new location." Both men found that most agreeable.

"What of the lost records? Surely, we must get them back or the line of documentation is broken," the king asked.

I decided to speak up, "You know, when this was set up way back when, we all knew that having the only records here in Nuadilan was going to be a problem. So many of the descendants were scattered across the mainland that it would not be feasible to have this as the sole location. We have one set of Holy Ledgers in Velona. I will see if the early records have been added to ours at some time in the past. I wonder if they did the same thing up in the Greenway, where I know a fair number of the descendants once lived? If so, they may have many more names to be added or even have copies of your early records."

King Argus agreed with me, "Yes, my father said to me once that he was told that our records were being copied and kept somewhere on the mainland just in case something like this should happen. I'm sorry that I do not know more."

"Excuse me," one of the other priests interrupted us. "Perhaps I know something; then again perhaps it is nothing."

"Speak up, father," Amos implored him.

"Well, it was early May. Sister Kelsi was ill, bedridden with the flu. A strange man arrived at the church asking for her. He carried a leather pouch. Anyway, I told him that she was too ill to see him. He then asked me to take her a message, saying that 'The One' had come again. I thought that a most strange message, but I delivered it as he asked. Sister Kelsi then told me that I was to allow him into the main chapel and see to it that no one was around for about ten minutes. After that, I was to take him into our basement library and again see to it that no one disturbed him. Once he was finished, again I was to allow him into the chapel alone. I did as she asked."

"Say, wasn't he that man who was here last fall?" asked another priest. Soon, Cosima learned from their combined, but dis-related observations that this same man had been coming here every fall and spring for years. It was not much of a stretch to conclude that this person was making a copy of the recent additions to the Holy Ledger.

"Can you describe this man?" Cosima asked, her pencil and notepad at the ready. Well, ask four witnesses what they saw and you get four somewhat different reports. At least, they all agreed that the man wore a weather stained leather cloak and carried a water proofpouch over his shoulder. He was both tall and of average height. He was thin and yet of average build. His hair was both black and dark brown. He carried a dagger, but he didn't carry a dagger. He had a gun, but didn't have a gun. Ah well, Cosima wrote down all four descriptions anyway. She was quite familiar with this phenomenon, having seen it repeatedly in her line of work.

At least they all claimed that he came up from Bregia. On that they were certain; he always arrived by carriage which originated from that city. Cosima then speculated that he came to Bregia by boat twice a year. "Under the current circumstances," she suggested, "when he comes back this September, we should contact him and tell him what has happened. He needs to be informed of the new location of your records. Also, perhaps he can tell us more information that we need." I resolved to have someone in Bregia waiting for this man, come September. Unfortunately, unforeseen events did not allow that to happen.

I decided to warn King Argus. "King Argus, the last time that the Mano del Dio had this kind of information about us, they went on an assassination binge, slaying quite a few of us descendants. At that time, they only had some clues as to our identities. Now they have an extensive list, presumably most of the living descendants are here on Cymry. I urge you and the others that you know to be exceptionally vigilant in the future. If 'accidents' or assassinations occur, then please send word to us in Velona. Perhaps we can find a way to help out."

"Lassie, I've already come to that conclusion as well. Yea take care over on the mainland. I'll pass on the word. If anyone sees anything about this, I'll hav'em relay it to you," King Argus concurred. "Worst part of it is, only my sister knew who all used to come here and log their new entries. I've no way to know all of our descendants who live outside of the Highlands. All those in Layamon are in grave danger, I fear. Still, I do have a few connections down here. I'll let them know about all this. Lassie, with some luck, they will notify the others here in Layamon. I best be getting back. Most honored to meet all of you. May the Blessed Holy Mother watch over you." He bowed and left.

After he left, Father Amos asked, "Now what do we do? About the missing bones, I mean?"

"Leave the investigation to us," Cosima answered for me. "It would seem that King Diget I had a hand in all this and his kingdom was on the mainland. Let us carry on the investigation on the mainland. I will keep you posted on any new developments. We must find those missing documents and what really happened to those remains of the Blessed Holy Mother." He smiled and gave her a warm thank you hug. We then left and returned to our inn. Since the hour was too late to begin the return trip to Bregia, we chose to relax the rest of the day.

Naturally, the trio decided to take a tour of the city and off they went, leaving us to chat and plan. "Should we case the Church of Jehosanity and look for the missing Holy Ledgers?" Renzo asked.

"Where would you look?" Cosima asked by way of an answer. He shrugged his shoulders. "No, we need more data. Those documents could well be on their way to the Pope as we speak. I find it a bit encouraging that there has been no reported assassinations or funny deaths reported yet. They've had the ledgers for over three weeks now."

"Ah, you'd expect that the Mano del Dio would have struck already," Alessa suggested. "Strike before everyone learns of the theft and can bolster their defenses, right?"

"Right, sis. It's been three plus weeks. Surely by now word of the theft has spread. At this point, the Mano del Dio has lost their element of surprise," Cosima explained. "Perhaps they have some different use in mind for these names. We ought to keep a sharp look out for unusual happenings to people here on West Reach, though I am not sure how we can do that."

"Well, I have been trying to recall the last time that I entered names in that stolen ledger. It was many years ago now. Honestly, unless someone copied all of Velona entered names onto the Cymry ledger, I don't think that we in Velona are in danger, probably not those in the Greenway either. Just those here are at risk," I concluded.

It was late when our three mischief boys finally returned, slightly intoxicated as expected. "Hey, we did learn something," Nicolo attempted their defense.

"Yeh, we did," Luigi added hastily.

"What?" asked Cosima coldly, as if scolding little boys who had just raided the cookie jar.

Pietro explained. "We visited the pubs. You know what's weird? Not a one person claimed that they were members of the Church of the Blessed Holy Mother. No one even said that they went to their church, for that matter. Not one. We visited six pubs."

"Well, that is a bit unlikely," Cosima had to admit.

"See, I told you we did some real detective work," Luigi added.

Cosima ignored him. "Look, the chapel could hold at least five hundred or more and the pews looked worn. The stone floor had wear marks from the passage of countless feet over the years. Someone, many someones must have attended services there. Why would folks claim that they didn't?"

"Hey, bet it's intimidation by the Jehosanity folks. The Mano del Dio probably threatens everyone," Pietro theorized.

"So what are we going to do about it? Take them out?" asked Nicolo.

"We're going home, that's what," Cosima said didactically. "Look, we don't have any legal authority in this country. We're just visitors. Besides, that is their own problem. Let them deal with it in their own way."

"Well, look what we are bringing home," Pietro proudly stated, "the find of the century. They call it a bi-wheel. See you sit on the seat and pedal. With this, you don't need a horse to travel around the city. They are perfect for the cobblestone streets of Velona. We each got one. Maybe we can go into business making and selling them." He sounded a hopeful note.

"It takes a bit of getting used to, though. We each fell off twice before we got the hang of it," Nicolo added. "We're going to put some side baskets on it, and you can use it to go shopping and such. I bet we make a fortune."

"Say, they just might," Renzo backed them up. Okay, so bi-wheels it is.

We arrived back home in four days, having had to accept a fishing trawler for the short return trip. All was quiet while we were gone and remained so for a time. During this period, Cosima and I began to make plans on how we could continue this interesting investigation. Everything pointed to the Greenway and its kingdoms. We'd have to travel there and see what could be found. Neither of us held out much hope. After all, my son Tegid, King Diget I, died over a century ago. It was likely that he took his secrets to the grave with him.

At least we knew the kingdom over which he once ruled. It was our old Santi fortress at Mont Blanc. In those early years, they took over the mountainous Langdoc region that butted against the impassable Appian Way. No one lived there, but as Mont Blanc's population grew, they built a whole series of new towns and cathedrals in those hills. Now sheep, wine, and wool were the main products they sent to the markets in Velona.

"Tegid, Tegid! Why didn't you leave me some clues?" I mused late at night.

Renzo grinned. "That would make everything too easy."

"I know that you are teasing me, but Renzo, you have a good point — all that was back in the era when the Mano del Dio were hunting us down and assassinating us all. Tegid knew that and probably hid things well so that they could not be found by the relentless searching of the Mano del Dio. He could not afford to make it too easy, for he suspected lives depended upon utmost secrecy. You know he always contended that being King was his birthright. Probably the most important thing to him was to ensure that birthright fell to his children. He'd do everything in his power to ensure that happened. It falls on us to discover what that was."

Chapter 3 In the Arad, It Begins

In January of 780, Father Kiros, his hands securely tied, his six traveling companion dead — their throats cut, prayed that he could meet his greatest and holiest challenge. He faced the barbarians, ready to attempt their conversion. Months ago, he recalled vividly receiving his Holy Orders from the Pope himself! Such a high honor he did not deserve, yet Pope Christos personally spoke with him, charging him with this most Holy Mission. How he could succeed where his nine predecessors had failed did not cross his mind that day.

No, the stark reality of the previous nine missions only struck home when he and his six companions finally set foot into the desert region of Juda Arad. Stark, bleak, sand and mesas dotted the landscape, forlorn at the very best. Nine similar parties had simply vanished from the face of Tarra. Yet, Father Kiros had suppressed those fears, those anxieties, and pressed on out into the semi-arid once Holy Land. He had his Holy Mission; he would not fail.

Now he faced his Holy Mission squarely. He stood tall and undaunted before the tent entrance of the barbarians, ready to fulfill his vows to the Church of Jehosanity. He would not fail. Prophet Qanun al'Tirsa, a heavily bearded holy man of the Arad, nodded to his lifelong friend and companion, Messiah Bani el Marina. Tamina el Marina, his wife, picked up the three teacups and bowed to the Holy Prophet. Once her face was out of sight of the two men, she grinned. Today, another of the foul, wicked, evil priests of the Church would die, giving his blood back to the desert sands, giving life to the desert. "It is time," Prophet Qanun said softly. The two men rose and opened the tent flap to face the captured priest.

Prophet Qanun was thirty years old; his friend, twenty-five. He spoke first, "Priest, you have entered upon the Holy Sands of Juda Arad, bringing with you lies and deceit. What have you to say in your defense?"

"I am Father Kiros of the most holy Church of Jehosanity, Megalos. I have come to bring the Holy Words of Lord Jehosa to all that live in this most Holy Land. Centuries ago, Lord Jehosa sent his Holy Son, Jes Amir, here to Juda Arad, to redeem your precious souls. Unto a Holy Virgin Mother was born the Son of God in Jerilum. He walked this land bringing faith, healing, and the Holy Redemption to all. I have come to teach you the ways of our Lord Jehosa, that your souls too shall be Redeemed, that they may enter Heaven and not Lucifer's Hell." He thought that this was a good beginning. Perhaps he would be successful after all.

"Already you lie," Prophet Qanun cursed and spat on the priest. "Jes was born as the second son to the Amirs. He was a man, just as you and I. We do not have souls; we are souls. You've already twisted his teachings!"

"No! No, his was an Immaculate Conception! The Son of God, Jes, was not a mere man! He was the Son of God! How could he be just a mere man? That is why I am here — to teach you the errors of your beliefs! You have a most precious soul. If you do not walk the path of Holy Righteousness, your soul will be cast out of Heaven and into the eternal Fires of Hell, Lucifer's Ungodly Domain, there to burn for all eternity! Please, you must listen to me," Father Kiros pleaded.

"Fool! Jes was born a normal man, just as you or I. You are your soul; you do not have one, fool. You are it! There is no such thing as Heaven or the Fires of Hell. There is no Lucifer. Jes was a man just as you or I. He married Bethany Madelyn and fathered children, just as Messiah Bani here. You and your Church are corrupting the word of God!" Prophet Qanun cursed at him, angrily.

"No! No! He was the Son of God. Bethany was a mere prostitute, a whore. He fathered no children. It says so in our Holy Gospels, written by his ten Holy Disciples! They, who traveled the Arad with him, preaching the Holy Word of God — they have written what took place. Jes was the Son of God; he was not a man as we. Bethany was a lowly, diseased whore whom Jes once healed of her sores. Do you not believe the Holy Writings of his own Holy Disciples?" Father Kiros felt that now he had made a strong argument. No one could doubt these Holy Scriptures!

"Are you a complete fool?" Prophet Qanun angrily replied. "Yes, the ten disciples did write their accounts of Jes. Yet, your people have totally rewritten them, altering, distorting, and outright changing their holy accounts to suit your own vile perversions. Your Holy Gospels are so badly altered that nothing in them is accurate whatsoever. A monkey might as well have written them using cow dung ink. They are worthless trash. Worse, you actually believe all this, don't you?" He gave the priest a pathetic look.

"Lord Jehosa, grant me the strength to convince these heathens of the errors of their ways. Grant me the strength to get them to see the Holy Truth, that their precious souls may yet be saved." Father Krios prayed, hoping that Lord Jehosa would hear him, even though his hands were tied behind his back and not in their proper supplicant position.

Prophet Qanun spoke solemnly, "So be it. In this, the Holy Land, the penalty for spreading heresy about our Lord Jehosa is death. Your flesh will help the desert survive. May you discover your own identity and repent of your evil wickedness done in the name of our Holy Lord Jehosa." Without further words, Messiah Bani's sword strike came swiftly, cutting his neck deeply. He pushed the fallen priest into a shallow grave in the sand and covered him up. Then, he rejoined the others inside the tent at this make shift encampment in the south of the Arad.

Father Kiros felt the cold steel on his neck, felt his warm blood gushing out streaming down his chest, and felt his legs go weak. He watched as his body collapsed to the ground. He watched as the messiah tossed it into a shallow grave in the sand, and then covered it up. Silence. Around him, the desert was totally silent. The hot sun shone down. Now a small rodent squirmed its way across the desert sands, oblivious to all that had gone on before.

"What's happening to me?" Father Kiros thought. "Lord Jehosa, take my soul. I am waiting for Holy Salvation." Nothing. Time passed. The rodent rushed back to his burrow; a snake undulated across the sands after it.

"I don't understand. What's happening to me? I still see things." Suddenly, he realized that he was not his dead body! "Somehow I am! I exist." Slowly, he began to have horrible thoughts. "Could it be that these men are right? That I am my soul? That the Holy Church is completely wrong?"

"Oh, Lord Jehosa! I have been so wrong! I have been misguided! I beg you; forgive me my sins, for they have been many. What must I do? How shall I do penance? I am at thy holy mercy." Silence. The snake slithered to the burrow's entrance and paused, its tongue flicking about, sensing its prey.

"I denounce the Church. So where do I go now? What do I do now?" An idea formed in his mind. "Yes, the new Perfect Society. Yes, we've all heard of this. That is what I must support, a perfect society in God's Holy Love. That is the answer." He took off at once for Hieras Anubis, the new town on at the tip of the Southlands, which used to be called South Port. He spotted the hospital and went through its walls. He found a woman giving birth and latched onto the new baby body as it was born. Now at last, Father Kiros relaxed. He was now going to be a member of the Perfect Society of Lord Jehosa. Nothing could go wrong this time. It was perfect. Then, he smelled something and his tiny body went unconscious. Pain! Pain in his left shoulder. Pain, pain in his right. "What is happening?" He backed out of the small body's head and saw the doctor who had just removed the arms of the baby girl. He was carefully sewing up the flesh on her shoulders. His stomach involuntarily lurched causing the doctor to miss a stitch.

"There, there, little one. I am almost done. You are perfect in all ways, little one," the kindly voice of the doctor said. *I am perfect!* The words echoed in Father Kiros' mind, repeatedly. He relaxed and felt at ease at last. *I am perfect now.*

"That's the tenth party from Megalos that we have encountered so far," Prophet Qanun said, once Messiah Bani joined him. "This has to stop."

"I know. Our numbers have grown. Last census makes us at five hundred thousand and some, but that is nothing compared to our adversaries on Megalos," Messiah Bani replied. "We've had little choice but to reoccupy many of the ancient towns. Water is so scarce here in the Arad. We've long outgrown the capacity of the hidden lands to support so many. Still, Qanun, we cannot hope to do battle with the soldiers of Megalos, holy or unholy. Daily, I pray for guidance."

"I know, Bani. The arm of this Church has grown long indeed. In Demokritos, they have tens of millions of supporters. That's more than ten times the whole population of Megalos. Worse, they have two Sea Prince Sectors, and now the ten Greenway Kingdoms have come under their control. We had so hoped that others would recognize the utter falsehoods of their religion. Alas, that has not happened. Rather the opposite, I'm afraid. If this keeps up, soon it will be only us, Bani, against the whole world. We must not fail; we must not let our Lord Jehosa down."

"You mean to go through with our plan then?" Bani asked.

"I can see no other choice, no other path that we can walk. If we do not do it soon, the world will be completely lost," Qanun replied. "Yes, we must acquire hard proof of their lies and deceit. Then, we use that to expose them all and finally bring down this wicked, evil Church of Jehosanity. It begins with what we know and have learned, Bani."

"We know from our own texts and scrolls that Bethany Madelyn Amir took their children and fled the Arad towards the Sea Princes, just after the Centurions crucified the Son of God, Jes Amir. Our lengthy research has led us to believe that she finally settled on the island of West Reach, as far from here as she could get, there to raise Jes' children in safety, out of the reach of the Centurions. Bani, your first task is to go there and find where her earthly remains are buried. Then, you must steal them and bring them back to the Holy Land, here in the Arad, where we will guard them with our very lives."

"That, my son, will be the easy part. The next action that you must accomplish is to locate the living descendants of Jes and Bethany Amir as well as those of his brother, Josh and Milla. Armed with her remains and their descendants, we can then prove to the world so many of their falsehoods and outright lies. Still, that is not enough, Bani."

"Your third challenge is to find and retrieve the actual Holy Scriptures written by the ten Holy Disciples of Jes Amir, Son of God. Here, we have some data, gathered and passed down to us from our ancestors. We know that Jes ordered each of them to write their own accounts of his life and teachings. Ten gospels they wrote and copies of them were made and stored in a safe place. This we now know for sure. Yet, we also suspect that the Church got a hold of the originals, when their Holy Paladins were raiding and scouring the Arad for Holy Relics. Thus, your third challenge is to find these copies and return with them that we may copy them and broadly distribute the true words of the ten disciples."

"As you know, Bani, I have devoted my life to tracing what may have become of these copies. Last year, I finally found our biggest lead yet. It seems the Santi del Dio discovered them and many other Holy Writings of our forefathers. They left the Arad with them in their possession. Yet, the Santi del Dio is no more. The organization is long gone. Somewhere, those precious documents must still reside. Your task is to find them and bring them back."

"But where do I search for them if the Santi are no more?" Bani asked. Already, it seemed that he had two impossible tasks placed upon him. This third seemed hopeless from the start.

Qanun sighed. "Put yourself in their boots. You have just discovered the most precious of all documents in the world. You must keep them safe from harm. Where would you take them?"

"Somewhere safe and secure," Bani replied, knowing that was little answer to the dilemma.

"Right. In those days, the Santi were strongest in Velona and a place called Mont Blanc, somewhere in the Greenway. That is the best starting location I can give you, Bani. While you are away, I will continue my efforts to glean more clues. If I find any, I will send them to you at once."

He continued, "Remember always that you have the full backing of the entire Qaam, all five hundred thousand of us." The Qaam was the holy name of their sect, derived from the ancient times of Jes Amir. Back then, there were four sects. Only the Qaam survived the destruction of the Arad.

Bani took comfort knowing that all within the Arad were supporting him, though he felt wholly unprepared for the three tasks set before him. Yet, he did not despair. He had faith, a strong, unyielding faith. Indeed, as a holy messiah, he was faith. "Though these tasks are long and difficult, Qanun, I shall not return until I have succeeded in all three."

"I know that you will not fail. You are the best messiah in the Arad. I believe in you, Bani. Now go help Tamina pack for your long journey. You leave at first light. We will use the Banca del Dio to transfer funds to you as you need them. Remember always that there are members of our sect out there in these foreign lands. Use them to help you as needed. Go with Lord Jehosa's blessing, my son." He said a brief prayer for Bani and then left the tent.

Tamina, who had listened in on their conversation, finished polishing her many weapons. As Bani joined her in the back of the tent, she carefully sheathed them. "I have my weapons ready, Bani." He saw that she had both her short swords ready, along with her three daggers and five knives, and he grinned.

"Well, you are armed, my love," he teased her.

"As befitting your right hand, my messiah. Once we set forth, it is only I who will have your back. I must not fail you," she said determinedly. Since ancient times, the wife of a messiah always was a fighter herself, always guarding the messiah's back. True, a messiah usually had many followers, but the wife was the most important of all.

"I know you will, Tamina. I just wish that we didn't have to leave our son, Ali, behind." Ali was only two years old now, and both knew that they could not bring him along on this Holy Quest. His brother and family promised to take care of Ali while they were gone. Already they had said goodbye to him, before they came here to intercept this latest evil priest who had entered the Arad.

"Our quest, Tamina, is to be known as the Quest for the Holy Graal. If we are intercepted, they will believe that we are seeking the Son of God's last drinking goblet that he shared when he was resurrected and held his last supper with his disciples. That grail is said to have given forth new life, yet it is the true life that we seek."

Tamina grinned, "Deceptive as always, my love. The Quest for the Holy Graal it shall be."

The next morning, while the others dismantled the camp, the two packed their saddlebags and said their final parting words. Six days later, tired and dusty, they rode into the thriving city of New Barq. Originally, centuries ago, this was the southern and only port city in Juda Arad. Then, the city fell into the hands of the Centurions of Megalos and was destroyed. They rebuilt the city just south of the ruins, calling it New Barq. Today, it was an independent city-state. While people from Megalos lived here, so did many from the Sea Prince lands and even a few from the Arad. As the two neared the outskirts of the city, they saw a most strange sight.

From the edge of the city, some new kind of road was under construction. A raised gravel bed, perhaps ten feet across, supported huge timbers evenly spaced a few feet apart. On top of these two metal rails stretched out across the land. "What kind of road is this?" Bani asked a passerby.

"Oh, it's the new railroad. Zargarb is extending their new line down to us in New Barq. Something called a steam engine pulls cars along that path. Never seen one yet, though. I hear when it's done, you can travel from here to Velona in four days' time! If that is true, it sure beats two weeks by caravel, when you can get one."

"Incredible. Most strange. What kind of thing can run on two tiny rails?" Bani asked.

The man shrugged his shoulders. "Some engineers in Velona thunked it up, I hear tell. That's not all. At the same time, they are installing a new communications system. They say that we will be able to send a message to Velona from here, and it will get there in a minute or less. Now *that* I simply cannot believe!"

Tamina interrupted, "Say, what's this metal stick that you have slung over your back?"

The man smiled, "My pride and joy. Another invention from Velona. Only this one is really a good one. It's the long-gun." He proudly took it off his shoulders. "You see, I aim it at something and pull this trigger thing here. It shoots a metal bullet a very long way. They claim that it can kill a man from a mile away! Me, I believe them! Here, I'll show you two." He pointed out a distant tree. "Now you watch that tree." Boom! The noise startled both of them, but they saw something hit the tree. Both went to investigate, followed by the smiling man.

"See, told you. Marvelous invention, this long-gun is." The two stared at a large hole in the tree, amazed.

"Are these long-guns expensive?" she asked.

"Ten gold, but then you have to buy the bullets that it fires too. You can get one at El Wadi's in town," he replied. They asked for directions and made El Wadi's their first stop.

Once they left the stranger and entered the city, Tamina commented, "We have to get a couple of these long-guns, Bani. Honestly, I don't know how I am going to be able to protect your back from one of these long-gun shots. A mile away — really, I am scared, Bani."

"Me too. Yes, we need to get some long-guns for ourselves and then learn how to use them. Something tells me that this will be very important for us. I will send word back to Qanun. I want him to start buying many of these new weapons for our people. If the soldiers from Megalos have them, then none of our people will be safe any longer. A mile away? Honestly, that is just frightening, Tamina!"

That afternoon, now toting a pair of long-guns and a goodly supply of ammunition, the two sold their horses and bought passage on the next caravel bound for Velona. They tried to get one to West Reach, but were told no caravel went directly there. Their best prospects would be to hitch a ride to that island from Velona, which was close to it.

On board the caravel, luck was with the pair. The captain had just received a dozen of the new long-guns for his ship's protection. Now he and his crew needed to learn to use them accurately. Thus, for two gold, the pair was allowed to join them. Old rotten gourds were tossed overboard. As they floated off in the caravel's wake, the crew and the two took turns attempting to hit one with their new long-guns. By the time that the two week trip to Velona was over, the crew and the two were very good shots with their new weapons. Both Bani and Tamina felt far more secure as they watched the impressive sight of Velona's harbor slowing coming into view. Neither had seen such a huge city and harbor. Indeed, there was no larger single harbor on Tarra at this time.

In fact, so many ships were waiting their turn to dock, that the caravel had to wait an entire day to get its chance to dock. During this waiting period, the captain, now friends with Bani, made an arrangement, via dingy-sent messages, for the two to get passage to West Reach. Once the dingy returned from the other boat, the two stowed their bags onto the small craft and were rowed over to an outgoing caravel bound for West Reach and beyond. Thus, this trip, the two never set foot in Velona and arrived in Bregia, West Reach, late that afternoon.

As they docked, the tallest building got their attention: the Bregia Church of Jehosanity; their enemy was here as well! They took a room at the Bally Inn and then had dinner there. After eating, Bani asked the innkeeper, "Say, where can we find the church where folks worship the wife of the Son of God? We've heard that there are worshipers of her in this land."

The innkeeper looked as if Bani had just uttered blasphemy! He put his fingers up to his lips. "Sh!" He lowered his voice to a whisper. "You don't want to go around openly talking about such things. People have been known to just disappear." In a louder voice, he said, "Nice evening for a walk." He lowered it again and suggested, "You might go ten blocks north and two east."

Bani thanked him and with their long-guns slung over their shoulders, the two headed out to take an early evening walk. They were prepared for the cold, just not the snow that covered the ground. Both slipped and nearly fell five times before they got the hang of walking slowly over the snow-covered streets. Both had never seen snow or really experienced such cold. It was late winter here in Bregia.

Soon they stood before a small, non-descript church. A strange symbol adorned its otherwise plain double doors. They saw a carved circle with an enclosed six-pointed star composed of two upside down, large, overlapping triangles. Neither knew what it meant, but they entered anyway. To their amazement, they saw twenty people inside. A service was ongoing. Both sat down on the back pews and listened.

Neither understood a word that was said. After a time, the service ended and the twenty rose to leave. One elder man with a full beard spied the two newcomers and paused beside them. "Hello. Strangers?" he asked in the Layamon dialect.

Bani shrugged his shoulders and replied, "I'm sorry, we don't speak your language." The man grinned.

To their surprise, the man now spoke in the Arad dialect. "Hello. Strangers. I am Khan Duhur. Pleased to meet you. You are from the Arad, right?"

"Yes," Bani could not conceal his relief at hearing words spoken in his own language. "I am Messiah Bani el Marina, my wife, Tamina. We just arrived from Juda Arad."

"Well, very pleased to meet you both! Say, where are you staying?" The two struck up a conversation.

"Yes, a lot of our ancestors immigrated here from Juda Arad, you know, after the fall. Quite a few of the locals do speak our language, particularly the innkeepers, who often get visitors such as yourselves. Say, my wife and I would be delighted to share our home with you."

"That would be most generous of you, Khan. We greatly appreciate your kind offer." The two arranged to meet the next morning, since they had already reserved their room at the inn.

The next morning as Khan led the two down the snow covered streets to his home, he could not help noticing how poorly the two's leather moccasins were on the snow. Both were slipping and sliding along. "You need proper winter boots," he teased them. Both could not agree more!

"Welcome to our humble home. My wife, Isi," he presented his wife to the duo. After warm introductions, they sat beside a warm fire while Isi served them all hot tea.

"What brings you to our island?" Khan asked politely.

"We've come in search of those who worship the wife of the Son of Jehosa, Jes Amir," Bani attempted to explain.

"Ah, now that is something. Yes, here on West Reach, you will find many of us who still worship the Blessed Holy Mother, that's our name for her, Bethany Madelyn Amir that is. However, I must caution you both! Our island has been taken over by our enemy Church of Jehosanity! They are everywhere these days. It is no longer safe to mention the Blessed Holy Mother in public! Some who have done so recently have completely disappeared from Bregia! No one knows what has happened to them."

Isi interrupted, "Khan, we do have our suspicions. Only two weeks ago, the Thawrah's were seen openly defying the evil Church. The next day, they both had disappeared completely! Their house went up for sale a couple days later. No one knows what happened to them, but many of us believe that the Church abducted the both of them! Around here, it is not safe to speak out against the wicked Church of Jehosanity, no indeed it is not!"

Khan continued, "Still, our churches exist. For some unknown reason, the Church of Jehosanity does not ever touch or harm our churches. None of us knows why that is. You can tell our churches anywhere. Just look for our holy symbol on the entrance doors."

"Oh, you mean that circle and star symbol?" Bani asked.

"Yes, once inside, then and only then is it safe to talk freely, that is outside your own home, I mean," Khan explained.

"What does it mean?" asked Tamina, curious about the symbol's connotation.

"It is the Circle of Life and the triangles represent the Holy Union of man and woman. You can see which is which," Khan explained. "It is said that our symbol goes all the way back to the lifetime of the Blessed Holy Mother, when she lived here among us."

"Fascinating. Say, where did she make her home? Here in Bregia?" Bani asked.

"Oh heavens no. When she and the brother of Jes Amir first came here, they found many other refugees also arriving, fleeing the slaughter in the Holy Land. She and Josh founded four cities from the wilderness of Layamon. She made Nuadilan her home. In good weather, it is but two day's ride from here. Right now, travel is difficult because of the snow and cold."

"How do you manage? This awful cold and snow — it's almost unbearable!" Tamina exclaimed. This was the worst she'd ever experienced, coming from a desert climate.

Khan and Isi chuckled, "Yes, I suppose for desert dwellers our climate is just awful," he agreed. "Yet, in the springtime, West Reach is positively a heaven." They chatted for some time.

At last, Bani decided to be frank with Khan. "The purpose of our visit to West Reach is to learn all that we can about the wife of the Son of God, Bethany Madelyn Amir. Back home, we know much about the life of Jes, but we know so very little about Bethany. Our mission is to learn all that we can about her life here after the Holy Resurrection of Jes."

"Well, you've certainly come to the right country," Khan replied.

Later that day, Khan took them to get better winter footwear and to get warmer, more suitable clothing. During the ensuing weeks, Khan took them to visit with the various Blessed Holy Mother priests and worshipers of Bregia. Slowly, the two began to learn more about Bethany's life here in West Reach.

When spring came, Khan took the two on a tour of the four closely related cities, founded by Bethany and Josh, namely Nuadilan, Amathon, Bedwyn, and Brea. Khan then left them in the care of a trusted priest in Brea, one Father Jasper. During the ensuing weeks, the two continued to meet with various priests and devout followers, slowly adding to their store of knowledge of the life and times of Bethany and Josh.

More than once, they heard the story of Bethany and her daughter Sarah dashing around Nuadilan, fleeing from some unknown man. After hearing many different versions, Bani compiled what he calculated to be the actual event. That is, Sarah came to warn Bethany that some evil man was after her. Bethany then fled Nuadilan, heading north and then west. She was never seen again. All agreed that this wicked man had finally caught up with her and had slain her.

In Nuadilan, they also heard stories about the coming of King Diget I, who claimed to have found the remains of the Blessed Holy Mother. Some said that he even made her final holy resting place, burying her with the honors that she deserved. This was precisely the information that Bani most wanted to hear!

In the middle of May, both had to agree that West Reach was almost heaven, at least what they might envision heaven to be. Now armed with the fact that King Diget I had played a vital role in recovering her body, Bani began discrete inquiries about this event. Finally, he was quietly directed to Father Amos Pitt of the Church of the Blessed Holy Mother in Nuadilan. This church was the oldest in West Reach. The original church at which Bethany had preached was on this very site, but had burned down. The current stone church was rebuilt shortly thereafter.

Bani quizzed Father Amos about these early legends. He impressed the priest with his knowledge and his quest to bring all of this information back to Juda Arad and to share it those in the Holy Land. So much so, that at the start of the last week of May, Father Amos took Bani aside and said, "My son, Holy Messiah, I want to share a secret with you, but you must give me your solemn, sacred word not to share this with others. When I share the secret, you will understand why this must be."

"I so swear, Father Amos," Bani replied, eager to hear this tightly kept secret.

"Our church here houses the remains of the Blessed Holy Mother herself! Yes, King Diget I did find her bones, and he had a special sarcophagus built to house them. Yes, he did perform a Holy Ceremony, giving her the High Honor and Respect that she deserved. Would you like to see her tomb?"

Bani could not believe his ears! His first Holy Quest was almost at an end! "Yes, it would be the greatest honor for me, a humble Holy Messiah, to touch and kiss and pray upon her!" As they went down the stone stairs into the subterranean vault, Bani could not help noticing that his and Tamina's local boots made quite a noise. Actually, it just seemed that way to the two desert dwellers.

As Father Amos brought the two to the central sarcophagus with the life-like rendition of the Blessed Holy Mother adorning it, both began crying. They sensed the intense holiness coming from this holiest of places. They realized that among the hundreds of millions of people on Tarra, they were almost unique in being able to be this close to Bethany Madelyn Amir, the wife and mother of the Son of God's children. Such was an honor for which to die! Both knelt and prayed for nearly an hour, before teary-eyed, they quietly left, following Father Amos up to the main chapel. After thanking him profusely, the two returned to their room at the nearby inn.

For an entire week, the two argued amongst themselves. "How can we possibly desecrate such a Holy Site?" Tamina wailed.

"I don't know," Bani wavered in his Holy Vow to Prophet Qanun. "To steal away her bones, her blessed remains, after King Diget I's Holy Burial Ceremony — to say nothing of his Holy Quest to find her remains, it is a sacrilege beyond words. How can I even think of doing this?" he wailed. So it went for seven days.

At last, Messiah Bani found inner strength. "Look, the entire world is about to be overrun and destroyed wholly by the evil, wicked Church of Jehosanity. I am sure that if we could talk with Bethany, she would want us to do this, if in doing so, it would help bring down this vile church. In her name, Tamina, we do this tonight." He finally reached his decision to fulfill his mission.

They put on their Arad moccasins, and late at night, the two stole into the ancient Church of the Blessed Holy Mother. Quietly, they made their way to the back private altar room. The ancient lock on the concealed door was easily picked, and the two descended into the subterranean vault. While Tamina held a small lantern, Bani used his strength to slide the heavy stone embossed lid off the granite box. Then, the two looked inside, scarcely daring to breathe!

"Oh my god!" Tamina whispered, almost dropping her lantern.

"Damn! Someone has gotten here before us! All is lost!" Bani wailed. Despair struck the two. Vainly attempting to keep from crying, the two made their way silently up the stairs, re-locked the door, and left the church. Neither said a word until they were safely inside their room at the inn.

"All is lost!" Tamina finally gushed.

Still reeling from the sudden blow, Bani ran his hands through his hair and beard. Inspiration struck. "Wait a minute. Look, from all that we have learned, which is an enormous amount when you consider this all happened centuries ago, everyone totally believes that her remains were buried here by King Diget I. Let's assume that is what happened. Then, at some later time, someone robbed the tomb or perhaps King Diget I lied and never did what he is supposed to have done or. . ." he paused in thought.

"Or what?" Tamina probed. "Surely the tales of King Diget I were not a complete fabrication. Father Amos showed us those ancient records."

"Or King Diget I only *pretended* to bury her remains here. Look, who would want to steal her remains? The Church of Jehosanity certainly would, but considering how carefully they have safeguarded this secret all these years, I doubt that they stole her bones. We must put this into the context of the times in which King Diget I lived. This burial was at most some twenty years after the Mano del Dio assassination of the young Queen Caitlyn Amir, the supposed mother of King Diget I, if those records can be believed. If you were this King Diget I, would you bury such Holy and Sacred Remains right here where your enemies lived?"

Tamina brightened up! "No way! I'd pretend to do so and then take them back with me to my kingdom and bury them in secret at a place that I could defend. He must have buried her remains near his own dwelling, wherever that may have been! Bani, you are brilliant!"

"Yes, tomorrow first thing, we must leave West Reach," he stated.

"Say, how are we going to find out where this ancient king lived?" she asked the obvious.

"In Velona. There they have a huge library. We know that he came from the mainland. So he must have had a kingdom somewhere in the Greenway or Sea Princes. I think the Sea Princes are out, because we've never heard of them having kings, only monarchs and high priests. Probably somewhere in the Greenway lies our Holy Graal."

As the two loaded down with their bags and long-guns left the inn, a shadowy figure moved up behind them. "This is a loaded gun in your back," the cold voice whispered. "Continue walking down the street if you want to live." Both did as he asked, Bani feeling the hard metal poking in his back.

"What do you want of us?" Bani asked in broken Layamon dialect.

"We know that you have been asking a whole lot of questions about Bethany Madelyn Amir, and we want to know why?" the icy voice replied quietly.

Bani said nothing; the gun barrel jabbed him hard in the small of his back; he winced. "We know that you are from Juda Arad and are infidels. What do you want with Bethany? Why are you here? Who sent you? What is your purpose? Answer me and your pretty wife lives."

Long had Bani and Tamina practiced just such a situation. He decided to reply. He purposely turned to face this man, knowing that with the gun in his hand, the assailant would not yet use it, because he was answering the man's questions. "We are seeking the Holy Graal."

Momentarily distracted by Bani turning around and seeming to be answering him, he took his eyes off both of them, giving Tamina the chance that she was waiting for. A dagger slipped from its sheath on her upper arm, sliding down into her hand. Her fingers gripped it tightly, and with one quick thrust, she stabbed the assailant in his neck. The robed man began to drop to the ground, vainly holding onto her dagger and his neck. She pulled it out as he fell. Both saw that the man was indeed Mano del Dio.

"Quick, let's get out of here before anyone sees us," Tamina urged. The two began running, ducking down a side street and then heading for the public stables.

"Thanks, my dear. You were perfect," Bani complimented his wife.

"Practice makes perfect," she replied. A few minutes later and a few gold well spent, the two galloped down the road from Nuadilan heading towards Bregia. The two rode non-stop the fifty miles to the port city. There they hopped a fishing trawler, which dropped them off at Fortress d'Grange the next day. There, they discovered the new passenger train line.

Marveling at the immense steam engine and passenger cars, the two spent a gold for a ride down to Velona, which took only one day. Both fully enjoyed this incredible new form of transportation. Now they understood the meaning of this new train line being constructed down in New Barq. Yes, this new train thing would be of great benefit in travel and the shipping of goods. To the two, the train seemed to make the world smaller, though at this point they were not sure if this was a good thing or not. This day, it was, since they had gotten to Velona rapidly.

Chapter 4 Solidification

In January of 765, Pope Christos called for a Cardinal Conclave, summoning all his cardinals worldwide to Constanza City. Now forty-three, Pope Christos had finally gotten all his preparations made. His complex plans he'd refined well, nothing was left to chance. Why summon the conclave now? Two things had come to fruition, and an unexpected positive development had occurred.

First, down at the bottom of the Southlands, his experiment in the creation of a perfect society, the city of Hieras Anubis, his Holy Children, his Bambini del Dio, was a legitimate success! There was no crime; there had not been any criminal actions since its founding. That was to be expected. All children were being properly educated, which was also to be expected. Rather the Pope, being a pragmatist by nature, needed the city to be financially sound, to be able to support itself. The fiscal report on the past year, 764, was in. Hieras Anubis was now profitable, no longer requiring the input of funds from the Church of Jehosanity for its survival. Pope Christos thought that this was entirely remarkable and only convinced him further that he had made the right decisions all along. Indeed, their population had grown to nearly eight thousand.

Second, the first batch of his newly formed, very special priests had completed their education and was ready to be posted to their new positions within the various countries. These were his very special Confessore del Dio. Their training had been exceedingly special. Their Holy Task was to take a person who defied either the Church or the tenets of Jehosanity and get them to confess their sins, their evil, wicked actions. Thus, they needed to be well versed in the tenets of church doctrine, to be able to spot easily those whose actions contradicted either one, and to be able to do what was needed to extract a confession from the guilty parties. These first fifty Confessore del Dio he had personally observed in action, guaranteeing their success in the field. These men combined many of the techniques used by the Mano del Dio as well as priests who performed Holy Confessions for the general worshipers. They were now competent and ready to go into action for the Church.

The unexpected development occurred in the healing profession. Apparently, one Doctor Yi in Tashien had perfected the art of surgery upon limbs, revolutionizing the treatment of injured arms and legs that could not be saved. Now all doctors were being uniformly trained in these new surgical procedures. The Church needed such services to support their Holy Women of the Eighth Degree Ceremony, which was still growing, albeit at a very, very slow rate. Now, Pope Christos had further plans for this surgery and had acquired fifty new Medico Santo who were to join with the

Confessore del Dio in handling those who insisted on defying the Church or its Holy Tenets. Pope Christos could scarcely believe his good luck that derived from this unexpected development. Thus, he called for his conclave of cardinals.

At nine in the morning, Pope Christos walked ceremoniously into the Holy Assembly Hall, where the many cardinals had gathered, talking among themselves. None had any idea why they had been summoned. None knew of any substantial, worldwide threat to their Church, and speculation ran wild.

"Thank you all for answering my summons. I have news of the greatest importance. We are now about to launch my Holy Plan for World Domination by the Church of Jehosanity. Yes, esteemed cardinals, we are about to take a giant step toward our goal of bringing the Holy Salvation of Lord Jehosa to the entire world. Let me outline the problems that we are facing in today's modern world."

"Within your areas back home, are there not still people who rail against our Holy Church? Condemn us; criticize our every action? Indeed, some among you are bombarded with such on a daily basis. Are there not many who do not believe in Lord Jehosa and our Holy Gospels, our Holy Teachings? Do some not rail against our Holy Tenets? Indeed, they do. My Holy Plan will begin to handle this once and for all."

"When you return to your countries and cities, I will be sending along with fifty of you one of our new Confessore del Dio men. These highly trained individuals are steeped in the Holy Tenets of our Church. Indeed, their vast knowledge may startle and rival some of you, my esteemed cardinals! I know. I personally trained each one of these men myself. Yet, they are more than just knowledgeable of our religious dogma. They are highly skilled to be able to take a person who has defied either the Church or the tenets of Jehosanity and get them to confess their sins, their evil, wicked actions. Yes, these Confessore del Dio are able to spot easily those whose actions contradict us or our tenets, and more importantly, they are able to do what is needed to extract a confession from the guilty parties!"

As expected, Pope Christos had to pause for a time, allowing the surprised cardinals to discuss this amazing revelation among themselves. A bit later, he continued, "With each of these Confessore del Dio, I will also be sending along one of our newly trained Medico Santo. These men are highly skilled surgeons, capable of handling any needed surgery and provide any needed medical care. While they are assigned specifically to the Confessore, when they are not needed by the Confessore, they will also attend to your needs and to those within your area, providing any desired medical care." Again, he had to pause while the cardinals reacted quite favorably to having their own medical doctors with them. This was a dramatic step forward in their estimations. "To safeguard and assist the Confessore del Dio and the Medico Santo, four Mano del Dio will always accompany them, providing any needed security and assistance."

"Now here is how this will work," Pope Christos then spent a good while outlining what the cardinals were to do. Essentially, it boiled down to alerting their Confessore of anyone who was particularly against their Church or its religious tenets. The Confessore would take it from there. Pope Christos did not elaborate just what would happen when the Confessore met with the offender, other than to say those who repented, would be salvaged, converted into worthy Church members.

"I know that only fifty Confessore are way too few. Many of you will not yet have one assigned to your country or city. Have faith. It takes time to train these men and to train the Medico Santo. Each year, I will be sending out more of these special teams. I hope that within ten years we will have enough for all our needs worldwide. I know that is a sweeping goal, but I will work hard to make this a reality."

"Now then, on a completely different front, I want to personally report on the incredible success of our special experiment which has proven most worthy and has exceeded all expectations. Only a few of you know about my personal experiment. Now it is time that you all hear of it. Down in the Southlands, the Church bought out all the people who used to live in the ravaged port town of South Port. There in the abandoned homes, I established a new city called Hieras Anubis, the Holy Children, my Bambini del Dio. Ever since the ill-fated arrival of the Elders of Dorota, we have been faced with the situation of how to deal with so many women who were deceived and gave up their arms for that religion. Unlike our Holy Women of the Eighth Degree, these were ordinary women and young girls. Many of you know how awful the situation was."

"Yet, we also know that originally on Dorota, they claimed to have a perfect society, one without criminality, without wars, where all children were properly educated, and where all were deeply religious. Their Elders failed in their vain attempts to bring their way of life to the other lands of Tarra. Our own Pope Leo, my predecessor, visited Dorota and we have his hand written accounts that indeed back up all the positive benefits that we have heard so often expressed by their Elders, that theirs was a perfect society in all ways."

"Thus, I took it upon myself to re-create their perfect society in Hieras Anubis. Yes, on the side, we gathered all those who yet remained on Megalos, in Demokritos, and other places and moved them to this new city, totally devoted to their unique needs. Yes, I have been personally funding them these past many years, allowing them to get themselves fully established and functioning. Today, I am very, very proud to announce to you that as of last year, Hieras Anubis is financially on their feet, totally self-sufficient, requiring no funds at all from me or the Church!"

"Cardinal Krios Panos has been there with the three Elders who agreed to oversee this establishment of a new city devoted to their needs. I call upon him to give you all a full report on this incredible success. Yes, in all these years, there has yet to be a single crime committed in that city! Cardinal Panos, I give you the podium!"

For over an hour, the young cardinal outlined what had taken place and the vast results. All were very impressed with the fact that all these people were now ardent supporters of the Church of Jehosanity and its tenets, which were originally so close to those back on Dorota. His glowing report inspired even more confidence in Pope Christos, who had the vision and ability to have brought this experiment into fruition.

Later that day, Pope Christos gave his farewell address to the assembled fifty Confessore. He instilled in them, "Please use caution and discretion for a few years until we have all the kinks worked out. I expect monthly reports from each of you. Tell me what is working and what is not. Tell me your suggestions for changes. In time, I am certain that we will have a smooth operation going. Above all, remember do not let any trace of those who refuse to repent be discovered! For now, secrecy is our best protection."

He looked upon the bright, young faces of these men, eager to fulfill their Holy Duties and knew that they would ultimately be successful. However, he also knew that if word got out about what really happened to those who did not repent, the backlash could totally undermine the whole project and his plans, hence his strong admonition to the Confessore.

The next day Pope Christos watched the many caravels departing for distant shores, carrying the cardinals and the new Confessore del Dio, Medico Santo, and their protectors. He grinned, for his plan was now set into motion. Next, he visited the Supreme Prelate of the Mano del Dio, Thales Deus, a man of thirty. Thales gave the pope a demonstration of the new long-guns. So impressed was Pope Christos that he gave the order to purchase one for every Mano del Dio.

A bit later, Thales also demonstrated the newly acquired powder bomb, imported from Tashien. That this small device could shatter a huge boulder, as well as moving it, greatly impressed the pope. He gave orders to begin manufacturing them here in Constanza City. He then added their use to Phase Two of his Holy Plan. In time, these would be incredibly useful, he rightly concluded. So much was going so right for him, and he was pleased.

During the next five years, Pope Christos continued to train more Confessore del Dio and more Medico Santo personnel. He monitored all the reports and continued to refine their methods and procedures. At this point, in Vito, Bonilla, and Megalos, the Confessore were fully operational and working at the intended rates. Now, Pope Christos began allowing the Confessore in the ten Greenway kingdoms to begin their full operations, unfettered by the extreme caution that the others had to observe.

Also by 770, the population of Hieras Anubis had swelled to nearly ten thousand, and the city now faced expansion problems and needed his attention once more. Pope Christos listened carefully to the suggestions of

Cardinal Krios and decided to accept his suggestions. Essentially, the Church would loan the city the funds to construct a second city three miles to the east at a bay conducive to harbor construction. They would also construct a third city three miles to the west, which would not have a port or docks, except for small fishing vessels. He christened them Anu East and Anu West.

In May of 770, Pope Christos received a message that he had been expecting for some years from Cardinal Danski of Demokritos. Emperor Kreon's wife, Frona, a Holy Woman of the Eighth Degree, was very ill and expected to die shortly. Pope Christos smiled and prepared to leave for Demokritos that very day.

The end of July, Pope Christos finally arrived at Emperor Kreon's Palace in Kefall. As expected, Empress Frona had passed away and been given a royal funeral. Accompanied by Cardinal Danski, Pope Christos was introduced to Emperor Kreon, who sat impressively on his throne. The two leaders were the same age, forty-eight. The pope looked resplendent in his purple robes with extensive and ornate gold trim. The Emperor looked virile and robust for his age. He wore a heavy cotton shirt and pants, both were Imperial Green. A jewel-encrusted crown adorned his head. The pope sensed a twinge of sadness in the Emperor's eyes.

"It is a high honor to meet with you at last, Emperor Kreon," the Pope said in welcome. "Please accept my sincere understanding on the death of your highly esteemed wife, Empress Frona. The world has indeed suffered a great loss." He made a guess that this was behind the Emperor's mood.

"Well met at last, Holy Pope Christos. Yes, it is a shame that we meet under such sad circumstances. May we speak in private?" the Emperor asked. Pope Christos, somewhat surprised by this request, nodded. The Emperor's three advisors quickly left the room, but Emperor Kreon held his hand up, bidding Cardinal Danski from also leaving. "Please, Your Holiness, stay a while that we may talk." Cardinal Danski bowed humbly.

"Indeed, your loss is great. Empress Frona was a role model for so many of your people. She was a brilliant statesman and had a deep love for your people. Her loss is great, Your Majesty," Pope Christos poured it on a little heavy to see the reaction of Kreon.

Kreon sighed, "Yes, yes, she was all that and so much more. I, I find this hard to say, but I truly miss her. I never expected to have such feelings — you know that my tastes are for young men?"

"Yes, of course. This is a great tribute to Empress Frona that she could so touch your heart, Your Highness," Pope Christos replied, being careful not to affront the leader over his unusual sexual practices.

"Indeed, that is so, that is so." He paused a moment before continuing, as if considering his position. "Pope Christos, never has Demokritos had such an ally as you have been to us. Your continuous monetary donations to the throne and me over these many years has most definitely endeared you and your Church of Jehosanity to me — particularly so to my Frona who never doubted you. With her passing, I find myself deeply in your debt — so much so that I am almost afraid to ask yet another favor of you and Cardinal Danski."

Pope Christos smiled; oh, this was so delicious! The Emperor acknowledged openly his debt to the Pope! Indeed, he should. Kreon had received many millions of gold from Christos! "Please, most worthy Emperor, please, you must ask. The whole purpose of the Church is to administer to the worthy of Tarra. Who is more worthy than the Emperor of the largest country in the world? None, I say. Please, how may the Church be of further service to you?" He especially liked how he had deftly inserted the word 'further.'

Emperor Kreon struggled with his inner thoughts a moment before replying. "While I prefer young men, always it is done discretely. My people must have an Empress on the throne at my side. Frona understood my needs and I hers. Ours, while not what you would consider a traditional marriage, ours was, well, ideal for us both. She was always satisfied and wanted for nothing, and in return, she allowed me to want and yearn for nothing. Now I do find that I miss her so very much. Such tolerance and love is so very rare."

"Oh indeed, Frona was a rare flower, a Holy Woman of the Eighth Degree, so rare indeed," Pope Christos backed him.

"Yes, we agree. How do I ask this?" Kreon fumbled, uncertain how to make his desire known without causing any affront to the Church and its holy men.

"Please, just ask it simply and directly, Your Highness," Pope Christos urged, still unable to grasp what the man might desire.

"For the good of my country and for me," Kreon finally just asked, "I would like a replacement Empress. I would like, no, I *need* another woman like Frona, if that is even possible. Yes, she should be a Holy Woman of the Eighth Degree, but she must understand my needs and my disposition and not be offended or upset by it. In turn, I swear to treat her with the same high respect and honor that I have done all these years to my dear Frona. Is this possible? Can you possibly find such a woman for me to share the throne of Demokritos?" There, he had actually vocalized his desire. Somehow, it didn't sound as badly as he had feared these many weeks. A small spark of hope lit his eyes as he looked at the two holy men.

"Your Majesty, we would be most honored indeed to assist you in this most vital matter of state and heart," Pope Christos replied. Oh, how he was savoring his victory over Demokritos! "Allow us some time to find the ideal woman for you."

"Oh thank you both! This is the most heartening news that I have had for weeks. Please, is there anything that Demokritos or I can do for the Church or yourselves, perhaps?" Emperor Kreon asked sincerely. He knew that men always wanted something. No one offered their aid unconditionally, not in Demokritos. Even Frona wanted something in return for her unconditional support of him.

"Well, Emperor, there is a little something. You see, there are those in Demokritos who are vehemently outspoken against the Church, even to the point of persecuting our followers and our priests," Pope Christos began quite carefully.

"Yes, of course. Isn't this always the case with religions?" Kreon asked. He already knew the answer to that. He wasn't the Emperor for lack of grasp of fundamentals.

"Yes, indeed it is so. However, are there not also some within Demokritos who still strike out against you? Some who openly condemn you or cause no end of trouble for the Imperial Throne?" he asked, knowing from the many reports over the years from Cardinal Danski that there were many such men and a few women.

"Yes, of course. Why?" Emperor Kreon asked, slightly annoyed that the Pope would bring up this minor flaw in his reign. He did his best to please the majority population. There would always be those that would be offended that he didn't please them, give them what they wanted. Kreon's Rule had always been give the most to the most and the population will be happy and support you. It mattered not whether what he gave them was good for them or not, only that it was what the majority wanted.

"What if I told you that the Church of Jehosanity has now become able to deal with all those who are so outspoken and rail against both the Church and also those who rail against yourself? Indeed, we now have very specially trained Confessore del Dio men who are able to do just that. They are able to work with these recalcitrant individuals and get them to see the errors of their ways, to confess their sins and seek Holy Redemption, changing their ways."

"That is very impressive indeed!" Emperor Kreon suddenly sat straight. This was very curious and hopeful news, that someone had actually found a solution to this nightmare problem that all rulers must face at one time or other. "Do tell me more!"

Pope Christos knew that he had him netted now. "Yes, already, our Confessore are succeeding very well in several northern countries. Once the Confessore pick up a person, that person will either repent and become a useful, supporting person or they simply disappear from the society that they lived in and are placed in another society, one in which they will be able to find their salvation. Of course, in this latter extreme case, their possessions in the society that they leave are turned over to the Church."

"This has proven to be a very workable method. If you are interested and will allow us free rein to implement our methods here in Demokritos, we will also work our magic on those whom you deem enemies of your throne. In these cases, should they not repent their sins, their possessions would, of course, become the property of the Emperor, not the Church, since they offended against you, not the Church."

"You would do this for me?" Kreon asked in disbelief. Oh how he was using this Church to his great advantage! His entire reign was based upon using the right people at the right time to further his ends. Now he had the Church of Jehosanity under his thumb as well, doing his dirty work for him! This was just too incredible for words. "Yes, I hereby grant you permission to allow your Confessore del Dio to work their magic in Demokritos. Pray, how do I notify them of those who, as you say, rail against the throne?"

"I believe the easiest way would be for you to send a message to Cardinal Danski, who will arrange for the Confessore to meet with you in private to discuss the person's situation and how it may best be handled for all concerned. Would that be satisfactory?"

"Absolutely. I will begin compiling a list. There are a number of men who simply will not cease their condemnation of all that I do. Obviously, they are in a tiny minority."

"Obviously, Your Majesty. Shall we shake on this?" Pope Christos asked. The two exchanged a hardy handshake, sealing the bargain.

"Understand, your country is large and it takes time to train these very special priests, these Confessore. I will do all that I can to send as many here as quickly as possible. Please for the immediate future, prioritize those whom you deem need to repent of their ways. In time, the Confessore will deal with all them."

"I understand fully. Yes, I will begin to compile the list."

"Perfect. I have brought six Confessore teams with me on this trip, and they will begin their work soon. Now, if you will excuse us, we must set to work to fulfill your special request. I am sure that within a few days we will be able to have just the right woman for you."

"Thank you, Your Holiness, thank you." The three men shook hands and the pair left. Kreon shouted for joy once the two were well out of earshot. His advisors came running fearing the worst had happened, only to discover a very cheerful Emperor waiting for them.

Once back at the Cardinal's residence, the two men conferred, having been lost in their own thoughts during the carriage ride there. "Cardinal Danski, I will need your assistance in locating the perfect woman for Kreon. She must, of course, be a Holy Woman of the Eighth Degree, preferably between thirty and forty, relatively attractive, but with the proper disposition. She also should be an ardent Church supporter and have a head on her shoulders."

"Of course, Your Holiness. I will begin my search at once. I maintain a complete list of all the Holy Women in Demokritos. I will set to work at once," Cardinal Danski replied.

"Good. Send in my six Confessore, please."

Selene Omela was an astute businesswoman who worshiped power. As a young girl in her teens, she had single-handedly turned her father's failing business around. As she learned the hard way, men are not always appreciative of a woman succeeding where they failed. For her efforts, she was quietly set aside after the business began to flourish once more. Selene was not one to let misfortune rule her life. She was not unattractive, though not exceptionally pretty either. Hence, with the Annelise fashions becoming the norm at all courtly affairs, Selene began to wear nothing but the most fashionable apparel. For years, she endured ever more constricting wasp waist corsets from Annelise until now at thirty she proudly displayed a fifteen-inch waist.

She had let her curly brown hair grow long. The combination of her ample bust, tiny waist, and billowing satin dresses, complete with staggeringly high heels from Annelise now made her a striking figure at any gathering. She had achieved her objective in this category.

When she was twenty, she endeared herself to Alkimos Omela, a wealthy bachelor who ran a thriving import-export business. Within a month, they were married. Her next objective was somehow to gain more power and control over Alkimos. Alkimos was fascinated with the Holy Women of the Eighth Degree, and Selene saw this as her golden opportunity. Such women commanded great respect and power. She celebrated her twenty-first birthday by becoming such a woman herself.

Of course, Alkimos now absolutely had to surround Selene with all manner of personal servants. For a time, he was quite smitten with Selene, as her power over him slowly grew. Then, disaster struck, she became pregnant and had to put her waist reduction on hold, to say nothing of losing her nightly pleasures. She groaned every day about the ever-increasing size of her belly. Worse, Alkimos now seemed to pay little attention to her! Oh, never should a man do that to a Woman of the Eighth Degree and certainly not to one of Selene's power.

Karpos Omela was born and christened by Selene, ignoring Alkimos' requests for his child's name. Now Selene put all her attention on reducing her waist back to where it had been before she had become pregnant. However, she enjoyed suckling her baby and grew overly fond of her child, something she had not anticipated nor expected for that matter. As Karpos grew, she doted over him, spending less and less time with Alkimos, whom she was certain was having affairs with other women now.

When she was twenty-five and Karpos, four, Alkimos met an unfortunate accident at the docks, where he was observing the unloading of some new imported acquisitions. Some whispered that Selene was somehow the cause of his unfortunate and untimely accident, but nothing was ever proven. Selene now took over total control of Omela Imports. Under her astute guidance, a micro-manager, the company's profits soared to new heights, proving that she was more than competent. Indeed, lacking arms, she made up for that by using her mind. She had an eidetic, nearly photographic, memory. She never forgot a face; she knew the precise tally of their entire inventory, all from memory, since she could not write anything down or even pick up a ledger to read such information.

For the last five years, she continued to get her waist size reduced to her desired goal. Now it was perfect and she was content with this aspect of her appearance. She made sure that Karpos received the very best education and fighter training, particularly with these new guns and long-guns that had begun making their appearance in Demokritos. Here in 770, Selene was well respected, highly successful, and quite wealthy. In short, she was most definitely a sought after woman by many men.

However, screwed by her father and then by Alkimos, to say nothing of having to endure being pregnant, Selene wanted nothing to do with the many suitors who flaunted themselves at her feet, more precisely, at the edge of her fourteen foot in diameter satin Annelise dress. Oh, she allowed some to dance with her; it would not be seemly to ignore all men totally; she'd lose power if she did that. It was just that no man ever got a second date, so to speak, with her, but all that was about to change on August 4, 770, during the late winter. (Here in the southern hemisphere, the seasons were opposite those in Velona.)

Her servant interrupted her morning hair brushing. "My Lady, Cardinal Danski is here! He wants to speak with you. He says that it is most urgent." The servant was most impressed. Never had she been even close to such a Holy Man. That the Cardinal himself chose to come to her mansion impressed Selene.

"Okay, take him into the drawing room. Prepare some tea. Estelle, how do I look? Is my long hair properly done now?" Estelle assured her that she looked perfect, though of course, Estelle would never tell her that she didn't, for she valued her job. It paid very well. Selene rose, found her balance on the extreme heels, slowly glided across her sitting room, and headed down the hall to the drawing room, prepared to make her grand entrance. Long ago, she had ordered all the doors in the mansion removed, allowing her freedom of movement throughout the large estate. Selene glided perfectly into the drawing room, where the Cardinal was just removing his heavy winter cloak, revealing his cardinal robes and skullcap, all embossed with golden threads.

"Ah, My Lady Selene! You look stunning today. Allow me," he carefully positioned her chair for her, adjusting it as she demurely sat down at the very expensive mahogany table, highly polished and with golden candlesticks positioned perfectly on it.

"Your Holiness, you give me great honor by your visit. Would you care for some tea?" Selene asked politely, knowing that this was the perfect way to begin their conversation. She reasoned that if he wanted to talk with her privately, he would have to hold the cup for her to sip, giving her power over him.

"Yes, please, it is so cold outside. I, for one, am quite ready for spring," he replied, sitting beside her. He too realized that if he wanted a private chat then he would have to wait on her needs. This he was prepared to do. Too much depended upon this meeting.

A minute later, a servant brought a tray with two fine china cups and pot imported from Tashien. She poured both cups, curtsied, and left the two alone. Cardinal Danski held the cup up for Selene, who took a demure sip. "What brings Your Holiness to my humble home on such a cold morning? Is there something that I can do for our Church, which has been so wonderful for me?" she asked coyly, knowing that whatever it was, it must be exceedingly important, for the Cardinal himself was holding her cup!

"Selene, I have a proposition for you," he began. Quietly, he outlined the situation with Emperor Kreon fully. "Knowing the situation with him, would you be interested in meeting with him? If he finds you acceptable and you find him acceptable, you can be married with the Church's blessing and become our new Empress. You have all the qualifications needed. You wear only the finest, height of fashion dresses. In my humble opinion, Selene, you would make a perfect Empress. What do you say?" Cardinal Danski kept his fingers crossed.

Selene prided herself on never, ever losing her self-control. Constricted in this tight outfit though, she nearly fainted. Never had she set her sights on so much power. Empress! She wanted to shriek, to yell, and to scream out "Oh Yes!" Fighting to keep from fainting, she said, "Yes, that would be most acceptable. When shall we meet?"

"Excellent, Selene, excellent. Let me arrange it. Would a dinner meeting this evening be too soon for you? Then, you could spend the evening getting to know each other."

"Yes, oh, yes. Perfect. Oh, will I need to bring along my servants? You know, to handle my needs at a meal and such?" Selene asked. No way did she want to embarrass the Emperor by making him feed her and helping her go to the bathroom, if she could avoid it.

"I do not believe that you will need to bring along any servants. However, I will check and if so, let you know soon. If you will excuse me, Selene, I must see to the arrangements for dinner. The Emperor will send a carriage for you, say around five?"

"Perfect. I will be ready and waiting. Thank you for giving me such an honor!"

"Oh you are most welcome, Holy Woman. You are the inspiration for so many women of our fine country." He bowed, donned his heavy cloak, and left. Selene sat there quite stunned by the suddenness of this incredible opportunity. She barely noticed her servants gathering around her, most curious about what transpired.

Selene fought to calm her racing heart, desperate to catch her breath.

At last, she managed to say, "Tonight, I am to dine with the Emperor. He, he is interested in my hand in marriage!" Of course, she had no hand to give, but that was beside the point. Her servants shrieked and danced around the room, just as excited as she was. "Oh, I must prepare! Draw a bath at once. What dress shall I wear?" The women enthusiastically set about their many tasks.

At four, she was ready and nervously awaiting the arrival of the carriage. She wore her light blue satin gown, which displayed her ample bosom rather well. Her long curly brown hair was perfectly done. She opted to wear a pair of the black silk hose imported at great expense from Tashien, the kind that felt extremely sensuous on her well-proportioned legs. She wore her finest black Annelise oxfords with their seven-inch heels. The fourteen-foot billowing gown greatly accentuated her tiny fifteen-inch waist. She wore a pair of blue sapphire earrings with a matching necklace, whose gemstone was the size of a baby's fist. In short, Selene looked absolutely stunning and felt that way, which was all that mattered to her. Her opinion of herself was all that really counted.

As the hour drew close, her servants put her heavy winter cloak over her shoulders, adjusting her hair properly. At last, the carriage arrived and a gentleman servant graciously escorted her and assisted her into the carriage. A short while later, he assisted her out and led her into the main entrance of the Imperial Palace, where Emperor Kreon stood waiting for her arrival.

He wore his finest satin suit, emerald green. His boots were highly polished and he looked remarkably fit and handsome. "Ah, you must be Selene. Allow me to take your cloak," he offered. Selene seldom had a man remove her cloak, but saw no other option now. Kreon totally surprise her, though. Not only did he properly remove her cloak, he adjusted her hair almost as well as her own servants would have. She found this intriguing. His arm around her thin waist, he led her into the expansive dining room. She smiled. There were only two places set side by side, candles were burning, and four musicians began playing soft music from a distant corner of the room.

In these heels, Selene had to walk very slowly, but Kreon seemed not to notice, escorting her perfectly to her seat. After getting her properly seated, he took the seat beside her. Selene realized that the Emperor would be actually feeding her and helping her dine, not some servant woman. How unusual she thought!

Selene was most impressed with just how able Kreon actually was at waiting on her needs during the delicious meal. Certainly, Alkimos never was able to do this remotely right! In Selene's mind, the dinner went absolutely perfectly. This she could not understand: a man could be this sensitive to her needs. Such she had never experienced.

With the meal finished, he suggested they move to his private sitting room. Again, he was the perfect gentleman, helping her as needed. In fact, she noted that so far she had not actually had to ask for a single thing. Always, Kreon seemed to know just what she would need next. Selene was impressed as she sat down on the velvet love sofa. Kreon sat beside her.

"You are an incredibly beautiful young woman, Selene. I am very impressed with you," he began. "I assume that the Cardinal has explained my situation, I mean my preferences and such?"

"Yes, he has. That is, you prefer young men," she replied, testing him.

"Aye, that I do. And that I prefer this does not bother you? I mean, you cannot expect me to physically love you as I do young men?"

"Not at all. I really don't like such done to me. I certainly do not want to get pregnant again, not even to bear the Emperor's child. I hope this will not be a problem for you," she said honestly.

He smiled, "Amazing. You are so like Frona in so many ways. She never said a word about my affairs with men. She was very content to be pleasured in bed. She never asked me to do what I cannot with her in our bed, if you follow me."

"That would be perfect. I do so love to be pleasured; having no arms makes that so difficult for me. Pleasure, I do desire greatly. The other — well, like you, I can do without," she replied.

"I promise you that I will always pleasure you properly and to your satisfaction. Yet you will not be upset if after that I leave the bed for a time?" he said inquisitively, rather beating around the bush, so to speak.

Selene knew what he meant. "Absolutely not! Actually, once I have been pleasured, I would feel just terrible if you did not obtain the pleasure that you need. I'd have to kick you out of the bed and make you go get it," she teased, bringing a broad smile to Kreon's face.

"I thought that this whole subject would be the ruin of me, of us. Once again, I owe the Cardinal my eternal thanks. You, Selene, are a rare flower!" With this rather embarrassing situation handled fully to both their satisfaction, the two entered into a long and friendly chat.

Selene then brought up the only other potential obstacle. "I do have a nine year old son that must stay with me for a few more years. As soon as he is fourteen, though, he will be moving into my mansion and taking over my import-export business. I do hope that you can deal with a nine year old running around for a few years."

"Certainly, I am sure the palace here is large enough for him," Kreon teased her. Selene was relieved to hear his acceptance. She did not need Kreon to play dad for Karpos, just not interfere with his raising. Four hours passed by rapidly and neither wanted to end this evening.

A week later, dressed in white satin wedding gown, Selene married Emperor Kreon and became Demokritos' next Empress. She thus achieved a goal of power beyond her original planning. Even more significantly, Pope Christos married them personally in a lavish ceremony in the largest Church of Jehosanity in Kefall. This huge honor had not befallen any other person in the entire country, and as such, it made an impression on a very large number of influential people, including Selene herself, who now felt a strong bond with Pope Christos.

When Pope Christos then set sail for home, he was extremely pleased with the outcome of his visit. Actually, the result far exceeded his fondest hopes. He had handpicked the next Empress of Demokritos. That she was a Holy Woman of the Eighth Degree was mandatory, and thus she was closely tied to the Church. No, that she was eighteen years younger than Kreon was brilliant! She would survive when Kreon died. Yes, this was really what had brought the Pope to Demokritos. Succession. Kreon was a fascist, a self-appointed emperor, the first ever, bypassing all the High Councilmen. Kreon was also forty-eight. In a few more years, Kreon would die, leaving this incredibly able woman on the throne. Perfect in all ways was this result! However, all this would be needed in Phase Four of his Holy Plan; yet he was only into Phase Two now.

Chapter 5 Confessore in Action

The date: February 14, 767. The place: Glantas, Megalos. The time: 3:30 p.m. The President of the ruling Senate rose for the tenth time. "Senators, senators, please. We are supposed to be deciding the fate of the bill before us. Again, I remind you, the Church of Jehosanity is requesting that Megalos construct new ten guns ships with three being dedicated to the protection of their Holy Vessels. Please, please, the day is hot. Keep your comments directly relating to the bill before us. The floor recognizes Senator Cestis Arantos."

The sixty year old senator rose. "We should oppose this bill completely. If the Church wants gun ships of its own, let them pay for them out of their own funds. Lords knows, they take in enough tithes from our citizens as it is. Hell, probably more than we tax them to run the government!" Other senators yelled and screamed, attempting to drown him out, but the acoustics of the amphitheater were such that they could not.

"Look, I am not saying that Megalos doesn't need gun ships. I'm saying that we should not pay for the Church's gun ships." He sat down.

Another Senator rose and yelled back, "The esteemed Senator Arantos is completely out of touch with the modern world. Look at all the incredible, valuable, and fantastic things the holy Church has done for all the people of Megalos. There's free education for our children. . ."

The President rose and cut him off; tempers flared; the heat stifling. "I just said: keep your arguments to the bill at hand. We all know what the Church has done for us in the past. Hell, I'm calling for a vote. All those in favor, raise your hands." Hastily, his assistant began counting. "All those opposed, raise your hands." Again, the sweating assistant rapidly counted these senators. He then whispered to the President, who looked incredibly annoyed with the results.

"Okay, tie vote. I am closing this session. Clearly, we all need time to cool off. We will take this bill up in the morning, when cooler heads may prevail. Good day." The Senators rapidly filed out, heading for their homes and a cooling bath, much needed after sitting and baking in the hot summer sun in the amphitheater all day.

"How did it go?" Hestia asked her husband, as he entered their marble home. As with many homes on Megalos, only thin cloths were used for walls, allowing maximal airflow through the home. Ornate marble columns supported the equally ornate, red tile roof. The smells of supper cooking were in the air.

Sweating like a pig and just as grumpy, Cestis growled, "Damn Church is trying to get us to pay for their damn gun ships! At least it didn't pass. I'll give them some credit, not all senators are idiots!"

"Dear, you need a cool bath. I have your waters drawn. Take your time; supper is not quite ready," Hestia replied. She knew how to handle her husband, get him cooled off and well fed, and then he'd become the loving husband that she had married. Hestia was young herself, barely thirty-five. She'd married the older senator to gain status, but had fallen in love with him over the six years of their marriage. Hestia definitely enjoyed the benefits that came with being a senator's wife! It certainly beat waiting on tables at the inn where she first met the senator shortly after his first wife died. She'd seen her chance and taken it, befriending him. Six months later, he proposed. Hestia set their table and began dishing out the evening meal, hoping to time everything just right.

She did. A cooled down Cestis walked into the dining room refreshed. "Ah, it smells good, my love. You are such a rose. Come, give an old man a kiss." Dutifully, she did just that.

While they were eating she asked, "Why should we pay for the Church's gun ships anyway? That doesn't sound fair to me. Besides, why do we need gun ships in the first place? Is there a war going on somewhere that I don't know about?"

"My point precisely, love, there is no need for a gun ship in the first place, and certainly our people should not have their taxes paying for gun ships for the stupid Church of Jehosanity," he replied.

Around midnight, four figures dressed entirely in black climbed over the walls surrounding the Arantos home. Stealthily, they moved through the complex to the bedroom, where the two were sleeping. One opened a jar and soaked two rags in some liquid, and then handed them to two others, while he carefully closed the jar. The two crept silently up beside the heads of the two sleeping forms. At precisely the same instant, both brought the cloths down over the nose and mouths of Cestis and Hestia. At once, both tried to get up and push the smelly cloth off their face, but the vapors were very fast acting. Within a few seconds, both sets of arms slumped uselessly back down onto the bed.

Meanwhile, the fourth man had already opened the main doors and moved a wagon up to the entrance. Two of the men carried the heavier Cestis out to the wagon, dumping him in its bed, while another carried the unconscious Hestia out as well, depositing her beside her husband. Three of the men then covered the unconscious forms and moved the wagon slowly on down the street, while the fourth double checked that they had left nothing behind to suggest anything had happened. Satisfied, he climbed back over the walls and joined his comrades on the wagon as it slowly made its way through the deserted streets of Galantas. All four men removed their masks and donned farmer's hats, pretending to be farmers, in case they were stopped by the city guards. They were in luck and saw none.

Cestis awoke and found himself bound securely to a chair, which was bolted to the floor. His hands were tied to the arms of the chair, palms out, fingers splayed. His lovely young wife, Hestia, was similarly tied in a chair next to him. She was just now regaining consciousness. "What is going on here? Where are we? I am a senator! You'll hang for this!" he bellowed loudly, while struggling futilely with his bonds. The room was dark.

Out of the shadows, a man dressed in hooded black robes stepped silently. Cestis tried to see his face, but could not. He spoke calmly and softly. "Cestis, this is your Judgment Day. I am Confessore del Dio, God's Holy Confessor. Hear now your confession of your unholy sins." He had a lengthy document in his hand, and he read it aloud to Cestis and Hestia.

"For over twenty years, I have been systematically fighting against the Holy Church of Jehosanity, cursing them, vetoing every bill that would benefit the Church in any way. I have railed against the Holy Church to everyone who would listen. I have argued with, and attempted to subvert and to disillusion, Holy Church members nearly every day for the last twenty or more years. I have publically humiliated our Holy Women of the Eighth Degree, even calling them fools and idiots." He read off a very lengthy list of similar offenses, which Cestis thought was amazingly accurate. He had fought against this wicked Church nearly all his adult life.

"I, Cestis Arantos, have finally come to my senses. I admit that I have committed all these wicked Unholy Sins and am now seeking Holy Repentance that my soul may be forgiven by our Lord Jehosa and his Holy Son Jes Amir, and be allowed to enter Jehosa's Realm, Heaven. I have been ignorant and foolish. I have been spiteful and hateful. Yet, I now seek the Holy Salvation of the Church that I have so long sinned against. To prove my undying faith in this Holy Church of Jehosanity and to prove my deep sorrow for my many past sins, I am donating three-quarters of my earthly wealth to said Church, in hopes that the funds will be able to help so many others who are deserving of the Church's Holy Help."

The Confessore then added, "It lacks but your signature, Cestis."

"I will not sign it! This is outrageous! You cannot get away with this! This is simple blackmail!"

"Oh you will sign it, Cestis. Furthermore, once you have signed it, the document will be copied and put on public display for a month. You will assign over three-quarters of your wealth to the Church. Once that is done, if you or your wife *ever* says so much as *one word* about this affair to anyone, you will be summarily executed. There is nowhere you can hide where we cannot find you, Cestis. We know everything about you. You will sign it."

"I will not! I will see you hanged for this — this is treasonous! Wait until the senators hear about this! Why, that wicked Church will be cast off Megalos!"

Wham! A leather strap smacked across the face of Cestis, delivering a painful, sharp sting. After more blows and he still refused to sign the document, sharp nails were thrust between his fingernails and his flesh, causing the old man to howl in great, intense pain. Still he refused to sign. A hammer came down on a giant spike position over the middle of his left hand, nailing his hand to the arm of the chair. He screamed in pain and passed out.

A while later, a foul smell woke him. He was still sitting in the chair, his hand still nailed to the arm. The Confessore spoke calmly and quietly, "Since you do not value your own well-being, perhaps you value that of your lovely wife, who has also committed treasonous acts against the Church of Jehosanity."

"You butcher! You leave Hestia alone," he screamed.

Now the Confessore moved over to Hestia. He produced a second document and read off the charges against her. Mostly they were speaking out publically against the Church and ridiculing Holy Women in public places. She too refused to sign the document. Instead of beating her, the Confessore went straight for her fingernails. She screamed and passed out when rough hands forced the needles into the soft flesh beneath her nails. She awoke and found both of her hands nailed to the chair arms.

"Now Cestis, will you sign voluntarily or must we harm your wife further?"

"You bastard! The hell with Hestia anyway. She's just a good lay and housekeeper. Hurt her all you want, but I'll never sign. I'll see you hanged first!"

This was too much for Hestia. The overwhelming pain combined with her husband rejecting her, leaving her at the mercy of these sadistic men was just too much. She fainted again. Hestia missed seeing her husband having all his fingers on his left hand broken, laid back flat against his palm. She missed seeing his toes likewise broken and his feet smashed. She missed seeing him die of a heart attack at this point. She missed seeing the Confessore signing their names to another slightly different set of documents. These new ones had an additional line that read, "We are now retiring to my country estate, and in seclusion we will be praying for our salvation." She missed seeing a stone slab on the floor being slid aside, the body of Cestis dumped into the pit filled with lime, and the slab shut again. She missed her body being handed over to the Medico Santo.

On the other hand, it was wise that she missed her surgical operation. When she did regain consciousness, it returned slowly. She felt a gentle rocking motion, a bit of nausea, and pain — intense pain in both of her shoulders. Hestia opened her eyes and tried to get up, tried to see where she was. Her arms didn't work. Panic struck; her stomach knotted; she could not feel her arms. Hestia was slightly propped up on a very narrow bed. She looked for her arms and saw none, but she did see heavy bandages on her shoulders. Her arms were gone. Hestia screamed as loudly as she could.

Almost at once, the small door opened and both a man and a woman entered. "There, there, Hestia, you will be all right," the woman's soothing voice attempted to calm the terrified Hestia down. She helped her sit up in bed. When she at last stopped yelling, the man spoke softly.

"Hestia, your worthless husband is dead. He died without repenting his sins. However, the Church has confiscated his wealth anyway. You, my dear, have been given a second chance at Holy Redemption. You are being sent to a special colony where you can work hard, learn how to deal with life, and help others. If you do so, you will be granted Holy Redemption, and your soul will be allowed into Lord Jehosa's Heavenly Realm when your body dies. You are being given a completely new chance at life in this special colony. Please, do not abuse this one last chance. We will be there in about ten more days. During this voyage, the nurse here will assist you with your needs. I wish you the very best of luck in your new life, and may God guide you on the path of righteousness and virtue." He bowed and left the two alone.

Hestia cried some and then sank into a deep apathy. She allowed the nurse to deal with her bodily functions and needs. Her mind reeled, trying to take in all that had happened. It was all just too much to comprehend.

The date: May 14, 769. The place: Leadtown, Kingdom of Brownsville, Greenway. The time: noon. Eve and Connor Byfield held a rally in the town square. Leadtown was home to five thousand, mostly shepherds and foresters. Connor, a thirty year old wool shearer, stood on a make shift podium, an empty wooden box. "It is time that we returned to the old ways of choosing our king. My grandfather remembers when the candidates used to travel to all the towns and villages in Southway campaigning for your vote. Yes, we, the people, used to have a say in who our leaders were. Yet for the last fifty plus years, the Church of Jehosanity and King Baltus have denied us our voting rights. This we cannot and should not stand for any longer. Now that Baltus is dead, you and I should choose our new king, not some church. We must not let this Church of Jehosanity gain any more power over our lives!"

"But what can we do, Connor?" a friend called out. At least a hundred people had gathered. Eve was right about the time. She'd said many would be on their lunch hour and noon was perfect.

"We all stand together and just say no to the Church. Sign my petition that says we want to choose our new king, not the Church. I'll take it to the other villages and towns. If we have thousands of signatures, the Church will know that we are not going to stand for this any longer."

"Yes, but what about the soldiers?" another asked.

"They will back us too. Many of us have our sons in the army. They will not shoot their own parents and family. It's time to stand up for our rights!" Connor did his best to enthuse his fellow townsfolk. By one, he had two hundred signatures on his petition. Eve and Connor walked back to his shearing shop, quite pleased with this, their first attempt.

"Tomorrow, we can do it again," Eve suggested. "Then, we can begin traveling to the five nearby towns. By the end of next week, I bet we have over a thousand signatures, Connor. We can do this."

"Hi mom, dad," their eight year old daughter, Jean, said, when the two walked into the store. They'd left her in charge while they were gone. "Amos came by and left a bundle for you dad. Otherwise, it was all quiet."

Connor was tall and lean, nearly six-two and rather handsome or so Eve thought. She was a year younger and wore her curly brown hair shoulder length. Her blue eyes took in everything around her. She was very proud of how mature Jean was — she looked so pretty in her cotton print dress. "Jean, look at this, we got two hundred signatures." She showed her daughter the papers and Jean admired them, before heading out to play. Both Connor and Eve had been very active for nearly two years, attempting to convince others to support a return to free elections of their leaders, something long ago suppressed by King Baltus. As he grew old and feeble, the Church began having an undue influence on his rulings, until last year when the Church effectively ran the whole kingdom — illegally, according to many, including Connor and Eve.

That evening, Eve lovingly tucked Jean into bed and kissed her forehead as she always did. Connor then leaned over and gave her a kiss as well. "Sleep tight, little princess," he whispered. He always whispered the same thing, ever since Jean could remember. She liked it. It made her feel good and special. Then, the two tucked their little boy, Tom, into his bed. He was only six, but felt somewhat proud that he was always tucked in second, after his older sister. This small gesture he felt made him feel special as well. A bit later, Eve and Connor turned down the last lantern, passionately embraced, and then retired themselves.

Around midnight, four men dressed from head to foot in black crept into their bedroom. Their living quarters were at the rear of his storefront. Almost no one in the town had a lock on their doors. There was no need, no reason to lock them. The Confessore mused on just how easy his job would be, simpletons, he thought. The four prepared their cloths, putting some liquid on each before moving into position near the heads of the four sleeping villagers. In unison, the four pressed the cloths down over the nose and faces of the sleeping family members. Yes, all four attempted to react, but the vapors were very fast acting. Within seconds, all resistance ended; all four were unconscious. Quickly, the four carried them outside to a waiting wagon, placing the limp forms in its bed. It took two each to carry the two adults, for Connor was a big man, though thin. Once the four were loaded and then covered up, one man went back inside to make sure that they left no trace behind. Finding none, he returned and the four climbed onto the wagon. A few minutes later, the wagon left Leadtown behind.

Daylight shone through a window, finally waking Connor. He found himself in a strange, unfamiliar room, mostly devoid of furniture save four chairs. He was tied securely to one, his arms strapped to the arms of the chair, his hands flat against the wooden arms. His legs too were strapped to the legs of the chair, and he noticed the chair legs were secured to the floor as well. He turned his head and saw Eve similarly tied in the chair next to him. Tom and Jean were likewise tied to chairs beyond Eve. "Eve! Eve! Wake up! We've been kidnaped or something!" He tried to wiggle out of his bindings but couldn't. She woke and let out a shriek of surprise mixed with a wave of fear flooding over her stomach.

Out of the shadows, a man dressed in hooded black robes stepped silently up to them. Connor and Eve tried to see his face but could not. He spoke calmly and softly. "Connor, Eve, this is your Judgment Day. I am Confessore del Dio, God's Holy Confessor. Hear now your confession of your unholy sins." He had a lengthy document in his hand and he began to read the aloud to Connor and Eve.

"You are both charged with High Treason against the King and the Church of Jehosanity. You are both guilty of preaching insurrection and sedition." He read a long list of charges, before turning the page. He continued, "I, Connor Byfield, and I, Eve Byfield, have finally come to our senses. We admit that we have committed all these wicked Unholy Sins, these acts of treason and sedition against the Church and King. We are now seeking Holy Repentance that our soul may be forgiven by our Lord Jehosa and his Holy Son Jes Amir and that we are allowed to enter Jehosa's Realm, Heaven. We hereby state for all to read that we have been ignorant and foolish. We have been spiteful and hateful. Yet, we now seek the Holy Salvation of the Church that we have so long sinned against. To prove our undying faith in this Holy Church of Jehosanity and to prove our deep sorrow for our many past sins, we are donating all of our earthly wealth to said Church in hopes that the funds will be able to help so many others who are deserving of the Church's Holy Help."

The Confessore then added, "It lacks but your signatures, Connor, Eve. Which one of you wants to sign it first?"

"Don't sign it, Connor. You are the one who is guilty — guilty of kidnaping and extortion! Wait until the sheriff hears about this! He'll have you drawn and quartered!" Eve spat out angrily.

The two argued and yelled, railing against the Confessore for quite some time, ignoring the numerous leather belt slaps to their faces and chests. Even the breaking of all their fingers on their left hands did not dissuade them. After being revived several times, spikes were driven through both their hands. Still they refused to sign. Now the Confessore threatened their children, who by now were crying and screaming. As the Confessore moved the hammer over to Jean's hand, Connor finally broke down, Eve too. "Please, please, do not harm the children! What kind of a monster are you to hurt innocent children?" Eve wailed, suppressing the enormous pain in her hand.

"I am glad that you have seen reason." He untied each of their right hands and had them each sign the lengthy document. Once done, he gave a hand signal and two men slipped up behind them and put the cloths over their faces once more. Then, the children were gassed as well. They did not see the Medico Santo and his nurses enter.

Connor awoke, confused, ill, and in great pain. His shoulders ached, but he quickly remembered their horrid abduction. He tried to sit up, but his arms failed him. He felt a strange sensation as if his arms were not there. He looked down and saw that he was in a foreign bed, far too narrow. Then, he screamed loudly; his arms were gone replaced with two heavy bandages, one on each shoulder. His cries woke Eve, whose screams of terror joined his, and shortly Jean too began screaming as well. Poor Tom woke terribly frightened; rubbing his eyes, the boy tried to figure out what had happened.

All four were in one very small room which somehow seemed to rock gently from side to side. A narrow door opened and a man and a woman entered. She spoke softly, "There, there, it will be all right in time." The man waited while the three finished their shocking screams, which eventually subsided to intense crying. Only then did he speak.

"Connor and Eve, you both have been given a second chance at life. In due time, you and your family will be taken to a new colony where you will be given a chance to learn how to live life once more and be part of a perfect society. Your Holy Repentance has been accepted by the Church of Jehosanity, and thus you are hereby given this golden opportunity to fully redeem yourselves. If you do not and continue your evil, wicked ways, further more drastic steps will be taken to ensure the Holy Salvation of your souls. Until you arrive at the new colony, the nurse here will attend to the needs of yourselves and your daughter. Your son, Tom, can also assist you three. May God guide you now on a path of true righteousness in your new home." With that, he turned and left. They never saw him again.

"Yes, yes, everything will be all right in time. You must heal your bodies and become strong. Your family now needs you more than ever before, Connor and Eve. Be strong for your children. You are on a boat. It will sail in a few more days, and I am told that it will take many days to reach your new home. Relax now and heal."

The date: May 14, 771. The place: Brago, Vito, Sea Princess. The time: 11 a.m. Avis Porto, twenty-eight, walked slowly to the rundown docks of the coastal town. The Castelo was about to sail and its captain, Viana, an old friend, had asked Avis to bring down the blessing of Tur on his voyage. Vito was the slums of the Sea Princes; it had been so for many, many years, ever since the Church of Jehosanity took over control when the Emperor of Demokritos had conquered most of the Sea Princes, over a century ago. The Castelo was a fishing boat, old, worn out, its timbers half-rotten with dry rot. Viana was barely able to keep the poor craft afloat, managing to bring in a load of fish, just enough to provide a living for his family.

Avis was a direct descendant of old Baca Porto, one of the original founders of Vito and its first High Priest of Tur, the God of the Sea. Baca had shared the ruling of Vito along with the Sea Prince Vito. Now that the Church of Jehosanity had nearly total control over Vito, they had outlawed the ancient religion of Tur, banning everyone from the worship of such false gods. Yet, these men were seamen, fishermen, whose lives depended upon the bounty and grace of the ever unpredictable Med Sea. While the Church banished the formal worship of Tur, they could not remove Tur from the minds of men. Years ago, Avis moved from Vito down the coast to the fishing village of Brago. In time, the fishermen discovered that Avis was a priest of Tur still and begged him for secret blessings. Avis could not refuse his people. Still, they maintained an air of secrecy out of fear of retribution from the Church of Jehosanity.

After giving the Castelo his official blessing and watching the rickety ship set sail, Avis headed home, where his wife, Mora had lunch waiting for him and their two children. Alvito was seven and a bright lad, who had already learned most of his father's prayers. Avis had always said that one day Alvito would become the High Priest of Tur. Alvito had a childish certainty that he would indeed. Hence, he memorized all the official prayers that his father taught him. His daughter, Tomara, was five. She now followed her mother's footsteps, always wanting to help. Mora often paused to give Tomara a chance to do just that, even though she could have done it far more quickly and better. Seeing Tomara working so hard to fulfill a task with pride brought joy to Mora's face. Yes, life was hard, life was harsh, yet life was good to this loving family. It seemed that everyone gave them what they needed when they needed it. Friends do that for friends.

"How did it go?" Mora asked as Avis entered their one room shack and hung his worn cloak on the hook by the door.

"Well. The Castelo is really in dire need of repairs. I do hope that old Viana has a good haul this time. Perhaps he can then afford to make some of the repairs. Ah, porridge for lunch, smells good."

Mora cringed a little, so little food and so many mouths to feed. Porridge was cheap and now funds were exceedingly low. Avis had not been able to find enough wild hemp with which to make rope to sell. Yes, Avis was a rope maker, if only he could find the hemp. Perhaps one day, he would have enough money saved up so that he could purchase a large quantity of hemp and thus make enough rope to pay their bills and just maybe be able to afford some new clothes for the children. Mora certainly hoped so.

Still, neither Mora nor Avis considered themselves poor. Everyone in Vito was just as well off as they were, except for those who ran the sector and the Church of Jehosanity. Instead, the Porto's were rich in love, a quantity that cannot be bought.

That night, after saying their prayers, during which proud, little Alvito said them for the whole family, they retired for the night. While the children were contented, both Avis and Mora were still hungry. They had given the greater portion of their meager supper to their kids. Avis promised Mora that tomorrow would be a better day.

Around midnight, four men dressed in black with dark masks covering all but their eyes stole quietly into the Porto's one room shanty. The creaky floorboards broke the stillness, waking Avis, who was a light sleeper. He listened to what had to be footsteps and cautiously grabbed his dagger, which he kept under his pillow. Holding it tightly, he crept out of bed. All five were startled. Avis saw four men creeping towards their beds here at the rear of the shanty; the four men were surprised to see Avis leaping to face them with a dagger in his hand. They had not counted on the rickety floor giving them away or on Avis being a light sleeper.

Avis moved to block the man who was dangerously close to his sleeping wife and stabbed at him with the dagger. Unprepared for a battle, the intruder barely leaped back out of the way, stumbling over the children's chamber pot. He lost his balance and fell hard on the floor, waking Mora as well as the two children.

The other three froze, momentarily attempting to grasp what had gone wrong. Bang! A fifth man standing quietly in the doorway fired his gun. Searing pain waved over Avis' head. His dagger fell to the floor, and then his body collapsed onto the floor as well. Mora screamed, and the two children echoed her a moment later, as they finally comprehended what was happening.

"Gas!" the man in the doorway barked, and the three quickly poured the liquid onto their cloths. While Mora put up a valiant struggle, the vapors from the rag over her face soon knocked her out. She slumped to the floor as did Alvito and Tomara. "Well, that didn't go as planned! Quickly, quickly, get them into the wagon! Him too. Clean up the blood rapidly. Damn!" He whirled on his feet and moved to the side of the wagon, listening intently to see if they had awakened the neighbors. A distant dog barked. The Confessore kept his eyes and ears trained on the silent darkness. Damn, he thought.

His men moved quickly, but in the darkness could not tell if they had wiped up the blood from Avis or not. In fact, they had only smeared it around on the floor some, but no one really saw it until a week later. Once the bodies were on the wagon, they quickly moved on down the dark streets of Brago. Once out of town, the Confessore spoke again, "We were exceptionally lucky tonight. Lord Jehosa has been looking out for us."

"What do we do now? He's dead," asked one of the masked men.

"Not a problem. He's been tried and found guilty in absentia. Mora, too. We'll go directly to the Medico Santo. I'll simply sign their names and the assistant can inform Mora what has been done when she is allowed to waken. This kind of error has been considered and has been planned for, so nothing is lost," the Confessore explained. The man breathed a sigh of relief.

They had botched the job.

Several days later, Mora and the children were allowed to wake from the drugs they had been given. After Mora's and Tomara's panicked screams of shock, pain, and terror had subsided, the assistant and the nurse entered their caravel's cabin. The nurse began assisting the two invalids to sit up; both had heavy bandages on their shoulders; their arms were gone. Little Alvito struggled to grasp what had happened to his mother and sister. "Where's dad?" his weak voice asked.

The assistant spoke solemnly. "Avis and Mora Porto have been found guilty of heresy and subversion of the Church of Jehosanity. Avis, unfortunately, has died. Your father is dead son. Now you must become the man of the family. Mora, you and your children have been spared death. The Church has bestowed upon you and your family a second chance at Holy Redemption for your many sins and heresy. You will be taken to a colony where there are others like you. There, you and your family will have a second chance to live a productive and useful life. No more of this wild heresy; no more idol worshiping of the non-existent Sea God. If you follow the guidance of others there and live a useful, holy life, then your soul and your children's souls will be granted Holy Redemption and will be allowed to enter Lord Jehosa's Holy Realm, Heaven. However, Mora, if you fail to do so, if you and your children continue with this heresy worshiping, you will lose that second chance and be severely dealt with."

"In Brago, documents that you have signed proclaim your full and complete guilt in this matter. The documents also say that you have left Brago to atone for your many sins. You will not be missed. Now then it will be many days before you arrive at your new home. Once there, you will both be taught how to do many things for yourselves. Until that time, Alvito and the nurse here will help you with your needs. May God guide you to his eternal salvation, Mora." He turned and left them in the care of the nurse.

While Mora and Tamara cried hopelessly, Alvito looked around at his new surroundings. From the gentle motion of the floor, he knew that they were on a ship, perhaps a caravel. That his father was gone slowly sunk into his mind, along with the echo of that man's harsh words. He saw the helplessness of his little sister and went to comfort her and help her sit up. "I'll be dad now, Tamara. Lean on me," he said bravely. Mora continued to cry softly to herself; her world had ended.

The date: June 21, 769. The place: Bregia, Layamon, West Reach. The time: 6 p.m. Dora Caher bowed her head and began the Last Holy Communion Ceremony for the family of Bandon Corky. She was a twenty-one year old Priestess of the Church of the Blessed Holy Mother. She was performing the ceremony begun centuries ago by the Holy Mother herself, Bethany Madelyn Amir, and carried on after her death by her daughter, Priestess Sarah. While Dora had no ability to commune with the dead as the Druwids used to be able to do here, the ceremony was still incredibly popular among the devout, because it really helped give them closure. The survivors spoke their final, parting words to their beloved who had died. The ceremony brought great relief to the survivors, and hence it was still done today.

Only these days the Last Holy Communion Ceremony had to be done in secret. The Church of Jehosanity had long ago outlawed the ceremony, calling it black witchcraft and worse. Still, among the faithful here in Bregia, Dora defied the Church and performed the ceremony when needed. At last finished, she shook hands and hugged each of the grieving family members as they left the front room. Then she too joined the family for a last meal in Bandon's honor before she headed on home.

"How did it go?" Cormac, her husband of three years asked. He was a twenty-three year old blacksmith here in Bregia. He had already tucked their two year old daughter into bed. He'd told little Shannon a bedtime tale about the Blessed Holy Mother and the little girl had quickly fallen asleep. Now he had a bedtime cup of cocoa prepared for his wife. He hugged her and she sat down at the table.

She sipped the cocoa and replied, "It went well. I believe that the family definitely found peace because of it."

"Ah, then you did well, my dearest. Honestly, I can't imagine why the despicable Church of Jehosanity refuses to allow us to do this kind gesture for the grieving families. They are so heartless! How can they call themselves religious folk?"

"They have their ways, Cormac, and we have ours," she replied. "Perhaps one day they will tire of our island and return to their homeland." Cormac really didn't believe that they would, but began lovingly rubbing his wife's back. Shortly after that, the two turned in for the night.

Around midnight, four men dressed entirely in black with hoods over their heads crept into the Caher home. The front lock was a simple one and easily picked by these well-trained men. One opened a jar and poured a bit of its liquid onto each of three cloths, handing them to his companions. Two stole silently up to the bed where the sleeping couple lay, the other moved into the side room where the small baby crib was located. He found it precisely as described. It was just where Garvan Corky, the eldest son of the late Bandon had said it would be.

The Confessore smiled, inwardly thanking Garvan Corky for his timely information. True, he had played upon the son's greed and anger when he'd learned that his father had split his business in thirds, giving his two sisters an equal third to his. He'd been expecting his dad to leave the family business to him alone. He was howling mad over this, drowning his ill fortunes at the pub when the Confessore had found him. It had been easy to get the young man to spill the beans about the secret, outlawed ceremony that was to be held the next evening. The Corky family had been close friends with the Caher's and thus Garvan was able to describe very accurately the home's layout, particularly where they all slept. This had been too easy. Now the Church would be rid of one of its worst offenders, this vile witch Dora.

Sometime later, Dora awoke and found herself secured to a chair fastened to the floor. She looked around and did not recognize the room. Fear swept over her as her eyes fell upon her husband who was also tied to a chair next to her. Frantic with worry, she looked around the room until at last her eyes lighted on a baby's bassinet. Relief, Shannon was safe, she thought. Cormac groaned and woke. As their eyes met, he whispered, "Shannon?"

"Over there," Dora moved her head towards the bassinet. Cormac relaxed slightly. He tried to break the bonds holding his arms tightly to the arms of the chair, hands flat against the arms. His huge muscles bulged, but the thick leather straps refused to break. Dora's fear began to grow once more.

"What's happening to us?" she whispered.

Just then a door opened and a man dressed in black robes and mask entered, carrying several pages of written material. He spoke softly and sternly, "Dora Caher, you are charged with being a Priestess of the outlawed Church of the Blessed Holy Mother. Worse, you are charged with practicing witchcraft."

"I am not a witch; those are only fairy tales. Witches don't exist. Let us go," Dora put on a brave face before this unknown man.

"Did you not conduct a ceremony last night at Corky's? We know that you did. One who was there has told us all about your evil witchcraft! You cannot lie to me." He then read off a very lengthy list, outlining her many so called crimes of blaspheme, heresy, witchcraft, and worse. "For these crimes, you and Cormac have been sentenced to death." He paused to allow his pronouncement to register fully in their minds. When he saw the proper reaction to their death sentences, he knew that the timing was right.

"However, the Church of Jehosanity does not want your souls to go into the Eternal Fires of Lucifer's Hell. We want all souls to have the chance to go to Lord Jehosa's Holy Realm of Heaven. Hence, the Church is offering you both a second chance at life. If you chose to take this second chance, you must forsake your wicked, evil ways and live a holy, blessed life, helping others as you can. If you live a holy second life, your soul will receive the Holy Redemption and Salvation that only the worthy may receive. Your souls will then be granted passage into Lord Jehosa's Holy Realm. The choice is yours to make: death or a Holy Second Chance at Redemption."

Cormac spoke up, "Dora, please, we must think of Shannon. What will happen to her if we are both slain?"

"What do you mean with this second chance thing?" Dora asked hesitantly. We could always run away to the mainland for a time, she thought.

"In a while you will be moved to a new city where you will be able to start your lives over with a clean slate. What will matter after that is your conduct. Your past witchcraft and vile, evil actions will not be held against you, only what you do after you arrive at your new home. If you persist in your practice of witchcraft or continue your evil ways, you will lose your second chance at life. Which will it be?"

"Will we still be living together as a family at this new place?" Dora asked what she thought was a vital question. "We will not be killed or harmed if we take this second chance?"

"Yes, you will remain as a family and you will not be slain."

"What choice do we really have?" she retorted. "Okay, we will take your second chance."

"All praise to Lord Jehosa for guiding you both! Please place your signatures here." Two more masked men appeared and freed their right arms.

"What's this say? We cannot read this writing," Cormac asked. It was written in the Megalos dialect on purpose. The Confessor knew that neither of them could read his language nor could they speak it. He smiled as he thought of their massive confusions ahead when they arrived at their new home and couldn't speak a word of the language spoken there.

"It merely says that you are acknowledging your guilt of said crimes and that you are accepting a Second Chance at a Holy Life so that your souls may receive the Holy Redemption," he replied. Both signed their names to the documents. Later, the Confessore would forge their signatures onto another set of document written the Layamon dialect and post them around Bregia for all to see.

Once they had signed, the two men again placed the cloths over their faces, knocking them unconscious once more. Cormac woke first; the assistant stood beside him. Cormac realized at once that he was onboard a ship of some kind. His universe gently rocked and swayed. "Ah, you are awake at last. You are now on your way to your new home and your second chance at living a proper, holy life. Cormac, you must be strong, your wife and daughter will now more than ever before need your undying love and strength. Go now and wake your wife. The nurse here will help you attend to her needs and those of your daughters." He turned and left the small cabin and a nurse entered.

Cormac sprang to his feet, still slightly dizzy from the ether and a bit nauseous. He screamed when he saw his wife, waking her. Momentarily, she too screamed long and loudly, both from the pain and terror and shock of discovering that her arms had been amputated. Little Shannon's had been too. Cormac smashed his fist into the table, splintering it.

Between 765 and 780, the Confessore continued to do their work according to Pope Christos' plan. As reported earlier, by 770 the population of Hieras Anubis swelled to over ten thousand. At that time, they began construction of two additional towns, East Anu and West Anu. East Anu had a small dock that could support one caravel at a time along with numerous fishing boats. West Anu became a farming community with no coastal access. Here the waters were too rough and the shore too rocky to support even fishing vessels.

By 780, the time of this story, the population there had grown to fifteen thousand. A fourth town had been formed about two miles to the north of the port city and not too far from the Coastal Mountains. Here, sheep were being raised. The many inhabitants chose to call this village Second Chance, and the Governor of Hieras Anubis allowed the name to stand. Several times a month, a caravel would dock at the main port city, depositing another load of newly arriving second chance victims. The Governor estimated that they were receiving around forty new people each month now, on the average. They came from the Greenway, the Sea Princes, Demokritos, West Reach, and Megalos.

However, the Governor now faced a new and unexpected problem. His colony now had a superabundance of single women who needed husbands to assist them. Two to one was the ratio of available women to men. His stopgap solution was barely working at best. Now he had many middle aged women who were single. Thus, he sent a lengthy message to the Pope, suggesting several possible solutions. One was to allow the men here in the colonies to have two wives and families. Something had to be done and done soon.

Chapter 6 Beginning Moves

Late May of 780, Prelate Mallow raced to the office of Cardinal Alexio Kinos, the fifty-five year old leader of the Church of Jehosanity, Bregia, Cymry. The news that he had just verified was astounding. Breathless from his run to see His Holiness, Mallow paused before the ornate door and caught his breath. He knocked and waited, then entered humbly.

"Ah, Prelate Mallow, what brings you to see me this fine afternoon?" Cardinal Alexio looked up from the many reports he'd just received from the assorted Churches scattered over the island. This new plan of the Pope's had really made quite a difference. Resistance to the Holy Church was at its lowest point ever. That was about to change.

"Your Holiness, I bring terrible and shocking news. The Blessed Holy Mother herself has been buried all these years right here in Layamon — right under our very noses. Her remains were in a sarcophagus beneath the Church of the Blessed Holy Mother in Nuadilan! Only now, someone has stolen her bones! I've overheard many talking about this in hushed tones. I just came back from there. It is true; their priests are terribly upset and frantically searching for clues. Honestly, they have no idea who may have stolen the remains."

The smug smile evaporated from the Cardinal's face. Long had he feared something like this would happen. That her remains, her bones, did in fact exist alone was staggeringly important. That they had been here for centuries right under his nose infuriated him. He had inherited all of his predecessor's records and journals and had made an extensive study of this whole field: the supposed prostitute whore of his Holy Son of God. He read extensively about the early Church's attempts to eradicate all the supposed heirs of theirs. That so many had been assassinated only lent credence to the myth that some woman had some kind of claim over the Church. Surely, their claims were just that, false claims of some long forgotten whore.

Now things took a wild, new turn. That her remains did exist would be a severe blow to his Church. His Pope would have to begin a completely new campaign of discrediting the whore mentioned in the Holy Gospels. Only someone who knew the incredible significance of these remains could have stolen them. Why else would anyone dig up centuries old bones? In his mind, Cardinal Alexio envisioned dozens of such descendants marching upon the many Churches of Jehosanity worldwide, demanding their destruction.

"What do we do?"

The voice of his Prelate, his Mano del Dio, pulled the Cardinal back into the present. Do? Yes, that was *the* question. True, he would have to dispatch the Pope at once, but his own job would then be on the line. No, he also needed to send along with that message his handling of the situation.

"The thief must be one of that whore's descendants," he explained to his chosen man, "who is going to make an attempt to use them to discredit our Holy Church. We must not let that happen."

"Absolutely not! That's why I raced back here from Nuadilan and ran all the way from the stables to inform you. This is a terribly serious business, is it not? Could they not use this to bring down our Holy Church?" he asked his mentor.

"Well, the whore's bones alone might not. No, I fear more the descendent children who may become embolden by this and attack our Holy Church. We must take action, although I will inform the Pope, of course."

"Come with me, let's examine our archives. Your Mano del Dio predecessors were very thorough in their information gathering," Cardinal Alexio suggested. For an hour, the two re-read all the documents that dated back over a century, pertaining to the assassinations of all the heirs of the Son of God.

"Your Holiness, they speak of these people as if they really were the children and grandchildren of our Holy Son of God. Can this be true?" the Prelate asked. If so, in his mind, the threat would be monumental in proportions! If this were true, the Church should have acted many years ago. Certainly, he, as their Prelate, ought to have acted ten years ago. He promised to deliver significant pain penance on his fleshly body later this evening while praying for forgiveness for the dereliction of his duties.

"Ah ha. I believe that it is time to make use of this detail that was discovered over a hundred years ago," Cardinal Alexio said, holding up a ledger. "It seems that these descendants have left birthing records of each generation. A previous Prelate traced this supposed ledger to the Church of the Blessed Holy Mother in Nuadilan, yes, the very place where her bones have lain! He was never able to ascertain their secret hiding place there."

"Prelate Mallow, I am going to give you a vitally important, most critical assignment. I want you to return to Nuadilan immediately! Seek out this church. Discover their secret hiding place. Bring those papers back to me. Then, we will have a list of all these supposed descendants, and we will know better who are enemies are."

"Brilliant Your Holiness! I will leave at once. I shall not fail you!"

"Bless you my son," The Cardinal quickly made the sign of the Holy Cross over the forehead of his Prelate. He watched as the man dashed out of his office. He noticed the usual tiny drops of blood on his rug and sent for his cleaning woman again.

During his long ride back to Nuadilan, Mallow began to work out just how he might discover this secret hiding place. Inspiration struck. Often foreigners would come to Bregia and some went north to Nuadilan for a time. Perhaps some of these were descendants from the mainland who had come to add more names to the list. If so, he could pretend to be one such person, from say, Velona. Ah, first, he would need appropriate attire.

Upon his arrival, Mallow visited a tailor and acquired a fine looking suit. Back at an inn, he altered it so that he could still carry the weapons of his trade. Satisfied that he looked presentable as one from Velona, he headed for the Church of the Blessed Holy Mother. He wondered just why the Church of Jehosanity continued to tolerate this church. Why had they not simply knocked the stone building down centuries ago? Why had they allowed it to stand? He knew not.

Evening mass ended and Mallow found the main chapel deserted when he arrived. He preferred working at night anyway, less chance of discovery. Inside, two lanterns dimly illuminated the huge space. As he walked up towards the High Altar, a Sister came in from a side door, a cleaning rag in hand. Sister Fiana had come to clean up after the mass. She saw the stranger looking around and asked, "May I help you, sir?"

"Yes, perhaps you can. I am from Velona and have come to add birth names to the records. Perhaps you can show me where it is hidden?" he said innocently, doubting that she could. It would be a start; she'd probably have to go get a priest.

"Certainly," she replied and walked across the chapel towards him. "You've traveled a long distance to do your Holy Duty," she said.

"Oh, yes, yes, I have indeed. Thank you so much." This was going to be incredibly easy, he thought.

"Wait! You are not from Velona! I have seen you around. You, you are the Cardinal's Mano del Dio! Help! Thief!" she began calling out.

Instantly, he acted, jumping over the pews, clasping his hand firmly over her mouth, silencing her. "Okay, woman, where is this secret hiding place." She refused all his attempts to make her divulge her secret. At last, he had little choice but to use force on the woman. One by one, he began breaking her fingers, and after each break, asking her where the secret hiding place was located. He continued to stifle her screams and twice had to rouse her from unconsciousness. At last, writhing in pain, she showed him the secret vault beneath the stone on the floor before the High Altar. He then put her out of her misery and carefully retrieved all the documents stored in the vault. He left quietly, returning briefly to the inn, where he changed clothes and hit the road back to Bregia.

Late the next day, after riding non-stop and dead tired, Prelate Mallow presented his Cardinal with the greatest prize imaginable. After many accolades, Mallow headed off to get some sleep, while the elated Cardinal began pouring over the stacks of records. "So many, so many," he muttered to himself, as the enormity of the problem began to sink into his mind.

The next evening, Prelate Mallow, now rested, was summoned to the Cardinal's office. "Ah, there you are. I've been going over these records. Incredibly valuable! However, it seems that they are very incomplete.

Apparently, there are a large number of descendants living in the Greenway and in Velona. Back in ancient times, they came over to West Reach to log their births and deaths in the ledger. However, that stopped shortly after the time of the assassinations. There are references in here about parallel ledgers being kept somewhere in the Greenway and in Velona. Where in the Greeenway is quite obtuse, but there are a number of mentions of this Mont Blanc. However, we've hit the jackpot in Velona. The location is somewhere in the Church of the Three Holy Roses!"

"Pack your things! I want you to take these documents and go at once to Velona and Cardinal Bosto Rems. Tell him what has happened here, about the theft of the bones and this ledger. You are charged with finding the Velona secret records and stealing them. Once that has been done, perhaps Cardinal Bosto will be able to give you guidance on where to look in Mont Blanc. I am dispatching the Pope, telling him of the Holy Mission that I am sending you on, plus, I will send along a dispatch for Cardinal Bosto, informing him as well of your Holy Mission and that the Pope has also been so informed. That way, Cardinal Bosto cannot shunt you aside, turning the matter and the glory over to his Prelate. You deserve the honor. This is your finest hour, my son. Go with God!" Again, he blessed him and made the sign on his forehead.

"This is utterly unbelievable! Who could possibly want to steal some whore's bones? This list of names, Prelate Marrow, doesn't mean a thing," Cardinal Bosto exclaimed. It was early June, and Prelate Marrow had just delivered the Holy Ledgers and his Cardinal's personal message to Cardinal Bosto Rems, a portly forty-five year old man. The significance of the message was totally lost on him.

Cardinal Alexio had failed to grasp the simple fact that other than the Pope only he knew that the whore mention in their Holy Gospels was in fact real and Jes Amir's wife, that their Son of God had sired children, and what impact those of that line would have on their Church! The only reason that Cardinal Alexio knew as much as he did was because West Reach was where the woman had settled and where their direct descendants were most likely to be found. Thus, Pope Christos had to keep Cardinal Alexio at least somewhat informed. Not so with all the other Cardinals, who knew nothing of all this. Hence, Cardinal Bosto's unexpected reaction.

No matter how he chose to handle the situation here in Velona, Cardinal Bosto knew that he had to keep Prelate Marrow involved. Only the Pope or the Supreme Prelate of the Mano del Dio could override a charge given to a Prelate by a Cardinal. No matter. This was of little importance. That some ancient whore's bones had been both discovered and stolen was trivial beyond trivial. These records — well they could be anyone's lineage. They proved nothing. He handed them back to the Prelate.

Cardinal Bosto then said gruffly, "Your Cardinal's letter mentions the

Holy Rose Church may be involved. I want to caution you to use extreme caution with this church. They run the entire country, and in this country our own Holy Church is not only in the minority, we are just barely tolerated by the monarch of Velona. So do not do anything to upset our precarious position here. Do you understand me?" he asked coldly. Prelate Morrow said that he did and left the Cardinal's office.

Morrow's first action, once he took a room at an inn relatively close to this Church of the Holy Rose was to case the church. At first, he was overwhelmed by the sheer size of this complex. While the nearby Church of Jehosanity was taller and vastly more elegant, trimmed with much gold, this church was vastly larger, occupying several city blocks. Numerous office quarters were attached to the main building; guards were everywhere, quite a lot of foot traffic entered and left at all times of the day.

The locks on the outer doors were complex, of the very latest make. Picking them to gain access would be tricky, perhaps not impossible though. He soon discovered that the church was never without some guards on duty, even at midnight. Until now, he'd never encountered a more heavily defended location.

Later in the week, he took a guided tour of the Church of the Three Holy Roses. This he found informative and he got a good look at the main chapel area, though he had no idea in this vast space where the secret vault may be located, if indeed it was within this portion of the giant complex. He found the descriptions of the guide fascinating. "These rose markers on the floor mark the north-south line for all navigation, using the new system developed by Velona's inventor Arsenio Bartolo, co-founder of the DAE Enterprises." He had no idea how this line could possibly affect navigation, though.

At last, he reached a conclusion and headed back to West Reach. "I have failed you, Cardinal Alexio," Prelate Marrow wailed. He explained what had happened and all that he had seen and carefully observed. At this point, Cardinal Alexio realized that Pope Christos had not told the other Cardinals about Bethany Madelyn Amir or her significance. Further, gaining clandestine access to the Holy Rose Church was likely impossible at this time. He sighed.

"Well, Prelate, let us use what God has delivered unto us, before we send it on to the Pope." The two began a serious study of the records. After pouring over them for several hours, Cardinal Alexio suddenly realized a key significant detail, one that he could exploit.

"Look at this, Prelate. Back in 628, Emil Amir, son of Justice Amir, son of Emil Amir, son of Jes and Bethany — he married Tonia Woodgrove Po! Ellaina Deitz Po was his daughter. That means probably the entire West Po line that now controls Velona are direct descendants of Jes Amir! They are direct heirs to his legacy and would be kings of Tarra! Perhaps they have stolen her bones and plan to use them against our church! We may not need the actual records stored in Velona after all. I will send our findings along to the Pope. This is extremely important data that we've discovered, though I can see that many others have not the knowledge to realize the importance of all this, but I'm sure that the Pope will."

"Will he give us some guidance on our next step?" asked Prelate Morrow.

"Let us hope so, my son." Cardinal sent a lengthy dispatch to the Pope and sent it off on the next caravel bound for Megalos. He continued to ponder the significance of another matter entirely. While Marrow was gone, strangers from Velona had come to West Reach, accompanied by the same Father Amos. They spent time at his church in Nuadilan. What did Elizabeth and Renzo Bartiana have to do with all this? They were accompanied by a Cosima West Po and several others. Were the Bartiana's somehow involved as well? He had many unanswered questions, too many. He prayed that his Pope would provide the necessary wisdom and guidance that he sorely needed now.

During these same weeks, Messiah Bani el Marina and Tamina arrived in Velona. For the first week, the two took carriage rides around the huge city, whose population had now swelled to nearly a million and a half inhabitants. The sector boasted a population well over four million, staggering considering its long history. The two were continually deeply impressed with what they saw. From electric streetlights to the trains, from the enormous docks to the impressive Laid Foundation for the Arts, such grandeur, such a civilization dwarfed anything that their imaginations could dream up!

However, the language barrier caused them their biggest problem, until finally they discovered an Arad sector of the city. Here, they took an inn and spent time chatting with those who had immigrated from Juda Arad or those whose parents had done so long ago. At last, they began to get information that they needed. On June 10, 780, the two took a carriage to the Laird Foundation. Acting on the best tip that they had yet had, they headed for the Laird Foundation Library. While the three towers of the Foundation were spectacular visually, neither were prepared for what they saw when they first entered the Laird Library!

"Oh my, Bani!" Tamina gasped, as she saw thousands of books lining the walls of this huge library. Bani just stared in complete disbelief. In his entire life he had seen ten whole books, but never more than two at the same place. Here were books and knowledge beyond imagination.

They stood completely awestruck. The librarian, Natale Angela, daughter of Kallisto Ann and Len and married to Dianna's son, Dante, saw their dismay and came over to help them. "Hello, I am Natale, the librarian. Welcome to the Laird Library. How can I help you?"

Of course, the two only understood a few words, enough to know that this young seventeen year old woman was seeking to help them. "Hello, I am Bani, my wife, Tamina. We are looking for information, for books that have to do with Jes Amir and his Holy Disciples." He spoke in his Arad tongue.

Natale smiled; she spoke four languages and was working on learning that spoken in Demokritos. "Ah, Juda Arad. Yes, I speak the Arad dialect myself. Let me begin again. I am Natale, the librarian. Welcome to the Laird Library. Books on the Great Messiah and his followers. Yes, we have some. If you will follow me, I will take you to them." She began explaining how the books were catalogued and how the two could find them on their own. However, since they didn't read the Velona dialect, she told them just to ask her.

"Ah, here we are. This collection is a translation of the original ten Gospels written by the ten disciples of the Great Messiah. They have been translated from the originals which, as I understand it, were written in Ancient Arad, terribly difficult to find anyone these days who can translate such."

Flabbergasted, the two stared at the ten volumes! Could it be that these were from the originals? No, more than likely, they were translations from those published by the evil Church of Jehosanity, Bani concluded. As he took one down to look at it, he again realized his ignorance. "I'm sorry, Natale. We cannot read these words. Is there someone who we could perhaps pay to read some of these to us? You see, we came here to learn more of our own history. There are so few books in Juda Arad."

"Sure, you two wait here and let me see if I can find someone," Natale replied. While the two marveled at the books, Natale went in search of someone who was free. Unfortunately, everyone was busy. She returned a bit later.

"I'm sorry. Now everyone is tied up. However, I know a man who loves to read to others. Mr. Kamal, he's sixty-five. His father emigrated here from the Arad, and he is very familiar with these books. I am sure that he would love to read these to you. Can you be here at say nine tomorrow morning? I'll see that Mr. Kamal is here then." The two thanked Natale profusely and promised to be here by nine.

On their way back to their inn, Tamina exclaimed, "Bani! If these are really translations from the originals as Natale claims, then the originals in our language must be here somewhere! The stories that the Santi del Dio found our precious scrolls and books must then be true!"

"I know, Tamina," Bani fought to restrain his elation. "Yet we must be cautious. These may well turn out to be vulgar translations of the distortions of the Church. But maybe, dare we hope?" She gave him a big hug.

At nine the next morning both were waiting right by the books. Natale spotted them and led an old man with greying hair and beard over to them. At once, Bani saw that he was a true Arad. His clothes were old and had been made in the Arad. Both felt very much at ease with him.

"So pleased to meet my countrymen. My dad came from the Arad. I still wear his clothes. While I have never been there myself, dad told me stories of the Arad ever since I was a wee lad. It is my great pleasure to read these to you. I often come here to the library and read books to the children, those who cannot see, and others, like yourselves, who cannot read the Velona writing. Which one should we begin with?"

"Bandar Dero's please," Bani suggested. He thanked Mr. Kamal profusely.

The three sat on comfortable chairs, and the old man began reading. Bani's hand found Tamina's, and they squeezed each other tightly, scarcely daring to breathe! By noon, they were certain that these precious books were indeed translated from the originals written by the ten disciples themselves. So much of what was said and described were so very different from what the wicked Church's Holy Gospels proclaimed that there was no comparison at all. It was as if someone had totally rewritten the entire book! Of course, I knew that a century ago.

At noon, Natale dropped by to see how the reading was working out. She found the two strangers nearly weeping. "Oh, you cannot imagine what hearing these true Holy Words means to us," Bani attempted put his intense feelings into words, but struggled mightily.

Mr. Kamal looked very pleased indeed. "If everyone was as interested in books as these two are, why, the world would be so much better indeed."

"I am so glad that this has worked out so well for you. Say, it is lunch time. How would you all like to grab a bite at Luigi's with me? My treat, Mr. Kamal. It is not often we get visitors from so far away to our prized library." All three joined her for lunch.

"Might I ask a question about those ten books?" Bani asked Natale as they ate at the open-air table looking out on the busy street.

"Sure, I might not know the answer, but I can see if I can find out for you," Natale said helpfully.

"It says that these books were translated from the originals written in the Ancient Arad language. Might we see these original books from which the translations were made? Do they exist still?" Bani asked the key question of his quest.

Natale smiled. "That I don't know, but when we return, Mr. Kamal can read a bit more to you while I see if I can find out. How's that?"

"Oh thank you! It would mean so much to us actually to see these originals. They are utterly priceless to us in the Arad," Tamina replied, hoping that she had not revealed too much.

Mr. Kamal read for another half hour before Natale returned to the trio. "Excuse me. I've brought our Curator Mr. Blanche, who is in charge of the extremely valuable, rare book collection. This is Mr. Blanche," she introduced the forty year old curator to the trio. She had already discussed their request with him.

"Yes, it is possible to see the originals," he spoke softly and reverently. Rare books were his entire life. He'd devoted the last thirty years to the collection and preservation of old, rare books, ever since he found his first one when he was ten.

"Now the rare book collection is extremely valuable. Here at the Laird Foundation, we pride ourselves on having the largest collection of old and rare books on the planet! Yet, due to their extreme value, they are very heavily guarded at all times. Plus, their preservation is of vital importance. We keep them in a very special vault. Even Mrs. Angela here has never been in that vault. If you would all follow me, I will take you on a tour and show you the originals."

Natale was just as excited. She'd never been down to the vault, though she had heard about it before. They followed him down into the basement and walked through a long hallway. Various rooms opened to their right, but these he ignored. At the end of the hallway, two men with guns stood guard. Both looked very bored, Natale thought. She couldn't imagine standing there all day long with nothing to do but guard!

"I am sorry, but you all must first be searched for concealed weapons and for chemicals that could be used to destroy or harm these priceless and irreplaceable rare books and scrolls," Mr. Blanche explained. Bani hated to be so disarmed; Tamina, even more so, as her task was to protect his rear. Nevertheless, they did as asked. The guards laid their weapons on a table and allowed them all to pass through the door.

To Natale's surprise, they then went down yet another long flight of stairs! At the bottom, an iron door blocked further passage. Mr. Blanche used three different keys to unlock the three locks on the door. Natale had never seen a door with three locks on it. Bani began to see that the theft of these books, assuming that they were real, would be most difficult indeed!

To everyone's surprise, the door only led a short way to yet another triply locked door. Mr. Blanche used an additional three keys to unlock this one. He then flipped a switch just inside the door and magically lights turned on. "One of Mr. Arsenio Bartolo's better inventions, the electric light, if I do say so myself. Welcome to our rare book collection. We take extreme measures in this room. As you can see and sense, we keep the humidity low in here and the lights off as much as possible to prevent the light from discoloring the pages even further."

"Now here is one of the very first novels ever penned. One of the Three Roses actually wrote this book! Incredible. However, let me take you to what you are more interested in." They walked past very carefully preserved books and scrolls neatly arranged on wooden shelves. "Ah, here we are: the ten volumes. I must warn you, no one is allowed physically to touch these books with your bare hands. Here, put these gloves on, please. We do not want oils from our bodies to deteriorate further these priceless volumes. Often the pages are extremely brittle and great care must be used."

He took down the Bandar Dero volume and the group crowded around the small reading table to examine it. After looking closely at it, Bani said, "Excuse me, Mr. Blanche, it says here in the beginning that this is actually a copy done by the translation unit, which made the books that Mr. Kamal was reading to us. We wanted to see the actual volume written by Bandar Dero himself, if that still exists."

"Ah, I understand you now. Yes, well, the best that I can do is to show you the official certification of these copies. You see, these are the original sworn statements by the Santi del Dio members, who found the Qaam Scrolls and the Gospels in northern Arad. In here are their sworn statements as to their authenticity. They then hired a number of Arads who were versed in the Ancient Arad language to make these official copies. I have their sworn statements in this packet as well. These that we have here before us were the copies that were then given to the translation unit who created the copies that we have in the main library, the ones that Mr. Kamal was reading to you. So you are asking about the original copies that the Santi del Dio uncovered."

Bani nodded and he continued. "Alas, the Santi del Dio were disbanded long before I was born. What they did with those original Gospels only the ages may know. I can tell you that in today's world, they would be priceless! I would give anything to get my hands on those originals, indeed I would."

"I understand, but are there any of the old Santi del Dio members still alive who might know what they did with those originals?" Bani asked.

"I hardly think so. Yet, I will ask around, but I would imagine that they would be a hundred years old or more if they existed. Still, I will make some inquiries. Natale will let you know if I find out anything. Give me a few days, please."

They examined these rare books for a while longer. Bani and Tamina were both pleased that they were able to read most of the words, which were close to the modern words. Some, however, they could not. Even Mr. Kamal enjoyed reading in his father's language. Natale noticed that one of the guards always kept them all in view at all times. Security, she realized, was tight down here. After an hour, they left the vault with Mr. Blanche re-locking the doors. After stowing their weapons, Bani promised to check back with Natale in a few days, hopeful that Mr. Blanche might have further information for him. Then the two left.

That evening over supper, Natale mentioned to me, "You know, Bethany, I got to see the rare book vault today. There were these two strangers from Juda Arad in town. They came to see the original copies of those old Ten Gospels written by the disciples of the Great Messiah, Jes Amir. They seemed keenly interested in seeing the real original copies, not the ones that we have. It seems our copies were made by some translation unit way back when and used to translate them into the Velona dialect.

These two wanted to see the originals from which the copies were made. Now, Mr. Blanche, our rare books curator, he told us that these books were found by the old Santi del Dio, way back when. According to him, they gave the copies to the library, but no one knows what ever happened to those originals. Mr. Blanche says that those ten books would be worth a fortune. The two from the Arad really do want to see those books or find out what happened to them. Mr. Blanche said he will look into it, but honestly, the Santi del Dio has been long gone. I don't suppose that he will find out anything more. Isn't this the strangest thing?" She gaily chatted about her day.

Renzo looked at me and said, "You don't suppose that these were the ones who tried to steal the bones in Nuadilan, do you?"

"Isn't this curious? Dear, could we meet these two visitors?" I asked, thinking along the same lines as he.

"I suppose, if they ever come back to see if Mr. Blanche has discovered something. I can tell them that you want to visit with them," Natale replied, suddenly feeling very important because I had actually taken an interest in what she was saying. Only Cosima and Alessa were also paying any real attention to her chat. The others were talking among themselves about other things. The three mischief boys were planning their bi-wheel company, for instance. Well, most of us were happy that the three mischief boys finally took a serious interest in something.

"If they are the ones, they might not want to have total strangers asking them questions," Renzo mused. "Perhaps we ought to entice them a little."

"Yes, good point, dear. Natale, when you see them again, tell them that Renzo and I would like to chat with them. Tell them that he and I are something of Santi del Dio scholars and know much about that ancient organization."

"Sure, Bethany. Honestly, you do know a lot about them, don't you?" Natale replied, beginning to wonder if there was more to all this than appearances.

"Some, yes," I answered truthfully. Well, I did found the Santi, but during its final years, Linda d'Grange ran it while I was off in the southern hemisphere dealing with crises there.

The next late afternoon, Cosima and Alessa returned from a lengthy shopping trip. At least once a week, the duo spent most of a day wandering through the myriad shops in our huge city, looking for the unusual, the surprise find, or even fancy dresses. You know women. They stopped by to show us their latest acquisitions.

"Bethany, you must have a look at these new cool rugs that Alessa and I discovered in a small shop this afternoon," Cosima declared as Enrico began carrying the rolls of carpet in from their carriage for the two women. "At first, we thought that these would look good on our bedroom floors, but wait until you see them. Yes, Enrico, could you please unroll that one right here, please? Thanks." She was very animated, while Alessa just grinned.

He did so and I got my first look at a Hieras Anubis rug made by someone called Mora. "Wow! Why, dear, this is beautiful. Isn't that the Med Sea there? A coastline, perhaps?" I was caught up in the beautiful scene depicted in the rug. It was about ten feet long and six wide, perfect for beside the bed uses, Cosima indicated.

"Well, yes, we thought so, but honestly, it is such a work of art that now I am thinking of turning it into a wall hanging. What do you think?" Cosima asked.

"Yes, dear, I agree. The craftsmanship is superb, but the artwork is what so sets this one apart from just rugs," I concurred.

"See, she agrees with us, Alessa," Cosima gaily pointed out to her sister. "Bethany, wait until you hear the story behind these rugs. The woman who made this rug has no arms! She did it all with her feet. Incredible, isn't it?"

"Well, yes, fabulous," I replied, but at the mention of armless, my mind took off onto other avenues of thought.

Cosima continued, "The shopkeeper explained that this Hieras Anubis is a whole colony of armless women. He thinks that they moved there from Demokritos, you know, some of the ones from Dorota and from Demokritos who chose to stay behind and not go back to Dorota, many years ago. Apparently, they have now formed their own town. I think that is a very good idea. Anyway, Alessa and I just could not resist buying all the rugs that they made."

"Yes, we feel that in some small way that we are helping to support those women," Alessa explained. "We have six rugs; this one and another one are by this Mora person. Admittedly, the other four are more like just rugs, but they do look like fine rugs."

When Enrico brought the rest of the rugs inside, Cosima unrolled the others, and asked, "Okay, Bethany, point out the other Mora-made rug."

I grinned and said, "Okay, Madam Detective, let's see how good I am." I looked at the other five and knew immediately which one was the Mora rug. Four looked like rugs, but the fifth contained images of flowers scattered at random locations on the rug's surface. She chose not to have them be predictable but randomly spaced, giving the illusion of real flowers in the wild.

"Yes, that's the one, not hard to tell is it?" Cosima declared. "Now I must see if Enrico and Arturo can get these hanged for us, if not, Gerardo can later tonight. Sorry, Enrico, can you roll them up and put them back in our carriage for us, please?"

Enrico chuckled and did as she asked. "Good to still feel that I am useful," he teased her, winking at me.

At eight that evening, Gerardo came knocking at our door. "Excuse me for waking you this late, but it's Cosima. She has discovered something of vital importance and needs you to come see it at once." He seemed a bit concerned, and we agreed. He left and Renzo and I got dressed to go next door to their house. Yes, they had bought a large estate at 44 Hampton Way; Gerardo and Cosima shared the estate with Alessa and Arsenio.

"Sorry, but you have to see this, Bethany!" Cosima declared animatedly. "Honestly, you have to see it at night. It isn't so clear in the daylight. Come, it's in my room." She led us down the hall to her bedroom, where Gerardo was standing. He had Arsenio's fancy electric lights on in the room. Alessa and Arsenio came dashing up to us.

"You are not going to believe this, Bethany," Alessa exclaimed. We saw that Cosima had the seascape Mora rug nicely hung on the wall. "I've got the flower one in my room. You have to see it next!"

"Well, yes, Cosima, it looks fabulous on your wall. We were right about using it as a tapestry," I said, unable to see what they were so excited about.

Cosima grinned mischievously. "Kill the lights, Gerardo. I came in with my small bed lantern, like this. Now look at it carefully please." Her dim lantern cast a focused beam of light in mostly one direction. She sat it on her bedroom table and pointed it just so at the tapestry hanging beside her bed.

Suddenly, my eyes picked up something shiny — no a whole lot of shiny reflections coming back at me. I moved my head around. Could they be letters? Yes, tiny letters. "See them, the letters?" Cosima could restrain herself no longer. "There is writing hidden in the rug — secret writing! You can only really see it like this. I know. Gerardo, Alessa, and Arsenio, we've tried many different ways to see them. This lantern is the best. Can you see them?" She asked impatiently.

"Yes, it is definitely writing. Sea Prince I think," I replied. "There is an H and there is an e," I began to say.

Cosima just couldn't wait for me to get the letters worked out. She turned on the electric lights and held a paper for me to see. "I copied the message down." Renzo and I read over her shoulder: Help Me. Mora Porto of Brago. Heiras.

Now Alessa could stand it no longer. "Mom, come and look at my flower one. It's got her message embedded in it too!" We quickly moved to her room and she showed us the similar message.

Cosima then declared, "Look, this incredible artist must be Mora Porta, and she is in dire straits and has resorted to this incredibly secretive way to deliver a message to the outside world. Help me. She must be in dire trouble. Bethany, we have to go help her out!"

Alessa added, "Look, mom, we know that this Hieras Anubis is a whole colony of armless women. There must be more to it than that, if Mora is sending out this secret plea for help. We have to go to her rescue!"

"I've examined the reflective threads," Cosima interrupted, insisting on laying out all that she had discovered from her examination of the rugs. "She has woven a single metallic-like thread to form the letters. It is so thin that you don't see it under normal lighting. I've examined it closely and believe that it may be a silver satin. I can't be sure without taking a sample, and that would be destructive, so I won't so it unless it's necessary. Now, the maker of the rug has attached a small patch on the back. See, it reads Mora Porto, Hieras Anubis. So we know the maker and the sender of the message are one in the same. The rug is predominately wool, dyed of course, nothing unusual about that. In fact, cross-comparing the six rugs, I believe they used the same batch of wool and the same dying techniques."

"Now as far as the message is concern, Bethany, she has left us her name and perhaps an origin city, Brago. There is a Brago in Vito, but there may be more towns with that name. Now I know that Dianna said that the Trans Sea Prince Line passes through Brago, Vito. It's a small fishing town on the Med. Prudence would suggest that we go there and make some inquiries before we jump to too many conclusions," Cosima suggested, ending her insistent report of the facts.

I smiled and replied, "Good work, Cosima. Yes, we ought to check first before making conclusions and acting. Let's hold a family meeting in the morning to discuss it."

Snug in our bed a bit later, Renzo whispered, "Dear, I don't want you getting involved down there. I've had all the armless Bethany's I can handle." I grinned and snuggled close. That was an understatement. I certainly didn't want to risk living through that kind of lifestyle again either. I had hoped that we were done with that nasty aberration having left it behind in Tashien.

The next morning we discussed this amazing plea for help with our extended family group. Renzo came up with the best plan, which we adopted. Brago was about two hundred seventy miles east of Velona. Next came Barcella, our close ally and then Vito, our enemy Sea Prince. Brago was further on down the coast from Vito. However, the new steam train line went through there, and Renzo would travel by train. We all found it amazing when Dianna said that the trip would take less than two days! My, how our world was shrinking because of her invention.

"I'll use a cover story that I am an Estate Trustee and that I am looking for a Mora Porto. A distant relative of hers had passed away leaving her a small sum," Renzo explained his grand idea. "That way, no one will think twice about talking with me." Dianna then explained that the next train leaving for Zargarb was tomorrow morning, and more importantly, its return trip would pick him up in Brago seven days after dropping him off. However, she also said that he might be able to hitch a ride back sooner on a cargo train.

Natale volunteered to see if there was any information on this Hieras

Anubis place in the library. Gerardo said that he would speak with Adolfo and others on the chance that, as their monarch, he may have heard of this place. Dante, who was just starting up his own import-export business, said that he would check on who was importing what from this town and get more details for us.

Early next morning, Renzo was packed and ready to set off on his little trip. "Now be careful. I don't want to have to come and rescue you," I teased him and we hugged. Later that morning, Gerardo sent word that all he could find out from Adolfo was that Hieras Anubis was the old South Port, renamed and taken over by the Church of Jehosanity on Megalos. Well, that figured.

At lunch, Dante came bounding into the dining room. "Well, have I scored a hit or not! Listen to what all I have found out!" He sat down and helped himself to part of our lunch. "Something like twenty years ago, the Pope bought out all the remaining people who lived in South Port, Southlands. Then, he moved all those Dorota immigrants who still lived on Megalos there and also added more from Demokritos as well. Today, my source claims that the place had quadrupled in population and that they have had to build more towns. He thinks that there are four, all within walking distance of each other. What's interesting is that apparently most all the women are as you suspected armless, but some of the men are as well. Further, and this is the very interesting bit: it is a closed city! No outsider is allowed beyond the docks!"

He guzzled some juice and continued rapid fire, "One trader, who sold him some things made there, says that there is a huge sign posted in several languages that says, No Admittance Beyond This Point. Trespassers Will Be Shot. No Exceptions. Now isn't that just fascinating? Why would they go to such extremes to keep visitors out? Something nefarious is going on down there." He sat back, smug with his discoveries.

"Well done, Dante. Well done indeed. Now we are getting somewhere. What I find even more interesting, Dante, is the fact that you said their population has quadrupled. Where are they finding all these new armless men and women? There are so few of them still alive here in Velona."

"Are they coming from Dorota perhaps?" he asked naively.

"Not a chance. I bet that somehow we've stumbled into something that we are not supposed to know about. It must be that damnable Church of Jehosanity at it again," I theorized. He returned to work and I began to ponder this damning information. If they were at it again, where were the victims coming from? I decided to pay a visit to Cosima at her headquarters. Enrico insisted on driving me.

"No, Bethany, there are no reports of people being abducted by the Church of Jehosanity here in Velona. However, I will keep a sharp eye out for such events," Cosima replied, after making a thorough search of her records, just to make sure that she had not missed anything. As I rode back home, I began to have a bad feeling about all this.

That evening, Natale brought the two strangers around to see me, volunteering to stay in case my Arad was too rusty. She introduced the two. "Bethany, this is Messiah Bani el Marina and his wife, Tamina. Tamina, Bani, this is Bethany Bartiana. Her husband is away on an assignment. Both of them do know a good deal about the old Santi del Dio." She rattled off in the Arad dialect. I caught most of her words and suddenly was grateful for her deciding to stick around. If you don't speak or use a language for a century or more, duh, it gets a little rusty.

After shaking hands, I offered them some tea and dates, which they seemed to enjoy. "How can I help you?" I said, trying to keep my words simple. Natale grinned, I guess my Arad was crude, but the two seemed to understand me so far. He was heavily bearded, which reminded me of those who used to be of the old Qaam Sect, when I was with Jes Amir. I guessed that he was in his mid-twenties, but I also noticed that both wore the traditional leather moccasin-style boots so common in the Arad.

He spoke slowly for my benefit. "We have come from Juda Arad seeking knowledge of our heritage. We want to learn all we can about the Great Messiah, Jes Amir — not the lies and corruption spouted by the evil Church of Jehosanity, who have so perverted our Great Messiah. Our records back home, as dismal as they are, considering the looting done by all the Church's Holy Relic Seekers of the past, suggest that his wife, Bethany Madelyn Amir, fled the Arad and brought their children to the west. They settled on West Reach that much we do know."

"Yes, I agree that much we do know," I agreed with him.

He continued, "The Great Messiah had ten disciples with him, and with his passing, they were instructed to write down his Holy Teachings. They are known as the Ten Holy Gospels."

"Yes, we are fortunate to have translated copies of those works in our Laird Library," I stated the obvious. I also added, "We know that the Church of Jehosanity has totally altered those books. The Holy Gospels of that Church have almost nothing in common with the real Gospels written by the ten. That Church has always been an enemy of us in Velona, though we have not been able to keep them completely out of our country. Velona prides itself on being tolerant of all religions. Freedom of religion."

He got closer to his point, "Indeed, I am glad that you also see the falsehoods being propagated around the world by these vile men. We have also heard from some of our people tales of the Santi del Dio having come into the Arad and discovering the ancient scrolls and the original ten Gospels."

"Yes, the Santi del Dio actually did discover that secret cache. It was buried in the ruins of a town. They brought them back to Velona. Knowing the importance of the Holy Gospels, the Santi had them copied and then had very accurate translations made. Those translations are readily available in our library," I again said the obvious.

Natale added, "Yes, but so few actually read those originals these days."

"Yes, Natale has shown us the copies of the originals held in their very secure underground vault," Bani continued. "Yet, you must understand our position. We must really see firsthand the original Gospels so that we can verify that the copies are accurate and not drastically altered as the vile Church has done."

"Yes, I can see your point, Bani."

"Yet, while there are hundreds of scrolls that are even older than the Gospels in the vault, rare and valuable though they may be, it seems that the originals are not there. No one seems to know what the Santi del Dio did with them. It is my quest to find them and read them. Perhaps you may know where they may be found?"

"Not exactly, I am afraid. I do know that the Santi del Dio was the archenemy of the Church of Jehosanity and that they were highly afraid of the Church stealing and destroying those precious ten Gospels. So much so, that after the copies were made, they decided to put them in a secret, safe, secure place. They left the copies made for the translators available in the Laird Library instead. As I understand it, those copies were very painstakingly made, and completely accurately done, with no alterations. However, I have no proof of that," I attempted to answer honestly.

"But where would they have secreted away these most precious Gospels?" he asked, a pain in his voice.

"That is a good question; I am afraid that I do not know the answer," I said honestly.

He looked crestfallen for a moment, and then asked, "Where was their main headquarters located? We have been told that there were a lot of Santi del Dio based here in Velona."

"Yes, they were. The Santi del Dio used to have a huge complex beside the Laird Foundation, but that has all been torn down and new buildings raised. No secret vaults were ever discovered there. However, I do know that they also had another major base at Mont Blanc in the Greenway, just across the border from Fortress d'Grange."

"Ah, is that not where the King Diget I used to rule?" he asked. I was not at all surprised to hear that name mentioned. I was sure that it had been these two who had broken into the Church of the Blessed Holy Mother and had opened the sarcophagus. Whether or not they had murdered the Sister and stolen our ledgers I was not sure yet. Neither seemed to me to be assassins, but merely truth seekers.

"Yes, that was his kingdom over a century ago. You know of this ancient king?" I decided to probe a little.

"A little. According to those on Cymry, he discovered the remains of

Bethany Madelyn Amir and gave her the proper Holy Burial that she deserved. Perhaps he has buried her remains in some secret location. Perhaps that may also be found at this Mont Blanc place," he suggested back at me.

I decided to be a little more to the point. "You know, we in Velona have just heard that her remains were thought to have been buried in a small church in Nuadilan, the Church of the Blessed Holy Mother." I detected a slight flush in Bani and pressed on. "The priest there believed that someone broke into their church and stole her remains a couple weeks ago."

I definitely got a rise out of him on this one, but not quite what I expected. "Perhaps the remains were stolen a long time ago," he replied slightly defensively.

"Oh indeed they were. You see, the priest came to me for assistance. We went there to see for ourselves and to investigate the supposed theft. However, we discovered concrete proof that the remains of Bethany Madelyn Amir were never in that sarcophagus. In fact, nothing was ever buried in it, not ever."

He seemed visibly relaxed, as if I had somehow taken a burden off him. "You wouldn't know anything about that, now would you?" I asked him.

Tamina blushed noticeably and whispered to Bani, "You might as well tell her; she knows it already."

"You are right. When we heard that her bones were buried there, we just have to see them for ourselves. Can you imagine my shock when I discovered the crypt was empty? I feared that the Church of Jehosanity had beaten us to them and that her remains were lost to us forever. We in the Arad would greatly desire to have her remains buried in Juda Arad, where she may be honored for the Great Woman that she was, not some perverted whore the Jehosanity priests claim."

"Yes, I guessed that it was you who opened the crypt. Did you also have a hand in the slaying of their Sister a week later?" I asked directly.

Both became very defensive. "No, we know nothing of that! We left for Velona that very night! A Mano del Dio man tried to kill us right after that. Tamina killed him and we fled that same night. We have been here in Velona at the time of the murder. You can ask the innkeeper, if you like."

"No need, I already suspected that it was a Mano del Dio assassin who did it."

"Why? Why would they kill a humble sister of the church?" Tamina asked, completely mystified.

"They tortured her into showing them the secret location of the ledgers. You see, Bethany charged her children and grandchildren with keeping a ledger of their lineage. All births and deaths of all the descendants of Jes and Bethany as well as Josh and Milla have been dutifully recorded down through the centuries. They stole those records."

The sheer magnitude of this shocked both. "You, you mean there is a complete record of all the descendants?" he asked.

"Yes, but in the early years, many were assassinated by the Mano del Dio. That was around the time of King Digit I. Perhaps that is why he kept things so secret, to keep them from falling into the hands of the hated Mano del Dio," I explained, guessing what my son's reasoning probably was.

"Such a tragic loss!"

"Well, it may not be a total loss. We have kept similar records here in Velona, and I know the descendants who lived in the Greenway also kept records there, though I do not know where that location is," I explained.

"Does this mean that you are one of those descendants?" Bani asked. He was bright and quickly had caught my deeper meaning.

"Yes, I am and so are many of us as well."

"We are most honored and humbled to be in the presence of such royal blood!" Both rose and bowed to me. I motioned to Natale, who grinned. Her mother was a direct descendant as well. They bowed to her too.

"Might it be possible for us to actually see these Holy Ledgers? We have traveled so far and would treasure such a sight," he asked. Well, I figured that was coming.

"Honestly, I have no problem with your viewing them, but it is not my decision to make. Let me check with others and get back to you on your request."

"Thank you, thank you, holy women," Bani effused towards us. The two promised that we could find them at the library each day. After they left, Natale returned home as well. I, on the other hand, headed off to pay a call on Velona's High Priestess, Daria Benz West Po.

She and I discussed the matter for an hour, after which she agreed with me. What harm was there in letting these two Arads see the documents? She suggested that I bring them by her private office around six tomorrow night. On my way home, I dropped by Natale and Dante's place to have her relay the message to the two from the Arad.

At six, Cosima, Alessa, and I were already at the Church of the Holy Rose waiting for Natale to arrive with our guests. Daria had carefully retrieved our documents and had them arranged in a proper sequence on her drawing table. She wore gloves to handle them, especially the oldest ones, which were yellowed with age and brittle. Natale arrived right on time and brought the two into Daria's private office. After a brief introduction and admonition not to touch the documents without wearing gloves, Daria allowed Bani and Tamina to examine them.

"These here we copied long ago from the originals on West Reach so that you can see our direct line over here on the mainland. As you can see, we go back to Ellaina Deitz Amir, the great-great granddaughter of the Great Messiah and Bethany. Now Bethany's line goes all the way back to the Great

Messiah's daughter Sarah Elizabeth. As far as we can tell, those on West Reach trace their lineage back to his brother, Josh and Milla Amir," Daria explained and showed the two the connections.

After an hour's study, Bani asked, "But what about those who live in the Greenway? What is their lineage?"

"That we do not know," Daria admitted.

I decided to cast a little light on this point. "Very likely those in the Greenway trace theirs back primarily to King Diget I, who was really Tegid, the twin son of Caitlyn Amir, daughter of Jes' son Ahmad. Caitlyn was assassinated hours after she gave birth to the twins. The Mano del Dio assassins did not realize that she had given birth, and we kept their lineage a secret to protect the babies' lives. That's why I suspect those in the Greenway go back to King Diget I, or Tegid."

"Incredible! Natale was not wrong when she said that you were really knowledgeable about these things," Bani was most impressed with the way that I rattled all this off. Little did he know that I was Caitlyn's husband and the babies' father. Of course, I knew all this.

At last, they were satisfied with the documents. While Daria repackaged them and put them back in their secret hiding place, I led them to another room for tea. Over tea, I asked Bani, "So now what are your plans?"

"We must learn more about this Mont Blanc and King Diget I. Then, we must go to this place and see if we can discover where Bethany Madelyn's remains now lie," he replied. Daria joined us and we had a nice chat before they left. I thought that all this had gone very well indeed. No more mystery or problems. Little did I know how wrong I was!

Some days later Renzo returned from his little outing. He was quite invigorated and had been successful. Over lunch he explained, "You are all going to have to take a train trip to Zargarb! It's the greatest. Hitched a ride on a cargo train coming back, not so good. Anyway, you won't believe how slummy Vito actually is these days. Everything is rundown; the people are quite poor, but the coming of the train line has given many better paying jobs. Okay, to the point. I spent a day going around the town of several thousand. My cover was perfect. I learned very soon that indeed an Avis and Mora Porto had lived in Brago, along with their son, Alvito, and daughter, Tomara. She should be about thirty-seven now and their children sixteen and fourteen. Anyway, one night, the entire family just disappeared! No trace of them has ever been found."

"I learned that Avis Porto was a Priest of Tur, the Sea God, a religion that has been outlawed in Vito for many, many years. Naturally, all my questioning got me in a bit of trouble with the local Church of Jehosanity. However, I explained that I was an Estate Trustee just looking for some proof that they were deceased or were no longer able to be contacted so that I could close the estate. The priest there gave me a copy of this official document as proof. Wait until you read what it says!"

We gathered around and read the most vile, disgusting diatribes imaginable, followed by an equally unbelievable confession on their part. "What I find interesting is that the document says that they have accepted a 'second chance' at living a holy life so that their souls may go to heaven. I bet they kidnaped the family, amputated the women's arms, and sent them to this Hieras place!" Renzo finished his presentation. I relayed what Dante had already found out about the town in the Southlands.

"Wow! Shot and killed just for walking into the town! Now that only tells me that they are hiding something awful that they do not want the world to know about! When do we leave?" he asked. I gave him a poke.

It was time for a family council. Obviously, we needed to respond to this plea for help, assuming that Mora was still alive. It was indeed a lively discussion. Ania decided that she would go. "Although I am fifty-four, and I still have the luxury of having my Alex body. I'm expendable, so to speak, only don't tell Dianna that." Her wife, Dianna giggled; she was fifty-three now. I agreed with her decision; besides she was a Judger and very able to handle complex negotiations should that be needed.

They flatly refused to allow me to go. "Bethany, you have been through way too much of this amputation business. No way are we going to let you go there!" Enrico stated sternly, and they all agreed with him. Renzo, however, wanted to go along as the senior Protector of the group. Regrettably, I thought this was a wise move, but I would really miss him. Besides, there seemed little danger in Velona at all at this time.

Kallisto Ann and Len volunteered to go as well. "Look, we speak the Megalos and Demokritos dialects. That may be crucial, to say nothing of having another Judger and Protector along," Kallisto insisted. After some discussion, we agreed on those two as well.

Surprisingly my son, Marco spoke up, "Say, how about Rosina and I tagging along too." I bristled and Rezno said, "Wait son. This could be very dangerous. You and Rosina are just getting started in life. Look how awful your mom and my lives became with all the underhanded treachery cast our way. You don't want Rosina to lose her arms, now do you?"

"Of course not dad. But what if there are a whole lot of children there that need help? Rosina and I are good with kids. We're everyone's baby sitters as it is."

Kallisto spoke up for her daughter, "Renzo, he has a point. We know that Mora did have two children who are about our kids' ages now. They would relate to the young ones better than we old fogies." Again, after some discussion, we agreed that they could go also.

Cosima spoke up, "Before you all get too far gone on this, how about waiting another couple of weeks before you set sail? The importer is supposed to get another shipment of rugs from Hieras Anubis in by then. I've already paid in advance for all the rugs that come in this time. Let's see if she sends out a further message or even a repeat message." We agreed with her suggestion. However, in the meantime, Renzo, Ania, Kallisto, Len, Marco, and Rosina began to make their preparations. I did insist that they take three of the Grey Creature's blasters with them to help prevent their being shot by guns.

Adolfo kindly allowed us to hire one of his caravels for an indeterminate period. He too was worried about this new nefarious scheme of the enemy Church. I donated a thousand gold to his emergency fund, and the Portly Prince was ours for as long as we needed it. On July 1, we said our farewells and they set sail. Yes, the next batch of rugs did have another one made by Mora among them. It too held the same "help me" message. I rather wished she'd said more.

Chapter 7 The Message

Sometimes, I am amazed at just how fast people can react in an emergency. I was reminded of this at noon on July 3, 780. Renzo and the others had been gone barely two days now. As we ate our noon meal, complementing our cook on her delicious chocolate pie, Bianca contacted me from d'Grange.

Bethany. Emergency here! Queen Ann Penton Hammersmith has just been kidnaped by the Confessore del Dio of Mont Blanc! They are going to either kill her as they did her handmaiden or cut off her arms and send her to Hieras or worse! Her Forze Secrete member rode all night to get to me. We must get to Queen Ann immediately! She tried to send us a dire warning, but her message was intercepted, and her handmaiden who was delivering it was killed outright! I'll prepare horses and gear; get here with some stealth forces as fast as possible, if you want any chance of saving Queen Ann Penton!

Okay. Contact you with specifics shortly! I went into action. I explained what Bianca had relayed, and Enrico said, "I'm coming with you. Who else can do we dare get on such short notice?"

The three mischief boys looked up, glanced at each other, and Luigi said, "Hey, how about us? We are all dead shots with the long-gun. Sounds like you might need us. Count is in on this! Besides, she's a Penton."

"It might be good for the boys," Enrico suggested, taking their side. I didn't have time for an argument.

"Okay, you three, go pack your things. Bring along what you think you may need, but plan to be able to carry it on horseback. Enrico, pack your stuff, mine too. I'm going to see about getting us there fast." He saluted me, and the three mischief-makers chuckled and saluted me as well, before dashing off to find their stuff, debating among themselves just what to bring along with them.

I focused and contacted Dianna at DAE Enterprises. After telling her about our emergency, I sent, *Anyway you can get us up to d'Grange in a big hurry on one of those trains?*

You bet. Head for the station. I'll make the arrangements and meet you there to make sure the orders are followed! After thanking her, I made a dash to my room to change into my leather traveling outfit, thankful to be out of the damnable corset for an extended time. An hour later, we were packed and ready. I made Enrico take one blaster with him, while I carried another with me, leaving the three behind in case something else came up.

Arturo had the carriage ready, and we five climbed in, bags and all. Admittedly, the boys with their long-guns had an awkward time trying to stow them and finally just held them. Ten minutes later, we arrived at the main train station near the docks of Velona. As promised, Dianna was waiting for us.

"Okay, this is your train, only one passenger car. The engineer knows he is to go at top speed. We've already used the signal system of Arsenio's to alert the other stations along the way. You are clear to go from here to d'Grange. Please, do be careful, Bethany. If you need something or some help, let us know. We'll bring an army if we need to." I gave her a big hug, and she hugged Enrico as well.

"Hey aunt, don't I get a hug too," Luigi teased her. He was Enyo's son, but Dianna was also Enyo. To avoid total confusion, he always called her his aunt. She gave him a hug and an unexpected kiss, telling him it was from his mother. He laughed at the jest. Having two bodies at the same time can be confusing and interesting too. We boarded and stowed our packs, admiring the fact that we had the entire twenty seats to ourselves. Naturally, the boys spread out, each taking their own seat.

As the train began moving, Luigi asked, "What's the plan? Can we shoot King Hammersmith if we see him?"

"You can shoot anyone who tries to stop us or harm Queen Ann," I replied. "First, we are rendezvousing in d'Grange with Bianca. She will have some horses for us. Somehow, we have to sneak across the border and get to wherever they are holding Queen Ann. The plan is to snatch her from this Confessore fellow and bring her back with us to Velona."

"Hey, can we shoot this Confessore fellow?" asked Pietro. "That would be a blow to that damnable church."

"No, I get to shoot the Confessore fellow," Nicolo protested. "I said it first!"

"First one who sees him gets first shot," Luigi settled their dispute. I began to regret having allowed the boys to come with us.

As suppertime came, Enrico pulled out some dried beef, rolls, and a jug of juice, while I set a seat as if it was our table. As we began, I looked up at the three faces staring hungrily at us. Coyly, I said, "We told you to bring what you needed."

"Yeh, but," Luigi started to say, but thought better of it.

"Here, help your selves," Enrico laughed, and showed the boys the small bag of food he'd scraped up in a big rush from the pantry. We looked at each other and smiled.

We arrived at the station in Fortress d'Grange in less than ten hours. What I found interesting were the periodic stops every four hours to take on more water and coal. During these hour delays, we stretched our legs and took in the sights. These way stations were usually just outside a town. We arrived at midnight, dead tired. Both Louis and Bianca met us at their station.

They put us up in their castle tower for the night, but we were too sleepy to observe much. We rose at first light and ate a hasty meal. Lena Groves, one of Queen Ann's handmaidens and a Forze Secrete member assigned to look after Ann, briefed us while we ate.

"Things are taking a bad turn at Mont Blanc. Ann decided to warn all of you in Velona, and Lena Tompson, her other handmaiden, volunteered to sneak her message out of the palace and send it off to Adolfo. That was on the first. Her dead body was found later that night and the message was gone. We feared for Ann after that, and our team stood watch over her from then on. We know that the king sent word to the Cardinal. Alec, he's another of us, spotted the Confessore and his crew of assassins meeting with the Cardinal later that afternoon."

She took a long drink of tea and continued, "We suspected something was up and again kept a secret vigil over Ann as best we could. The king suspects some of us, so we had to remain pretty much in the background. It was around midnight when I heard whispered voices outside Ann's room. I pretended to be asleep when someone opened my door. Apparently, they thought that I was. Anyway, I kept alert and heard Ann suddenly struggling with them, but it was over in less than a minute. I heard footsteps, ventured a peek, and saw them carrying her body down the hall. I lit my candle and signaled Arlie. He took over for me and discretely followed them. According to him, they put her in a wagon, covered her up, and then headed out of town."

He roused Fred, who then followed the wagon. I snuck out, met up with Arlie who told me what he'd seen, and I decided to come for help. I rode all night and all day to get here as fast as I could. I just barely made it through the lines of soldiers that the king has out on patrol, blocking all the roads that lead south into d'Grange. Fred, Alec, and Arlie are monitoring where Ann is currently located. All we have to do is get to Mont Blanc. One of them will be there to meet us and lead us to Ann. We must hurry! Whenever the Confessore gets a hold of someone, they just totally disappear from Mont Blanc!"

The mischief boys groaned that they didn't get a chance to see the sights of Fortress d'Grange, but mounted up, nevertheless. Louis gave me a hug and kissed Bianca goodbye. "Send word, dear, and I'll send an army to the rescue," he offered. I could see from his eyes that he really wanted to ride with us, but that he also knew that he had the responsibility of his country on his shoulders and dare not leave.

We rode hard that morning, and at noon, the border with Mont Blanc lay ahead of us. Enrico and Lena urged caution, and we halted at a position from where we could see the crossing ahead without easily being seen ourselves. Sure enough, we spotted at least fifty soldiers guarding this main road into Mont Blanc. While I was debating whether I ought to pick up the fifty and give them a toss, Bianca whispered, "I know another way across." We backed up and climbed higher into the mountainous terrain. She led us essentially around the peak, and we crossed easily into the Kingdom of Mont Blanc unseen.

An hour later, we spied the city-fortress high on the low mountain of its namesake, Mont Blanc. Now we were dependent upon Lena making contact with one of the three others. As we paused to survey the scene before us, I noticed an alarming number of mounted soldiers patrolling the outskirts of the walled city-fortress. Some galloped off to the north, some to the west towards Calgary. It didn't look good for us to be able to sneak into the city at all.

Once the soldiers galloped on off to the west, a lone rider came out of a side gully. "That's Le Ann. What's she doing here?" Lena waved to her. "She's one of us," Lena added quickly. We rode to meet her.

"Thank god you've come," Le Ann, fired off rapidly. Very worried, the young woman added, "This way, we have to go around the city way to the west. The king has more patrols out than normal. Don't know why." We followed her lead.

Less than an hour later, we had traveled a semicircle around the towering fortress and were due east of it. Here, Le Ann halted and explained. "It's safe to stop here a bit. The Confessore have taken her to a small village just east of Mont Blanc. The men are there keeping an eye on them. Alec says that there are ten soldiers standing guard, and the Confessore has four of his henchmen with him plus the Medico Santo and his nurses. We think that they are planning something awful for Ann, but the men are far too outnumbered to stop them. If we ride hard, we can be at Bywindle before dark."

"Let's ride then," I replied, and we all galloped after Le Ann. We made good time, though at least four times, we hear the approaching of riders and took countermeasures. Here in the Langdoc region, the country is very rocky and filled with limestone caverns. We were able to stay pretty much out of sight of the patrols. However, soon we entered that section where there were huge, wide valleys that offered little cover from someone viewing from a distant hillcrest. I felt particularly vulnerable now.

As the sun began to ride low in the west, we spotted the village of Bywindle ahead. We also saw olive groves and rows upon rows of grape vines on either side of the chalky white road. Just then, we heard a strange bird whistle and Le Ann gave a whistle in reply. Her husband came trotting out from his concealed position in the olive grove. He nodded to us and I introduced ourselves.

"I'm afraid that you are too late. Last night, we think that these evil men operated on Queen Ann," Alec said softly. Le Ann put her hand to her mouth to stifle her cry. Lena lost it and began crying.

"Arms?" I hazarded a guess.

He nodded. "Arlie saw one man toss two arms outside their building at first light. Later, a man dug a hole, tossed them in, and covered them up. Arlie almost was caught trying to catch a glimpse of Ann. They are holding her in a shack at the east edge of the village. There are ten of the king's soldiers there too. Worse, Fred overheard some talking about another dozen men coming at dawn. I think that the king suspects someone will be trying to rescue Ann. He may be on to us, but I just don't know for sure. Le Ann, I don't think that it is safe for us to return to Mont Blanc anymore."

He added, "They killed Fred's wife, you know. Lea Tompson was carrying the message to you from Queen Ann. Fred's sworn to kill the king now, but now he's also sworn to kill this Confessore fellow. Come on. I'll take you to our meeting and hiding place. It's not too far from that shack. Just be very quiet, please."

We did as he asked and circled well to the south of the village before cutting back north and east. We found their campsite behind a large limestone formation. Here, we tied up our horses with theirs and unloaded our gear. The three boys attended to their guns, making sure that they were ready. Me, I still kept my short sword with me. I didn't like guns at all. Enrico and I made sure that our blasters were set to the proper setting to shield us from flying bullets. Then, we crept on our stomachs around the formation to get our first view of the shack.

We spotted Fred down as close as he dare to the shack, lying prone behind a small boulder about a hundred feet from the shack. Several lanterns were in use; stray beams came out of the un-shuttered windows. A wagon was parked in front of the building. I counted ten soldiers with guns milling around outside, but there was also a horse and buggy parked there. I counted five more horses than there were soldiers, assuming one for the wagon. Five others, presumably the Confessore and his crew were inside, along with an unknown number of the medical group.

While we watched, suddenly the door opened. A man with a doctor's bag came out, along with a woman. They climbed onto the buggy and drove off to the west, back towards Mont Blanc. I spotted a man in black standing in the doorway watching them leave. Alec whispered, "That's the Confessore fellow."

"What's the plan?" Luigi whispered. "I can take him from here. Can I shoot now?"

Ah the enthusiasm of youth! Yes, we needed a plan, and I knew without asking that the others were waiting on my wisdom. "Bianca, fire ball the densest pack of soldiers. Pietro, Nicolo, take out two soldiers. Luigi, take out the Confessore fellow. On my mark." Well, I was too slow in saying on my mark. Luigi didn't hesitate. Bang! The noise of his gun so close to my ear unnerved me. Bang! Bang!

As I watched, at first I thought that Luigi missed the Confessore fellow entirely. Then as I watched, his body slumped to the ground, blocking the door. Two soldiers also dropped to the ground a second later. A giant ball of flames engulfed five soldiers. Mass pandemonium broke out down at the cabin. It took all of my intention to keep everyone perfectly still and not go charging down there. There were four extremely deadly assassins still in that cabin!

"Reload your guns. Everyone, stay absolutely still!" I ordered. Poor Fred couldn't believe what he was witnessing. At last, he turned his head and saw us. Arlie gave him a sign to stay put. I hoped that he would. Three of the soldiers, using their horses as shields and looking around in all directions for us, slowly moved away from the cabin. Once out of our direct line of sight, they mounted up and galloped off.

I spotted two men peering out from the doorway. I kept everyone very still. "Wait," I whispered. Time seemed to take an eternity to move! Everyone's urge was to rush down there and finish this. I had to keep them from doing that. They would be no match for these skilled assassins. After a time, one of them stuck his head outside and surveyed the scene, but he didn't see us. A bit later, he stepped outside, his long-gun in his hands, ready to shoot anything that moved. "Wait!" I whispered.

Eventually, he waved his hand and another man with a long-gun stepped out, just as cautiously. The first man went over to the burning soldiers but didn't attempt to put out the flames, ignoring one man's begging for help. The two fanned out, looking for us. Then a third man appeared in the doorway. We waited. After an eternity, he too joined his buddies, moving dangerously close to Fred's position. Finally, I saw what I wanted; the fourth man stepped into the doorway, back lit from the lanterns. "Fire!" I barked the order. Three shots fired off rapidly. Fred took his clue and fired his at the man close to him. All four men dropped to the ground, and we got up and raced down the slope to the cabin.

While the men made very sure that the enemy were dead, I led us women into the shack. I expected the worst and thus was not surprised. The nurse that they left behind certainly was, as I raced inside, my sword drawn. She shrieked and began shaking. "Don't kill me. Don't kill me. I am supposed to look after her. Please, don't kill me."

"Get out of here and run back to town," I ordered. She didn't hesitate, leaving as fast as her legs could go. Le Ann and Lena did shriek, though, bringing the men running inside, fearing some additional trouble. For once, my mischief boys stopped; all three gagged and left quickly, vomiting just outside the door. On a crude bed lay Queen Ann; large, bloody bandages covered her empty shoulders. She was unconscious still.

I took a quick survey of the room and its contents. "Enrico, go bring our horses down here and get them ready to ride. Get the boys to help you. Le Ann, Lena, grab all the medical supplies that you can find in here, stow them into bags to bring with us; use anything you can find. Alec, you and the others, hitch the wagon and get it ready to move. We have maybe a half hour to get out of here."

At once, everyone did as I asked, while I rapidly looked over the room's contents, adding this and that to the growing pile of bandages and items the women were stowing into two large bags. Five minutes later, Alec called out, "Bethany, we're ready. Now what?"

"Everyone, inside a moment. Soon we can expect more soldiers to come riding here. We have one break; it is getting dark quickly, and they will probably have to wait until morning to track us. Is there any chance that we can slip across the border to d'Grange?"

"No, there is supposed to be a large buildup of forces along the border," Alec answered. "I think the king suspects or fears an attack from d'Grange."

"Okay, is there any way we can circle around to the north and somehow get to Calgary?"

"No, the northern areas are very heavily patrolled. King John Penton is an archenemy of King Victor Hammersmith. We've got even less of a chance if we go that way. I think that we are doomed," Alec admitted.

"Yes, he's got us really boxed in here," Fred added. "That is why they chose this location. I knew that we were in deep trouble when they came here. We cannot go north or west or south to escape. There's no way over the mountains of the Appian Way. We're as good as caught now. But we can make a stand here, take as many of them with us as we can," he exclaimed vehemently.

I had an idea. Long ago when I had my first lifetime here on Tarra, my Lightning Circle found a passage through the Appian Way using a long series of tunnels. Could I find that entrance again? If so, we had a chance. With Ann in dire shape, we couldn't try to outrun the soldiers.

"Okay, I know another way. Here's the plan. Alec, I want you to tie your horse to the back of the wagon and head off to the north and then circle around to the west, as if you were trying to make for the border of Mont Blanc and d'Grange. As soon as you've laid in that trail, ditch the wagon and ride back east, here in the Langdoc area. We are going up as close to the mountains as we can get and then head due east. Remember; get as close to the mountains as your horse can go and then head due east, and pick up our trail. Now, Fred, Arlie. You two take a couple extra horses with you; circle around the village and head due west, as if making for Mont Blanc. As soon as you have laid in a good trail that the soldiers can follow, let the extra horses go and double back yourselves."

"But what about Queen Ann? Don't you need the wagon for her?" Le Ann asked, very worried for her Queen.

"That will be what the others will also assume. Enrico, you take Ann in your saddle; hold her before you. She's just dead weight right now and when she wakes, she will be in intense pain. Yet, with you holding her, she can ride. They won't be expecting that move. Okay, let's get going before the soldiers come."

Our three young men gently lifted Ann up and got her positioned before Enrico. As I watched the other three head off in their directions, I mounted up and asked, "Guys, with your guns, hang back behind us a ways and be our rear guard."

"You got it. We've confiscated their long-guns, so we now have two each, plus Fred's got an extra one too," Luigi explained. "Is she going to live?"

"If the surgeon did his job properly, then she has a chance. If he did not, she may well get blood poisoning, and he's left me nothing more that I can cut off to halt it. Pray that he did a proper job of it boys. Let's get riding."

I led us due south as the sun finally set. As twilight came, I had to slow down. Picking our way through the boulder field took care. I could not afford to lame a horse. We needed them. I saw that we had a quarter moon and guessed that we could ride on for a few more miles. Eventually, it set behind the dark Appian Way, and I was forced to halt for the night. We hazarded a tiny campfire, particularly so I could see Ann's condition and examine the medical supplies that they had taken. Thank god for the sleeping powders! Yes, they had intended to give her sips of it periodically until she healed a bit. As Ann moaned a little tending towards consciousness, I quickly prepared a little of the powders and got her to take about a teaspoon. As expected, she fell into a deep sleep.

Meanwhile Lena and Le Ann took advantage of the tiny fire to rustle up some dinner, before I dowsed the light. We were too close to civilization to gamble on being detected by our campfire. Near dawn, we heard approaching horses. The others had now caught up to us, but they were dead tired and simply collapsed on the ground asleep where they lay.

At dawn, the three mischief-boys rose and built us a small fire. As I lay wakening up, I heard them whispering. Luigi said, "Well, we are in a pickle now. We can't go back the way we came, can we?"

Nicolo whispered back, "No chance. These long-guns are cool, but we only get one shot. There are far too many soldiers, and they all have guns too. We don't stand a chance trying to run through them."

Pietro added, "What we need is a gun that fires bullets one after the other bang, bang, bang. Where's she leading us? Are we going to go all across the Langdoc and come back via Zargarb? That'll take months. Sh. She's stirring." I rose, but pretended not to have overheard them.

"Ah, thanks for the fire. Get some water boiling, while I check on Ann," I whispered. Soon the other women rose, but let their three men sleep in as long as needed. Ann was resting fitfully. She was nineteen, with long blonde hair and blue eyes. I thought I saw traces of Percival Penton in her face, but maybe I was only imagining it. She was pretty. Lena, her handmaiden, was twenty with curly brown hair and a charming smile, though of late, we'd see little of it. Her husband, Arlie was a year older with black hair and a thin, wiry frame, a rather handsome fellow, I thought.

Le Ann was thirty with dirty brown hair kept relatively short with eyes to match. She looked like a tough matronly woman, while her husband Alec was a year older with dark brown hair and a gruff face that tended to intimidate others. Fred was twenty and his face was twisted in grief over the premature death of his wife, who had volunteered to carry Queen Ann's message. Considering our three fifteen year old boys, though they claimed that they were really men now and well past being of age, they still had the playful attitude of young teens. Now they were going to grow up fast!

Bianca stirred. She and I were the two older women, with her at thirty-nine and me at thirty-four. Enrico was our old man at fifty-seven, and I purposely allowed him to sleep in this morning. As the fire began crackling, Enrico woke, though I could tell that sleeping on the hard ground was taking a toll on his old joints. He rose stiffly, but full of spirit, still feeling responsible for all of our safety.

"Boys, fan out and take up a guard position. Keep a sharp lookout; I'll call you when breakfast is ready," Enrico ordered. They grabbed their long-guns and silently moved off a ways to several larger limestone slabs that so marked this Langdoc region. He pulled out his folded map of the region and sat down beside me. "Reckon that we are about here, south of Le'Ours, maybe ten miles from Middleton, which is right up against the Appian Way."

"We're going to need a whole lot of supplies and a couple of packhorses, Enrico," I said what I was thinking.

Bianca brought us a hot tea and sat beside us, while the two young women began making a meager breakfast. "Zargarb?" she suggested, working out our return trip.

"No, I have something else in mind. I've not told this to anyone, but back in the 550's, my Lightning Circle found a set of tunnels that led through the Appian Way. If they are still there, we can cut this trip short, sneaking back into d'Grange and Velona. Only seven people ever knew of this, my Circle. I don't know if it is still passable, and it took every ounce of skill our Loremaster had to get us through that maze of tunnels and caverns. However, Bianca, you and I can leave our bodies behind and work out the route by trial and error if need be."

"Way cool!" she replied enthusiastically. "Count me in."

"It comes out somewhere between Barcella and Velona, so my guess that the entrance is about a hundred fifty miles from the seacoast or maybe a hundred from here. It took us eight days of trial and error to get through the tunnels, but if you and I can scout out the path, we may be able to cut that down significantly."

"Well, then that puts the entrance perhaps seventy miles further east than Drillon," Enrico stared at his map. "Drillon is the last town anywhere near where you are saying, Bethany. If we don't push it too hard, we should make your cave in two to three days. Allowing for eight days to pass through, then it's five more days to Alta and safety. Sixteen days supplies for a dozen of us. We'll need lantern oil, and several water kegs too. Oh, yes, some firewood or charcoal; probably charcoal would be easiest to carry.

We're close to Middleton. The boys and I should make a detour there and fetch what we need."

"Where are we going?" muttered Alec, who finally rose, hearing the sound of pancakes on his wife's griddle. The others began stirring too. Ann began moaning and I told them I'd explain after tending to her needs.

Everyone gathered around the fire, sitting on limestone slabs eating their breakfast, while I explained my plan. "What? There is an underground passage through the Appian Way?" exclaimed Alec, quite surprised. Actually, they all were to varying degrees. "This is a monumental find."

"Yes, but I must swear you all to secrecy about this passage. Use of it by enemies could be devastating to the security of the Sea Princes, particularly Barcella and Velona," I countered. "We are about three miles west of Middleton. After we eat, the boys and Enrico will go into town and get our supplies while the rest of us take a wide detour around that area. It is imperative that we not be seen. They'll catch up to us on the other side."

"I'll lag behind and cover our trail," Bianca volunteered, ever the Protector. "Don't worry, we'll have you all safely in d'Grange or Velona in less than three weeks." She sounded a hopeful note to these gloomy faces.

"Wow, did you hear that, Luigi?" Nicolo whispered, "A secret tunnel! Boy, are we going to have fun!" I smiled and pretended not to hear that.

A half hour later, the boys carefully lifted Ann up onto my horse and me with her. I held her with one arm and the others then mounted up. Bianca stayed behind, wiping out traces of our campsite. Enrico led the three boys on eastward, while Arlie led the rest of us south by a little east. I relied upon his knowledge of this area of the Langdoc to get us safely around the Middleton valley. Ten miles later, we were back at the Appian Way edge some three miles east of Middleton. Not long after that and leading two packhorses, Enrico and the boys caught up to us.

I grinned, as Luigi came up last. Enrico had been teaching him how to cover their trail. Bianca teased him, "You missed a hoof print." He hastily erased it, grinning. We rode on, with the three boys riding behind us, keeping a sharp eye out for anyone following us. Bianca was with them, erasing our trail.

Around three in the afternoon, we heard three gunshots from behind us, and I saw a puff of smoke. Just as I was about to telepathically contact Bianca, she contacted me. *It's okay. We had to take care of an armed patrol. Not sure if they were after us, but we didn't want to take any chances. We'll catch up after we clean up the mess. We're all okay. Boys did great.* I relayed the info to the others, but Enrico grimaced. He didn't like how this was going. However, we only passed by one shepherd all that day.

Around the meager campfire that night, Fred suggested, "What about us? Do you want us to head back to Mont Blanc and see if we can shoot this treasonous king or the damnable Cardinal?" I sensed that he wanted to get revenge for the slaying of his wife.

"Do any of you have children back there? Are we taking you away from your families?" I asked, realizing that may well be the case.

Le Ann spoke up, "No, Bethany. The situation in Mont Blanc has been really deteriorating for the last ten years. None of us dared start our families yet. Honestly, we've been too scared to make a life for ourselves. I mean, look what happened to Lea. We all knew that might happen when we signed up to be Forze Segrete. That's rather affected our plans, you know. Well, we've got parents and siblings, but none of us have any children yet, if that's what you mean."

"Okay, thanks. I think that it will be wisest for you to come with us to Velona or d'Grange for a while until this blows over. Then, we can sneak you back into Mont Blanc, if you like. Still, it might be too dangerous to stay there; perhaps a different town might provide you with better safety. This king will certainly know something is up when Lena turns up missing," I suggested. They accepted this, all except Fred, who wanted revenge. He grumbled, but said nothing.

Late the next afternoon close to sunset, I spied the large, dark opening of a cavern. It looked like what I remembered of the exit tunnel from over two centuries ago. In we all went. "We'll have a nice fire tonight and use the lanterns. We don't have enough oil to burn the lanterns constantly. Don't panic. Enrico, Bianca, and I can create a pale blue light that we can use while we stretch out our lamp oil. Tonight, I'm going to try to rose Ann and change her dressings. I warn you in advance: this will not be pleasant. Don't be alarmed if she screams. You probably would too; it is going to be a terrible shock to Ann, to say nothing of the pain. I ought to have a pot of sterile water too."

I lifted Ann and leaned her against the back wall of the cavern. I spread out the medical supplies and got the water ready. The medical supplies also contained a small amount of opium to help deaden the pain, but I had already decided against using it unless her pain was too great for her to bear. I took a deep breath and moved the smelling salts by her nose to rouse her.

Ann stirred and tried to wipe her eyes and face, before realizing her arms were completely gone. Her shriek of terror and shock echoed off the cavern's walls, shocking everyone with its intensity. I let her scream and get it out of her system. Soon she stopped and began crying, as the stark reality of her condition sunk home. She slumped down into a deep grief, as I anticipated. Still, I remained silent, knowing that whatever I or anyone said at this point would be recorded in her still ongoing trauma. Those very words might come back to haunt her. Silence now was golden, though I heard Bianca in the background urging the others to remain silent a little longer.

Finally, Ann stopped crying and looked at me. "Hi Ann. I am Bethany Bartiana, head of the Forze Segrete from Velona. You are safe with us now.

Lena got to us in time to save you from further harm. I want to examine your shoulders now and change the bandages. If it is too painful, let me know. We must make sure that there is no infection. Be brave a little longer, Ann." She whimpered a little, and I carefully began my work. I took my time and was very thorough.

An hour later, with fresh bandages in place, I sat back and cleaned up. "Well, so far so good, Ann. There is no sign of infection yet and that is very good indeed. It looks like the surgeon has done a remarkable job; there will be almost no ugly scars when you heal. Now then do you need to go to the bathroom? Then, let's see if we can get some warm food in you, okay?" She sniffled and agreed, though she was still in some shock and trying to come to terms with her mutilation.

"I am so utterly helpless like this," she wailed and began to cry as I got her up.

Lena rushed to us to lend a hand. "I am still your handmaiden, Ann. I will always be here to help you," she promised repeatedly. Still, she was a big help to me in handling Ann. A bit later, we had her sitting around our fire, and Lena and Le Ann took turns feeding her.

Luigi said, "Queen Ann, I killed that wicked Confessore fellow who did this to you. My buddies — they got the other Mano del Dio assassins. We got them all for you." He looked terrible sympathetic towards her. His eyes were being opened to the harsh cruelty found in some places on Tarra. She managed to say thanks.

While the women were cleaning up, Nicolo said, "Say, look what I've found. Some kind of strange looking rocks on the floor." His two buddies joined him, looking at the strange looking stones on the floor. Enrico came over to have a look and chuckled.

"Boys, that's quite a find. It's dried horse dung. Looks like we've found the right cave," he commented.

"Yes, but it is hard as a rock."

"Well, it's been in a dry cave for a couple hundred years," he teased.

"So much for your find, sleuth Nicolo," Pietro teased him.

"Hey, actually it may well be important. As we move through the tunnels and caverns, boys, keep your eyes peeled for more. It may give us a clear route through here," Enrico wisely commented.

As we laid down for the night, Bianca said, "Look after me for a while. I'm going to go on ahead and check on the route."

"Hey, you want me to come with?" Nicolo asked.

"No silly. I'm leaving my body here and going myself. If you can do that, sure you can come," Bianca replied, casting her blue light Druwid spell, further impressing everyone. Enrico and I also cast ours as the lanterns were extinguished.

"Hey, super cool! How do you all do that?" asked Pietro, very much impressed.

I knew that it would be a little unnerving for all them to waken in total darkness, but that is what we would be facing after we left this entrance cavern, where the dim light of dawn roused us all. As they fixed breakfast, Bianca said, "Well, mom, I scouted out the tunnels quite a ways. The boys are right, you did leave a horse dug trail that is pretty clear."

"Hey, why do you call her mom?" asked Lena. "Aren't you Lady d'Grange?"

Bianca grinned. I wondered how she would explain this incredible mess, her being the adopted daughter of Dita, who was my wife, but Dita was also Renzo and I, Bethany. She couldn't call Renzo mom any longer and had taken to calling him dad and me, mom. "Oh, she's like my second mom," she gaily bypassed the whole mess. I grinned.

"Well, we're off to follow the dung trail!" Nicolo cheerily called out as we packed up to begin.

I lifted Ann onto my horse. "While we are going to walk, Ann, it will be better for you to ride some." She was too weak to do much walking.

I was surprised with Luigi, though. He came up to her other side and said, "Queen Ann, I will be walking right beside you to make sure you don't fall or slip off. You can count on me." Ann managed a slight smile, ever so slight.

Bianca whispered to me, "You know, the sooner we give her some therapy, the better it will be. Fred needs it too."

"I know. I thought that I'd do it while we ride along. Take charge dear." She grinned.

"Okay, off we go. Follow my blue light. Save the lanterns until we really need them," she ordered and led the way. I cast my blue light and kept it around us in the middle, as I walked on one side of Ann's horse and Luigi, the other. Enrico with his blue light brought up the very rear. While everyone could just barely see, this was preferable to burning up all our lamp oil too quickly.

I proceeded to explain what I was about to do to Ann, and then I began the first of her therapy sessions. While her occasional shrieks were unnerving to everyone, they all listened in as much as possible, curious about what I was doing. Soon, they were caught up in Ann's experience. The more times we went over the traumatic events, the more data she recovered and told me, and thus everyone else — fascinating for these people for sure.

Now the thing about being in an underground tunnel complex with little or no light is the loss of your time sense. It's amazing how much we depend upon the sun to establish our daily rhythms. Here in the near dark, our stomachs dictated when lunchtime came and dinner too. Having little else to do but walk along in the dark and avoid obstacles, Bianca pushed us as much as she could, hoping to minimize the number of days in this pitch black tunnel complex. Later, we estimated that she had us walking twenty plus miles each day!

Halfway through the tunnel, Bianca made contact with me telepathically. *Mom, I've found a side tunnel that goes up, way up. I think it may lead to the Grey Creatures hideout. There is a storage room there with stuff in it!*

Wow! We should find a way to come back here and explore this further. Thanks! Now this is an interesting find, I thought. Then, I wondered why all these years I had not come back here to check on such things myself? Well, I had other pressing things to handle, I justified.

By the fifth day, Ann was finally laughing about her ordeal and I ended her therapy sessions. The others were now chatting about how I had just worked a Holy Miracle. Yes, I can see how the incredible results would seem that way to others. Now I took Fred into a therapy session. I needed to knock out the shocking loss of his young wife. He was cheerful by the end of that day. What I found encouraging during his session, Ann actually wanted to spend most of the day walking along, not riding. Her strength was definitely returning, and I encouraged it. Luigi, however, continued to walk at her side just in case she needed anything. He refused to be parted from his self-appointed task. Even Lena grinned at him several times.

The sixth day we saw daylight ahead and reached the exit cavern near sunset! Everyone let out a very loud cheer and clapped loudly for Bianca. Nicolo exclaimed, relaying the heartfelt relief and thanks that all were experiencing, "Way to go Bianca!" Six days beneath the mountains was more than enough for all of us. Even Ann joined in cheering her.

At dawn on July 16, we set foot onto the Paese di Dio. All stood still for some time, admiring the expansive view of green grasslands void of all human touch, God's Highway, spiritually uplifting for all. Okay nearly starving by now, our horses made a beeline to the grass and refused to budge for some time. We allowed them to graze while we basked in the sunlight, crystal clear air, and the smell of the virgin grasslands.

For six days, we rode along the Paese contented with life. Even Ann stopped worrying about how utterly helpless she was and how awful and useless her life would now be. God's Highway affected everyone, as it has always had, in my humble opinion.

On July 21, Bianca announced, "Tonight, we will be sleeping in real beds in Louis and my country estate. Louis is there awaiting us with a hot supper; I hope you like his cooking. It is our country home, our getaway place, about as close to the Paese as you can get. I know that you are going to love it there."

Sure enough near dusk, we spied a single smoke curl drifting into the sky just down from the Paese as it came to an end in the rugged mountains that was Fortress d'Grange. She led us down a well-worn path to their huge stone mansion. Of course, my group had been here several times; Enrico and I, many times. Bianca had alerted him and Louis stood before their front door, which opened facing the Paese. A huge front room window faced the Paese di Dio, just as he had always wanted.

"Welcome Queen Ann. You look very well considering your ordeal. I am Louis d'Grange, monarch of Fortress d'Grange. You are completely safe now. Bethany, Enrico, glad that you could make it too. Boys," he nodded to our three mischief-boys, who grinned back at Louis. "Come on in; the boys can take care of the horses. I have a fine meal just waiting to be devoured. I do hope that you are all hungry." The trio of boys groaned, but did as the monarch asked, though Luigi made haste so that he could be beside Ann to help her as needed.

"Louis, I tried to get a message to you. I think that King Victor is planning to attack Fortress d'Grange and then Velona," Queen Ann said as soon as she was close to him. His welcoming smile vanished, but momentarily returned.

Chapter 8 Queen Ann's Tale

"Well, come in and let's eat first, Queen Ann. Then, you can take your time and tell me all about this new threat," Louis played gracious host in spite of the shocking news. Luigi helped Ann dismount and raced through the horse chores to get inside as fast as possible. Lena grinned as Luigi entered and looked at the dining room arrangement. She had saved the chair on the other side of Ann for him. He smiled and whispered "thanks."

After a really good and filling meal, we took tea and Ann began her tale. "I don't know where to really begin, King Louis," she began.

"Just Louis, please, Queen Ann," he insisted. Louis hated courtly formalities, likewise Bianca, who finally allowed them to call her Lady Bianca.

She smiled, "Just Ann now, if everyone pleases. I am no longer a queen. For years, the unholy Church of Jehosanity has been gaining increasingly stronger grasp on all the kingdoms of the Greenway. Now they have almost total control of all the thrones. Only my brother, King John Penton of Southway, is still resisting and can be counted to be on our side. Only three of the northernmost kingdoms remain relatively neutral, namely Calgary, Westfold, and Blaine. My cousin Carol Penton Blaine is doing her very best to keep King James Blaine and the Kingdom of Blaine neutral, but I don't know how much longer they can hold out against the Church."

"My cousin, Mary Beth Penton Witherspoon, has failed to convince King Henry of Karka, and now he has joined the enemy alliance against d'Grange and Velona too. She is a virtual prisoner in her own castle. I hope that she doesn't meet the same fate as I have."

"Queen Kathleen (d'Aine) Mir, wife of King Diget III of Brownsville, Amos Mir, is in the same mess as Mary Beth. She is on our side, coming from a long line of d'Aine's of the Highlands of West Reach. They both are in dire danger. I tried to warn them two years ago, but I have not been able to see them since or get word to or from either since then. I fear all is too late for them as well."

"His cousin, Phil Mir, is the Cardinal of Brownsville, a double whammy. But then his cousin Cecil Mir is now the Cardinal of Mont Blanc. So too their sisters. I mean Winnie Mir Claghorn is Queen of Calgary and doing her best to convince King Bill Claghorn to join the conspiracy. Yet their cousin Sara Mir Penton is staunchly supporting us, along with her husband, King John Penton of Southway. But then Phil's sister, Mary Mir Williams, is solidly behind her husband, King Ros Williams of Avon. Yet, Ros' brother Edward Williams is now the Cardinal of Urkurt, backing King James Smythe who is against us too. So is his wife, Rose, who is a cousin of James Blaine. But then her sister, Betsy Blaine Westfold is remaining neutral still, along with her husband King Hugo Westfold of the Kingdom of Westfold. Yet her cousin, Cardinal Sam Westfold of Calgary is heavily pushing this war with you, Louis."

Suddenly Louis broke out laughing. "Whoa! Whoa! My head is swimming in names. Is everyone in the Greenway related? Talk about confusion. Are any of you following all this?"

I grinned, glad that someone else called a halt. "I've completely lost track of all these people, Ann."

She giggled, "Well, so many of us are of the Amir lineage you know, and over the centuries so many of us have become kings and queens. These days, the kings and queens intermarry frequently so that the Amir line remains the kings and queens. I know that it is terribly confusing, but they are planning to conquer d'Grange and Velona!" Ann protested.

"I know," Bianca spoke up. "Let's draw us up a map and put the kingdoms on there and then the kings and queens and cardinals. I'll use three colors. Blue is on our side, red are against us, and grey will be those who are neutral. I assume that all the cardinals will be against us, that's a given. Okay, Ann, as I draw in the kingdoms, you supply the names and their status, okay."

"Hey, that's perfect, I wanted to do something like that, but now I am utterly helpless to do so. She fought back a watering eye, and Bianca carefully allowed her time to gain control over her emotions. Bianca drew out a large rectangle. Across the bottom, she wrote in Appian Way. Just above that, she drew another line across the whole bottom and labeled it Langdoc Region. Across the whole top, she drew a jagged line and labeled it Dnu River and Volgost Mountains. Down the right side, she wrote Elbe River, while she label ocean along the left side, marking the boundaries of the Greenway.

Down near the bottom left corner she drew in Calgary, their sole main port. Fortress d'Grange lay in the mountains just below that point with a bit of Mont Blanc lying between Calgary and d'Grange. Then, she drew an arc line from Calgary due northeast and labeled another dot Brownsville. She then extended the line over to the Elbe River and added another dot there, the city of Melantas. This was the ancient Centurion paved road, the major highway across the Greenway over which grain was shipped to Calgary and beyond.

The Kingdom of Mont Blanc she drew in next, covering the Langdoc Region about halfway across the bottom. No one owned the eastern portion of the Langdoc; there was nothing there that anyone desired to own. Ann then gave the data. King Victor Hammersmith, her husband, ruled along with Cardinal Cecil Mir. Both were against us.

Southway was drawn in next, a small rectangular kingdom directly above Mont Blanc and she drew in the rest of the kingdom of Calgary, which rose on up the coast halfway up the left side of the map. Ann then filled in the names. King John Penton and Queen Sara were on our side, but Cardinal Hank Johns was not. In Calgary, King Bill Claghorn was neutral but his wife, Queen Winnie (Mir) was against us, as was their Cardinal Sam Westfold.

Even with the top of Calgary, Bianca drew a line over about half way across the Greenway and then down to touch Southway, forming another rectangular kingdom, Brownsville. Here King Diget III or Amos Mir ruled and was against us, while his wife Queen Kathleen (d'Aine) was on our side. Cardinal Phil Mir was against us, of course.

She extended the top line of Brownsville on over covering half of what remained and then drew a line down to the Langdoc. Here was the Kingdom of Redun, where King Helmut Johns and Queen Elaine (Williams) ruled; both were against us as was their Cardinal Sly Smythe.

She extended the top line of Redun on over to the Elbe. Here was the Kingdom of Avon, ruled by King Ros Williams and Mary (Mir). Both were against us, as was their Cardinal Frank Ames.

Next, Bianca divided the top half of the Greenway into roughly quarters. The westernmost quarter above Calgary was the Kingdom of Westfold, ruled by King Hugo Westfold and Queen Betsy (Blaine), both of whom were neutral. Their Cardinal Tom Cider was not.

The next quarter was the Kingdom of Blaine, lying above Brownsville. King James Blaine and queen Carol (Penton) ruled here. While he was neutral, she was on our side. Their Cardinal Tom Montrechet was our enemy.

The next quarter was the Kingdom of Karka, where King Henry Witherspoon ruled along with Mary Beth (Penton). She was in grave danger and supported us, while he was against us, as was his Cardinal Hank Johns.

Finally, the last quarter by the Elbe was the Kingdom of Urkut. King James Smythe ruled here and was against us, while his wife, Rose (Blaine) was neutral. Their Cardinal Edward Williams was against us as expected.

As I looked at the map, I felt sorry for the Pentons and King John in particular. Our only ally was surrounded on three sides with our enemies and thus his. Only neutral Calgary lay on his western border. How had we allowed such a mess to form, I asked myself repeatedly? I'd never seen this coming! I'd been too preoccupied with other areas of the world! Damn it anyway!

Worse, two more women, two queens, probably desperately needed our help and there was little that I could do for them, if they were still alive. I sighed heavily. Maybe if we could get safe passage through Calgary, we could sneak into Brownsville to get to Queen Kathleen and then on up into Karka to get to Queen Mary Beth. I saw little hope, though.

Now with a clearer picture, Ann picked up her tale again. "For many years, the kings have been building up their armies. The Cardinals and their unholy Churches have been helping to fund their armies. They are equipping their soldiers with long-guns and cannonae too."

"Do you have any idea of the size of their armies?" Louis asked the key question. His own Fortress d'Grange was a tiny country, hardly able to withstand such a large attack. I knew that Louis was now facing a crisis.

Tears streamed down Ann's cheeks. "I don't know. Lots of them. He would never tell me his numbers." After Lena wiped her cheeks, Ann added, "But I did overhear Victor saying that there is going to be a Council of Kings on September 1 at King Diget III's palace in Brownsville. All the kings and cardinals will be there. Victor was saying that they'd be making their attack plans then. That's when I decided I just had to get a message to d'Grange and sent Lea off with it. Poor Lea, I sent her to her death!" Ann lost control of her emotions once more, and Louis graciously allowed her time to deal with it.

Louis then spoke like a true monarch. "Queen Ann, you have done Fortress d'Grange and Velona the highest possible service. Your timely warning has given us time to prepare and has definitely saved thousands of lives, had we been taken by a surprise attack. Our countries owe you the highest possible thanks. I give you my word that for the rest of your life, you shall not lack for anything. Speak, and it shall be yours or done. I know that I also speak for Adolfo West Po of Velona as well. We owe you our lives. Thank you, Queen Ann. I am humbled by your selfless sacrifice for the free peoples of Tarra."

I think that Ann was deeply impressed with his little speech. She had received a good acknowledgment for her ultimate sacrifice. She managed a smile. He added, "Bianca, make a copy of your map. We must get this to Adolfo immediately. He and I must meet soon to consider our preparations. Bethany, I leave the potential rescue of these two queens who are in grave danger up to you and your forces. Ann, you will always have a home in Fortress d'Grange. I will reserve a secure room there in your name. Come anytime. However, under the present circumstance, I believe that you will be safer if you go with Bethany to Velona. Fortress d'Grange is very small and will be facing these armies first. You have better chances of survival in Velona."

I added, "Please, Ann, you should come with us. I also want to help you learn new ways to do the ordinary things of life so that you are not helpless. I give you my word that in time you will not be feeling helpless any longer. While we both know that your life will never be the same as before, but at least you will be able to do things on your own and not be utterly dependent on others. I give you my solemn promise on this. Will you come with us to Velona?" Ann agreed.

The next morning after a short ride into Alta, we were pleased to discover that Louis had arranged for a passenger train to take us down to the city of Velona. He'd contacted Dianna who had arranged it, stopping all other trains, and allowing ours to have unrestricted travel.

As Luigi helped Ann board, he eagerly said, "Ann, you are going to get your very first train ride! This is something else! It's fabulous. I'll sit with you and point out the sights." He did just that, though his mischievous companions snickered at him behind his back. I think that the two were a little jealous of him spending so much time with Ann. For now, I had her Forze Segrete members come along as well. I was not sure yet what to do with them. Certainly, they could not return to Mont Blanc.

Chapter 9 Timetable Shifted

On July 10, a caravel from Calgary docked in Vito. A messenger raced to deliver his message to General Franca Mafra. The fifty year old general was the sole ruler of Vito, had been for some thirty years now. He ruled with an iron fist, but was forced to share power with Cardinal Branco Beja, now just turning sixty.

Franca knew that he was an important man. He'd known it for years, but when he received his personal meeting with Pope Christos some three years ago, he knew that the world also knew just how important a man he was! Indeed, he had received very special orders from the Pope. Yet, those orders had been given to him in the strictest confidence, one that he would not break. The first sealed packet he'd opened in the presence of the Pope himself. The second sealed one contained a stern warning not to open until 779. Again, he obeyed his Pope's wishes. However, part of those orders contained a set of special circumstances which if met would allow him to open this third packet before March 781. Again, he had far too much to do to meet the first two sets of orders to worry much about what might or might not be contained in the third. He only knew that they would be highly important.

His aide called out, "General, there's a special courier from King Victor of Mont Blanc."

"Send him in," General Franca barked.

A breathless young man rushed in, handing a sealed packet to the General. "I was told this is critical and to await any reply, sir." The general smirked. After verifying the seal was unbroken, he opened it and read.

General,

The Confessore here failed in his assignment. Yes, he and his men got to Ann and had the Medico do his thing, but before they could ship her off to Hieras, someone got to them. Killed the Confessore and all his men and escaped with the Queen. As you read this, we have an all-out manhunt for them and the queen. However, prudence dictates that as of this writing, d'Grange and Velona have become aware of the military buildup here in the Greenway. All is still set for the Council of Kings on September 1.

King Victor Hammersmith

The general noted the key words "become aware of the military buildup." He said, "If you will please wait outside. I must check on something." He flicked his hand as if the messenger was a fly. Hastily, the man obeyed, leaving the general alone in his elegant office. Once he was sure no one was looking, he took his desk key from his waist key band and unlocked a drawer. Inside, he found the second packet's documents. He opened them and compared the wording. Satisfied, he grinned. "Ah, the Pope has thought of everything." He greedily tore open the third sealed pouch and read the Pope's secret message.

He read it through three times, pleasantly shocked with what he now saw was the full, complete plan. Operation Squash was its official title, well, he'd have called it something else. He hastily jotted a note to King Victor, paused to check his calendar and that of the new train, which came through Vito on a regular basis. He chuckled, "You will be the victim of your own inventions." He added a few more lines to the reply. He sealed it and placed his hot wax seal over the packet. He then went to his door and summoned the courier.

"Take this back to King Victor. If you are intercepted, you are to burn this packet. Under no circumstances should this packet ever leave your hands. Understood?"

"Yes sir!" He took the packed and raced out of the palace. From his bay window, the general saw the caravel slipping out of the dock just ten minutes later. He smiled and set to work.

A half hour later, he had his ten aides in attendance. "Gentlemen, the timetable has been moved up by six months. We are now entering Phase Three. Here is what we must do immediately and without fail." He began outlining in detail what he needed carried out yet today.

Chapter 10 The Death Blow

On July 17, we began our train ride down from Alta, Velona, to the city proper, a ten hour trip. Meanwhile in Velona, Torres got off the train at the station in Velona. He began walking down the main street, checking street signs. At last oriented, he quickened his pace. I am coming, he thought to himself. I am coming soon, Lord Jehosa. A half hour later, he paused before the large estate mansion. He took out his opium pipe as instructed and took his last hit.

Then, he walked up to the door and knocked. A servant answered and he said, "I have a message for Adolfo West Po."

"I'll take it to him," she replied.

"I must give it to him personally," he replied in a monotone. She asked him to step inside and went to fetch Adolfo. His extended family had just sat down to lunch together.

"Yes, you have a message for me," he said, looking the stranger over. The man rose and pulled a string, which ignited a huge black powder explosion. Boom! Shortly after that, the mansion went up in flames.

Chief Inspector Basilio was supposed to dine with his family as usual. However, a group of thugs had just been arrested, and he had to see to their arrests. Thus, his lunch was delayed. He was not home when a human bomb blew up his house and extended family.

Gerardo, who was supposed to dine with his folks, canceled at the last minute to be with Cosima at our estate, hoping to be filled in on this incredible news of an army about to attack Velona from the Greenway. He missed the explosion, which leveled his parent's home.

Within the space of thirty minutes, ten bombs exploded within the wealthier district of Velona. Mass pandemonium broke out, as the fire crews, able to deal with one fire, found themselves facing ten huge blazes. There was little they could do except keep the flames from spreading to neighboring houses.

Bethany! Ten bombs just went off in Velona! Gerardo and I are going to investigate! Cosima alerted me. My face turned ashen; my stomach felt like someone had just gripped it in a vice.

"Bethany, what's wrong?" Enrico asked.

"Cosima. She just reported that ten bombs have gone off in Velona! She and Gerardo are going to investigate. I have an awful feeling about his, Enrico. Can't this train go any faster?" I said near panic.

"Damn! I'll go see," Enrico decided to try something.

"What's that, Bethany?" Pietro asked; he'd overheard us. I explained what little I knew. The three boys turned rather pale too.

Fearfully, Ann asked, "Has the war begun already?"

"I don't think so. Velona is hundreds of miles from Mont Blanc. They have not had time to march an army there. This is something different Ann, but I don't know what yet."

Enrico returned and said that the engineer was pouring it on, whatever that meant. Very restless, I decided to act. "Enrico, watch over my body. I'm going to go to Velona and see what is going on." He sat down beside me and I took off, deciding that I was now high above Velona and so I was.

I looked down and saw ten huge smoke clouds drifting up towards me. They were all clustered together in the wealthier district, I observed. Then, I began to swoop down for a closer look. Could I identify the houses? Oh my god! That was monarch Adolfo's home! Fire crews were throwing water on nearby houses, ignoring the roaring flames from his. One by one, I moved in on the other fires. They all were homes, which I knew. They belonged to the various members of the West Po clan! Now I was even more terrified than before. Surely, no one could survive those blazes. Had anyone gotten out? I felt sick and returned to my body. Enrico said that I was white as a sheet.

"It's ten of the West Po homes. They — they are totally destroyed!"

The silence in the passenger car was total. Not even the mischief boys spoke; they were lost in their own private thoughts. I took a deep breath and reached out to Cosima.

Cosima, all ten houses belong to the West Po's. Someone is out to kill all them.

I knew that she was crying. *All ten?* She whimpered. *We are at Adolfo's now. We think that they are all dead. All ten? My god!*

Listen, honey. Here's what I want you to do. You and Gerardo go around and find all the West Po clan who have somehow survived this attack. Get them all to the safety of our estate. We have the trainman making this thing go as fast as possible. Be there with you as soon as we can. It is vital that you find all the remaining West Po's and get them to the safety of my estate. Hurry!

Okay. Will tell Gerardo now. He's bawling like a baby. She didn't need to tell me that she was crying as well.

I sat back. Considering the size of the West Po clan, it would be some time before I could possibly know who was killed and who was still alive. I felt so helpless sitting here in a train car, when they needed me so desperately in Velona. "Can't this train go any faster?" I growled. Enrico rubbed my shoulders and I relaxed a bit.

Four-thirty in the afternoon, the train pulled into the station at the docks. People were running around everywhere, many carrying buckets of water from the Med Sea and handing them via a human line down the streets to where they eventually reached the surrounding homes. There were no carriages to be had, but Arturo was waiting for us. "Over here, quickly," he called out. We raced over to the carriage. Luigi helped Ann safely aboard and then he helped me, though I didn't need it. After getting Le Ann and Lena inside, he joined us. The others piled up on top with Arturo; we headed to our home, taking a circuitous route to avoid the long lines of volunteer fire fighters.

As we pulled into the gates at 42 Hampton Way, red-eyed Gerardo and Cosima met us at the doors. "It's bad, really bad," Cosima said trying desperately to keep from crying again. "We got them all inside."

As we entered the living room, I saw Chief Inspector Basilio West Po slumped on a chair, holding his head in his hands, crying to himself. Dianna, her eyes bloodshot, was going around to the many others offering words of hope as she could. There was no older Po's present in the room! Oh my god! I thought, not all them!

Alessa came up to me; she too had been crying. Silently, she handed me a list of names. Adolfo and his family, Giana and her whole family, Basilio's family, Lona, Daria and her whole family, Lucinda and her family, Marcella and her family, Tom and his family, Suzana and her family, Tonia and her family. All told, I counted thirty-three names, staggering. Someone had wiped out nearly all the rulers and potential rulers of Velona, just as a war was about to break out with the Greenway!

Alessa spoke at last. "Gerardo was here waiting on information from you about the war in the Greenway. Basilio was delayed because he had to deal with the arrest of some thugs. The younger set, all these here, were out on the town on dates and such. At least the teens survived."

With uncontrollable tears now trickling down my face, I walked before the assembled group. I had to address them, and knew that I had to get order brought back to the country immediately. I just could not allow Velona to fall into chaos, not with a war looming on the horizon.

"I am so sorry for each and every one of you. All your lost ones were dear friends of mine too. In this time of terrible personal tragedy, our whole country is on the brink of destruction. Someone has very nearly succeeded in wiping out our rulers. All Velona will soon know the utter depths of this tragedy. We must have new leaders in place immediately to help bring back order and to show the world that we are not destroyed yet. I don't know if any of you have given any thought to lines of succession, but we need a strong, able leader and a strong able High Priestess. The rest can wait."

Felix spoke up, "Gerardo is the best of us qualified to run the country. Everyone else is dead." He broke down and couldn't say more.

"I can't do it," Basilio wailed. "I want to find out who did this heinous act and kill them! I will not rest until I do. Kids, I give you my solemn word that I will devote the rest of my life to finding the guilty parties and killing them personally! Just don't ask me to lead the country. Gerardo should take over." The young teens all began nodding.

"Okay, then Gerardo, you are now the monarch of Velona," I stated, trying my best to keep my flowing eyes clear enough to see. "We need someone to take over our church."

Dianna whimpered, "I can't do it. I don't know anything about it. I've failed everyone now."

I looked at the remaining women: Adrianne (fifteen), Elaina (sixteen), and Justine (fifteen). Her eyes swollen almost shut, Elaina looked up and said, "Mom has been teaching me."

"Good for her. Elaina, you are now the High Priestess. However, I will be glad to lend you a hand, especially with these painful duties that we all now are facing." The look of thanks that she gave me told all.

"Okay. The first thing in the morning, Gerardo, you must make all this widely known. Basilio and Cosima, I want every resource you have investigating these bombings. We must know who was behind them and soon, very soon. Until further notice, all of you will be staying under my roof here. I am taking your personal safety on as my responsibility. Your parents would not want any less of me."

"If we all have not had enough bad news, I have just returned with Queen Ann. It cost her her arms to get this to us. The Greenway kingdoms have built up a large army with the intention of invading and conquering Fortress d'Grange and Velona. How soon they will attack us we do not know yet. Indeed, we have entered a very dark hour indeed. Now, let's see if we can find a place for all of you to sleep, if any of us can sleep right now."

While everyone began to help our guests, Dianna took me aside. "They tried to bomb me too, at the DEA, but as I came to the door and the guy detonated his bomb, the Grey Creature's blaster forced the whole explosion back onto the man, incinerating him, but nothing else caught fire. I wasn't harmed in the slightest. I thought that you ought to know," she added and headed off to help her nieces and nephews find a spot for the night.

A bit later, Jules and Danielle came up to me arm in arm. Felix and Justine were right behind them, as were Gervaise and Julianne. He said pleadingly, "Bethany, can you somehow marry us right away, before anything else happens? We want to be together if the worst happens." I knew that all three couples had been dating for well over a year at least and that they were serious about each other before this horrid day. I could not help but give them my consent.

After we all got the young couples situated, I called asked the others to join me. Besides our two sets of parents, Gerardo, Cosima, Alessa, Arsenio, Enyo, Alex, Dianna, and our many teens joined us. "Gang, tomorrow three things must happen. First, we must demonstrate to the country that there has been a clean transition of power to Gerardo here. How do we best inform everyone?"

After working out some details, I then said, "Second, we need to gather the other priests and priestesses here in Velona and set them to work on both assisting Elaina in getting herself established as the High Priestess and on recovering the many remains and funeral arrangements. This also ties in with the third objective. We must allow Cosima and Basilio time to fully examine the crime scenes before the bodies are removed."

"Okay, four things. We need to get some constant protection details around all the rest of the West Po family and any other critical targets that more suicide bombers may attack."

"Let me tackle that one," Dianna suggested. "I know pretty well who is key now and what places must be protected."

"Okay. Now kids, I want you all to pair up with the remaining West Po's. From now on, you are on the buddy system. If Jules and Danielle decide to go shopping, then Pietro you tag along. I will leave it to you to work out who will buddy with whom. From now on, I don't want any of the West Po clan to be without one of us nearby."

Luigi protested, "But I have already promised Ann that I would be looking after her."

I realized that he had given her his word, though I knew she'd understand if he was needed elsewhere. "Okay, when you are not needed with her, lend a hand with the other teens, please. Until we know the source of these terrorists, we must take every imaginable precaution against more attacks. Who knows, maybe tomorrow they will go after the ones that they missed."

In hindsight, I was the one who first used the word terrorist in regards to this heinous crime. After the meeting broke up, Gerardo pulled me aside. "Do you realize the damage these terrorists could have caused if they had exploded their devices in the public markets? We'd have hundreds of dead and hundreds more wounded. If I was behind these attacks, that would be my next logical step. Frankly, I am scared, Bethany. How do we protect our open society from these insane suicide bombers?"

"Gerardo, for once I don't yet have an answer. We need to let Cosima and Basilio do their jobs first. We need to know who the attackers were and why, if possible."

"Well, the why is obvious. They want to disrupt our leadership before they launch a full scale invasion," he replied. I nodded my agreement.

Now that Renzo was off at sea, I put Ann in my room. Lena got her dressed and ready for bed. "Okay, thanks, Lena. I'll take over from here. Ann, you are sleeping with me tonight."

"I am going to be so much trouble," she started to protest.

"Ann, if you become trouble, I will personally kick you in your rear! Now come on, into bed with you. The first thing to realize and come to grips with is that many things will now simply take more time to accomplish. Do not let anyone rush you. Work out how you can do something and then do it. See, you got yourself into bed by yourself. I'll look at your bandages in the morning."

I woke early and helped Ann use the chamber pot. Before attempting to get her dressed, I removed the bandages and looked at her shoulders closely. "Interesting," I mused.

"What do you mean, interesting?" she asked, wondering if she ought to be worried.

"Look in the mirror for yourself. You really don't need any bandages any longer. Amazing. Usually such drastic surgery takes from six to ten weeks to heal to this degree. Yet, you have healed in about half to a third that time. Therapy done early on really makes an incredible difference in healing rates of our bodies," I explained.

"Here, today, wear this loose fitting dress. See if you can wiggle yourself into it," I suggested, while setting about getting myself dressed. Ann worked at it and managed to get it on by herself. Now then, let's see if you can slip on these flats. From now on, you will be using your feet and toes as you used to use your hands and fingers."

"What were they going to do with me? That Confessore fellow?" she asked.

"My guess is that they would send you to a town called Hieras Anubis, down in the Southlands. We think that all the women there are like you, armless. Say, see the rug that you are standing on? Well, Cosima bought it for me. It was made by an armless woman in Hieras. Pretty amazing, eh? So you see we just need to help you learn new ways to do things. Luigi will also be around quite a lot to assist you as well."

"Say, Luigi has been incredibly kind to me, hasn't he?"

"Yes, unusually so. He's part of our trio of mischievous fifteen year old boys. I brought them along on our rescue mission partly in hopes that they would mature a little. They got more than they bargained for, that's for sure. You should have seen their reactions when they first saw you. All three actually vomited, that's how badly it impacted them."

She grinned, "Well, we were all once teens ourselves."

After breakfast, I took Gerardo aside and made him take a blaster. I showed him how to use it and insisted he carry it in his pocket all the time. He grinned and agreed, especially after I explained how it had saved Dianna's life yesterday. Soon, everyone headed off to begin the awful day's work. I sent our parents off to lay in a whole lot of supplies, while I remained here acting as coordinator for everyone. In addition, I sent the Forze Segrete off to help protect Gerardo, Dianna, and the DAE Enterprises. They were glad to have an immediate assignment that they could do.

At last, it was just Ann, Luigi, and me who remained, along with our cook, who set about cleaning up and then preparing lunch. "Okay, Ann, it's time for some lessons. I'll show you what to do and then leave Luigi to help you work out the details. I got them started on learning how to feed herself using her feet and toes. Once I had shown her the methods, I left them to practice.

I spent some time bringing Bianca up to date and then spent even more time with Renzo and his group. Yes, they almost insisted on turning around and heading back, but I convinced them to complete their mission. I had no idea what they would encounter down there, but I knew it had to be bad.

Not long after that, Elaina came back with another Priestess, and we held a long, frank talk. She was willing to help Elaina learn what her mother had yet to teach her about the powerful position, as well as marry the three young couples and perform the funeral services. We spent the better part of the morning going over these details.

Late morning, Enrico and the others returned from shopping, having bought the entire market or so it appeared. "Here, look at the headlines in the extra edition of the Velona News." He tossed the newspaper at me. The top headline read: Terrorists Strike a Deadly Blow. The second line read: Gerardo West Po Assumes the Monarchy. Elaina West Po New High Priestess. Well, the news certainly traveled quickly.

Not far away, Cosima and Basilio decided to work together. Surrounded by fifty of their policemen, they began the gruesome task of examining each of the ten crime scenes. Today, Cosima wore her traveling leathers, knowing that she would be scrambling through rubble. She did however bring along a huge supply of evidence bags along with her usual black bag, her detective kit. Their first stop was Adolfo's home. Only smoldering embers remained. Nevertheless, Cosima was thorough, with Basilio assisting her at every step.

"Well, this is the terrorist's body. It holds a wealth of clues. It was not totally burned up, just blasted to pieces in his middle. We have top and bottom parts filled with clues," she said, steeling her mind against what this man had done and what his corpse now looked like. She knew that she was working on the most important crime of her career. She had to find the answers that everyone wanted to know. After spending an hour here, they released the site. Others now gathered up what remained for burials later on. Neither wanted to watch that grim action, and they moved on to the next site.

A weary Cosima and Basilio finally returned home almost missing supper. They had an entire carriage full of evidence bags. There was no lack of willing hands to carry them all into her office, for which she was grateful. As she finally joined us for supper, Gerardo asked, "Well, love, any news yet?"

"I am pretty certain that they came from Vito or Bonito sectors. Basilio will be tracking that down tomorrow. There were ten of them and I suspect all ten were opium addicts. I found traces on five of their remains. All were likely between fifteen and twenty years old; all were male. All carried the explosive devices strapped around their waists. All were suicide bombers. What is curious, I found several bits of papers, which contained the address of the home they bombed. The handwriting is the same on each. One person wrote out all their orders. If we ever had a sample of that person's handwriting, I could match it to them. Just how I am going to get that handwriting sample from the guilty party is another question entirely."

"What makes you think that they came from Vito?" Gerardo asked.

"We found a number of caps and boots that are typical of the crude boots made and worn there. Bits of pant legs also tend to support that theory, though I will know more after I have had time to process the evidence. I will get onto it tonight, dear."

Gerardo then explained, "In case something happens to me, I want someone prepared to fill my shoes. As of now, I am pulling Adrien, Felix, Jules, Gervaise, and Dante from their current jobs and businesses and putting them to work in our government. Who knows who will succeed me, but I want all five to know as much as possible, just in case. I am going to let Felix continue with his dock expansion project, though. Honestly, the power transition went as well as could be hoped today."

"Heck, Gerardo, it went super well! You are a genius at this stuff," Dante exclaimed, very impressed with how skilled Gerardo actually was. "He's a perfect choice to replace Uncle Adolfo." Of course, the mere mention of that name brought immediate tears, but that was to be expected.

"Wow! Will you look at Ann!" Gerardo shifted the focus. Ann flushed as everyone turned to look at her. "She's doing rather well at feeding herself! Way to go Ann," he praised her efforts. Indeed, Luigi had worked all day long with her on this one thing, using a spoon and handling a mug with a large handle.

After supper, the three mischief-boys ducked into the basement, the first time that Luigi had left Ann all day. Lena and Le Ann were hovering over her, so I could see why he decided to take some time off. Little did I know what those three were up to in our basement! Before the terrorist strike, I knew that they were working on a design for their bi-wheel contraption that they intended to market.

In the basement, Pietro explained, "Okay, we all agree. These long-guns are great, but have a terrible liability in that it takes us ages to reload."

"Right, ages that we didn't have," Luigi added.

"So what if we could have a contraption that held say a dozen of them. One could fire twelve shots before reloading?" Pietro asked.

"Yes, that's much better, but then it will be twelve forevers reloading them," Nicolo countered. "What if we could simply swap out the used twelve for a fresh set of twelve and then continue firing?"

"I like that. Then, we could have others who are behind some protections going to town reloading the dozen guns while we continue to shoot," Pietro extended the idea. Thus was born the initial idea for the multi-fire gun. They tore apart one of the long-guns that they had confiscated from the soldiers that they had shot.

"Look, all that we really need out of this is the long barrel. If we can come up with some way to fire it without all this extra stuff. . ." Pietro suggested.

"Right! We could mount a dozen of these in a cylinder mounting, with this end ready to fire. After firing, rotate the cylinder so the next one comes into the firing position. Should only take seconds to be ready to fire again. I like this; now we are getting somewhere," Nicolo added.

"Maybe we can get Arsenio to lend us a hand in getting this thing made," Luigi suggested. "Mums the word until we get it built. I'll go see if I can sneak him down here."

The next day was grief filled. Thousands upon thousands passed through the Church of the Three Holy Roses, paying their last respects for their lost rulers and their families. They buried all the remains of each household in one crypt, because identification of whose remains were whose was nearly impossible. The survivors were not allowed to be present during the long public visitation. The risk of another terrorist bombing was too great. We escorted them through before the church was opened to the public.

Priestess Agnese officiated, and I stood in for the family for many hours that long, long day. The outpouring of grief was incredible, and I relayed this to the children, giving them some small comfort. I found it interesting that Cardinal Bosto Rems, resplendent in his red robes, also passed through the line, paying his respects as well. During the next two weeks, condolence cards and letters flowed into Gerardo, who began making a pile of them in one corner of their room.

After the funeral, I had Priestess Agnese sit down with the three young couples to discuss their wishes to be married before anything further happened. She got them to agree to marry in one month. "Children, you need to give yourselves time to grieve. August is soon enough to begin married life," she counseled the six. Thankfully, they went along with her suggestion and began planning their wedding.

The fourth day after the bombings, Cosima finally finished her analyses of the piles of evidence that she had gathered. That combined with Basilio's investigations yielded some definitive conclusions. Cosima and Basilio presented their summary to the survivors first. Briefly, it boiled down to ten men from Vito. They had taken the train the day before the bombings, arriving together shortly before noon. Witnesses saw them walking off in various directions from the station. All described them as appearing to be rather obese around the waist. Cosima added her suspicions that they all smoked opium before they detonated their bombs.

"Someone in Vito has gone to a whole lot of trouble to somehow convince young men to blow themselves up to kill our relatives. My guess is that they were addicted to opium and had been convinced that they would wind up in some kind of opium heaven if they would just do this simple thing," Cosima outlined her theory. "These men did not make the bombs themselves and probably had no idea that they were actually committing suicide. Probably just told that pull this string and you will arrive in heaven or some such drivel."

"As I said before, all of them apparently had pieces of paper with precise directions to the home to blow up. One person wrote those notes. One day, I hope to discover his or her identity. Yet, that also leads me to conclude that someone had to have been here spying on our families to know their routines. From now on, keep an eye out for strangers milling around wherever you are at. If you see anyone suspicious, report it at once."

By the end of July, Gerardo pretty well had the reins of government back to normal. However, the newspapers continued discussing this terrorist strike. Everyone now knew that someone in Vito had been behind the terrorist assassinations and tempers were rising.

August 1 was the date that Gerardo arranged to meet with both Louis d'Grange and Andriano Barcella to discuss the Greenway threat. The meeting would be held at my estate in secret. No one but Louis and Gerardo knew where we'd hold the meeting. Both men arrived by train and were to be escorted directly to 42 Hampton Way. That was the plan.

A bit bored that morning, Cosima looked at the large pile of condolences that Gerardo had been tossing into a corner of their room. She decided to clean it up, what with the conference to be held here later this afternoon. With Alessa's help, the two began going through them. At Alessa's suggestion, they intended to store them in a large folder and store it at the church for posterity.

"Oh my god!" exclaimed Cosima. Her long red talons held up a fancy condolence letter.

"What's the matter?" asked Alessa, taken completely by surprise. Cosima didn't answer but rushed to her evidence collection and hastily searched through the bags. At last, she found the right one and opened it. She laid the scorched papers down and then lay the condolence letter beside them. She opened her evidence collecting bag and took out her magnifying lens. Bending over, she began a careful comparison. Shortly, she looked up and exclaimed, "I know who wrote these directions!"

"Oh my god! Who?" asked Alessa. She didn't wait for Cosima to reply, but bent over the table and saw for herself. She stared at the signature. "Cardinal Branco Beja of Vito!"

"Yes, and I wonder who gave him the information?" Cosima spat out.

"Cardinal Bosto Rems! I'll bet anything it was he and his Mano del Dio who kept tabs on all the West Po's and then passed that information on to Beja," Alessa theorized. "Where are you going?"

Cosima was already out the door, heading down the hallway, her heels clicking rapidly on our floor. "To tell Basilio!"

Chapter 11 Defensive Plans

Just after lunch, a carriage pulled up outside our estate, along with a hundred mounted soldiers, who joined the fifty who were already on guard around the perimeter of our estate. Cosima, wearing her blue satin ball gown dress and Annelise heels, stood awaiting the arrival of the leaders. Gerardo stepped down first, dressed in his finest suit. He held his hand out for Lady Bianca, who wore a red satin gown; Louis followed her out of the carriage and took her arm. Then, Gerardo assisted Adelina Barcella step down; she wore a similar gown of red satin. Soon, Andriano Barcella stepped out and took his wife's arm. He was thirty and she a year younger.

From their speed of movement, Cosima relaxed, both women had to be also wearing Annelise high heels; they were moving extremely slowly, although extremely elegantly. "My charming wife, Chief Detective Inspector Cosima," Gerardo proudly introduced her to the Barcella's. This was the first time that Cosima had met these monarchs from Barcella.

Once inside, Gerardo introduced me to the Barcella's and I, wearing my red satin gown, led them all into my private study — well, Renzo's and my private study, that is. I had a large map of our area of the world on the wall and had added Bianca's notations to it. Once seated, I opened the meeting.

"I have asked you all here to outline perhaps the gravest threats to our countries in over a century. First, let me have Cosima explain her findings about the terrorist bombings, which very nearly wiped out Velona's ruling families." She rose and went through the details of the evidence gathered, ending with her finding this morning of the author of the directions to the homes that the bombers struck. As I expected, the Barcella's were shocked and outraged.

Andriano angrily asked, "Do you expect more of these suicide bombings? Ought Barcella close its borders with Vito? The nerve of that Church!"

I didn't directly answer him. "Sir, there is far more to consider before you discuss your options. Almost a month ago now, we received a plea for help from Queen Ann Penton Hammersmith of Mont Blanc. She has been an outspoken critic of her husband's and other's plans to attack the Sea Princes. The Church of Jehosanity's Confessore del Dio had kidnaped her. While we got to her as fast as possible, we were a bit late. They had already mutilated her and were about to ship her off to Hieras Anubis. At this time, I would like to present Queen Ann Penton and let her tell you her story. She has paid an awful price to get this dire warning to us all." I called out an okay and Luigi escorted Ann into our room. I didn't want to waste a lot of time moving slowly to the door.

I had dressed Ann in one of our old style slinky dresses that did not try to hide her bare shoulders. Her new form was her form, and she had to get comfortable with others seeing her body as it now was. I had her looking as queenly as possible, including wearing our lower Alexa heels. After all, she was a queen and on par with the three monarch families in the room. Luigi, wearing his fancy twin tails suit, escorted her to her chair and got her seated. I had him take a chair near the door so that he could assist her out when she was finished. He looked extremely pleased to be so honored by this. I began to think that this mischief boy was growing up after all.

Yes, the Barcella's were shocked by Ann's appearance and humbly gave her sympathy, which she didn't want. Yet, it served my purpose to drive home the terrible sacrifice Ann had made to get us this critical information. This way, I knew the Barcella's would take it seriously. If we stood any chance at all, we three had to be working together as one, though only Gerardo already knew this intuitively.

Ann again relayed her story, while Bianca pointed each out on the large wall map. An hour later and many questions as well, Ann finally finished up. "My brother, King John Penton of Southway, will fight on our side; I know he will; only he is surrounded on three sides by the enemies, maybe four sides if Calgary drops its neutrality. Plus Queen Mary Beth and Queen Kathleen are in as much trouble as I was."

With that, I had Luigi escort her out of the meeting for now. "Thank you, Queen Ann. Thank you. Your sacrifice will be rewarded somehow, I know it will. Have faith in God," Monarch Andriano proclaimed humbly as she rose. She bowed and Luigi's arm went around her waist, gently leading her out. I had told her beforehand that we might need her back later on. Luigi nodded to me, indicating that he would be ready with her, if needed.

"Now then, I believe this casts the recent bombings in a different light," I began my attempt to tie these two acts together into a bigger picture. I need not have.

Andriano broke in, "You bet it does! Why, it looks like they have a grand plan to assail us from both sides! Vito and Bonito attack us from the east, while the Greenway comes down from the north and then the west! Worse, what if the eastern armies of the Greenway push down through the Northern Steppes? Why, that would seem very likely to me, then they could sweep into Zargarb from the east while Bonito pushed into Pieta from the west! We will likely be attacked from four sides at once! This is indeed the worst news in centuries!" He was highly animated, and I realized that I shouldn't have worried so much. He sized up the situation just as Louis and Gerardo had.

I was about to sit down and allow Gerardo to run the meeting from this point, but Adelina Barcella asked me an astute question, one that I had to answer. "Excuse me, I know that we are about to launch into what our actions will be. Mrs. Bartiana, we are grateful that you have rescued Queen

Ann and that you are graciously allowing us to meet in your secure home where we do not have to worry about more terrorist bombings. However, may I ask what is your position in these matters? Concerned citizen? If you are to remain in the meeting, what it is it that you bring to the table in our time of need?"

Gerardo and Louis looked at me, wondering how I would answer her. Gerardo was prepared to proclaim me as his top advisor, if need be. "In my position, secrecy is beyond critical. I will tell you, if I have your sworn word not to repeat what I tell you beyond those in this room."

A secret! Now I had them. Adelina did a double take, and stared at me most curiously. Both swore that they would not reveal a word. "I am not a ruler of a country. However, I bring two things to the table. First, I am the top leader of the Forze Segrete." I paused to let that sink in. I knew that there were six of our members looking after these two rulers in Barcella. A smile of recognition pierced her lips and she winked and nodded. Andriano merely smiled.

"Second, I am the leader of another worldwide organization that may find a role to play, the Banca del Dio."

"What? You? The entire banking system of Tarra? The whole network of banks?" exclaimed Andriano in total disbelief. Even Louis raised his eyebrows; he had not known this detail. Only Gerardo did, by virtue of being the husband of Cosima.

Gerardo smiled, "Yes, you are looking at the very top of the Banca del Dio. I cannot tell you how critical her information has been to Velona over these many years."

"Well, Gerardo, you sly old fox! No wonder Velona has always been one step ahead of the rest of us! This explains so much! So that is how you were on to the cardinal in Barcella dealing opium some years back. Dad certainly was dependent upon your guidance in that matter. You fox!" Gerardo looked pleased.

I added, "As you begin your discussions, let me be forthright with you. You have the full support and backing of the Banca del Dio. We will help you finance your defenses." I chuckled and added, "I'll be using some of our own enemies' gold to pay for your needs."

All six roared with laughter as they grasped my full intent. I added, "It is my intent that when this war, assuming it comes to that, is over, the Church of Jehosanity will be bankrupt!" All six broke into spontaneous applause. "Gentlemen, simply give your bills for war expenses to your local Banca, and they will forward it up the lines to me. I will pay them from the Church's funds."

Now came the hard part, how to defend and when to expect the attack. Would they attack soon before any real preparations could be made? Gerardo pointed out that Ann had said that there would be a Council of Kings on September 1. "I don't think that they will try anything until after

130

that meeting. My educated guess is that at this council, they will announce their plans and timetable in an attempt to convert the remaining neutral kings to back them."

Louis added, "Given that the fall harvest will just about be beginning shortly after that, I doubt that they will launch their attacks during the fall. I don't think that they want also to fight the winter's ice and snow. Winter comes early in the mountains of d'Grange and in the Steppes. Their army would be quickly bogged down. No, I am looking for a spring offensive and probably as you have said on four fronts simultaneously — a coordinated series of attacks."

"So, we either have a month to prepare or we have eight months," Andriano asked and stated. "If they attack in a month, Louis, how are you fixed to withstand them?"

"Already, I have been making plans, but you are right. If they attack in September, I will be very hard pressed. Fortress d'Grange is a small country with only two hundred thousand people. Given eight months, I hope to be able to field an army of perhaps forty thousand. Right now, I have been calling up the reserves and bringing back to active duty those who have retired. My forces number maybe five thousand at most. Five thousand cannot hope but to delay the combined Greenway armies. Delay yes, they must pass through our mountain valleys, but delay is the best I can hope for today. In eight months, I can promise you a longer delay. Without a very significant number of soldiers from some other country, I can only delay the inevitable passage of their army through d'Grange."

Andriano wiped his brow. "I cannot see how Barcella can help you, Louis. If Vito strikes against us, we too are going to need all our soldiers to defend our two hundred mile long border with Vito, ignoring the possibility that they might come at us from the Paese di Dio. Even in eight months, Barcella will be hard pressed to stop an army from Vito and possibly Bonito. I'm sorry, Louis."

"I understand. I already assumed that you would need every man to defend Barcella. While I have only to defend perhaps fifty miles, you have hundreds of open miles. Yours will be the more difficult defense," Louis acknowledged, and Andriano sighed in relief.

Gerardo then spoke up, "Look, if Velona sits back and attempts to solely defend itself, we will ultimately face two armies, one coming at us from the north and the other from the east. It is not in our best interests to fight such a two-pronged battle. While Velona has the largest population, fighting in that manner would spread our forces exceedingly thin. No, Velona's best defense will be to move many of our soldiers to d'Grange and Barcella. If our combined armies can hold the lines there, all three of our countries might have a chance of surviving this war."

Both Louis and Andriano looked incredibly relieved to hear this! Indeed, that Velona would be coming directly to their aid and in force would make all the difference. Gerardo then added, "I believe that we ought to immediately inform the Czar in the Northern Steppes, along with Pieta, Solamina, and Zargarb as well. We need to acquire as many allies in this defense as possible."

"Will the Czar really help us?" asked Andriano. He doubted that very much.

Louis answered that one, "You bet he will. He owes me big time. Leave the Czar to me. I'll have him onboard soon."

"Of course, Zargarb will be with us, we only have to ask," Gerardo continued. "I believe that the same will go for Pieta and Solamina, though I have not had any contact with them."

Louis asked, "Okay, beyond these, who else may be joining them in attacking us? Will Megalos again send its Centurions north? Will Demokritos join in the battle against us?"

"If Demokritos joins, we are doomed!" Andriano exclaimed. "That country has ten times the number of people in all the Sea Princesses combined!"

I ventured a guess, "If Megalos sends Centurions north up the Southlands into the Arad, I believe that I can get them stopped by our new allies, the immigrants from Tashien who have settled there on the border between the Arad and the Southlands. Of necessity, marching Centurions would have to pass by them. If so, I will do my best to gain the assistance of those folks to stop or delay the Centurions."

"Well, that is a relief. Still, the might of Demokritos could be brought to bear nearly anywhere," Andriano worried. Indeed, he ought to have been. If they joined in, we would have little hope unless somehow I could get the armies of Tashien involved on our side, making this truly a worldwide war.

Gerardo scratched his head, deep in thought. At last, he spoke up, "You know, I've been thinking. We all are going to have to begin a massive buildup of soldiers. How are we going to get them? While we could order all able bodied men into our forces, that removes their power of choice, and as such, they make poorer soldiers. True, once we go public with this threat, we will have a surge of patriots who want to fight to defend their countries, but those initial volunteers will hardly be enough."

"True, what did you have in mind?" Louis asked.

"I am a student of history," Gerardo explained. "Ages ago, we faced a similar crisis. At that time, they called it the First Crusade for Religious Freedom on Tarra. That brought a huge number of volunteers onboard. Admittedly, many died in those battles. Yet, why don't we do the same thing now? Let's call this the Second Crusade for Religious Freedom. After all, it is the Church of Jehosanity, which is determined to wipe out all other religions on Tarra."

"Perfect!" Louis exclaimed.

"Brilliant, Gerardo!" put in Andriano.

I relaxed, any doubts and concerns that I had, about these men not grasping the situation or not coming to terms with what really had to be done if we were to survive this, vanished. They all were intelligent and wise. Now that they were diving into the details, my mind began to wonder what might be done for the two Queens and for King John Penton. If Calgary could be convinced to join us and not the Mont Blanc force, then perhaps a counter attack could be launched through Calgary into Mont Blanc and from Southway north to Brownsville. The more that I stared at the map, the more that I saw Calgary as being pivotal, the key.

I decided that we ought to attempt to convince King Bill Claghorn to either join us or at least remain neutral. "Excuse me. I have another idea to toss onto the table." They looked up from their sketches, having forgotten that I was there. I explained my thoughts about Calgary and they agreed with me.

"Brilliant as usual, Bethany. We ought to send a negotiator to Calgary at once, before their supposed council," Gerardo replied. "Leave that to me." I did so, but left to go chat with Ann. I found Luigi and Ann sitting in the living room, trading jokes of all things! Ann was actually laughing; what a change in her outlook, I thought.

"Excuse me, Ann. We are thinking of sending someone to Calgary to see if we can convince King Bill Claghorn to join us or at least remain neutral. What can you tell me about him? How set is he on remaining neutral in this?"

"He is actually leaning towards supporting you, but his wife, Queen Winnie — she's a Mir, you know. She is actively pushing her husband to join the fight against you. She is a cold, contriving woman, from what I've seen of her. I don't think that you have much chance of getting King Bill to go against her completely. Maybe you might be able to convince him to remain neutral, but that's just my opinion, Bethany."

"Thanks. Ann, this information that you brought us is saving all our countries." She grinned. I left them to find my records of the Forze Segrete. Luisa, my mother this lifetime, kept them up to date for me, and she took me to where she had them stored in her desk.

"Remember dear, any given group only has a single contact person above them. So from your view down, you are only going to see a few key members in the different countries. What are we after?" she asked.

I looked at the names for those in the Greenway. "What do these lines through the names mean?" I asked.

"Oh, those are the ones that I have confirmed have died. Yes, we have lost contact temporarily with four of the kingdoms. I've sent word to some of the others to attempt to find and make contact with those who remain. That is the real problem with this organization. I don't think that Linda considered this when she set it up way back when," Luisa explained. Naturally, we had lost our contacts in Brownsville, Karka, and Mont Blanc, just the ones that I wanted to contact. Still I had one in Calgary.

"Mom, get word to him that I would like a secret meeting with him as soon as possible. I can go to Calgary if need be." Luisa didn't like the sound of that, but agreed to do so.

The six rulers continued to meet all afternoon and decided to continue tomorrow as well. Now that the planning was underway, the next day while they met, I took Ann and Luigi with me to visit the Banca del Dio here in Velona. Already Sandra had given me the information that I needed, but Luigi would not hear of Ann going out in public without him as her escort. Enrico drove us to the bank. Oh, I was being devious, but I wanted King Victor to pay for what he'd done to Ann. Since she was still his wife for a few more hours, she had the right to transfer some of their funds.

That is precisely what we did. Acting as her guardian now, we transferred five hundred thousand gold from their account in Mont Blanc to a new account for her in Velona. This new account was in her maiden name only, and as their monarch, their queen, the bank naturally allowed her to drain nearly every gold from their joint account. We left him ten gold.

On the way to our next stop, Luigi rolled with continuous laughter. "Way to go, My Lady! Ten gold! Magnificent!" Even Ann was pleased, though I knew that she knew that she now at least had the funds to support herself in her new life, which was going to be difficult at best. Neither knew what I had planned next.

We stopped at the Church of Jehosanity! "What are you doing?" Luigi fairly screamed. Even Ann looked pale.

"Trust me," I grinned. We entered the grandiose cathedral, the largest in Velona, dwarfing our own pride and joy, the Holy Rose Church. "We need to see Cardinal Rems, please," I said to the priest who met us as we entered.

"Who should I say is calling?" he asked politely, noticing Ann's missing arms.

"Mrs. Bartiana and Queen Ann Hammersmith." He bowed and we waited briefly.

Soon the overweight aging cardinal in his gold embroidered scarlet robes waddled along the red carpet towards us, his hands opening wide in a welcome. "Welcome, Queen Ann, welcome." He seemed surprised to see that she was armless, however. He and I had never met. We shook formally and I introduced Luigi as her assistant. He led us to a side office and bade us sit. Luigi carefully assisted Queen Ann.

"I must admit, Queen Ann, I did not know that you were one of our Holy Women of the Eighth Degree. I am honored to be in your presence. How may I be of service?"

I spoke for her. "Your Holiness. What would you say if a man married a wife under false pretenses and then, against her will, had her kidnaped and had her arms cut off and intended to send her to some other country to life in utter disgrace? What is the Church's position on such atrocities?"

"Oh dear me! That would be a Holy Sin of magnitude! Indeed, it would. Marriage is a Holy Union, not to be so mistreated! The Church's position would be to grant an annulment. We do not believe in the vulgar divorce that so many heathens do. Once joined in Holy Matrimony under Lord Jehosa's eyes, the two are bound, for better or for worse, until death do them part. Yet, we also recognize that such marriages can be contrived, as in your example. In that case, the man married under false pretenses, and thus the marriage is a falsehood. The marriage should be annulled as if it had never taken place, which in Lord Jehosa's eyes, it had not. Why do you ask, if I may be so bold?"

"Your Holiness, Queen Ann requests that her marriage be annulled. That is precisely what has happened to her. King Victor Hammersmith married her under false pretenses. On July 2, he had the Confessore del Dio of Mont Blanc kidnap her from her bed. He took her to a distant, remote shack and had a doctor remove her arms without her consent. She was unconscious the entire time. Friends rescued her just as they were about to transport her to some place called Hieras Anubis, wherever that may be. She has been wrongly mistreated by her so called husband and wishes her marriage to be annulled."

"Oh Queen Ann, is this all true? How can this be?" he asked, feigning sympathy which he did not feel.

"Yes, every word of it! I was taken around midnight. They came into my room and put a rag over my face. I fought back but fell unconscious from some smelly thing on the rag. I awoke to find myself like this, crippled for life and in total disgrace, headed for some country that I have never heard of before, never to see my brother again. How am I to live like this? At least, I wish my ill-fated marriage annulled."

"My dear Queen Ann, yes. I will get the papers drawn up immediately." He rose and left us for a moment. When he returned, he continued, "I will have them for you shortly. In the meantime, have you given any thought to joining our glorious Church of Jehosanity here in Velona? It would be my great honor to award you the highest status we can, that of a Holy Woman of the Eighth Degree. We have a goodly number of women like you. They are given the highest honor and respect by our church members. Indeed, you will be allowed to always sit in the very front row during services." He rattled on about how great this would be for her.

Feeling jovial since the episode at the bank, Ann replied, "I mean no offense, Your Holiness. But do you have any idea at all how horrible it is to be like this? I cannot even itch my nose! I have to have someone helping me with everything. It is so embarrassing to have to go to the bathroom. You have no idea how horrible this is!" His face flushed slightly; I knew that he actually didn't. Just then and aide entered with the formal papers. He quickly signed them, avoiding facing her about her comments.

He handed them to me and said, "There, this is the very least that we can do for you, Ann. But I do wish you would give this some serious thought. A Holy Woman of the Eighth Degree is a very high honor. All Velona will give you the respect that you deserve."

Not wanting to affront him, Ann agreed to do so, which pleased him and we left. Once in our carriage, Ann let loose. "I am free of Victor finally! I feel like a lead weight has lifted off my chest." Indeed, it had.

Chapter 12 Now What?

August 2, Renzo and crew arrived off South Port, now renamed Hieras Anubis, for reasons unknown to us. It was the heat of the summer, unbearably hot below deck. For the last week, they all spent as much time on deck as possible. At last, they saw their objective on the horizon.

As they slowly glided into the small docks of the town, Renzo began observing what details he could using a spyglass. Actually, they all were using spyglasses to gather as much intelligence as they could on this first encounter. Renzo had been here before, when as Dita, we had taken the Utu Princesses back to their homeland further inland past the coastal range. Here on a narrow fifty-mile wide strip of good cropland was the town. Just beyond that were the foothills of the coastal mountains, which ultimately rose to at least eight thousand feet, all but impassable except for a few valleys which led upwards and onto the vast savannah of the Southlands.

Renzo began carefully noting what had changed since our visit. Gone were the rickety shanties and people. They'd been bought out and moved on elsewhere, counting theirs as an amazing stroke of good luck. On the contrary, neat new homes dotted the gently rolling lands. Crop fields dotted the outskirts of the town. Somehow, the town had undergone a total transformation, physically for the better, he thought. Still, somewhere in there was Mora who had been sending out secret messages for help embedded in the rugs that she made.

They all knew that this was a closed city. That is, no outsider was allowed beyond the docks, under penalty of death — an extremely unusual declaration. Renzo concentrated his observations on the docks now. Yes, he spied the usual dockworkers, nothing unusual there, save that there were so few of them. That was understandable; only one other ship was currently docked, and the port was small; only another two caravels could dock now.

Then, Renzo began spotting soldiers, a garrison force of men with guns strapped to their waists. They were patrolling just beyond the docks. To their right, he spotted their garrison house. Ania called his attention to the far right and left. Now he too saw them. Two cannone were pointed out into the bay, where they could easily blow apart a caravel! "Damn, these people mean business!" he cursed. A gun ship might have a chance at knocking out the two shore batteries before they sunk it, perhaps anyway. Theirs was not a gun ship, Renzo mused.

Ania spoke softly, "This place is locked up tighter than a drum. One gets the impression that it is a prison, not a town. Be very careful what you do and say, Renzo. Stick to your plan."

An hour later, the Portly Prince finally slid into the dock and its crew caught the mooring lines, securing the ship to the wooden pylons. Six soldiers with long-guns had some time ago come marching to this berth and stood waiting them. Some welcoming committee, Renzo thought.

"Ahoy, Portly Prince. This is a closed port. State your purpose in docking," one of the soldiers barked loudly.

"Ahoy there. Fresh water. We are low on water," the captain called out truthfully.

"How many barrels?" the soldier replied.

"Three."

"Fifteen gold plus your three barrels or fifty and no barrels," the man replied.

"Three barrels it is. Bosun, raise the three empties for these men. Sir," he said addressing the soldier, "we have a trader that wishes to make contact with someone in charge to arrange trading deals."

"Send him ashore. We'll take him to see the Governor," came the reply.

Renzo, wearing his finest twin tails suit, carefully stepped off the ship. At once, three men surrounded him. One said, "This way. Closed port. You try anything and you will be shot, no questions asked."

"Is this any way to treat a merchant looking to open up new trading partners? Honestly, I have half a mind to forget this place," Renzo acted as if he was terribly affronted by their actions.

"Well, if you want to leave, let's return now," the soldier replied, halting the group.

"Okay, okay, I'm here. I might as well see this governor of yours while they are loading the fresh water." Renzo resisted the temptation to twist their necks.

Talk about strange. Renzo entered the very same pub where we met the man who took us to the Utu! Only now, the place had been redone and was more like a rich man's palace or estate! Everything inside was top quality from the furniture to the drapes. A pudgy but well-dressed man entered from another room. "Trader here to talk, Governor." The soldier then stepped outside.

"Welcome, I am Governor Ariston Horus. Please, sit down. You are in the import business?" he said, pulling out a very fine cigar, though he didn't offer one to Renzo.

"Yes, import-export out of Velona. First, I rather wanted to meet a rug maker of yours, goes by the name Mora. You see, her rugs are selling for ten times what the other rugs from here are fetching. Ten gold is the usual price they are fetching, but those by Mora, well, they're going for one hundred. In fact, they have been sold out, and he's gone so far as to take pre-orders for her next ones charging them two hundred gold! Incredible. Now, I thought that if I could meet her, I might offer her more than she's currently getting. Then, I could turn a tidy profit."

"Yes, I see. Well, I am afraid that is out of the question. If I let you meet this woman, then my soldiers would have to shoot you. I'm afraid that you would not then make your profit," he replied, rather nastily.

"Well, does someone handle her sales then? Could I talk to them? I am prepared to offer substantially more than what she is now getting?" Renzo countered, resisting the strong temptation to twist this fat man's neck.

"Certainly, I'll send for Damon."

"Excellent. Say, could I interest you in some fine black tea from the Spice Islands? Fine silk from Tashien? Surely, the women of your town would like fine silks? Perhaps even some of those fancy ball gowns from Annelise?" Renzo toyed with him.

"No, we already get goodly supplies of tea. Our women have no need for such fancy things. Sorry."

"Well, how about cotton then?"

"Let me get Damon for you." He rose and called out to one of the soldiers, "Get Damon now." The soldier took off at a trot. Governor Ariston returned to his chair, but then the door opened again. Renzo saw a man wearing scarlet robes standing there and knew there had to be a cardinal here in this place.

"Ah, Cardinal Krios, come in. We have us a trader here who is looking to establish some arrangements with us." He quickly stamped out his cigar, however, and rose as the cardinal entered.

"Excellent. We can always use more trading arrangements. I am Cardinal Krios Panos." He extended his hand.

"Renzo from Velona, Your Holiness. I've been asking the Governor if there were any items that he might desire that I can provide. To his credit, he has none, but how about you, Your Holiness? Might there be something that a worldwide trader such as me might be able to provide for you?"

"Thank you my son, but no, the Church kindly provides for all my earthly needs. Here in Hieras Anubis, our flock only needs the simple basics of life," Cardinal Krios replied.

"Ah, cotton, sewing needles, spinning wheels, perhaps?" Renzo suggested still playing the role of trader.

"Yes, now you have the right point of view," Cardinal Krios suggested. Just then, the door opened and Elder Damon entered, slightly out of breath. Renzo suspected that he had to run to get here. After a brief introduction, the governor asked Renzo to explain about the Mora rugs and the other types of goods that he might be able to offer in trades. Renzo did his best to keep them talking, but it was quite obvious that the cardinal and governor could not be less interested, while Elder Damon actually seemed keenly interested, perhaps a little too much so, Renzo thought.

Just then, a soldier knocked and shouted for the Governor. "Come at once. Another damn fight has just broken out!" The Governor cursed and waddled out the door followed by a concerned cardinal.

To Renzo's complete surprise, Damon became deadly serious. "We've only got a minute. Renzo. How far do you travel around on Tarra?"

"Hey all over. Just heading off to Tashien for a load of their finest silks next. Why?" he played along.

"Good. This is a matter of life and death. Can you deliver a message to Dorota? I will pay you. Here is a thousand gold; hide it fast. Take this sealed letter to Dorota and give it to someone in charge." He slid a sealed envelope into Renzo's hand. Quickly, he stuffed both inside his shirt and pants.

"Absolutely, consider it done," Renzo replied, as the door opened. "I will pay this Mora woman ten times what her current offer is for the exclusive rights to all the rugs that she makes. Do we have a deal then?"

Damon smiled and shook Renzo's hand. "We certainly do." Looking up at the governor and cardinal, he added, "Twenty gold per rug, that's forty per month. Very tidy profit for us. Yes, bring as many plain white cotton bolts as you can when you return and we will deal then." He rose, signifying the meeting was over.

Renzo nodded to the other two and left; the soldiers fell in line and escorted him back to the ship. The crew was in the process of hoisting the three heavy water barrels onto their ship and lowering them into the cargo hold, when Renzo stepped back onto the ship. Playing along, the captain called out loudly, "Mr. Renzo, we are ready to set sail as soon as these barrels are stowed. Have you finished your business here?"

"Yes, captain. Finished. Tashien is our next stop. We must pick up those silk bolts there." Renzo replied and ambled slowly into the cabins off the poop deck. Once safely inside his cabin, he took out the pouch and saw a number of gold coins and several smaller value gems. He guessed it was probably a grand. Then, he pulled the envelope out of his shirt and looked at it.

Ania stepped into the cabin. "Well?" she asked, eyeing the envelope and coin pouch.

"Talk about strange," he answered. "Let's wait until we are clear of this port. Best we are seen on deck." The two headed back on deck to watch the departure. A half hour later, the mooring lines were dropped, and slowly the large caravel drifted free and began to gracefully tack out of the bay. "Head south until we are out of sight of land and of the usual coastal shipping lanes," Renzo ordered.

An hour later, only the peaks of the coastal range could be seen and Renzo, Ania, Kallisto, Len, Marco, and Rosina gathered in the hot galley. Renzo quickly explained what had happened. "That was really weird. The instant that the soldier came to announce that a fight had broken out, the governor and cardinal left in a big hurry. The demeanor of this Elder Damon changed drastically." He described the brief conversation and showed them the money pouch and the sealed letter.

Ania said, "It's addressed to the High Council of Elders, Dorota. This man desperately wanted to get this message sent off in secret. Something is very rotten here. The question is: do we merely act as messengers and go deliver the message or do we open it, read it, and then decide what to do?"

"Open it!" they all said in unison! Ania chuckled. "Okay, then on the off chance that this is merely some kind of religious report, let me open it properly so that we can redo it if need be. I'll need a steaming teapot, please."

A half hour later, the steam softened the glue binding the sides of the envelope and she was able to open it leaving the seal in place. This way, she could merely apply more glue and no one would be the wiser. The candle wax seal would remain intact.

It was written in the Dorota language. Only Ania and Renzo could read it, though Ania was better at it and read aloud for all.

To High Council, Dorota

January 12, 780

Elders Damon Doros and Esais Cadmus

Help! We have been horribly deceived by the Church of Jehosanity. Some twenty-five years ago, Pope Christos came to us, along with the now traitor Elder Ariston Horus, with a proposition. He wanted to found a perfect society based on the principles we used on Dorota. He offered us full financial support and bought us a town called South Port on the southern edge of the Southlands. Here we took all of our people who yet remained on Megalos and later from Demokritos and established a town similar to what we had on Dorota. A perfect town it was, at first. Hieras Anubis.

He sent Cardinal Krios Panos along to supervise us. The goal was for us to re-establish a Dorota-like perfect society, all funded by the Pope. For the first decade, all went well. We re-built the rundown homes, planted crops, began the education of our children, and in all ways, returned to those ways that we were all used to on Dorota. Our women were particularly happy with the arrangement. After a few years of constant financial support, we have become independent, making a solid living for us all.

Then, something happened, though we only know pieces of it. Beginning around the late 760's, caravels began arriving with cargos of new immigrants or so we were told. These were women and girls whose arms had been amputated. Their boys were not touched. Even a handful of men arrived without their arms. These so-called immigrants came from all over the world: Vito, the Greenway, Megalos, Demokritos, Bonito, and West Reach, to name the major contributors.

Most of the time these new arrivals did not speak our language or that of Megalos and had an awful time adapting to our ways. Our women were told to take in these strangers and to teach them the ways of our women. Of course, we did so. Yet, soon we began to hear the stories of these people, once they had learned our language sufficiently to tell us.

They usually had committed some offense against the Church of Jehosanity or those who ruled said countries. They said that they were abducted in the middle of the night, and their husbands tortured into confessing to the most alarming crimes, crimes with these people claim were untrue. They were forced and tortured in the most barbaric ways into signing false confessions of their guilt.

Frequently, their husbands were killed thereafter. Sometimes, their husbands had their arms amputated, as did all the women and their female children. Other times, the husbands survived whole. The sheer hated and anger these new arrivals hold for the Church is literally overwhelming.

Within the past few years, the number of these new so-called immigrants has increased enormously. So much so, that we have had to build three more towns nearby just to house them. Currently, we number twenty thousand six hundred fifty-three. At least twenty or more come each month now quite regularly.

Elder Ariston protested this to the Cardinal. When he returned from that meeting, he was a changed man. He was appointed governor and is now in league with the Cardinal. Our towns are called a closed port. Any outsider who enters is shot dead. Five men have been killed attempting to walk past the docks! We are virtual prisoners in our own homes, forced to work to produce products, which the Cardinal and Governor then sell, keeping three-quarters of the profits for themselves.

Over a hundred soldiers now guard our towns, with orders to shoot to kill any outsider who may wander in or any of us who may try to leave! We saw one man trying to lead his wife and son out. All three were shot to death.

Please help us. We are virtual prisoners in some diabolical prison camp. Each month, this evil Church is mutilating more innocent women and children and dumping them here in our town. Please help us. Esais and I are begging you.

Elder Damon Doros

The creaking of the timbers was the only sound anyone heard when Ania stopped reading the letter. She added, "Damn, it had taken them three-fourths of a year to get this letter even posted!"

"Wow, this is really bad, isn't it?" Rosina said more than a little shocked.

Renzo sighed deeply. "It is about what Bethany and I rather feared, I'm afraid, perhaps a little worse."

"So, pop, what are we going to do about it? Rescue them?" our son Marco asked eagerly, completely ignoring the fact that they had two cannonae ready to sink our caravel, to say nothing of at least a hundred soldiers with long-guns guarding the place against us. He also completely ignored the fact that even if they rescued them, they would need two hundred caravels to ferry them all to safety somewhere else.

"We can't go in by boat; they'll sink the Portly Prince," Renzo began thinking aloud.

Len added, "I scouted out their other port town, just east of there, maybe two or three miles. There is a cannonae there too. Their town to the west has no port. Perhaps we could begin there."

"The problem is that this spot is right in the middle of the big shipping lanes," Kallisto added her observations to the mix. We cannot remain stationary for any length of time or passing ships will get curious. Besides, some may be armed and bringing more victims here. Even if we could close this place down, what about all those women who are in transport? What will they do if they arrive and the place is deserted? Their captors would probably just kill them. Besides, we need two hundred caravels at the very least to move all these people to safety once we eliminate the soldiers."

"Pop, how about bringing in a gun ship and blowing up the cannonae?" Marco asked.

"In all likelihood, many innocent and perhaps helpless people might get hurt son. The guns are not very accurate and care not whom they hit. If we just start destroying houses, we are likely to kill those we are trying to rescue," Renzo explained. Marco realized his idea was foolish.

Len commented, "If they didn't have those damnable long-guns, we probably could take them out. Now they could shoot us from a mile away, before we could hope to get close enough to attack them back."

"If we can somehow take this place quick enough before they can send word to the Pope for help, we could pretend to be running Hieras Anubis and take on any new victims that incoming caravels dump on them. Then, we can work on how to get them evacuated, perhaps a few at a time," Renzo continued thinking aloud.

"You know, that sounds plausible, Renzo," Kallisto jumped in. "Take the place quickly, eliminating the guards and the two leaders. With the help of the two Elders, we pretend all is perfectly normal. Heck, we can even protect ourselves with their cannonae. Say, does anyone know how to operate one of those?" No one did, but Renzo guessed he could figure it out.

After discussing the problem for the rest of the day, they had no better ideas. "Okay, then that will be our overall plan," Renzo concluded as they all gathered around the galley for supper with the crew as usual. "Captain, somehow as yet not determined, we are going to take over Hieras. With the soldiers and two leaders out of the way, we'll use the Elders to help make things look normal. We can even use their cannonae to help protect them. That way, we can then work out the best way to truly help them all as well as take on more victims that the Church brings here. It will not be wise to evacuate Hieras totally until the Church stops sending poor victims here."

"Then, we will be hanging around here a while longer," the captain grinned.

Len commented, "Any attack by us ought to occur when there are no caravels in either port. That way, they cannot get any messages out."

"Good point, Len. Now tonight, I want you all to start thinking about how we can take them all out safely. I don't want to get any of us killed. Bethany will have my hide if I do," Renzo teased them.

That night, he relayed all that he had discovered. I agreed with him on the overall plan and that he should hold onto that letter for now. No use getting Dorota involved just yet.

Over breakfast, most looked glum, except Len. "Well, Renzo, as your field commander, I say that we need more accurate ground information. How many troops are located where? What are their routines? There are four towns. How distributed are these soldiers?"

"True, very true, Len. Reconnoiter?" Renzo asked.

Len nodded. "Yes, probably the least defended area will be that town on the west side of Hieras; there are only a few fishing boats there. No large ships can dock or even get close. If I were in command, I'd have fewer stationed there."

The captain showed us his sailing map of the area. Only a sliver about twenty miles deep beginning at the shoreline had any detail drawn on it. The interior was entirely blank space. "With a dingy, I could put you ashore somewhere around here, several miles from that western village. From there, you'd be on your own. When you need to be picked up, we can arrange lantern signals or something."

"We'd better pack along plenty of food and water," Len added. "No telling how long we will be, and there is obviously no way to resupply. According to the map, the nearest town is something like fifty miles either way."

For the next few hours, they began packing what they thought they might need. Plan for a week, Len suggested and they did. Meanwhile, the captain headed up north back into the shipping lanes and carefully navigated as close to the shore as he dared. Here west of the little fishing village, the shore was boulder filled and its waters quite choppy. To get the six ashore, the crew had to make two trips — it was that treacherous. More than once, the little dingy nearly capsized. At last, Renzo, Marco, Rosina, Kallisto, Len, and Ania were safely deposited onto the shore. They slipped into the trees and watched the dingy return and the caravel head off to the south once more.

"Gee, pop, it kind of feels awfully funny seeing our ship going off like that," Marco whispered.

"That's called scary, son," Renzo teased him. Rosina agreed with her father-in-law. It was scary and spooky too, but she was determined to help these poor people too. All six carried a long-gun, ammunition, and a pack stuffed with food and a little water. Len hoped that they could find springs; water was just too heavy to carry in any quantity without a horse.

"Okay, Len, you lead. I'd like to get to an observation point above and north of this first small village. We don't want to be seen by those fishing boats either," Renzo requested. Len grinned, he already figured that.

For the next four hours, the six scrambled over the terrain, sometimes dealing with a boulder field, others fighting dense tropical underbrush, rarely a smooth walk through grasslands. Here beyond the village the coastal land was not too conducive to habitation. Near dusk, Len called a halt, as he crested a rocky ridge and quickly ducked down. The others quickly crept up to see for themselves. This was a perfect spot to observe the village located in a fertile basin just below this ridge. Renzo estimated that they could farm for roughly a mile in all directions from the village here near the rugged coast. A dozen fishing boats were pulled up onto the shore for the night. Already half of the acreage was planted in crops. Some banana trees grew around the edge of the basin.

They backed up and made a camp, hurrying to fix something cold to eat before dark. Renzo would not risk any light, for that was far too dangerous. By the time they finished eating, the village also went dark; its inhabitants turned in at sunset, avoiding the need for lots of lamp oil, he concluded. The six then curled up in a blanket and tried to get some sleep on the rocky ground, mostly unsuccessfully, that is.

The next morning they began to watch the village closely. Rosina appointed herself their record keeper, jotting down the observations of the others. The objective was to learn as much about the placement and activities of the soldiers as possible, before moving to another location closer to Hieras itself.

Rosina cried softly to herself as she watched the armless women and children down below valiantly trying to do the normal actions of life, while several men worked the fields, some set sail to go fishing, and a few constructing more buildings. After a day's observation, they counted six soldiers who wandered about, but did little. Occasionally, they did help a woman in need. No other soldiers came or left during the day. Len decided to move on the next day.

Though the Hieras Anubis basin was three miles further east, its fertile basin stretched inland for some twenty miles. This forced the group into a major detour. Len insisted that they scout the well-worn road that connected the two towns. Of necessity then, they had to follow the wide rim of the basin up to the trail that Renzo knew led to the coastal mountain pass and on out onto the high savannah lands beyond.

Now their spying became far more difficult. Six soldiers guarded the northern road that led down into the Hieras basin. Once during the day, another six came to replace them. The next day, Len led the party around to the east of the road some ten miles. From this eastern side, using their spyglasses they got a good view of the whole basin. They spent two days studying the situation. They estimated that some fifty plus soldiers guarded this main town, some manning the cannonae.

Of the fifty, ten were assigned to watch over a fourth village being constructed two miles up the road toward the mountains. That left something like forty men in Hieras proper. After watching from here for two days, Len led them on down the coast to the second, smaller port. Again, situated in a fertile basin, though only a quarter the size of that of Hieras, the small bay was ideal for a single caravel. Here they observed another eighteen soldiers on duty.

Satisfied with their observations, Len moved them back into the rugged foothills, where they could at last light a campfire, near a bubbling stream. Now they began to work out their plan of attack. Sitting around their campfire and quite full for a change, Len noted, "Well, one thing is for sure, we cannot shoot our guns. One gunshot will bring them all a'runnen! In fact, whatever we do, we cannot let them fire off a shot either. Same reason."

Kallisto suggested, "If Ania and I can get close enough, we can put them to sleep."

"I figure I will twist a few necks," Renzo added.

"We have one thing in our favor, pop," Marco jumped in, "the soldiers don't move around a lot. Those in Hieras don't walk up to the other places every few hours. If we take some out in one area, their losses may not be noticed for some time."

We had just finished breakfast the next day when we heard a loud bell clang once. Naturally, he headed off to see what was happening. A bit later and in position once more, we spied a caravel slowly coming in to dock at this single dock. All the women and children were nowhere to be seen. Curious. We watched as the dockhands slowly unloaded some large crates. Later afternoon, the caravel slipped away from the docks. Once it was distant, the bell sounded twice. To our amazement, some women and children reappeared from their homes, continuing with their delayed chores. Now they knew why they had not seen the women. When caravel arrivals were announced, they were ushered indoors.

On August 12, Renzo contacted me to tell me they were about to make their take-over move. *Want me to lend a hand?* I sent. I hated not being a part of this.

Watch over us and help if we need it. I want to use total stealth if possible, he sent back. After asking Luisa to watch over my body, I appeared above the six and surveyed the small eastern port, three miles further east from Hieras Anubis.

Six of the eighteen men were milling around the cannonae, playing cards. The installation was at the eastern edge of the basin. Len said that he could sneak up on them and take them out. Renzo sent Marco along with him. Four were scattered about the town. Kallisto and Ania would take them out, with Rosina going with them. That left eight who were close to the docks patrolling the area. Those would be Renzo's. A half hour, I reported that Len and Marco were in place.

Ania and Kallisto began their Judger chants. Then, they and Rosina began calmly walking down the side of the basin and into the town, heading for the four soldiers. Everyone who looked at them simply saw three soldiers and gave them a wide berth. As they came upon a soldier, Kallisto put him to sleep and Ania did the dirty work of finishing him off.

Len and Marco crawled to within five feet of the six who were playing cards. They quietly stole up closer and slit two throats before they realized what was happening. Two more went down before they could figure out what to do, and the remaining two were forced to draw their swords, but Len and Marco were upon them too quickly. Their battle lasted sixty seconds from start to finish.

Renzo's body remained at the top of the basin, along with the six backpacks. He and I floated over the eight soldiers. One by one, Renzo began twisting their necks — their dead body's dropping to the ground. The eighth one saw several of his comrades in trouble and raised his rifle. I latched onto the gun and pulled it out of his hands. Renzo then twisted the startled man's neck.

A couple of dockhands spotted the fallen soldiers. "What happened to them? They are dead! They are going to think we had something to do with this! Come on; we best hide and tell the others to hide too."

Len and Marco had not been seen by the townsfolk, and they quietly crept back to their starting point. The three women returned as well and finally cancelled their Druwid spells. Already, the many bodies had been discovered, and the general reaction was to rush into their homes. A bit later, not a single person could be seen in this village.

Renzo asked me to follow the road to Hieras and alert them if any soldiers were headed this way. Meanwhile, with packs retrieved, Renzo and Len decided to make a dash across the open valley. It would be quicker to get to Hieras this way; besides, everyone was in hiding, afraid of some nasty retribution from other soldiers. Two hours later, they approached Hieras itself.

Following Renzo's orders, I floated on up the valley to verify the location of the eighteen soldiers. I found them more or less where he said they would be and relayed this to him. This time, Renzo and Len's plan changed. Ania headed to the easternmost cannonae station where six soldiers were playing craps to pass the time. Her job was to sleep them all. Len and Marco would follow and eliminate them, with Kallisto accompanying them using her spells if they were spotted. With all the buildings in the way, they had no trouble dispatching that group.

Now they faced two problems. If they attacked the dozen on the docks, the other cannonae group on the far side would likely see them. It would take far too long to go through the whole town to get to that western cannonae installation. The second problem was where were the remaining thirty-four soldiers? Renzo solved the cannonae installation by floating over the men and rapidly twisting their necks. As he appeared back over the docks, Ania and Kallisto had just walked there and slowly the men slumped to the ground asleep. Renzo then took care of them.

Now they had to find the thirty-four. Ania and Kallisto fanned out walking the streets of the large town, looking for soldiers. While the streets were filled with a few men, mostly women and children were out. Via their spells, none saw anything unusual about them. From above, Renzo guided them toward a group of six soldiers, while he twisted another six who were scattered about the city. Uniformly, when the folks saw a soldier's body drop inexplicably to the ground, they quickly left the area. No one raised any alarm. Soon, twelve were dealt with.

Me? I handled my assigned eighteen rapidly in my own manner. Bodies shot high into the air and came crashing down. Exit soldier. I know that we were being particularly brutal, but these men were holding nearly helpless women and children prisoners and forcing their labors for money. Intolerable in my mind.

How about checking inside the barracks? I sent Renzo. He and I appeared inside and spotted a large number. Several card games were in progress, a few were milling around. While Renzo did his thing, I did mine, only mine went smashing into the ceiling and then down. When no more remained, he double-checked mine just to make sure. Then we counted them, twenty-two. At last, he was satisfied.

We still have six more at the western village. Will you take care of them for me while I deal with the governor and cardinal?

You bet. Back in a bit.

Renzo contacted Marco and Rosina. About a half hour later, the six finally met near the old pub, now the palace of the governor. I returned in time to see Renzo boldly knocking on his door. "Come in," Governor Ariston called out. Renzo smiled, this was too easy. Still, he made sure that his blaster was turned on, just in case the man had a handgun. He and his group walked inside. I alerted him to the fact that two men were running this way, but that they were not soldiers.

The overweight man was smoking a cigar and sipping a beer. "Ah, back so soon? Oh, who are they? Guards! Only one person is allowed on shore at a time."

"Sorry governor, there are no more guards. It seems that we've killed them all," Renzo stated flatly.

"That's impossible! I haven't heard a single gunshot. Guard! Guards! Infernal guards, where the blazes are you?" he yelled, spilling his beer on his overly large belly.

"Governor," Renzo began, but was interrupted.

"You, you are back? What's happening? The soldiers — they are dead. How? What's happening?" a very confused Elder Damon asked, completely bewildered.

"I've answered Mora's request as well as yours, Elder Damon. I am about to arrest Governor Ariston here for high treason."

"No you don't!" the governor yelled. Having turned to talk to Elder Damon, Renzo didn't see the governor draw a gun from beneath the table. He pointed it at Renzo. "Out of here. Get out of here or I will shoot!"

Renzo didn't move, but stared coldly at the treasonous man who had betrayed his own people, armless women who had depended upon him. "Hand over that gun before you get hurt," he said angrily.

"I'm warning you for the last time, get out of here. All of you. Now!" Marco slowly lowered his long-gun. At this distance, he didn't even have to aim to hit the man. Marco watched the trigger finger of the governor. So did I for that matter. Body language announced his intention to fire. Simultaneously, I pulled his arm up, and the gun discharged into the ceiling. Marco squeezed off his round. Bang! Bang! Two shots echoed almost at the same instant. The governor's body jerked back, and he fell off his chair, bleeding profusely from his overly large belly. Renzo twisted his neck, putting him out of his misery.

"Okay, one more to go. Where is the cardinal?" Renzo asked. Poor Elder Damon was speechless. Mechanically, he motioned to the church. "Okay, stay here, back in a jiffy," Renzo ordered. The six and I headed to the church. As we approached it, Cardinal Krios in his gold embroidered scarlet robes came rushing out to find out what the gunshots were about.

"What? How? Who are you?" he asked, his eyes moving from dead soldier to dead soldier lying on the ground near the docks.

"Cardinal Krios you are hereby charged with high treason to the people of Tarra. You have been victimizing those who most desperately needed your help. How do you plead?"

"But, but, but I. . ." he was unable to articulate his confused thoughts.

"Ah, hell with this," Len said and ran his sword through the man's heart. "Enough of his dribble. We have a city to rescue, and time may be precious to us." Renzo smiled, Len was thorough and didn't waste time.

They returned to the shocked Elders who had come outside and just saw the Cardinal slain. "Hello again. I am Renzo Bartiana from Velona. I hope that you will forgive me for opening your letter to the High Council on Dorota. We had come in answer to Mora Porto's plea for help. We suspected something like this was going on down here, and so I took the liberty of opening your letter. Here we are. All one hundred soldiers are dead along with the governor and cardinal. Are there others that need to be handled?"

"Er, no, all hundred? Incredible. A miracle, Esais, this is a Holy Miracle indeed!" Damon finally grasped the fact that it was over.

"We must spread the word to everyone! Thank you, thank you; twenty thousand will thank you and praise you!" Elder Esais exclaimed.

"Yes, spread the word. You are now free of the iron hand of the

Church. We have much to discuss and perhaps little time before another caravel comes. Will one of you send for this Mora Porto and her family, if she still lives, please?" Renzo asked.

Elder Esias raced off yelling at the top of his voice, "We're free! We're free at last! Our saviors have come finally!"

Chapter 13 Dealing with the Church's Mess

Timidly, people began opening their doors, with men peering out first, making sure that it was safe for their families to come outside. Then, they did so, swarming into the streets, straining to get a glimpse of what was going on down by the docks. Marco and Rosina were wholly unprepared for what they saw! Waves upon waves of armless females of all ages took to the streets, watched over by a few men and boys. They were shocked — not so for Renzo, Ania, Kallisto, and Len, who in their last lives, all had to deal with this mess.

Now came the language barrier. They heard the dialects of the Sea Princes, the Greenway, Megalos, and Dorota and a wild mixture of all four. Renzo decided to address the growing crowd. He spoke in the Sea Prince dialect, while Ania repeated it in Dorota, and Kallisto shortly thereafter in the Megalos tongue. He said a sentence and waited for the two echoes to finish.

"We have come from Velona and have killed the soldiers, governor, and cardinal who have held you prisoners here." Renzo paused. "You are now a free people, but we will all need to work together a little longer." After another pause, he added, "We will be meeting with each one of you during the coming days to sort out what you wish to do." A bit later, he said, "We cannot take you all back to say Velona immediately; we do not have two hundred plus caravels." After the two echoed this, he added, "A war may be about to break out in the north, a war against this wicked Church of Jehosanity. We want to keep you safe until it's settled." Then he ended with, "Give us time; continue to do what your two Elders ask, and we will do all that is possible to help each and every one of you."

Those in the front of the crowd began relaying the messages to others in the rear and those still walking towards the docks from the more outlying streets. Elder Esais came wiggling through the throng, leading three behind him. At last, he made his way to us. "I have brought Mora Porto. This is she and her children, Alvito and Tomara."

Renzo looked at the sad faced, but proud, woman of thirty-seven. She, like all the other women, wore a plain white cotton short dress, a simple affair that she could slip on herself. She had long brown hair, rather disheveled. Her daughter was fourteen now and looked very much like her mother. Alvito was sixteen and a fine looking young lad.

"Mora, my daughter found your secret message in your rugs. We came at once and have killed those who have been imprisoning you all. Bless you for having had the courage to send out your message. Twenty thousand here owe their freedom to you." He leaned over and gave her a kiss on her forehead. Tears trickled down her cheers; she barely was able to mumble a thank you.

"Mom, is now the time that I can finally openly pray?" asked Alvito. She nodded. He got down on his knees, clasped his hands together, and prayed aloud for the first time in nine years. "Lord God Tur, it is I, your humble servant, Alvito. I give you my undying thank you for at last answering our many prayers. Bless Mora for her unfailing faith and dedication to finding a way to get all of us help. Bless my sister Tomara for not giving up and for helping all that she can. Finally, Lord Tur, bless these strangers who have taken time out of their lives to come to rescue all of us in our times of greatest need. I thank you, Lord Tur. Amen." He slowly rose.

"Well said, Alvito. Well said indeed!" Renzo complimented the lad and shook his hand.

"My dad taught me many of Tur's prayers. Now I can try to follow in my dad's footsteps as a Priest of Tur," he said proudly.

"I'm sure that you will. Your dad would be very proud of you today, Alvito." He smiled. "Oh, by the way, Mora, how much did you receive for your beautiful rugs?"

"Two gold," she timidly replied.

"Criminal! Do you realize that they are works of art? In Velona, they are selling for a hundred gold each! If you make any more of those fabulous rugs, Mora, I will see that you get at least eighty gold each," Renzo added. She nearly fainted.

Tamara whispered, "Mom! We could live on that much money! Thank you, sir." Renzo smiled and gave her a hug too.

A short while later, the six met in the opulent quarters of the governor along with the two Elders. "Please, do not call us Elders any longer. We are not worthy of such a title. We have led our people into slavery and disgrace," Elder Damon explained.

"You kept your people alive and did everything you could to get help, such as the letter," Ania replied diplomatically. "As I see it, you are most worthy of remaining Elders." Both men held their heads bent low, however.

"Now then, we have extremely critical things that we must know," Ania took charge. "Are there any other soldiers around? How often do you get ships from Megalos? We cannot get you all out of here; we only have a single caravel. Besides, a war is about to break out across the Sea Princes. We are fighting against this unholy Church of Jehosanity. So it would seem that your people are going to have to stay here for some months. How are your supplies holding out? Do you have enough food? What are the medical needs here? Any doctors? We can get in some supplies, but we need information. How many able bodied men are there here?"

"Once a month a caravel comes from the Pope. The governor and cardinal send back reports and receive new orders. It is due here again around September 1," Elder Esais explained. Slowly the picture began to emerge. This caravel only stayed long enough to deliver the dispatches and take on two barrels of fresh water. Ania and Kallisto decided that they would fabricate the reports to the Pope and use their illusion skills to impersonate the governor and cardinal to these men from Megalos.

At random intervals, other caravels would arrive with new victims, usually around ten per ship, though there was no predictable pattern to their arrivals. They would stay long enough to unload the victims and take on water. However, the town had three caravels of its own, handling trading for the towns, making runs between Megalos, the Southlands, and the Sea Princes. Elder Damon was in charge of their scheduling. They also had a few random ships come by, mostly to pick up water. Here across the Southlands, Hieras Anubis was widely known to be a closed port, and caravels abided by that.

Young teens were given the job of watching for incoming caravels. Once sighted, they rang the bell once. The soldiers would take up their defensive positions, while all the women and girls had to move at once indoors. Renzo then asked for volunteers to wear the soldier's uniforms and pretend to be soldiers when caravels came. He had no shortage of volunteers for this task. The men were all heavily into protecting their wives and children, who were so utterly dependent upon them now. For practical reasons, we had our Portly Prince dock at the lone dock of Anu East. That way, no other ships could dock there, forcing them to dock at Hieras only. This way, we could concentrate our forces there.

They discovered that there were only two doctors here and thus, Renzo, Ania, Kallisto, and Len took on more duties as medical helpers, with Marco and Rosina helping. In each of the towns, one building was the medical center, usually visited only when needed by the two overworked doctors. Both were greatly relieved to have four more that could help with lesser emergencies. Their most serious cases were usually the new arrivals. More than one woman died from complications following their surgery and long transport on the caravels to Hieras.

With the critical aspects sorted out, Ania began to take stock of the people here. As of their arrival, there were now twenty thousand six hundred fifty-three people in the four towns. Of these, sixteen hundred were infants; over six hundred babies had been born here. Counting all able-bodied men above the age of fifteen, there were only around five thousand of them. Ninety-five men also had no arms, while the rest were boys. There were nearly thirteen thousand five hundred armless women and girls.

Esais explained that originally, there were about seven thousand who founded Hieras. In those days, everything went according to plan, and they very nearly had recreated their perfect society. However, he pointed out that they had steadfastly refused to amputate the arms of any new baby girls born here. Yes, in time, the armless state of their society would have become a thing of the past; that was the Elder's intention as well as the inhabitants.

Their harmony was slowly eroded and eventually destroyed by the caravels bringing in so many more new victims of the Church's great purge of "undesirables." These men and women brought with them language barriers and intense grief, hatred, and anger. Worse, these women had no idea of how to do anything for themselves. Many women and their children arrived without their husbands, who had been murdered. In this society, a husband was essential for their survival, because someone had to have arms and hands.

At first, many of the original Dorota families took these poor victims into their homes. There they cared for them and taught them the alternative ways of caring for themselves and their children. However, this soon put a huge strain on their husbands as well as themselves. Over time, the problem only got worse. At this time, these new arrivals outnumbered the originals by three to one. Now their anger, hatred, and grief dominated life in these towns. Women who knew these alternative ways of living were very hard pressed and spent most of their hours working with the newer women and tending to their desperate needs. Yes, everyone here was under some form of stress of one kind or another.

Yet, all was not total gloom and doom. Two bright spots emerged. First, all children were now going to school every day. As a result, the children and teens were exceptionally literate and bright. The next generation was optimistic for a better future. Second, the younger folks had in time grown into young adults and had been marrying other young teens, starting families of their own.

Once Renzo had a grip on the situation, they set Marco and Rosina the task of bringing every family to meet with them. Renzo, Ania, Kallisto, and Len began drafting a document containing the names of everyone, where they came from, what had happened to them, what their livelihood now was, what they would prefer doing if they had a choice, and most importantly what they wanted to do now that they had been freed.

This latter was the most critical, Ania considered. Why? Because she eventually had to deal with this massive resettling problem. Of course, some just wanted to go back to their homes; only they also realized that this was impossible now; they'd just be captured and tortured once again. Repeatedly, these people explained that they wanted revenge or justice done on their abductors and torturers. However, a great many wanted to just be left alone to have their desired perfect society. Ania discovered that it was not just the original folks from Dorota who wanted this, but now many of the new arrivals also desired this as well. Perhaps, she thought, it was because these new women were more comfortable being with and living with others who were as they were, armless.

The four also noted on a scale of one to ten just how badly each person needed therapy sessions, either to handle their losses or their surgeries. That nearly everyone would benefit from therapy session Ania found appallingly dismal. While the four of them could deliver the needed sessions, twenty thousand patients would be impossible to handle. It took the four of them nearly two months to interview every person in the towns.

The only factor that Renzo found helpful was that the towns were independent with regards to food. Between the men's diligent fishing, growing of crops, and herding of sheep and a few cattle, all families had enough to eat all year round.

Finally, I had them ask around to see if either Queen Kathleen d'Aine Mir or Queen Mary Beth Penton Witherspoon was there. This I had to know. If they were there, then no rescue in the Greenway was needed. If they were not there, perhaps there might still be time to save them. By the fourth week of August, Renzo reported neither woman was here, but that he would let me know if either showed up on arriving caravels.

On August 28, a caravel arrived, bringing another nine victims. Renzo and Len orchestrated the masquerade, pretending that nothing in Hieras had changed. Fortunately, the Elders were supposed to deal with the ship's captain, nurse, and the new immigrants, that is, victims, being off loaded. They were all from the Greenway. One woman came with two young boys and a daughter. Another woman had two daughters, just as helpless as she was. The third woman had to be carried off the ship; she was quite ill. The nurse carried her two year old daughter for her.

All the females looked in terrible shape, long overdue for a bath, their bandages dirty, their hair a complete mess. Following their usual routine, the Elders took them to their hospital building not far from the docks. Meanwhile, dockworkers helped the crew load three fresh water barrels onto the ship. Two hours after docking, the caravel left, none the wiser, as far as Renzo could tell. He then joined the others at the hospital.

Here, volunteer women were giving the new arrivals a hot bath, while the doctors were examining their shoulders. Ania and Kallisto were hovering over the unconscious woman, while Marco and Rosina were bathing her little girl, being very careful around her shoulders. "Don't think she'll make it," Ania whispered to Renzo as he walked up.

"Her little girl is called Carmela Terina," Kallisto added. "I think that we ought to try to rouse her and let her know that we will take good care of Carmela for her. Give her some peace of mind; there's nothing much else we can do — blood poisoning." Renzo nodded and relayed word to Marco and Rosina, who were now drying off the two year old, who was giggling as Rosina tickled her a little.

"Dad, her shoulders are healing nicely. She's going to make it. How's her mom?" From the look on his face, Marco knew the answer; so did Rosina, who began brushing out the girl's clean hair.

With a clean diaper, now wearing a simple dress and a yellow ribbon in her hair, Rosina pronounced Carmela finished. "Now let's go see your mommy, shall we?" Carmela giggled and said "mommy." Holding her, Rosina walked over to where her mother lay. Ania then used smelling salts to revive the woman, who was running a high fever.

"We've brought you your little Carmela. She's had her bath and look how pretty she looks?" Ania said as the young mother woke and saw her child.

"Carmela," she whispered.

"We want you to know that we will take very good care of Carmela for you," Ania explained.

"I'm dying, aren't I?" she whispered. Ania nodded. "Who will look after her? She's so helpless now."

Rosina sighed and said determinedly, "I will, Marco and I will raise Carmela as our own child. We will see that she gets a good education and has everything that she needs. I promise you that we will always look after her."

The woman smiled. Silently, she mouthed, "Thank you," her eyes closed, and she died.

"That is what she was waiting for," Ania said softly, trying to hold back her watering eyes. "She was hanging on to life just to make sure that her daughter would be cared for. Rosina, that was very generous of you."

"Well, Marco and I now have a little girl, don't we?"

"Yes and a pretty one at that. Right Carmela?" Marco replied, backing Rosina all the way. Yes, Renzo was a proud father at that moment, so was I when I heard about it later. Later on, the other women told Marco that she had come from Mont Blanc and that the mother's name was Luisa Terina. I swore that one day I would find out her mother's story and any living relatives for my granddaughter.

On September 2, the caravel from the Pope arrived. Ania and Kallisto used their spells to make the visitors believe that they were seeing the cardinal and governor. It went surprisingly well. The messenger handed them a pair of mail pouches, and the two handed a pair of fake reports to be taken back. That they were supposed to take theirs out of the pouches and put theirs back into the pouches was the only awkward moment, which the two cleverly made the messenger forget had happened. After three nerve-wracking hours, the caravel set sail, and they all breathed a sigh of relief.

The messages said that they were to expect more immigrants until April. After that, the Pope hinted that the immigrations would likely dry up for some time. However, he did ask if they would like to double their population in say a couple years. I suspected this might be a hint about what he intended to do in the theoretically conquered countries.

Chapter 14 Into the Greenway

On August 6, I heard back from the Forze Segrete member in Calgary, Able Farthington. Take a room at Bywaters Inn near the docks. That was the entirety of his message. I took this as a hopeful sign.

"You cannot go alone, Bethany!" Enrico insisted.

"I know, but Enrico, you are needed here. I have to have my best Protector looking out for the Po clan or all is lost."

"I'll go," Arturo said dryly. "Besides, Enrico went last time. Who knows, maybe you will need a Loremaster this trip."

"Hey mom, I'll go," Nico, my youngest son, volunteered. "Pop's taught me everything. Isabella will understand."

"I volunteer Phillipe and myself," Ania's daughter, Enrica, spoke up, seeing an opportunity to get in a little traveling. Phillipe was Elena's son. Both were seventeen, while Nico was only fourteen. Still, I knew that Nico was good with a sword, so was Phillipe for that matter. Enrica didn't take after her mother so much as Len. She was a dead shot with the longbow.

"Okay, okay. We are only going to Calgary. Five should be enough for this simple meeting," I agreed to take them. "We should wear our leathers, no dresses. I am not sure where this inn is located, but it might be in the seedier section of Calgary. We don't want to draw undo attention to ourselves. We leave in the morning."

I already knew that caravels traveled frequently up the coast to Calgary; it was a short haul of three days, if the winds cooperated. While we could have gotten there sooner overland, the border beyond d'Grange was effectively closed now. One had to pass through the southwest corner of Mont Blanc to get to Calgary. Caravel was our best bet. Hence, I'd had Felix West Po place a hold for us on one caravel bound for Calgary to pick up a load of early harvest. Loading would take several days, more than enough for me to make my local inquiries.

"Better cut your nails, mom," Alessa advised. She was right, if I went around with my two-inch talons, folks would get suspicious. The next morning, dressed in traveling leathers with cotton shirts, we headed for our carriage. Each carried a duffle bag with a change of clothes and various weapons, though Enrica carried her longbow across her back. Enrico kindly drove us to the docks.

There we boarded the Hampton Express, based out of Calgary. I paid the captain our fare, ten gold, which covered a round trip. The kids had an enjoyable trip, watching the coast of Velona float by and then the craggy peaks of d'Grange. Soon the large port of Calgary came into view late afternoon on August 9.

Once we docked, I asked for directions to the Bywaters Inn. As I suspected, the inn was very near the docks and offered inexpensive quarters. Wealthier visitors would travel to the better section of town. Since it was only about ten blocks, we chose to walk there. However, we noticed a fair number of mounted soldiers riding the streets, and a number of seedier looking men lurking in the alleyways, most likely waiting for nightfall. We had rather wished that we'd gotten our weapons out of our bags first.

The Bywaters Inn was a large wooden establishment, which had seen a large number of "enlargements" and remodeling over the years. Actually, if the term patchwork could be applied to a building, the Bywaters was it. We entered and choked slightly on all the smoke coming from the men's pipes and cigars. At least twenty were already here, mostly drinking and smoking.

Arturo walked up to the innkeeper and asked, "We need three rooms, please."

A burly man with an apron replied, "Six gold. Yea be out of towners."

"Well, yes, from Velona, actually," Arturo replied, handing him the six coins. As the man counted them, I noticed he was eyeing us. I took a guess and drew a circle in the air such that only he could see it. Cleverly, as he was counting, he duplicated that and added a triangle. I smiled and finished our secret signal.

"Rooms 9, 10, and 11. Meals are extry." Arturo gave him another gold for our supper and breakfast. After heading to our rooms and quickly donning some of our weapons, we headed down to eat dinner. While not the best, it was wholesome food. Then, we returned to our rooms. Now there was nothing to do but wait. I expected he would drop by later at night, once he closed the bar. I was right.

Around midnight, he knocked on my door. Nico let him in, and he sat on a chair while we all sat on my bed. After introducing ourselves, Able was very impressed to meet the "top lady" as he put it. Then, we got down to business.

"First, Able, what's the position of King Claghorn on the proposed war with Velona? I asked.

"Still claims to be neutral, though the queen has been pressuring him something fierce. We've heard reports of violent arguments between the two."

"Is there much chance that he could be convinced to support Velona and King Penton of Southway? Would it do any good to have someone from Velona talk with him about it?" I asked.

"Only if you can eliminate Queen Winnie. Honestly, she's a real cold bitch. No offense ma'am's."

"None taken. I do need you to be frank with us. I know that they are going to hold a Council of Kings in Brownsville on the 1st. Any chance King Claghorn will remain neutral? Any chance we could persuade him to remain neutral?"

"You want my honest opinion? I've heard tons of scuttlebutt, especially from the dandy's at his court. If the seven decide to go to war, Claghorn has almost no chance of remaining neutral. I wouldn't put it past them to invade our kingdom if he remains neutral. They need our port and southern lands for their war and staging areas."

Well, that was what I needed to know. "Another matter. We believe that Queen Mary Beth of Karka and Queen Ann of Mont Blanc are in grave danger. They are supporting us, while their husbands are vehemently against us."

"Aye, that they are. That they are." He repeated himself, nodding his head sadly.

"We've also lost contact with our man in Brownsville, Alan Lee Jones. By any chance. . ." I began. He interrupted me.

With a big grin on his face, he said, "You wait here a minute. Got a surprise for you." He ducked out of the room and reappeared a minute later, leading another man, who had a bandage wrapped around his head.

"Alan Lee Jones, meet our boss lady from Velona," Able said proudly.

"Well met indeed. What a surprise," Alan said shaking my hand and then the others.

Able explained, "They came into his home and shot his wife and kid and him, left 'em for dead. They were, but not Alan. Only man I know who is carrying around a bullet in his head!"

"Yes, the damn Confessore and his men murdered my wife and son. Shot me in the head. I woke up sometime later. I was mostly blind, massive headache, and very dizzy. Somehow I managed to get to my horse and get away before they came back to finish the job. Nowhere in Brownsville was safe for me, so I lit out for Calgary. I don't know how I made it here, but I ended up on Able's doorstep. He fixed me up. Still have these headaches from time to time, but I am getting better."

"Are any of the rest of your Forze Segrete group still alive?" I asked.

"Dunno." I had him give me the names of his contacts, just so that the chain of command would not be broken. Then, I related our worries about the two queens.

"They will probably be safe enough until the Council of Kings. They all have to appear there with their queens for appearance's sake. Kind of an unwritten rule, you see. Once they declare war, which I'm sure they will, then the kings can dispose of the two queens, legally, since they will undoubtedly not back them in going to war," Alan stated factually.

"Will they shoot them? Murder them?" I asked.

"You know, twenty years ago, if you had asked me that, I'd of said you bet, sure thing. Now, I am not so sure at all. It's these darn Confessore squads that are roaming the kingdoms. People just seem to disappear. No bodies are ever found, just weird confessions of treasonous guilt get posted and something about getting a second chance at Holy Redemption or some such drivel," Alan explained.

"Damn, damn, damn," I replied, knowing now just what the Confessore were doing. I quickly explained what Renzo had discovered in Hieras Anubis.

"Do you think that there is any way we can get to the queens and rescue them?" I asked directly.

"Probably not. They have so darn many soldiers out on patrol now it is even hard to travel down the roads. They go from village to village yanking out young men, forcing them into their ever-growing armies. It isn't safe to be on the main roads. I got here by going cross-country."

Able broke in, "I told them that I thought they'd be safe enough until the Council of Kings is done. After that, they're gone'rs."

"He's probably right about that," Alan agreed with him.

"Will the Confessore wait until Queen Mary Beth returns to Karka?" I wondered aloud.

"You know," Alan said thoughtfully, "now that you mention it, I bet they won't! Why waste all that time? Both would be in Brownsville at the castle there. If the Confessore go after Queen Kathleen, why not take two for one? My guess is that they take them both together, right after the council is over and before the kings depart for home. Sure would be more efficient that way. Guess maybe your husband can be alerted to look for them at this Hieras place."

"I wish I knew who to contact in Karka. We've lost our primary contact person. I'd like to at least try to get a message through," I said mostly dreaming.

"Well, there is still Howard Littleton; he's Queen Mary Beth's personal coachman," Alan suggested. Again, we noted this. At last, we had at least one contact there.

"Thanks. You know, I suppose as long as we are here, we ought to try to visit with King John Penton and let him know that we are backing him in his stand. It's only some fifty miles to his border. Once we cross, we should be quite safe," I proposed.

"Now whatever gave me the idea that this would be just a quick trip to Calgary?" Arturo teased me.

"Let's do it, mom," Nico said eagerly.

"Well, if you are going, let me at least lead you there. I know a bunch of back roads, which will bypass most of King Claghorn's soldiers. We have to stay north of the main paved road, because soldiers from Mont Blanc often cross over into Calgary and patrol there. I think they are scouting out staging areas for their armies," Alan explained.

"Are you well enough to ride?" I asked.

"Sure, still get headaches, and sometimes I'm a little dizzy, but I'm mostly okay. We need some horses. Once we get into Southway, we can stay at inns. I'll get us six horses. Be ready in the morning," Alan replied. I think that he was eager to have something to do once more. Perhaps the loss of his family was eating him up while he was just sitting around this inn. "We ought to be in Middleton in four days at the most."

True to his word, Alan had six horses saddled and ready for us around eight the next morning. This time, we were all armed, and our duffle bags were stowed on our horses. He still wore a bandage around his head and I vowed to examine it at the first inn that we would stay in for the night. Travel was trickier than anticipated, and it took us until noon to leave Calgary by heading north. Soldiers were everywhere, and we took many detours until finally the rolling farmlands appeared.

We rode all that day and were forced to camp out that night, far from any village. Without proper gear, we were a bit uncomfortable to say the least. However, by evening of the next day, we crossed into Southway and found a small village inn. After dining, I took Alan aside to my room, while the others listened to the chatting of the locals around the bar.

"I know a bit about healing, Alan. I want to check on how your wound is doing." He allowed me to examine it. A round bullet hole was clearly visible nearly dead center between and above his eyes. The edges of the wound were starting to heal and I saw no signs of blood poisoning, but I thought I could see the bullet itself just beneath the skull bone, barely inside his head. No way was I going to attempt to remove it. There was too much of a chance that it would kill him. I cleaned it up and put a fresh bandage on it. I wondered how long a person could live with a lead bullet stuck inside their head.

On August 14, we arrived at Middleton, the capital city of Southway. The city was swarming with soldiers, however. We headed to the main castle gatehouse where we were stopped. "We would like to see King John Penton. We bring news of his sister Queen Ann," I announced to the gatekeeper.

"Wait here. Take some time to relay your request. These days, only those on official business are allowed onto the castle commons. Nasty business, I say," the man said. He was missing two front teeth and looked rather gruff. We dismounted and moved aside for some soldiers, who came riding up and were allowed inside. While we waited, we all took in the sights of this city. It was large, probably a couple hundred thousand people, maybe more. Everywhere, people were making preparations for a siege, stockpiling straw, hay, and all manner of produce from the start of their late summer harvest. I spotted a large pile of pumpkins and smiled, thinking of pumpkin pie.

An hour later, the gatekeeper returned along with a courtier. "Follow me. I will take you to the king," he said formally. We did as he asked, but watched a dozen soldiers surrounded us. King John took no chances with strangers, and I saw this as a prudent move and was not offended in the least.

King John and Queen Sara met us in their Royal Court Hall. He was tall and well-muscled, with long blonde, curly hair and small moustache. I guessed he was in his thirties. Queen Sara was perhaps two years younger, with domineering raven hair and matching eyes, but with a disarming smile. She had a radiance about her, and I could see why King John had fallen for her. We were escorted to their thrones.

After I did the introductions, he said, "Well met indeed. My father has mentioned you and Renzo or is it Dita often to us. Well met indeed. Yet, I was told that you have news of my sister, Ann? We were told that she posted a document announcing her treasonous sins against the Church of Jehosanity and God, that she had accepted a second chance at living a Holy Life so that her soul could receive Holy Redemption. We believed that she had been slain, rather."

"I am afraid that she is alive, but has been horribly treated by the Church and their Confessore del Dio," I found no easy way to tell him. I told him about how we had gone to rescue her but had arrived too late. He was pleased that we had killed the Confessore and his henchmen. That she was doing as well as could be expected in Velona greatly pleased him, especially since she was living in my home.

"There are not words with which to thank you enough for what you selflessly did for her and our family," he began expressing his heartfelt thanks. I also explained that her marriage had been annulled and that I had cleverly taken all the current gold in King Victor's account and transferred it to her private account. "Then, because of your efforts and genius, my sister will not want for funds. That is perhaps the best that I can hope for her now. I owe you greatly. How can I ever repay you for what you have done for us?"

"Keep on fighting against these other kings who are dead set on starting a war with us," I grinned.

"But I will do that anyway. Please, there must be something that I can do to repay this uncommon kindness on your part."

"Let's work on strategies. If they go to war with us," I began, turning the subject to what was really needed at this time. We talked long, at least an hour. He was particularly pleased to hear that he had no financial worries, for the funds he spent for his defense would ultimately come from his enemies, once this conflict was over. Queen Sara particularly like the idea that we were calling this the Second Crusade for Religious Freedom. I also told him that now that I had met him, I could contact him telepathically from Velona, keeping him and his queen informed. This, both found quite intriguing and fascinating indeed.

He then asked us to dine with them and we did so. Over dinner, I brought up the plight of the other two queens. He agreed with our conclusions that both queens would be safe until the conclusion of the council. After that, all bets were off. His words backed up everything that we had heard or concluded thus far. Indeed, the two queens' lives were in the gravest of danger. But what to do about it?

"King Diget III will have Brownsville and the whole surrounding lands under an incredibly tight lock down before, during, and after the council. There is just no way you could even get close to his castle, let alone inside to meet with the queens," King John explained. "As cold and calloused as this sounds, perhaps their best chances of survival is to rescue them when they are taken to this Hieras place, assuming that is where they are taken."

Somehow, I just couldn't let this go. Queen Ann was trying her best to adapt, but it was a horrible thing to have happen to anyone. I didn't want it to happen to these two queens, if somehow I could prevent it. At last, I got his agreement to allow us to accompany them to the border of Brownsville. There, he said, we could see for ourselves just how impossible it would be to even enter the kingdom, let alone get to the queens. He promised to see what he could do to keep the two queens close to him once the council ended.

"I will insist that they stay with Sara and me, saying we are planning a birthday party for their husbands or something. If I can keep them with me, maybe they will have a chance," King John suggested.

"If we could only somehow have them return here with us," Sara added, "we might be able to keep them safe, unless our castle falls too."

For the next week, we were allowed the run of the city, given official passes to come and go as we pleased. Every evening we dined with our hosts. Meanwhile, I had Arturo lay in a goodly supply of trail food and supplies. Honestly, Brownsville was barely forty miles north and slightly west of Middleton. Surely, we could find some way to get there and keep watch, though what we could actually do then I had no idea or plan.

On August 30, we halted at the border of the two kingdoms. From here, we could see just what King John meant. A mile further on down the road at least a hundred cavalry stood guard; all had long-guns as well as swords. We saw some riding both east and west along the border as well. Here we parted company with the king and his group, and he promised once again to do all that he could to save the two queens. He was not worried about his cousin Queen Carol Penton Blaine, because King James had no intention of ever going to war with anyone.

Sadly, we watched as his party crossed the border and was escorted on up the road towards Brownsville. We headed off the road to regroup and decide our next move. I bit my lip, so close and yet so far. While the others chatted about our situation, I tried to think logically about all this. I was risking so much for two women. Was it worth it? I was desperately needed in Velona, now more than ever.

While I was debating my few choices, we spotted a large band of gypsies and their many colorful wagons rolling down the road. One young lad was perched high beside his father, who was driving. He was playing a guitar and making up a song. His tenor voice carried well to us.

Oh, we're off to play for the kings and queens.

Oh mighty minstrels are we you don't say.
Tis music, dance, and revelry bold
That we do on the morrow's eve.

His ditty was ended abruptly as they approached the soldiers. To our surprise, they were allowed to pass! However, mounted soldiers moved in beside the wagons. I heard the captain explain, "You will have to camp outside the castle proper, though you may bring your instruments inside with you, subject to a thorough search, that is. Security is very tight. You will be playing for ten kings and queens tomorrow night." The rest of his words were lost as the distance became too great, but I did hear the young lad begin his ditty once more before the noise of the passing wagons drowned his faint voice out. I counted two dozen brightly colored wagons roll by and on up the road towards Brownsville.

This gave me an idea. If we could somehow get to the gypsies, perhaps we could join them and get ourselves inside the castle and to the queens. Of course, Arturo asked, "Then what do we do? Fight our way out against untold long-guns?" Well, it was an idea anyway. Yet, if they could get close to the castle, perhaps so could we, with a little luck.

Nico asked, "Mom, why are you so intent on getting into the castle? Look, the Confessore have all been following the same scenario. They abduct their victims and drive them to a distant town. Only then do they call in their Medicos to do their dirty work. We don't have to get inside the castle. We only have to watch for the Confessore and their wagon leaving the castle. We follow them and take them out and rescue the queens."

"Hey, my grandson might have something there, Bethany," Arturo admitted. "From all that we have learned about their operations, he's right. The Confessore will certainly have to move the victims from the castle and take them most likely to some remote location before they do their dirty work. It shouldn't be too big a barrier for us to keep watch for that wagon leaving. It is always in the middle of the night, from all accounts."

"Okay, I like it too, son. Good thinking. How are we going to get to Brownsville in the first place?" I asked.

"Leave that to your Loremaster. There are many routes into any city. Come on; let's ride east a ways and see what we can find," Arturo suggested.

An hour later, we were in a dense patch of timber. For some time, we had not heard any soldiers about and chose this point to cross over into the Kingdom of Brownsville. Now Arturo practiced his trade. Unerringly, he led us along deer paths, slowly moving us towards our objective of the capital city itself. I admired his skills, which until now I had not known that he had! Imagine, ignoring his specialty for nearly fifty years! I felt very foolish this whole day, though I must admit now that I would be even more impressed in the very near future.

We camped for the night in a stand of dense pines, beyond which farmlands lay in the valley, which surrounded Brownsville. Here on the southeast corner, ours was the last patch of trees. For a time, we spied on the far distant town through our spyglasses, but could see very little from this distance, save for the moving cavalry dots.

At dawn, a cavalry patrol came dangerously close to our position, but moved on, not before giving us all a panic awakening. Now we all crept to the edge and looked down upon the valley as the sun climbed. Somewhere in that far distant brown stone castle, which rose above the brown stone outer walls, the Council of Kings was being held. Brownsville itself was a large city, perhaps some two hundred thousand lived here.

"Okay, it looks like the main Centurion built, paved road comes in from the southwest and goes off more to the north of east," Arturo pointed out. "There are smaller roads heading north, west, and south. I count dozens of farmhouses around this valley, at least those close to us. Ah ha, there is our way into the city!" He pointed to a distant farmhouse. I didn't see what he meant, but we mounted up and followed him.

As we drew closer, I spotted the farmer and his wife arguing; he kept pointing to their wagon, which had broken an axle. They had a load of squash in its bed. Arturo rode up and asked, "Hello. Bad day to have your axle break. Can we lend you a hand?"

Gushing as if he was the savior of God, the woman replied, "Yes! Oh thank you. We have to get these squash to the castle before noon! The king's cooks are expecting them. There will be utter hell to pay if we don't get them there, and Bill's stupid wagon decided to break on this morning of all mornings! I told you a thousand times, Bill, get that wagon fixed properly. But no, you said it'll hold together. Now look what you have done! The king will have our heads when he finds out about this." She ranted on while Bill looked very embarrassed about the whole affair.

"Well, have you some sacks or blankets or sheets that we can use to tie up bundles of your squash to our horses? We can walk them there with you," Arturo offered, knowing they would jump at the timely rescue. A half hour later, with bulging bags of squash tied to either side of our saddles, we followed Bill and Linda as they walked into the city, each also carrying a bag of squash. Although there were many soldiers about, we walked right past them up to the gatehouse of the castle. Here Bill and Linda began unloading their produce. A kitchen hand came running with a cart and was forced to make several lengthy trips to the kitchen.

Once we had unloaded our horses and been properly thanked by the two grateful farmers, we then began wandering the streets of Brownsville. Evidently, all those now in the city proper had been checked out, and the soldiers were only stopping others who were entering. For now, we were safely inside. The next step was to scout out the castle entrances. This proved easy; there were only four ways in, four heavily guarded gate houses. Near one, the two dozen gypsy wagons were parked in a circle, but heavily watched by thirty soldiers. We had no chance of meeting them.

At noon, we stopped at an inn to get something to eat and make some plans of our own. Inside, I imagined the fiery meeting between the kings was going on, eventually deciding to wage war with us. Then would come the celebration dinner and entertainment. Sometime after dark, they would all retire for the night. In the middle of the night, the Confessore would strike, hauling the two queens out of the castle through one of these four gate houses, but which one, and where would they be heading? This is what we discussed at length in hushed, whispered voices.

For a time I considered having them watch over my body and go float into the castle and listen in. For a moment, I had the wild idea of going in there and lifting these enemy kings and smashing their bodies into the ceilings or some such. Yes, I could outright kill these men, and no one would be the wiser. Think of the thousands of soldiers who might get killed or maimed and the grieving of untold families. All this I could avoid if I chose just to kill these men right here!

Yes, wouldn't being pro-active be better than always being reactive after the fact? I could stop the war by killing these kings; perhaps I ought to kill the cardinals as well. I recalled the horrors of the First Crusade for Religious Freedom fought over a century ago, when I had my Ket Bethany body. Did I want to have to pick up such horrid pieces yet once again? I could prevent it by doing this simple thing. I almost had myself convinced to do just that.

Then it struck me like a bolt of lightning! God. If I chose to do this thing, I was playing God. I was being all-knowing. These men had not yet actually done anything harmful to us. It had been the Confessore who were guilty thus far. What if cooler heads prevailed at the conference, and they decided it was a bad idea to wage war against us? I would have killed innocent men.

I was floating high above the pub in which our bodies were sitting sipping mead. Right there, I realized that more than likely not one of these kings was ultimately the single source behind this proposed war. I remembered my old training. If two men are fighting each other, look for a hidden, behind the scenes, third person who is actively fomenting the conflict by telling lies to each side about the other side or worse. No, as culpable these men may ultimately become, someone else wanted this war and was going all out to make it happen. That was the person I ought to eliminate at once, only I had no idea who. Good guess would be this Pope Christos, but I had no proof at all, only a suspicion.

Men ultimately have to take responsibility for their own lives and actions. If these kings allowed themselves to be so manipulated into causing such carnage and destruction and pain among their people and ours, they had to take the consequences of their own actions. It is not my responsibility to play god. It was my responsibility to find out the true source of this war and bring them to justice, even if I had to do it after the fact of the war.

People had to learn their lessons, even if it was the hard way.

After all, those who lived in Mont Blanc had allowed this king and church to take over control of their country. True, at this point, the king and church appeared to have total control over the country and the lives of its people, but long ago during their rise to power, the people had a choice and did not act, did not exercise their own responsibility to do the right things. These men did not overnight suddenly have total power over all the people of the country. No, the citizens of these countries failed to take responsibility in the past and now were suffering the consequences of their own failures. Mont Blanc used to be the staunchest ally in the crusade for personal freedoms on Tarra. Now they had fallen so low!

Just then, I saw something that fairly scared me, and I shot back to my body. "Gang, we have got to leave the town *now*! Move!" Startled, all obeyed at once. Grabbing bags, they followed me outside to our horses. Walking them along the street to avoid suspicious activity, I explained, "I just saw that there are thousands upon thousands of soldiers riding into the valley from both directions on the main Centurion road! In an hour, there will be more soldiers per street than people.

As we approached the edge of the city where we had entered, guards were now setting up roadblocks. Arturo handled it well. "Hi, more squash. Sure wish Bill's stupid wagon had not broken down this morning. Now we have to make another trip to bring the rest. Hope we don't miss all the fun."

The guard who had seen us entering earlier in the morning chuckled, "That'll teach Bill to keep his wagon fixed. Go on ahead. Fireworks won't be until nine tonight; gypsies are not scheduled until six, so you probably won't miss them. Sure wish I could get a peek at them; I hear they are something else."

A half hour later, we were well down the dirt lanes that led to the myriad farmsteads here in the Brownsville basin. We mounted up and rode on down to Bill's farm, though over our shoulders we could see ranks upon ranks of soldiers fanning out around the edges of the city. Most ended up in the farm fields near the outskirts of the city. I hoped that they didn't destroy their crops.

Once at the farm, we paused to look back. "That was a close one," Arturo commented. "Let's get into the woods."

From the ridge line woods, we made camp and took up spying positions. While we were five miles from the castle, with the spyglasses we could see a little. "There are only four ways that the Confessore can exit the castle at midnight with its wagon. I saw it briefly just inside the walls. It looks like a black hearse with the same two small Church of Jehosanity flags on its top front corners. Probably sometime after midnight, it will come out of one of those four gate houses. The question is which one."

We divided the task between us. During the night, one of us would focus all our attention on a specific gate or area. Since we could not directly see the northern gatehouse from our southeastern position on the rim of the valley, I'd have to do it myself, so hence the others would stand guard over us. The day passed slowly, though we did get to see thousands of soldiers on parade, albeit from an extreme distance. At nightfall, we were treated to a beautiful fireworks display, though from our extreme distance, they looked very small. Once the distant booming ceased, we began our vigil in earnest. Sometime in the next several hours, a horrible crime was about to be committed, a crime we intended to prevent.

Chapter 15 The Council of Kings

In the huge Great Hall of King Diget III, the critical council opened. Ten kings of Greenway sat at the table, with ten queens sitting to the right of their husbands and ten cardinals sitting to the left of their respective king. On the wall prominently displayed were the portraits of the three King Digets.

King Diget III spoke first, "Welcome one and all. You have all met King Victor's new queen, the lovely Queen Josie Mir." She was a second cousin of King Diget III and barely seventeen, ten years younger than her new husband, King Victor Hammersmith of Mont Blanc. Hers had been a very hasty marriage indeed. Victor had to have a queen at his side for this council. Josie was an excellent choice, since she was an active supporter of Amos Mir, that is, King Diget III.

After the opening formalities were conducted, Cardinal Cecil Mir of Mont Blanc discussed the recent events. "Our allies in Vito have nearly destroyed all the leadership in Velona. Now Velona sits ripe for our taking. Vito only awaits your decision to launch the invasions and they will begin assaulting Barcella. Likewise, Bonito awaits your decision; they are poised and ready to invade Pieta. Of course, neither will act if you do not act." He then spent a half hour elaborating on the damaging results that Vito had inflicted upon Velona, softening it up for the Greenway armies.

They then discussed the status of their ever-growing armies, kingdom by kingdom. All had reached their current targets of fifty thousand men. However, acquiring that many long-guns had still not been achieved. Cardinal Phil Mir reported that the Church was delivering another twenty thousand long-guns and ammunition due here later this fall, just before the winter freeze in Calgary. After mid-November, the only Greenway port capable of handling a caravel would be iced over until March. Another twenty thousand long-guns were scheduled to arrive as soon as the ice broke sufficiently to allow a caravel to dock.

All told, the kings anticipated fielding at least a half million soldiers come spring, though more than half would not yet be armed with these new long-guns. Next, they had a report on the number of assault cannonae. Mont Blanc and Brownsville each had ten, while the others had only a couple each. Again, the Church of Jehosanity promised delivery of another two dozen by March.

The remainder of the morning session was filled with various reports concerning the stockpiling of necessary provisions, wagons, and support staff. Of note, the cardinals promised that their entire Medico Santo groups would be deployed with the armies acting as their field doctors. "Indeed, these are the finest surgeons on Tarra," Cardinal Cecil Mir explained. "All have studied extensively the famous surgical techniques pioneered by the famous Doctor Yi of Tashien. They will be able to save the lives of many of your wounded men." This appealed to the kings.

After a long lunch, the afternoon session began. Now came the critical decisions. King Diget III and King Victor Hammersmith made impassioned speeches in an attempt to sway the three neutral kings and King John over to their side. Then, King John rose.

"Kings, Queens, have you all lost your senses? Have you all become mad with the hunger for power and wealth? This is madness that you are proposing. Throughout history, Velona has always been on our side. Even now, they are working on extending their new train lines up to Calgary that we might get our grain to market faster and thus our money sooner. What more can you ask of a friend?"

"Nay, I say that you are all just peons of the Church of Jehosanity. They say jump and you jump. I say that it is they who want Velona destroyed for their own diabolical purposes and are just using you to accomplish their goals. Once more, Queen Sara and I beg you to think this through. Do not allow yourselves to be used by these wicked men disguised in priestly robes."

Cardinal Cecil Mir countered, "Careful what blaspheme thou speaketh. Many sinners have been known to just disappear."

"Is that a threat?" King John fumed.

"No, it is just a statement of fact," Cecil replied.

King Diget III called for a vote, but King Bill Claghorn steadfastly refused to budge from his position of neutrality. He rose, "Look, Calgary is our only port of entry to the wide world. Already you have heard the expected shipments of guns, cannonae, and ammunition that will be arriving in Calgary come spring. I say that it is mandatory that Calgary remain neutral. If Calgary openly joins your proposed war, then it is a certainty that Velona and her allies will blockade Calgary, and no more shipments of any kind will get through. Do you not think that such would be most harmful to your cause? I certainly do. No, it is in the best interests of all our kingdoms that Calgary remains neutral to all sides."

The other kings accepted his argument as a wise, precautionary move. "You will of course have no objection to our armies marching across your southern lands?" King Diget III explicitly asked.

"As long as you do not wage war against my subjects, how can I stop you?" he gave a wry smile.

The two northernmost kingdoms also remained neutral. Neither had many guns nor a large population from which to conscript an army. It had taken all their resources just to meet the quota of fifty thousand soldiers. This, they at least had done, if only to ensure that their kingdoms would not be overrun by these other kings on their quest for wealth and power. Mostly, they were ignored, which suited them.

"Now then, King John, you still refuse to either join us or remain neutral?" King Diget III took control once more. King John glared at him. "So be it. What remains is that your kingdom lies in my way to the battlefield. Is it your wish to attack our armies from the three sides of your kingdom? Must we conquer Southway first? You have a death wish?"

King John knew long ago that it all boiled down to the simple fact that Southway was smack in the middle of the route needed for the armies of the other kingdoms to get to the battle zone down by d'Grange in Mont Blanc. Geography and roads were important here. The Centurion paved road that arced through the entire Greenway went through Southway to Calgary and close to Mont Blanc and d'Grange. Obviously, the movement of the vast number of troops and supplies would best be done along this single road. The alternative was to travel overland through vast stretches of the relatively uninhabited Langdoc region, where food and water were scarce and thus ill-suited to support the passage of a half million soldiers and their supplies. Southway was a bottleneck to their plans.

However, King John had no death wish and was practical. His army of fifty thousand could not possible withstand an assault of ten times that number. He made his last concession, keeping his fingers crossed. "If you will give me your sworn word that you will stay on or close to the Centurion road and not harm my towns and villages, I will keep my army in Middleton and not harass your forces as they pass through my kingdom." It was vital what he did *not* say, though. King John was very careful in his choice of words.

King Diget III looked pleased. "If you keep your word, King John, then we will not attack your kingdom. We all know how important safe passage along that road is for our armies to get to the battlefield. I give you my sworn word that we will keep to that path through Southway and not attack your villages, unless they attack us first." One by one, the other kings also agreed to this proposal. None really wanted to fight against one of their own kingdoms. Such would not be popular as many soldiers had relatives who lived in that kingdom. Besides, such a conflict would both slow the starting of the real war and cost them many soldiers who were needed in the actual assault on d'Grange and Velona.

That last barrier solved, King Diget III outlined their assault plans. March 21, 781 was set as the date of the start of the war. By then, the other kings had to have their troops in position. By late afternoon, the logistics of just whose army would be staged where had been worked out. Cardinal Cecil Mir also told them that on that date, Vito would attack Barcella and Bonito would assault Pieta. Further, the kingdoms of Urkut, Redun, and Avon would move into the Northern Steppes from the easternmost city of Melantas on the Elbe River, heading south to assault Zargarb from the east. However, if they met any resistance from the horsemen, they would stop and destroy them first.

King Diget III then announced, "In celebration of our great plans, I have brought some fine entertainment for us all; the gypsies will be performing while we dine. Later, at nine when it is dark enough, I am treating you to a fine fireworks display. Let us all celebrate tonight. Victory and power shall be ours by summer!"

During the fireworks display, King John was startled to hear in his mind, *Hi, Bethany here. You only need to think your thoughts, and I will receive them. So how did the conference go?* King John reported what went on, complete with their assault plans for March 21.

I'll see that those two caravels bringing more guns and cannonae are sunk by gun ships before they get to Calgary. Clever of you on your agreement. You said nothing about counterattacking them while they are in Mont Blanc. I sensed him smiling.

I then asked about the two queens, and he told me that they were with him and Sara right now. He was working on having them stay in his quarters this night. *I will protect them with all my guards.* I hoped that would be enough.

Chapter 16 The Assassination Spark

Chief Inspector Basilio had sworn to avenge the many deaths of his extended family, the West Po's. Long he thought about the incredible evidence that Chief Detective Inspector Cosima had uncovered, that Cardinal Branco Beja of Vito had written out all the direction instructions that the suicide bombers had used to find their targets. While he had managed to muster the expected tears over the many deaths, his emotions were totally suppressed behind an immense wall of hatred and anger against those who perpetrated this crime, the most heinous crime that he had ever known or even read about.

He watched from the sidelines as Gerardo and the other young teen survivors worked hard to pick up the pieces of the government and keep Velona from chaos. In his own way, he had helped them. Now here near the latter part of August, everything seemed under control, as best it could be preparing for a massive war with the Greenway and the wicked Church of Jehosanity. Now was the time. He would not be missed. Everyone was busy with their tasks; no one would miss him for a few days.

Carefully, he checked over his three long-guns, and four pistols. They were in top condition. He measured out a goodly supply of ammunition and packed that along with a bit of food and a waterskin. All fit in one long duffle bag, nothing would look suspicious. He changed into some old work clothes and boots. Holding the bag, he took one last look around his quarters at 42 Hampton Way. Everyone was out or sleeping and he walked slowly out of the estate and into the bustling streets of the city he so loved.

A bit later, he bought a train ticket to Vito and sat at the station waiting for it to arrive. His mind had no thoughts as he sat there for several hours. During the three days of travel, he ate well at the various stops along the way, but still he had no thoughts. His mind was clear and focused on one single action.

He arrived in Vito in the late afternoon and began walking. Even from the station, he could see the top of the commanding Church of Jehosanity of Vito. While there were a number of their churches in the city, the mother church was the tallest and grandest. He headed towards it with determined steps, carrying his bag at his side. His eyes took in the slum conditions of Vito. Every large city had slums, that he knew, only Vito was nearly all slums, had been for over a half century. Still, it suited him.

The church occupied a huge city block, a second block held rectories and other offices. The main doors were opulent and ornate, magnificent in their grandiose splendor, as were all these evil churches. Yet so were these despicable cardinals. Eventually, Cardinal Branco Beja would step out of those doors.

His highly trained eyes surveyed the surroundings. Even though he had never been here before, his years as Chief Inspector had prepared him for just such a situation. Quickly, he spied what he needed. He quickened his pace and entered the Boar's Dust Inn, just across the street from the doors. He gave the innkeeper five gold for a week's stay and requested a specific top floor room.

He climbed up the steps to the third floor and found his room. Entering, he noticed some cockroaches scurrying for cover. He didn't mind; they would be his company for a while. He dropped his bag on the bed, a dust bunny floated out from beneath it. This he ignored and went to the window and gazed outside. Satisfied, he opened the two windows and let the fresh air inside the stuffy room. He then returned to the bed and began getting his weapons in order, sitting each long-gun beside the window. He strapped the four smaller guns around his waist and carried the box of ammunition over to the windows and then a chair. He sat down and aimed one of the long-guns. Satisfied, he sat it back down and began to watch and wait.

Chief Inspector Basilio was patient — his wife always had said that to him. He forced such thoughts out of his mind, focusing on one thing only, the distant doors. He waited until dark and then ate some of his dried rations and then laid down on the bed, without removing his clothes or going under the covers. At first light, he rose and resumed his position on his chair. He was determined and ready. All morning long, he watched and waited.

Around one that afternoon, he again saw the doors move and his long-gun raised automatically. He stared at the doors. Finally, he saw the red that he had been waiting for! Sunlight reflected off the gold trim sewn into the opulent scarlet robes of Cardinal Branco as he stepped out of the Church of Jehosanity on the afternoon of August 29.

Chief Inspector Basilio's arm was steady; his aim was high as he estimated the fall of the bullet across the space between them. Bang! He dropped the long-gun and picked up the second, aimed at the red lying on the ground. Bang! He dropped the second long-gun and picked up the third, aimed at the red lying on the ground. Bang! He dropped the third gun and returned to the bed and laid down, satisfied.

Outside, he heard yelling and screaming and a general commotion. Someone yelled, "The Cardinal has been shot! He's dead!" Other voices joined in. Chief Inspector Basilio smiled, "Revenge is sweet," he whispered. Now, he waited. Soon he expected the police would come crashing through his door. Well, he'd meet them with his small handguns, for what that was worth. His death was inconsequential. The man responsible for the slaughter of almost the entire West Po clan was dead, that was all that mattered to him. He waited patiently for the end to come.

The daylight was vanishing and his stomach growled. He sat up, ate the rest of his dried food, and finished off his waterskin. Then, he lay back waiting for the inevitable to come. Night fell and still no one came smashing through the door. At last, sleep overcame him and he dozed.

Sunlight woke him. He sat up like a bullet! He listened but heard only the ordinary sounds. He relieved himself in the chamber pot. Still no one came smashing through the door. Mechanically, he reloaded his three long-guns and stowed everything back into his duffle bag. He shrugged and headed down the stairs. Breakfast was being served, so he stopped to eat.

While he was filling up on bacon and pancakes, he could not help but overhear others gossiping about the latest news. "Someone assassinated Cardinal Branco Beja yesterday!"

"Did they catch who did it?"

"No, says it's a bunch of Velona rebels, that's what I hear."

Finished, Chief Inspector Basilio walked out of the inn and back to the train station where he bought a ticket to Velona. Once more, he found himself sitting for hours on the hard bench at the station waiting for the train to arrive. Near nightfall, it pulled in and he boarded.

He took a seat at the very rear and sat down. As the train rolled along through the night, the long built up hatred and anger dissolved; intense grief now took its place. He cried softly to himself all the way back to Velona.

On September 1, Chief Inspector Basilio walked slowly onto the grounds of 42 Hampton Way. "Where have you been?" Cosima implored him as he walked inside. "Everyone's been in a panic. Some thought that you had been murdered or worse!" Her concern was real, he noted.

Gerardo, overhearing his wife, rushed out of their room. "Basilio? Are you all right? We have been searching everywhere for you. You've given us all a fright."

"It is done," he finally spoke. He sighed, "It is done. I have killed Cardinal Branco Beja. Shot him three times with a long-gun. It is done, Gerardo, Cosima. I have kept my word to my family and yours. The man behind the murders of our families is dead. I am tired. I want to sleep a while." They stared at each other, while he went into his room and closed the door.

Word quickly spread around Velona and many cheered the news. Not so, Cardinal Bosto Rems; rather he began to become slightly worried.

Over in Vito, word spread rapidly. Although no one had any evidence of who had shot their highest religious leader, the priests and General Franca Mafra did nothing to stop the rumors that Velona fanatics had done this horrid deed. In fact, they tended to support this theory. The general's remark said it all, as far as he was concerned, "This will only help our cause. More will volunteer to join our army for the spring assault on these despicable countries." Unwittingly, Chief Inspector Basilio had ignited a spark of rebellion against Velona.

Prelate Pointe Sor met with his fellow Mano del Dio, "Plans continue as before." His men chuckled. "How many more do we have prepared?"

"Ten. When do we use them?"

"There is talk of closing the rail line. Let's send them on their way soon. How many will be ready for the spring offensive?" Ponte asked.

"Fifteen, Your Holiness."

"Ah, that is good. That should be enough to clinch our victory," the Prelate smiled. He had no idea of the unintended results these actions would have.

Chapter 17 Terrorists Strike Again

Cosima went to check on Chief Inspector Basilio later that evening and found him still crying. Gently, she began a therapy session right then on his grievous loss. She wished that she had had time to do this weeks ago, but had not. Two hours later, she ended for the night. Her patient was too hungry and tired to continue. She promised him that they would continue first thing in the morning.

Now she worried about me. Not all was going so well. I had not returned from Calgary as intended; rather I had taken everyone into the lion's den of Brownsville. Yet, there was nothing that she could do about it now. She vowed to chastise me when I returned.

Beginning on September 2, a series of ten suicide bombings occurred. Each time, the target was a densely populated public place. Markets and even the train station were targeted. For six days, Cosima and Basilio were worked to death trying to piece together these vicious crimes. By the seventh day, all Velona was shocked and frightened; commerce had completely come to a halt. No one ventured into the streets unless they absolutely had to do so. Everyone held their breaths, waiting for the next explosion.

"Six hundred forty-nine dead, four hundred three wounded," Cosima reported the final tallies to Gerardo as they met with his entire staff and that of High Priestess Elaina. "We have been extremely lucky in that there have been no catastrophic fires. All were mostly detonated out in the open. Again, I have found bits of papers at each site that gave the suicide bombers directions to follow. The same person has written out these ten orders, but it is not Cardinal Beja this time. The author is unknown. However, I am certain that all ten bombers came from Vito. Of that, there is no question. I also found traces of opium at each site, so that must play a role in this somehow."

Gerardo spoke up. "I have ordered a total discontinuation of all trains through Vito and Bonilla. Anyone coming from those countries and entering Velona will be stopped at our border with Barcella and thoroughly searched. Barcella has beefed up its security and is now closely monitoring its border with Vito. I have sent word of this to Pieta. Hopefully, they will do the same along their border with Bonito. There is not much more that we can do. We have been very lucky that no real damage to our infrastructure has been done; only our innocent women and children at the markets have been slain."

High Priestess Elaina spoke up, "Gerardo, my priests are reporting a growing hatred against these terrorists among our people. They are outraged and angry, demanding that we take decisive action against Vito. If we do not do something soon, I fear that they will do something we all might regret."

"Okay, I will order ten thousand soldiers to Barcella immediately. Maybe that will keep things calmer here," Gerardo suggested. At least he hoped it would.

Gervaise West Po, now almost sixteen, was overseeing the enlistments of new soldiers. "Well, these bombings had drastically increased our enlistments, Gerardo. We've added over a thousand in the last five days. That is a positive to all this."

"Hey, I've got the tallies," Jules West Po broke in. Now seventeen, he was overseeing their defenses and equipment. "We have one hundred six cannonae ready to go. I've ordered the manufacture of mostly explosive shrapnel shot for them, as I don't see us assaulting structures so much as wiping out masses of invading soldiers. We have ten gun ships now operational. One more may be ready by spring. Plus there is this fifth all metal prototype ship that Arsenio has been constructing. He wants to put some cannonae on it as well. He claims it will be ready for limited trials by spring. If what Bethany says is true, we need to intercept those caravels heading for Calgary with those long-guns and cannonae."

"Excellent, Jules," Gerardo validated his efforts. To his son, he said, "Adrien, you and Emile work up how we can intercept and capture those gun runners. We could use those weapons ourselves. Let's sink the ships only as a last resort. Put your heads together and see if you can come up with a plan to capture them for our use." Adrien grinned, for now he would have something to contribute. He and Alessa's son began to make their own plans. Sixteen and fifteen respectively, they had the enthusiasm of youth as well as the ability to think in a fresh manner, uninhibited by prior military training and discipline.

Across town near the docks, Rimmi Pesaro, a rugged, huge dock foreman held his own meeting. Three days ago, his own wife had died in one of the terrorist attacks. "I say we march on Vito and destroy the entire country. We all know that the terrorists come from there. Even our Chief Detective Inspector has proof of that. I say we annihilate every last person, remove that scourge of the Sea Princes once and for all!" Many in the growing crowd shouted and cheered him, fueling his passionate speech.

"I say too that there is no viler church on the planet than this Church of Jehosanity, who we all know is behind this war! Even the Chief Detective Inspector herself has proven their cardinals are behind these terrorists! I say we destroy this church and burn them down!" The crowd roared with approval.

"Still, we ought to give Gerardo West Po an opportunity to do this for us. I'll give him time, but if he doesn't have the balls to do it, then I say that we do it. We are not afraid of evil priests or opium addicts." He worked the crowd to a fevered pitch and then left them to help apply pressure on Gerardo actually to do something about it. He wondered if perhaps Gerardo already had, though. Word had reached them of the assassination of the cardinal who was behind the first set of bombings. Perhaps Gerardo had done that. If so, he was ready to give the lad a chance. Time will tell, he thought.

On September 14, Messiah Bani el Marina and Tamina came to our estate asking to see me. Cosima, acting in my stead, asked them to come inside the highly secure estate. Over a hundred soldiers patrolled the perimeter day and night now. Both looked agitated, she noted.

"Have a seat. Bethany is away on a mission of her own. I am taking her place. How can I help you?" Cosima asked formally.

"We have tried to get into Mont Blanc. You know of what we are seeking?" Messiah Bani asked, unsure if this woman was privy to our discussions.

"Yes, the original copies of the Holy Gospels and the bones of Bethany Amir, right?"

He smiled, "Ah yes, that's right. We wanted to continue our holy search but were turned back at the border by many soldiers. We have heard of this coming war. Is this true?"

"Yes," Cosima replied and briefly explained what had occurred at the Council of Kings.

"This is very bad," Bani acknowledged, "but it is what we expected. I came to make Bethany an offer."

"Well, you can make it to me and I can relay it to her," Cosima suggested, becoming curious about what exactly he meant.

"We in the Arad hate these Infidels who have so completely twisted our holy teachings and those of the Son of God. We would like to join this Second Crusade for Religious Freedom that everyone is talking about, but. . ."

"That's good, we can use all the help we need, but what?" she asked.

"We of the Arad would like something in return when this is over and we have defeated the Infidels. We would like to be allowed to search this Mont Blanc for our Gospels and the remains of Bethany Amir. In fact, we would like Bethany to assist us in our search. That is the bargain that we came to make."

"How many soldiers would the Arad be providing?" she asked what she thought I would be asking about now.

"We can get forty thousand ready to ride within a few months after we get back to the Arad. If more are needed to defeat these wicked Infidels, we can arm even more, if we can get swords and guns." Cosima smiled, this was more like it. Forty thousand on the flank of Zargarb offered even better chances of survival, especially if Centurions came up the long road from the Southlands.

"Okay, I will contact her. Just a minute." She concentrated and made contact with me. After relaying Messiah Bani's offer, I sighed, and agreed. "She says that you have a deal. Here I will join you both to her." Bani and Tamina's eyes opened wide as I made telepathic contact to them.

I give you my promise to help you search for them once the war is over and we control Mont Blanc. Until we control that country, it is not safe for any of us to enter. He agreed and the bargain, struck.

"Okay, you need to get back to the Arad as soon as possible," Cosima took charge. "Report to the docks in the morning, ask for Felix. I will tell him your urgent needs and he will arrange for you to be on the next caravel bound for New Barq." The two shook hands and left. Cosima then relayed this good news to Gerardo, who placed a pin with the number forty thousand on it squarely in the Arad. His next question that needed answering was Megalos or Demokritos planning to send soldiers to this war as well? He mused over how he could figure that one out.

Down in Constanza City, Pope Christos received a dispatch that troubled him. Emperor Kreon was in failing health. He paced his office. The news out of Velona was highly encouraging, though a bit mystifying. How had Queen Ann been rescued? She ought to have been in Hieras Anubis, but now she was in Velona. Well, he'd thought of such eventualities, that is, unexpected situations arising. His very detailed written plans had taken the possibility of Velona learning about the potential war before the surprise attack in the spring of 781. Such had been executed. While it would have been vastly better had the suicide bombers struck at the same time as the invasion of the Sea Princes started, still, they had worked their purpose. Velona was now in the hands of a bunch of kids.

By now, the kings would have met and agreed to the spring date for their offensive. He had no suspicions that King John would capitulate. Further, the three neutrals mattered not. Now all was ready. He'd just issued the orders for the forty legions of Centurions to begin their long march up the Southlands, arriving near Zargarb by the spring. Five gun ships of Megalos were also being dispatched to the Velona area and were due to arrive by November, taking up a position near Vito to await the spring offensive. The remaining two gun ships he kept stationed near Constanza City, ready to handle any emergency. He fully expected to have total control of all the Sea Princesses by summer, September at the very latest.

On the other hand, this business in Demokritos was critical. Emperor Kreon, the first fascist self-appointed emperor was dying. He had handpicked the current Empress Selene, an ambitious and keen headed businesswoman and a Holy Woman of the Eighth Degree as well. She was a perfect match for the old emperor. Now, Kreon was on his deathbed and the line of succession in a crisis. Pope Christos had spent a fortune on Kreon, buying the emperor's favor. For the last twenty years, the Pope had slowly been rebuilding the influence of the Church of Jehosanity all throughout Demokritos. The moment that Kreon passed away everything would come to a head. Pope Christos just could not afford to lose any hard fought gains that he had secured over these years with the millions in gold he's spent there. He made his decision. "Prepare my yacht. We sail for Demokritos at once."

On September 10, Pope Christos set sail from Constanza City. The weather was still hot, and he stayed on deck as much as he could.

Captain Dante of the Velona gun ship, the Grande Pistola, had just arrived off Megalos on the assignment to watch for signs of army activity there. Here, the Grande Pistola met up with a sister ship, the Sea Dog. The two captains and crew exchanged news and assignments. The topic of discussion for days had been the suicide bombers who killed so many of the West Po rulers and the coming war with the Greenway and the Church.

Thus, on September 11, when Captain Dante spotted the Pope's Royal Yacht heading south by west, he decided to take the initiative. He signaled the captain of the Sea Dog his plans to shadow the pope's yacht. Eagerly, his crew dropped the canvas covering over the ship's gun ports, disguising them, making the Grande Pistola appear from a distance as a normal caravel. Then, they set sail shadowing the pope's yacht as it headed south. He guessed that it was headed to Demokritos. If Pope Christos managed to get them to send soldiers and gun ships north to the coming war, he had to warn Velona as early as possible. That was his reasoning.

On December 11, the Holy Yacht put in at the large port of Patri, the closest port to the emperor's palace in Kefall. The Grande Pistola sailed on further south to the smaller port of Filantos, and there spent several days replenishing its stores of food and water. A month later, he set sail back north to see if the Royal Yacht was still in Patri. It was. During this month, he'd studied the coastal ports with his spyglass looking for any signs of an army being mobilized and sent north by a fleet of caravels. He saw no such signs as yet. It was January 11, 781.

Chapter 18 Rescue

The night was black as we kept our vigil watch on the castle gate houses from our concealed location five miles to the southeast of Brownsville. Since I saw that from our position we would very likely miss the departure of the Confessore with the two queens, I tried a new tactic. While the others continued their diligent watch, I floated high above the castle from where I could see all four gate houses at the same time. Satisfied, I kept watch, hoping not to fall asleep.

I could see endless rows of pup tents housing the thousands of soldiers now camping in the farmers' fields surrounding the city. Suddenly, I saw movement and moved down a bit to check it out. Yes! There was the black hearse moving out of the north gate and into the city. A buggy followed it along with four on horseback. Damn, they were heading north, not south, nor were they following the old Centurion paved road. We were completely out of position to begin our pursuit!

"North road. He's off; the buggy is following the hearse. Let's get moving," I ordered my small group. We had only gone a little ways when this patch of pine forest ended. To our dismay, right there in the direction that we wanted to go, north, lay another large group of pup tents with many sentries on duty. We had no choice but to head due east. After a five-mile detour, we finally headed north again. Unfortunately, we now needed to veer west to connect to that north road out of Brownsville so that we could follow the Confessore. Once more, we found our way blocked by a large company of soldiers and had to press on north for several more miles until we finally hit a ridge and could go west.

Luck was not with us this evening. As we neared the road, we spotted a large company of soldiers heading back down the road towards Brownsville, evidently the night patrol returning. Once more, we had to parallel the road from several miles away, usually following no trails at all or making use of farmer's lanes. Finally, as dawn came we reached the north road.

We stopped and looked for the telltale tracks of the hearse and the buggy. "Damn! Damn! Damn! We missed them," I cursed angrily.

"Yes, no sign of them coming this far, Bethany," Arturo added his keen observations to mine. We had been forced to go too far to the north. Somewhere back towards Brownsville, the Confessore and either had changed directions and gone somewhere else or he had stopped at the desired location. Now we faced certain detection in the broad daylight. Yet, we had no choice but to head back down the road towards the city. "This is dangerous, Bethany," he whispered to me.

"I know. I think that it will be best if I float up and out ahead of us a ways. I can alert you to oncoming soldiers and such. You watch over my body here." He agreed and I began playing forward lookout. Good thing that I did so, twice we almost ran into a large patrol of soldiers.

Worse, we soon had to dart off to the side and run for cover! Thousands of soldiers and carriages came up the road traveling at a good clip; the kings were heading home. Damn, they would completely obliterate the precious tracks that we needed to desperately to find. We had no choice but to dismount and wait it out. Three sets of kings and their soldiers passed by during the space of an hour or so. Meanwhile, we decided to eat a cold breakfast and think this through.

First, I contacted King John. Why wasn't I surprised to hear that the two queens had been abducted right out from under his very nose? Why wasn't I surprised to hear that a cardinal read off the two signed documents supposedly written by the queens admitting to their terrible sins and guilt, opting for a second chance at Holy Redemption? Damn! And we had missed them.

"Calm down, let's think about this," Arturo cautioned me after I related what King John said. "Surely, the Confessore will not risk traveling by daylight. Too many things could go wrong. Thus, they went under the cover of night. We know that they left around midnight and that sunrise was around six, with at least one early twilight patrol out. So that means they could only have traveled for around four to five hours maximum. Their vehicles probably only make four miles in an hour, so that means the maximum distance north that they could have gone would be maybe twenty some miles. We are a good thirty miles out. We've already seen that we have overshot. So let's get going and start looking around twenty miles out or closer. There were at least two villages that we had to get around along the way. Perhaps they stopped at one of those."

Good plan. As soon as we could, we began riding swiftly south until we thought that we were twenty miles out. The country was rolling hills, filled with patches of timber near the hilltops, pasture lands and farmlands in the valleys. Once more, we had to avoid a smaller patrol. At this point, Arturo had us fan out on either side of the road, looking for any signs that the Confessore had veered off the main road. There certainly were a lot of farmhouses that they could have used, if they were empty.

Around fifteen miles out of Brownsville, we came to a small village. I took a gamble and had us continue riding on through the town. Everyone kept a sharp eye out for the black hearse and buggy, but we exited the town without seeing anything remotely suspicious. On we rode for another four miles, past many fields. As we crested another hilltop and ridge line, Arturo called out, "Over here!" He was off to the west of the road.

We all halted and move to his position. "Look there. Those sure look like suspicious wagon wheel tracks. Two vehicles for sure. Let's check it out." I agreed and we rode on up the ridge line for several miles. Mostly we were following deer trails and going cross-country. The tracks were very plain to follow. Why would two wagons travel this route? It made no sense to me at all. Plainly, there were no farmsteads here on the ridge line. Soon, we entered a stand of forest, but the trail continued. Now on the forest floor, the trail was harder to follow, but Arturo continued doing well with his tracking.

Around two in the afternoon, we spotted an old cabin sitting alone in the trees. Suddenly, I realized what this place was! Centuries ago, we Druwids lived in the Greenway, and we built small shelter shacks like this very one. In them, we stored firewood, water, food, and blankets for emergencies. Any Druwid knew intuitively how to find these cabins placed periodically across the countryside. Evidently, the cabins were still being maintained, at least crudely. We spotted smoke coming from the chimney from a good distance away and dismounted.

Silently, we all began making our way up to the shack. Some distance away, we halted. There was the Confessore standing around outside the shack! As we watched, we spotted four other men milling around the area as well. The hearse and buggy were tied up near the shack. Now what, I wondered. I had to think quickly.

The doctor could well be operating on them at this very moment. If we fired our guns, that sudden noise might cause his scalpel to slip, causing far worse injuries. Yet, I dare not attempt to take them down with swords; the four men had long-guns nearby and would likely shoot first. We needed to take them silently.

"Elaina, can you take the Confessore from this distance without giving yourself away too much?" She nodded and readied her bow. "Okay, you take him out, and I will take out the four assassins. Our objective is to do this silently, in case the doctor is cutting away inside the cabin." Arturo grasped fully what I meant and moved the others to cover me, in case one or more got to their guns before I got to them. As Elaina fired her longbow, I latched onto one of the assassins and threw his head into a tree. I grabbed the next who was ten feet away and did the same. The other two looked up startled. Wham. A third's head collided with a pine tree. The fourth raced for his long-gun. Wham! I picked him up by his legs and swung him into a tree.

Slipping back to my body, I motioned everyone forward; the others had their guns at the ready, while Elaina kept an arrow notched. When we were about ten feet from the shack's door, their horses whinnied, and the door opened. A nurse stepped out and tossed a pair of arms off to one side and called out to the Confessore, "We heard a noise. Is. . ." She stopped mid-sentence, staring at the arrow sticking out of his head, and she saw us walking towards her. Fear swept over her and she raised her hands, "Doctor, you'd better come out here," she said in a shaking voice that nearly cracked.

We arrived before her as the doctor stepped out, wiping his bloody hands off on a clean towel. He nearly fainted, but tried to go to the aid of the Confessore. "Hold, doctor." I barked. Just then, another nurse came out, and she shrieked and raised her hands as well. Both began begging us not to shoot.

"Damn, we are too late," I spat on the ground. "Any others of you inside?" I asked the doctor, who shook his head no. "Check those and make sure that they are dead," I ordered and stuck my head inside.

Queen Kathleen lay on a side bed, her clothes removed to her waist, but her arms were bare but intact. On the main table lay Queen Mary Beth. Blood covered both sides of the table near her shoulders. Both shoulders were now heavily bandaged; he had just finished up with her and was in the process of cleaning up before starting the other queen. A large kettle of water was boiling and several of his surgical tools were immersed in the boiling water. I will give him some credit for following good procedures. Both women were unconscious, of course.

I stepped back out and spat on the doctor, "You beast!"

His face went red, and I knew that he felt guilty about what he had done. Elaina ducked inside and came out white as a sheet. "You foul pig. I ought to cut off your arms and see how you like it. You nurses too. Let's see how you like a second chance to live a horrible life." Elaina ranted out her rage, as the color slowly returned to her face.

"Doctor, you are supposed to be saving lives and helping those in need not cutting arms off healthy women who have no say," I growled.

"Just doing as I am told. Following orders," he tried to justify.

"Yes, we are just following the Confessore's orders," both nurses echoed.

By now, the others had peeked inside and were equally revolted. Alan holding his head, said, "Bethany, these three ought to be brought to justice for what they have done to Queen Mary Beth. I vote with Elaina; let's cut off their arms too. I'll do it with my sword, if you like."

Nico whispered in my ear, "Mom, why not do your pressure point thing? That way we don't have a bloody mess to handle as well. We need to get out of here somehow." I smiled. My boy was right.

"We find you guilty of misusing your surgical skills to amputate the healthy arms of unwilling victims. You must pay the price, doctor."

"Please, I was just following orders! You can't do this. I am a surgeon."

"You have given up your surgeon status for that of a sadist." I touched his left shoulder, gave a solid pinch, and held it. While he was trying to figure out what I was doing, I pinched his right shoulder. Then, I stepped back.

"What have you done? My arms — I can't move them," he looked shocked. I pinched each nurse on her right shoulder and paralyzed those arms as well.

"There, justice is served. Your arms will remain paralyzed for the rest of your lives. Now, good doctor you can experience firsthand what it is that you have done to your patients. Nurses, if you want to live, you will take the good doctor and yourselves out of here in your buggy. Don't look back or I will change my mind."

I headed back inside to see what could be done now. "Grab all the medical supplies and get Kathleen's dress back on, please. Fifteen minutes later, they had all the items stowed on their horses. "Okay, Arturo, you will lead us. Nico, I am going to lift Kathleen onto your horse in front of you. Put one arm around her to hold her while you ride. Alan, hold my horse while I get Mary Beth onto my horse and mount behind her." A few awkward minutes later, we were ready to ride. However, to my surprise, Arturo had also taken the liberty of bringing along a spare horse for Kathleen to ride once she awakened.

"Which way?" he asked. "Look, Bethany, heading back to Calgary is going to be incredibly risky."

I looked back at the cabin and inspiration struck. "Let's head north cross-country, keep a look out for another of these emergency cabins. There ought to be more of them." He smiled and led us off to the north. He also decided to follow the ridge lines as much as possible, avoiding the populated, fertile valleys and villages as well.

I noticed that Alan lagged behind us. He tied some brush to his horse and walked along after us, doing his best to wipe or hide our trail. However, I did notice that his head must be hurting and he was dizzy again. I didn't like what I saw, but concentrated on keeping Mary Beth balanced on my horse as we went up and down along the ridge line.

Towards evening, Arturo spotted another of the old emergency shacks. This one was particularly rundown, but it was isolated and would serve us well. The shack was ten by twelve, tight quarters for so many of us. After bringing in the two unconscious women and placing them on the crude beds, the rest began handling chores. I searched the compartments beneath the wood box and found several bags of dried food no longer edible. However, the blankets were usable, though mice had found them. Between what we had and what was here, we made do. Our supper was a cold one, for we dare not use a fire, but did keep a low lantern on for a while.

As we ate, Kathleen finally roused. She was shocked and very surprised to find herself where she was. The last thing she knew was that someone was holding a rag over her nose. I quickly explained who we were and what had happened. Then, she saw Queen Mary Beth and shrieked, then held her hand over her mouth. I won't repeat what she then said. It wasn't very nice. As she grasped the complete picture, she realized that it if wasn't for us, she too would be armless like Mary Beth. Now she repeatedly thanked us repeatedly, heaping all manner of praise on us.

"We are not out of this yet," Arturo cautioned her. "We are in the middle of Brownsville with no real way to escape yet." That calmed her down, and she asked what she could do to help. Good start.

"I hate to put a damper on things, but we probably have only a half-day's head start. Certainly, the king will send an army after us. With so many horses, our trail will be easy to pick up even with Alan's precautions. Besides, they will be able to ride faster than we can. I give us a day or two before we find ourselves surrounded by soldiers." I didn't like his prognosis, but I slept on it, trying to find a way out of this for us.

In the middle of the night a high pitched shriek awoke us all. Mary Beth woke up and discovered what had happened to her. Fear, terror, pain, mingled with utter helplessness and total darkness shocked her. Only after we got the lantern going and I talked soothingly to her and helped her sit up did she finally calm down a little. I waited until the shock wore off and then let her cry for some time. At last, I was able to explain to her what had happened. I helped her go outside to the bathroom and then got some fluids in her, but I did not want to risk solids so soon. Near dawn, she finally fell asleep again.

Over breakfast, I discovered we had another problem. Alan wasn't stirring! I checked on him only to discover that he had passed away during the night. He had died helping others. We were saddened by his loss and took timeout to properly bury him by the cabin. One day, I hoped to return with a suitable marker for this selfless man.

As we got ready to leave, I sensed fear, terror, and anxiety rising in Mary Beth. Standing beside a tall horse feeling utterly helpless with no arms and confronting doing what seemed hopelessly impossible, Mary Beth froze. Panic seized her. "Relax, I have you and I will not let any harm come to you. I will lift you gently onto the horse and ride behind you with one arm securely around you. I won't let you fall. Even if the horse stumbles, I will lift us both to safety. See, like this." I gently lifted her up, sat her on my horse, and then did the same with my body. Only when my arm snaked around her waist did I sense her panic diminish slightly.

Off we went. Arturo took it slow at first, giving Mary Beth time to face her terror. He and I both knew that we had to get as far from here as possible, because by now soldiers would probably be riding up to the shack and finding the dead men. Soon, they would pick up our trail with a vengeance.

Around noon, our ridge line drew close to the north road. I spotted a long line of gypsy wagons, the very same ones who had been at the castle. I decided to take a gamble. "Arturo, head down to the gypsies. I want to talk to their leader a minute. I've an idea."

Three minutes later, we rode alongside a gaily-colored wagon. "I'd like to talk to your leader, please?" A woman with a front tooth missing grinned and called out the color of the wagon and pointed on ahead. We trotted on up, though Mary Beth's fears only escalated as we bounced up and down.

"Banja Silbini, leader of the Zupana Gypsies," he replied when I asked if he was the leader of this band.

"I'm Bethany from Velona. We've just rescued Queen Mary Beth here. As you can see, the evil Confessore of the Church of Jehosanity has done this to her. We got to Queen Kathleen in time. I am afraid that soldiers will soon be picking up our trail."

He grinned, "Ah, so you want the help of the gypsy, eh?"

"Yes, do you suppose that you could hide us in your wagons for several days? At least until we know that we are no longer being followed. We can pay you for you assistance."

At that, his grin broadened. "Aye, now you are talking gypsy. Yes, I have room in my wagon. Zeni will make you comfortable. Then, come up and sit with me. We shall talk. Have the others get in the next two wagons. Here, we will stop." Quickly, we did as he asked. I struggled a bit to help Mary Beth figure out how to get up the two steps into the wagon. Zeni was a woman who was always cheerful, and she began hovering over Mary Beth as if she was her baby girl.

Soon our horses were unsaddled and tied behind other wagons along with their spare horses. Ten minutes later, we began rolling along the north road once more. Zeni showed me the sliding wall between the back living quarters of their wagon and the driver's box. I scooted on up and sat beside the forty-five year old leader.

"Well, you have come a long way into the heart of your enemy. For what? To rescue two queens?" he asked.

"Yes, to us, life is precious, and I wanted to prevent what has happened to Mary Beth. A few months ago, we rescued another queen, but again we were too late to prevent her mutilation as well. I now have her living with me at my home in Velona."

"There is honor in you, that is plain. To risk so much for these women — they are your friends, your kin?" he inquired.

"No, I've never met them before. I only heard that they were in dire need, and I came to help. I am sorry that all those soldiers delayed us so that we couldn't get to Mary Beth in time."

"Much honor in you. Still. . ."

"Would five hundred gold help you and your family out?" I asked, knowing that it would.

He grinned and said, "Deal. We will take you with us, though you may not like where we are going. Are we not going the wrong way? Velona is that way," he pointed back the way we had come.

"No, we cannot go back the way that we came; there are now too many soldiers there. We need to go north for quite a while. Where are you headed?"

"With all that talk of wars, we are going up into Blaine all the way to the Volgost. There we will wait out this war. Gypsies want no part of battles."

"Perfect. I figured that we could go that far north and then head west and head down the Dnu River to the coast. Thank you for giving us sanctuary, Banja. You are an honorable man too." He grinned.

During the day, we passed through two towns, were met by four patrols of soldiers, and one large group that came riding up from behind us. Those I guessed were following our trail. The asked Banja if he had seen a party of riders. He told them all about the four patrols, and the man nodded and left, riding on ahead of us. At a crossroad, his men split up and rode off to the east and west. I guess that they didn't figure that we would really be going the wrong way for very long.

We made camp in the shelter of a patch of forest off the ridge line not far from the road. A small creek ran past us and the wagons formed into a circle. I had forgotten how full of life these people were. While I changed Mary Beth's bandages, other women brought us all gypsy clothes to wear. Soon we all looked like we belonged with them. While some played fiery music and others danced about the blazing bonfires, other women prepared the evening meal.

Mary Beth cried again as she saw the meal being prepared. "I cannot even eat any more."

"Of course you can eat. They didn't do anything to your mouth. I will feed you until you heal. Then, I will be teaching you to use your feet where we use our hands. I'm taking you both to my estate in Velona. Queen Ann is living with me too, and she is just like you, having to learn how to do everything with her feet. Trust me. Life is not over just yet. I will get you to safety. Now come on; let's go watch them dance, shall we?"

Beginning the next morning as we began traveling north once more, I began therapy sessions on Mary Beth. Of course, Zeni just had to listen in on the whole thing. I think that she got a bit more than she bargained for during the next several days as Mary Beth began to confront the deep trauma that she had experienced.

After four days, Mary Beth was finally laughing about something that the nurse had said while she was in great pain and unconscious. "She'll never be able to do anything anymore. Well, that is stupid. I sure had that attitude, but that was hers not mine. I can still walk and talk and think and dance and, well I don't know what all."

Zeni added her two bits, "And you are still young. You will find a handsome new man. Zeni is sure of that!" Mary Beth doubted that, but her attitude sure changed, even to the point of asking me how she could do things for herself.

"Let's wait a bit until your shoulders have healed fully. I don't want to risk any possible infection," I replied.

By now, Nico and Elaina were out dancing with the other youngsters at every opportunity. At last, I consented to try my hand at dancing as well. Kathleen and Arturo joined in and Mary Beth surprised us all, joining in and enjoying herself as well. Yes, traveling with the gypsies was more like one continuous party.

Thanks to the gypsies, we traded the women's fine nightgowns for practical leather pants and cotton shirts. Queen Kathleen was twenty with shoulder length red hair and hazel eyes. Though not a beauty, she had a sharp mind and was very learned. During her ill-fated, but brief, marriage to King Diget III, she had "grown" in wisdom. She spent most of her time helping Queen Mary Beth.

Mary Beth was twenty-one and very pretty, with long, very blonde hair and engaging blue eyes. Her face was round, and she had her brother's nose, slightly pointed. She looked remarkably like Queen Ann Penton. They could have been twins, not cousins.

Three times the gypsies stopped and did a show for a larger town, raking in a hundred gold. For two weeks we partied, danced, and really enjoyed their company. I invited them to come to Velona once the war threat was over. On September 19, we finally reached the foothills of the Volgost Mountains. Their high granite peaks formed a natural barrier between the Greenway and the home of the Axemen. Here, the gypsies made their permanent winter camp, far from civilization, prepared to wait out the war, of which they wanted no part.

During this time, I used my telepathy to chat with King John, who was terribly upset with what had happened to his sister. He swore that he would get his revenge one day. I also contacted the King d'Aine. He was extremely relieved to hear that I had rescued her before the surgeon had done his work on her. Both men wondered why I was heading to the very north of the Greenway, but they realized that the sheer number of soldiers on patrol in the south would make it exceedingly difficult for us to get to Calgary. My question was simple: go east into the Steppes and perhaps meet up with the Czar and enlist his aid personally or go west to the coast and try to find some way back home from there.

King d'Aine answered it for me. He promised to have a fishing trawler waiting off the coast by Coopersburg, where the Dnu River met the ocean. Now all that we would have to do is ride across some two hundred fifty miles of forested hills, following the river. I hoped that Queen Mary Beth would be up to such a challenge. Her wounds were now pinkish and I had removed all stitches. Because of having given her therapy so soon after the surgery, her body was healing far more rapidly than one might expect. Yet, she was still very helpless, having no skills with her feet yet. There had really been no time for us to sit down and quietly practice. If she could just sit in a saddle by herself, we could make it. Riding double this distance would be uncomfortable for both of us. At least, the gypsies had given them both practical clothing. In the last village, I had also purchased them two warm cloaks.

Winter was fast approaching; the fall colors were brilliant this far north. As beautiful and invigorating as the scenery was, Mary Beth was still afraid as we lifted her onto her horse. "I don't think that I can do this. I can't hold on!"

"Sure you can, use your legs. If you want, I can tie the reins into a knot and you can bite down on them and neck rein your horse all by yourself," I suggested.

"Oh no! I can't do that. Please, someone lead my horse. I'll try to stay on," Mary Beth hastily pleaded with me, her complexion paling. I nodded to Arturo, who took the lead. Nico led her horse, while Enrica and I rode on either side of her, and Kathleen and Phillipe brought up the rear.

I needed to keep her attention off herself. "Mary Beth, I couldn't help noticing that so many of the Amir line are either kings or queens here in the Greenway. Why is that?"

"Oh that's easy. As everyone knows, we of the Holy Amir Line were deigned to be kings and queens. So we tend to marry into our positions. That's why I married Henry — so that I could take my rightful place, you know, as queen. My children would then be in line for the throne later on, only I haven't had any yet. I think that is Henry's fault; something's not right with him."

Kathleen added, "She's right, I came over here from the Highlands to marry King Diget III. There wasn't any real opportunities for me back on West Reach, you see. Besides, I thought this would be a great opportunity for me. King Diget I was really powerful and famous, so I thought Amos would be just like him. Boy was I ever wrong!"

My mind wandered a bit. "So for a century there has been all this intermarrying between cousins and such here in the Greenway. Curious. I wonder if that may be Henry's problem of not being able to sire children."

"Don't know about that," Kathleen replied, "but Amos was a pig in bed and nothing ever came of it. I guess, Mary Beth, you and I are luck in that respect. If we had to have left children behind us now, leaving would be almost too much to bear."

"Yes, but I wanted to have children," Mary Beth replied, her voice choking up. "And now I can never have any." Her emotions got the better of her; tears began swelling up in her eyes.

"Why not?" I asked, figuring that she was not telling me some critical piece of information. Had Henry done something else to her?

"Who'd marry me now, like this, completely helpless? I couldn't even change the baby's diapers or even hug him or hold him or anything," Mary Beth let her feelings out and began crying.

Kathleen and I could see her point. While Kathleen was about to give her some sympathy, I spoke first. "Well, I've seen plenty of Dorota mothers who do just fine with their many babies. True, they have very different ways of dealing with their children's needs. Still, they do handle them, messy diapers and all. Lack of arms shouldn't stop you from having children, Mary

Beth. You will just have to meet the right man for you, someone who will love you and respect you and care deeply for you, not like that Witherspoon character. Marry for love next time, not for the throne; that's the best advice I can give you." She stopped crying and sniffled a bit; I leaned over and wiped her cheeks for her, and she braved a slight smile.

"Look, you are riding along just fine, so here's a little something that you can do," I pointed out.

"Well, it seems I can sit on a horse as long as nothing goes wrong. Only I have no way to grab hold if it doesn't," she pointed out her sense of helplessness once again.

Ten long days later, we finally reached the coastal town of Coopersburg. By then, I had heard Mary Beth recite all the inner-relationships of the many kings and queens, present and past. She was something of a history buff when it came to this topic. However, by the time we arrived, I had Mary Beth holding the reins of her own horse between her teeth and neck reining him all by herself. She'd gained some desperately needed self-confidence, along with the idea that things might not be quite so impossible for her now.

Coopersburg was a fishing village, the northernmost one of the Greenway. Perhaps fifty small craft were out in the bay working these last few weeks before the ice came. October was here and the weather was becoming quite chilly. By the first week of November, they expected their first heavy snowfall. The home of the Axemen lay just across the river to the north. None of us had brought warm clothes, and we were very glad to see the fishing trawler that King d'Aine had sent for us.

Two days later, we docked at a small coastal village on West Reach, where a large patrol from the Highlands awaited Kathleen. After leaving her there, we finally arrived in d'Grange on October 4 and took the train down to Velona and home.

While Nico, Phillipe, and Enrica gaily began telling everyone about our trip, I introduced Mary Beth to Ann and her constant companion Luigi, who eagerly began to explain to Mary Beth all the many things that Ann was able to do for herself now. He also promised to assist her as well, which pleased her, I believed. Perhaps, it was more that I began to do as I promised her — showing her alternate ways to accomplish life's tasks. Maybe it was a little of all of us. Much to my surprise, Pietro now began to hover around Mary Beth, volunteering to help her. Ah well, boys.

Chapter 19 October Surprises

Renzo let out a whoopee, "That's the last ones!" Ania, Kallisto, and Len smiled. For nearly two months now, they had been interviewing everyone here in Hieras Anubis. Marco and Rosina pumped their fists into the air, a sign of success. It had been their task to organize the visits, making sure that no one was omitted. Now they had their tallies, the names of everyone, their country of origin, their stories, and their level of adaption to their life without arms if such was the case with the person, and most of all what they desired to do now that they had been freed from this pseudo-prison.

We had some four thousand five hundred ninety-five families, that is, where there was both a husband and wife. Of these, ninety-five men and all their wives had no arms. One thousand of their boys were fine, while four hundred of their girls were also fine. Yet, they had one thousand sixty-three girls who also had lost their arms. Many of those who were fine, either were born here or were children of the original families from Dorota who began this colony.

That left some five hundred young men who were single and looking to marry; all were teens. All were waiting for someone to marry them. The pool of unmarried women was a staggering six thousand seventy-five of which only seventy still had their arms. These seventy were the teenaged daughters of the original settlers. Many of these unmarried women were mothers, and they had some one thousand twenty daughters in the same mess as they, while they had five hundred and five sons who were fine. Of these unmarried women, only eight hundred were teens. The rest had had their husbands brutally tortured and murdered, before they themselves had fallen victim to the knives of the Medico Santo of the Confessore del Dio.

By March of the next year when they stopped sending more victims to Hieras Anubis, Renzo added another four hundred four widows with their two hundred seventy daughters and three hundred one boys. All these females were similarly victimized, bringing the total to twenty-one thousand seven hundred twenty-eight people here in the Hieras Anubis area.

Based on conversations with the two Elders and many of the older Dorota women, Renzo estimated that it took the average woman or girl four years to adapt fully to their new life style and to learn the Alternative Ways of dealing with life. Of note, the Elders had ceased calling them the Women's Ways and Men's Ways because now there were men similarly victimized. The new term that was adopted here was Alternative Ways. He was then able to estimate that there were some nine hundred in their first year of learning, seven hundred in their second, six hundred in their third, and five hundred in their fourth year. This was a key datum. Twenty seven hundred women had yet to learn how to care for themselves fully.

Why all these numbers? I am trying to give you a feel for the immensity of the problems facing Renzo, Ania, Kallisto, Len, Marco, and Rosina. These twenty-seven hundred had to be assisted in daily living chores by someone else, particularly with those nine hundred in their first year of learning. Who would be assisting them?

Worse still, the old Dorota "Perfect Society" always had a husband for each family. This was critical, for he had to handle all the heavier chores around the home. Long ago, we had seen in the old Dorota society that their men were so overworked between their jobs and caring for their families that they had no time left over for anything else, such as the arts or creative works.

Here, Renzo and the Elders faced the nasty proposition of six thousand four hundred seventy-nine fatherless families, all who desperately needed a man about the house for obvious reasons. Quickly, Renzo arranged for the five hundred teens to marry their sweethearts, removing five hundred from the total households that lacked an able-bodied man. Still the numbers were staggering, and someone had to help these desperate women raise their families.

To that end, five years ago, the Elders had requested of the governor that the able-bodied men be allowed to have two wives and families, since already the men's hearts had gone out to the plight of these new arrivals. Every able-bodied man and his wife had taken in one of these unmarried women and her children. They had to do so, if only out of humanity. Polygamy was against church doctrines, and the Pope had vetoed the idea. Still, the men continued to provide not only for their own family, but also for another woman's family as well. Indeed, they were so overworked that it is a wonder that they did not suffer ill effects from it all.

That left one thousand four hundred seventy-nine manless families with no help whatsoever. Most of these were the newer arrivals that could not care for themselves anyway. Thus, the already overworked original families from Dorota took in these victims as well. Many men now attempted to support three households!

Renzo just could not believe their grim statistics. He did feel overwhelmed by the magnitude of the atrocities being committed by the Church of Jehosanity. Looking over these numbers, Renzo nearly cried. Ania and Kallisto were deeply impressed with what the selfless men of Hieras were doing for all the women. With the arrival of each new batch of victims, the problem only grew worse. Late October 780, Renzo drafted a lengthy letter outlining the atrocity that was Hieras Anubis and sent it by caravel to Velona. His orders were followed. The document was printed in volume and delivered to nearly every country on Tarra. His objective was to make this crime widely known throughout the civilized world. Its impact would not be felt for several months, however.

Rather what was felt was the thunder of a ship's cannonae sliding into Hieras Anubis' port on October 31! Boom! The Megalos gun ship fired a warning shot as it began its run into the docks. Already the warning bell had sounded. Women dashed indoors as usual, while a hundred men hastily donned the old uniforms of the soldiers. They took up their expected positions, pretending to be the Megalos soldiers guarding the city. However, Renzo quickly realized that something had gone wrong.

"Well, I guess they finally figured out about our fake monthly messages," Ania declared. "What do we do now? That's a gun ship there, and they probably have a hold full of soldiers, Renzo."

Len didn't wait for Renzo. He yelled, "We fight!" Renzo smiled. Len wouldn't think of doing otherwise.

"Okay, have all the fake soldiers run for cover. Have the two cannonae crews return fire. Len, you and Kallisto head to the western cannonae. Ania and I will take the east one. Marco, Rosina, you go organize the soldiers and their long-guns. If the gun ship docks and soldiers disembark, you and the others do what you can to shoot them. Action."

The six rushed to get to their positions, while the pretend soldiers were very glad to head into the relative safety of nearby warehouses. Shortly, the initial warning shot was returned. Both cannone crews fired off a salvo of their own. Untrained as they were, both shots went wide of their caravel target, much to the disappointment of Renzo and Len.

The only advantage these crews had was that the gun ship could not fire upon them if it continued to head into the docks. To fire, it would have to swing to the east or west, so that it could fire its broadside of ten shots. "Damn! Take cover!" Len yelled as the gun ship turned so that its starboard set of five guns could take shots at his position. Five thunderous booms were followed by hideous sounds of splintering wood. The heavy lead balls ripped into the westernmost wooden docks, smashing holes wherever they landed. "Idiots! Solid shots!" Len called out. Had they used shrapnel balls, his brave crew might have been decimated on the spot. As it was, only one man was injured with a broken arm.

Seeing the open gun ports, Renzo had a brilliant idea. "Balls of fire on the sides where the five gun ports are located. Fire away!" he yelled as loudly as he could. He concentrated and let loose his own Druwid spell. Within seconds, five blazing balls of fire exploded around the sides of the gun ship. Ania wondered why they were not casting them onto the deck, where the rigging and sails would likely catch fire, perhaps injuring some of the crew, disabling the ship's maneuverability for a time. Even Kallisto thought these five balls of fire were completely wasted; however, she did as ordered. Five explosions of fire swept up the side of the gun ship, and some of the flames and heat entered the gun ports. Seconds later, black whips of smoke curled upwards into the sky, the remnants of the five spells. Nothing seemed to have happened. Ania was just about to order a strike on the deck of the ship where the sails and crew might be impacted, when a massive explosion deafened everyone!

Half of the wooden starboard side of the ship seemed to fly off in a giant arc into the bay! Huge red flames then shot out of the massive holes. The ship, which at first rocked heavily to port from the explosion, now rolled back and over on to its side. Water came gushing in the holes, great mountains of steam soared into the sky from every open crack in the boat. Thirty seconds later, only the port gun ports remained visible, as it sank rapidly into the waters of the bay. A minute later, the bay was filled with an enormous quantity of flotsam and jetsam. Occasionally, bodies of the dead popped up onto the surface amid the debris. Those on shore just stared at the spectacle, speechless for several minutes. Then, the pretend soldiers manning the two cannonae yelled and cheered. They jumped up and down and shook hands with any hand in sight. Marco, Rosina, and the remainder of the pretend soldiers came rushing out to add to the noise of celebration.

Ania looked at Renzo and commented, "Well, that was brilliant, I'll give you that!" He smiled, greatly relieved.

Len, who had bounded over to Renzo, shook his hand, "I bow to the master! Incredible thinking, Renzo, incredible!"

Kallisto put a damper on their festivities. "They'll be back you know. When they find out this gun ship fails to return, they'll send in an army! Now what do we do?" The Elders had just run up and overheard her comment, which took the festivities and relief out of their faces.

"I don't know, but it looks like we cannot stay here much longer," Renzo admitted. He sent a telepathic message to Gerardo begging for immediate help. Two days later, the Velona gun ship, the Sea Dog, anchored off the bay at Hieras Anubis, a most welcome sight indeed. The Grande Pistola was far off to the south. Gerardo promised to send another gun ship, two caravels of soldiers, and two more cannonae, arriving in five weeks at most. Somehow, Renzo had to hold out until then.

With the assistance of the Elders, the group began analyzing the most important results of their massive survey of the inhabitants. Three quarters of the population needed their traumas handled. Anger and hatred seethed in nearly all but the young. The original settlers, who had wanted to found their version of a perfect society, felt utterly betrayed. Three quarters were victims who expressed anger and hatred against the Church of Jehosanity and the men in their employ who had murdered their husbands, kidnaped them, and mutilated themselves and/or their children.

Many of the more recent arrivals wanted somehow to return to their home country, where possible. In many cases, such was not possible, for they would only be subsequently captured once more, possibly killed. The original seven thousand or so wanted to move to another place where they could try yet again to build their society in safety. Another large block of those who had been here for at least six years also thought that this was a good idea. In their home countries, they would not do well. Here among so many others like them, they felt at ease and comfortable, though they wanted their children who were not mutilated to have a chance at a better life. Worse, so many needed an able-bodied man around the home. Yes, it was a strange mixture of feelings and desires.

Renzo scratched his head. Assuming that one could somehow cram a hundred people into one caravel, a fleet of some two hundred twenty ships would be needed to move everyone. That was ignoring all their needed possessions, livestock, and household items specially constructed for the women, who could not deal with life without them. What to do?

Kallisto pointed out, "We cannot just abandon Hieras. We keep on getting more victims dropped off here every month. It won't be humane to leave here until they stop dumping off more on us." Renzo agreed that she had a valid point, which only complicated matters. What to do? What to do?

Chapter 20 November's Preparations

By November 1, I had Mary Beth's marriage annulled as well. I also sneakily transferred some two hundred thousand gold from King Diget III and her court account to her own private account. She now had the funds by which she could support herself.

A month around Ann and Luigi was working miracles on Mary Beth's outlook. She saw firsthand the many things that Ann had learned to do, such as feeding herself, and did her best to emulate her cousin. That Pietro now hovered around her, helping her just as Luigi constantly did for Ann, was a great help in boosting her low morale. While I had hoped that our three mischief-makers were now growing up, such was not the case.

One day, Luigi playfully tickled Ann and then began running around the mansion with Ann chasing after him, trying to get him back. Ann and Luigi got me good one morning. I put what I thought was a spoonful of sugar in my black tea, only to gag on it. "Salt! Who put salt in the sugar bowl?" I cried out, upset and spitting the undrinkable mouthful back into my favorite mug.

Ann and Luigi giggled and then burst out laughing. "You should have seen your face, Bethany!" Luigi cackled. Ann roared with laughter as did the others sitting around the table. Okay, I calmed down and resigned myself to having been the brunt of another joke.

At dinner a day later, I took the saltshaker and shook a bit onto my fish. The top fell off and half of the salt poured out. Again, the mischievous trio cackled along with Ann and Mary Beth. Later Ann confided in me, "You know, I feel years younger when I am around Luigi. I wonder why? You know, I used to have fun doing things like the salt switch with my folks. I usually was sent to my room as a result. Still, it was just good fun. I feel like a teen again. Isn't that strange?"

I grinned, "Don't go messing with the salt again or I will send you to your room." She giggled.

Later that week, I had the four together with me in the basement. With Enrico and Arturo's aid, I had reassembled the old low kitchen that we had used years ago when we all were armless. My plan was to show them how they could fix meals and carry things with the old yokes that we used to use.

"This stuff is amazing, Aunt Bethany," Pietro declared. "Now they could actually cook their own meals!"

"Ann, now you have no excuses anymore for not making me your specialty of roast pheasant," Luigi teased her.

"Hey, give her a break, Luigi! She has to learn how to use all these things. We'll have the stove operational tomorrow. Arturo will hook it into the chimney there. You can bring her down a lot of charcoal and take her grocery shopping, Luigi." He grinned.

"This is all rather fantastic," Mary Beth proclaimed hesitantly. "We really can do all these things ourselves?" she asked.

"You bet. Just remember that it will take a lot more time than you were normally used to spending on doing a task," I answered her honestly.

"Okay, I'll take your word for it," Mary Beth said unconvinced. "You know what I miss most?"

"What? Not being able to tickle me back so easily?" Pietro teased her.

"No silly. It's running. Back home when we were all growing up, you remember this Ann, we used to all go running a couple miles every day. Uncle John always said a fit body leads to healthy body and mind," Mary Beth recalled.

"Sure. In fact, until I got abducted, I still did run around the castle grounds every morning," Ann admitted.

"Same with me; drove King Diget III nuts. I could out run him. I think that really ticked him off," Mary Beth confided.

"So why don't you both take up running around the estate here every morning? I am sure the boys here would love to run with you," I finally got back at the boys for their mischief! I knew that none of the three mischief boys liked to run, especially in the morning and especially more than a few feet. Both Luigi and Pietro groaned.

"You really think that we can?" Ann asked. "I mean like we are now?"

"Perhaps not, if you used to run on your arms," I half-jested.

"No, on our feet," Mary Beth tried to explain and then realized that I was putting her on. She giggled as she picked up on it.

A bit later, I had all four outside. Though the weather was a little chilly, a good run would warm them up. "Okay, twice around the very perimeter is a mile. Have at it," I called out. Ann and Mary Beth began to run hesitantly and very cautiously. Soon they left caution to the wind. Groaning and complaining, Luigi and Pietro attempted to keep up but fell behind.

When they finally stopped, Ann teased Luigi, "You are going to have to really practice running if you are ever going to catch up to me! Now I know how to handle you, run." Mary Beth giggled along with her, while the boys groaned once more. After that, every morning the four took a several mile run around the estate.

Even more positive, around the end of November, the two women cooked the evening meal for everyone in the house. Using their yokes, they also carried the many dishes to the makeshift tables there in the basement, though they let their mischief boys cut up their meat and actually serve the dishes. Radiant pride beamed from their young faces that evening. After that, I suggested they fix dinner for us all once a week, which pleased them considerably. Now they were contributing to our large group.

When the mischief boys were not assisting the two women, they were in the basement working on their inventions. Mid-November, Nicolo, Pietro, and Luigi took us all out to the northern edge of Velona, where Gerardo had established a gun training firing range. While some twenty of us stood and watched, the trio demonstrated their invention.

"It's called a multi-barreled long-gun," Nicolo explained. Essentially, they had taken a dozen long-gun barrels and fastened them together by two circular metal rings into a cylinder. A makeshift firing mechanism allowed one gun to be fired at a time. One then rotated the cylinder until the next barrel came into position before firing again. "You can get off twelve shots without reloading," Nicolo went on. "Watch the targets."

Bang. Bang. Bang. Within a minute, Nicolo got off a dozen shots. More importantly, he hit twelve different targets, although they were positioned closely together. Gerardo was very impressed, as were others who were working on the city defenses.

"Now we are addressing the problem of reloading," Pietro explained. "Everyone knows that it takes several minutes to reload one barrel properly. With twelve to reload, this is not too practical, especially since it is so heavy that it has to be mounted on this metal tripod. We've made the barrel cylinder exchangeable. See, Nicolo is taking out the fired cylinder and inserting the next cylinder. Now in two minutes time, he can fire off another twelve shots in rapid succession." More noise and smoke punctuated his explanation; the mischief-boys were having fun.

"We figure that if you had a goodly supply of the cylinders at hand and a reloading crew, one of these MBGs could fire nearly continuously, and the loading crew could be somewhere nearby that was protected from enemy fire," Pietro explained, primarily to Gerardo, who they hoped would fund their invention. Fortunately, for our ears and noses, they only had the two cylinders.

When they finished, Gerardo was most impressed and set the trio up in business. He wanted these guns available for the coming war and I could see why. We were going to be greatly outnumbered. This new invention might level the field a bit. Nicolo eagerly setup a company to begin the production of the MBGs. By the start of the war in the spring, Velona had fifty of these new weapons, while d'Grange and Barcella each had ten.

As we began heading back to the carriages, I overheard Pietro and Luigi talking to Ann and Mary Beth. Pietro said, "See, Mary Beth, I promised you that I would help you retake your country."

"Yes, Ann, with these new MBGs, we stand a very good chance of getting your kingdom back for you," Luigi added. Both women were very impressed and chatted with them all the way back to the estate.

Up north, Bianca and Louis were also not idle. Daily, they took long rides to the north of their small, mountainous country, looking for ways to stop or at least delay the mighty army massing on their border. Louis knew that they could not totally stop them; his idea was to delay them and then hold up within the two huge stone fortresses. Of course, the enemy would bring on their cannonae and eventually breach the walls, but Louis promised to make such a siege as costly to the enemy as possible.

"See, the only roads into d'Grange lie in these three valleys, with this one being the lowest and most easily traveled," Louis pointed out the obvious main road winding down the steep sided mountain valley rather like some giant snake. "Now if we can somehow let some slabs of rock fall down, we ought to be able to slow them down and inflict some casualties on them as well." Bianca liked that idea.

However, she, like most in Velona, only rarely saw snow. Now that November came, she saw mountains of the white stuff building up on the taller mountain slopes nearby. That gave her an idea. "When does all that snow melt, Louis?"

"Oh, the valley floor will be gone by mid-March, but up there, why, it lasts until early June, especially at the higher elevations. Why?"

"What if we made some barriers to trap and hold back a bunch of snow? Then, when the army comes marching down the valley there, we let it loose."

"Ah, an avalanche! Great thinking. Avalanches are common in the high country. Yes, brilliant, Bianca."

During November and the ensuing cold months, Louis had work crews building barrier walls and constructing rock slides that could easily be triggered into an avalanche of falling stone as well.

In late November when he got his first of the new MBGs and saw it in operation, he got another clever idea. His work crews began building stone blockhouses to house these MBGs in such a manner to allow the guns to shoot the enemy, while at the same time protecting his men from the hail of enemy bullets. Each blockhouse held a dozen men and one MBG. One would shoot while the others worked on reloading.

Stonemasons were perhaps the most common workers in the country, whose main export, besides ores, were stone blocks used in all forms of construction. Louis and his planners began working out just where to position these defenses and how many they needed, based upon the estimates of MBGs that Velona would make and/or send to d'Grange.

By late November, Renzo's little pamphlet entitled <u>The Hieras Anubis Experiment of the Church of Jehosanity</u> became widely available throughout Velona and copies were shipped off to the other Sea Prince sectors as well as to the Greenway, Megalos, and Tashien. Later editions were also sent to Demokritos and Annelise as well.

As one might imagine, his little booklet caused quite a stir. Some used it as further fuel to attack the church, while others including the

Church defended it as being the humanitarian thing to do with those women who had lost their arms for whatever reason. Almost none of those in Hieras Anubis had come from Velona or d'Grange. Yet, in the other sectors, the publisher and thus I as being Renzo's wife rapidly became besieged with letters of inquiry from friends and relatives seeking word on their "vanished" loved ones.

Here in Velona, down by the docks, the rugged, huge dock foreman Rimmi Pesaro continued to hold his own meetings. Still grieving and angry over the terrorist bombing which killed his wife, he used this pamphlet to enrage further all who would listen to him. Many more now listened to him. So much so that Rimmi began to have to hold several meetings each day, just to accommodate all those who wanted to hear his take on all this. So outraged were these men that they began to enlist in Rimmi's Militia, a band organized to combat the terrorists and the Church of Jehosanity.

Further fueling the flames were another two suicide bombers who struck late November, killing a number of women at an open-air market. Cosima and Basilio quickly examined the grizzly crime scene. Once more, she found indisputable evidence that these bombers came from Vito.

Rimmi's call for death to all those from Vito began to be heard around the docks. Velona did have a small number of immigrants from Vito living together in a poorer section of town, the Vito Neighborhood it was called. Rimmi's Militia now began to hang out there, threatening those poor folks and keeping them under close surveillance. So much so, that Gerardo was forced to ask Basilio to station a hundred policemen in that neighborhood to maintain the peace. This action did not bode well on the members of Rimmi's Milita, who began to have suspicions that Gerardo was not totally on Velona's side. He was lapping up with these from Vito.

If Gerardo made one mistake during these months, it was not taking Rimmi's Militia seriously.

Chapter 21 Power Change

On December 20, 780, Pope Christos arrived at the Emperor's Palace in Kefall, Demokritos. At once, he was taken to the Empress' Throne Room, where Empress Selene awaited him. She had heard of his arrival and took heart in it. After all, the Pope had married her and Kreon. Such honor had never been bestowed on anyone in Demokritos.

As usual, Selene wore her light blue satin gown, which displayed her ample bosom rather well. She had allowed her hair to grow and her long curly brown hair was perfectly done, draped somewhat provocatively over her left armless shoulder falling into her lap. As always now, she wore a pair of the black silk hose imported from Tashien. She loved that extremely sensuous feeling on her well-proportioned legs. She never wore anything except the finest black Annelise oxfords with their seven-inch heels. As Empress, she only wore sixteen-foot billowing gowns which greatly accentuated her tiny fifteen-inch waist. Yes, for the last ten years she prided herself on maintaining her tiny waistline, the envy of many courtly partisans. Indeed, her sense of style and elegance was now legendary throughout those in the know in Kefall.

As Pope Christos entered, Selene rose, took two tiny steps towards him, and welcomed him. "Oh, Your Most Holiness, it is so good of you to come during my time of great sadness and sorrow. Emperor Kreon is in failing health and cannot get out of bed any longer. It is such an embarrassment. Staff must change his pants and bedding twice a day now. It's just awful, I'm sure." Selene had never made but one visit to her husband's bedroom and that one was to see for herself that he was actually bedridden. Honestly, she thought, who would want to take care of and sit with someone who is slowly dying? Certainly not herself. Why, she needed to run the country, get her hair brushed properly, her make up done right, and always be well dressed, setting an example.

Pope Christos put his hands on her shoulders and gave her a fake kiss on both cheeks and a slight hug. "I am so sorry for you, Empress. I came as soon as I heard, though it takes three months to sail between Megalos and Demokritos. I do hope that I am in time to give him his Last Parting Rights."

"Oh yes, he is still breathing, I am told. My maiden here will take you to see him. Then, you must join me in my Royal Dining Hall for some refreshments," Selene said demurely, wondering what the Pope's real reason for this visit must be. She had a guess, but wanted to make sure.

Pope Christos followed the young woman to the Emperor's bedroom, which stank something awful. No one was really doing a whole lot for the gravely ill man. "Leave us now," he whispered. She dutifully left, closing the door behind her. Only the doctor remained. "How is he doing?"

The doctor explained how hopeless it was and that it was a miracle that Kreon had held on so long. Then he too was dismissed so that Pope Christos could perform the Last Parting Rights on Emperor Kreon. Cardinal Danski had informed him of the long illness as soon as he had arrived in Kefall; thus Pope Christos was prepared. He performed the holy ceremony and then pulled out a small vial. Carefully, he poured the contents into the mouth of the Emperor and rubbed the man's neck until he swallowed. Next, he poured a little water into the dying man's mouth to help wash it down. Satisfied, he rose and left the room. The young woman then led him to the Royal Dining Hall, where the very slow moving Selene had just entered herself, though she had ordered her servants to prepare a light snack for her and her guest.

As he moved around the palace, Pope Christos did notice the distinct absence of doors on most rooms. He smiled, assuming that it was Selene's orders, allowing her to move freely about the palace. He arrived in time to assist Selene in sitting down at the huge table. He then took his place on her left, while her servant woman sat on her right to feed her as usual.

"We can speak privately here," Selene began. "Hester here has no tongue and cannot read or write. That was part of her job requirements, to have her tongue removed. This way, she can help me at all secret meetings and be counted upon to be unable to repeat what was said to anyone. Yes, Your Holiness, she is very well paid for her services, aren't you Hester?" The thirty year old woman nodded vigorously. Indeed she was well paid, making a hundred gold a month, an immense amount for a woman of the street, which she was when Selene found her and hired her.

"I thank Holy Lord Jehosa that I was in time to give Emperor Kreon Deimos his Last Parting Rights. I do not believe that he will be long in this world and that Lord Jehosa will be welcoming his soul into Holy Heaven shortly." Selene demurely took another small sip of tea and smiled.

"That is so very kind of you, Pope Christos."

"Thank you, Empress Selene. I see that you are in excellent health and looking exceptionally beautiful. The years have been kind to you, most Holy Woman of the Eighth Degree."

She blushed, "Yes, they have indeed, though a woman must always watch her waist. It is so easy to be tempted by earthly pleasures and gorge oneself on royal food and wine. I do try to set a good example for other noble women, while I run the country. Men do listen to me and obey me. If I were ugly or fat or did not dress properly, I am sure that they would not."

"Of course, of course, Empress Selene. What man would dare offend such a Holy Woman as yourself? Indeed, none. May I ask, how has the enormous task of running Demokritos been for you?"

"Oh, it was a bit challenging for a week, but you know with my memory for all things, why that only lasted a week. Smoothly. That's how I would describe it. Everything has been running just fine under my astute and able leadership and has been for nearly nine months now." She wanted to ask him why he was so interested, but thought better of it. Allow a man to hang himself; they always did, especially so when around an elegantly dressed, beautiful woman.

"Now that *is* good news to hear. I was afraid that you might not be up to the task, but now I see that you are even more able than I had ever imagined you were, dearest Selene. That is quite a compliment, if I do say so myself," he said rather pompously to himself. She smiled demurely and chose not to reply.

"Have you made any plans for what will happen when Emperor Kreon passes away?" Pope Christos finally approached the real reason for his visit. That Kreon was still alive was a small bother that he'd just taken care of; he wanted to make this trip as short as possible and get back to the upcoming war. Still, it was critical that he leave Demokritos in the perfect situation.

"Yes, I have," Selene replied with a smile. Oh, he was not coming right out with it, she noted. Well, two can play the game. "When he passes, I will unveil a life-sized bronze statue of Emperor Kreon. It is outside before the main gates. Perhaps you saw the canvas covering when you entered." He nodded. "He sits astride his horse. It was done by one of our very best bronze sculptors. Now the entire world can reflect in the greatness that was Emperor Kreon." She smiled; touché she thought.

Pope Christos smiled appreciatively. Keen mind here. "I am most humbled by your kindness to Emperor Kreon. I was also wondering about who will lead Demokritos once he has passed away. Is there any chance that you wish to remain as Empress and rule?" There, she had forced him to come right out with it.

Ah, there we have it. She smiled, "Of course, I have already proven that I am perfectly capable of running Demokritos. I will retain my throne and the love of my subjects."

Feigning immense relief, Pope Christos exclaimed, "Oh that is music to my soul, Selene. I know of no one better qualified to run Demokritos than you. How can I possibly thank you for choosing to stay on as Empress?" He bowed to her, since he could not kiss her hand. She had none.

Still, Selene was not satisfied. She replied graciously, "Why, thank you, Pope Christos for your wonderful support! The Church has done so much for me all these years. That alone is more than thanks enough. Now it is my turn to give back. I will continue to rule this, the greatest country on Tarra." She knew very well that this was a man's world. A woman, that is, a beautiful woman who dressed properly and was a Holy Woman of the Eighth Degree alone could command the respect of men, but she had to have a keen mind and be a solid judge of men and their often hidden motives. Either that or dole out sexual favors. Selene was loathed to do that. She might get pregnant again and that would ruin her waistline as it had before. Not a chance of that, she swore.

"Excellent, excellent. I know that you will continue to do a fabulous job of running the country properly, Selene," he replied. "I wonder, have you given any consideration to perhaps remarrying and having a man become Emperor and lending you a hand with this important job?"

Ah, now it comes out! This is his real reason for this visit, she thought to herself. Men. So predictable. He wants to know if I will marry and put another man on the throne. Not a chance in Hell of that happening! Smiling, she replied demurely, "No, Your Holiness. I have not. I am too old to remarry; besides one day, I wish my son Karpos to become the Emperor. Is this not acceptable to the Church? I know that when Frona died, the Church assisted Kreon in marrying me. Does the Church insist that I remarry?"

"Oh no. Not at all, Empress. The Church feels that you are doing a perfect job of running Demokritos. It is only that if you found it too much to handle, we would graciously assist you in finding the perfect man to marry — you know, a man who fits your most personal desires. Since you do not want to remarry, the point is moot. However, Empress Selene, if later on you should change your mind, please let us know. The Church is always here to help and assist the Most Holiest of Holy Women of the Eighth Degree." He poured it on thick to avoid giving her the impression that he wanted her to marry and allow him to hand pick that man, that new Emperor.

"Why thank you so much, Your Holiness. I certainly will let Cardinal Danski know if I should reconsider. I am so glad that I can count on the support of the Church when Emperor Kreon dies. That is a big relief to not have that to also worry about when I have to bury my husband." Selene felt greatly relieved at last. Everything was going perfectly, well not perfectly. Kreon was taking forever to die.

"You are most welcome, my Holy Child, most welcome indeed. I want you to know that the Church is always here to assist you in any way that we can," he replied.

"Thank you as always, Your Holiness." Since he rose, she assumed that the meeting was finished. "Thank you so much for coming. I know that the Last Parting Rites meant so much to Kreon. Will you be staying long in Kefall?"

"Only until our Emperor is buried, and I know that you are securely at the helm of Demokritos, Your Highness. To leave sooner would be a terrible disgrace to you, our Most Holiest of Women! That I cannot do to you — to desert you in your hour of need!"

She smiled and rose to see him out. He bowed and hugged her once again and then a servant entered to show him out. Selene sat down to finish her tea, quite satisfied in what she had achieved. That the Church would support her in being the sole ruler of Demokritos was precisely what she most desired. Already the taste of ultimate power had been hers. For the last nine months, in fact, she wielded that ultimate power and she thirsted for it.

Now it was to be hers and she was pleased!

As the Pope neared the main entrance of the palace, near where the kings and queens used to stay during their councils, a young lad stepped out, blocking his way. The lad's face seemed somehow familiar, though the Pope could not place him. "Excuse me Your Holiness. I am Karpos Omela, Selene's son. May I have a word with you before you leave? A word in private?" he added.

Fascinated by the boy's abruptness, he followed the nineteen year old into his private quarters, one of the old king's quarters, where he had been forced to stay all these years. Out of sight, out of mind, more or less. That was Selene's way. Once inside, Karpos shut the door and offered the Pope a seat. He sat across from the pontiff.

"May I be quite frank and honest with you, Your Holiness?" he asked. Christos nodded.

"Emperor Kreon is dying any day now. My question is who will ascend to the throne? I know that my mother greatly desires to be the sole ruler of Demokritos, but she is a real bitch! You couldn't pick a worse ruler! She thinks only of herself and her desires, never anyone else's. Do you realize that she had Hester's tongue cut out so she can't reveal what is said in private meetings, while she helps mom eat and drink? Savage and uncalled for, I say. Obviously, we must have a male ruler. No other country has only a female as sole ruler. Such is preposterous."

"Now I figure that Selene could be forced into picking a new husband to become the Emperor. That's one possibility. Have you come to tell her to pick a new husband?" he asked.

Pope Christos replied, "No son. I asked her if she wanted the Church's assistance, but she stated quite clearly that she is more than capable of running the country." He kept it simple, wondering what the lad wanted.

He replied, "I thought as much. Another possibility, and one that many noblemen have been talking about for the last year now, is that they revert to the customary method of having the Noble Houses choose our next Emperor — that's the way it has been done since the beginning. The nobles definitely want a return to power. However, Your Holiness, I also know that the Church has donated considerable funds to Emperor Kreon over the years and took great pains to marry him to mom, to fill the beloved Frona's shoes when she passed away."

The lad continued, "I find this intriguing — that the Church so supports them. Now the way that I figure this is that you have a very strong interest in just who ascends the throne of Demokritos. I asked myself what would happen if the noblemen elected someone who was not, say, a believer in Jehosanity, not an ardent supporter?"

"How did you answer yourself?" Pope Christos asked, suddenly taking a keen interest in the lad. Perhaps there was more to him than he thought at first.

"I said to myself, if I had vested some twenty million in gold in the throne, I certainly would want a say in who sat on it. I believe that the Church would be very, shall we say, upset, if the noblemen elected a new Emperor." Pope Christos smiled.

"Look, you have a self-centered bitch on the throne right now. If she remains the sole ruler of Demokritos, how long do you think it will be before the men of this country revolt and insist that the noblemen elect a *male* ruler?" He placed heavy emphasis on the word male. "Not long at all, I say. In such a case, your twenty million may well have been utterly wasted."

"Obviously, Karpos, you have done your homework. Yes, twenty million is a lot of assistance that the Church has provided over these many years. And yes, we benefit greatly by having someone on the throne of Demokritos who is an ardent supporter of our Church. That is, in part, why I came to see your mother today. I wanted to see if she would be amenable to remarrying. If so, we could handpick Kreon's successor. However, as we both know, Selene has a mind of her own and wants no part of remarrying. Perhaps, young Karpos, you have a suggestion to make here?" Pope Christos asked the leading question that he knew the lad could not resist answering. Now, he would at last know what the lad had in mind.

"I do. I am like Kreon in some ways. I don't like the noblemen having a vested interest in what I do or say. Religion, now that is another story. Of course, the Church only wants to help us all be holy and righteous, that our souls can be saved. I have always been a supporter of the Church and will remain so. If Selene is allowed to be sole ruler, in less than a year, there will be a revolt against a helpless woman running the entire country. She cannot even feed herself. I do not want the noblemen to regain their lost control over our country — not any more than the Church does, if I read our history correctly. So, Your Holiness, my proposal is simple. Put me on the throne as Emperor." He smiled; at last, he had said what his heart greatly desired — that he wanted to be the Emperor.

Pope Christos smiled, but did not reply. He knew he could get more from the lad. Quickly, Karpos added, "I swear to always be loyal to the Church. I will back you in all things, always. I give you my solemn word."

"I agree with your analysis, young Karpos. Indeed, you would make an excellent choice for the next Emperor. You are right. We should act before it is too late. I am afraid that time is very rapidly approaching. If I went along with your proposal, Karpos, there would be two problems that must be faced and handled."

Seeing some agreement, his face lit up. "What problems?"

"First, what to do about Selene?"

"Well, ship her off to that place where you send other helpless women. What's it called? Oh yes, Hieras Anubis. You know, kidnap her in the night or something. I can let men in to the palace and take them to her quarters. It would be the simplest of matters to remove her."

The Pope smiled. "I see, yes that would be fitting for her. Yet, she is a Holy Woman. The second problem, young Karpos, is that there must also be an Empress. You are not married yet?" He shook his head no. "I see. Further, there is now a great tradition that the Empress be one of our Most Holy Women of the Eighth Degree. If you are to ascend to the throne, you would need to be married to one such as your mother."

He looked crestfallen for a moment. "I don't know anyone like that, besides mom."

"If we should do this, put you on the throne, then would you allow the Church to find you the right woman for you to marry? Of course, you must fulfill your husband duties to her. There can be no signs ever of disgrace upon her by you. The Church and all of Demokritos highly frowns on even the slightest mistreatment of its Holy Women of the Eighth Degree, who are so dependent on their loving, kind husbands."

Karpos smiled, "We all have to make sacrifices to achieve what we desire. Mine will be taking such a wife and seeing that she is properly treated at all times. Is that acceptable?"

"Absolutely, son. It certainly is. Will you allow me to do some research of my own and get back to you on this? I am sure that we can work this out to our mutual advantage." He shook the lad's hand, sealing the bargain. Then, he left, having far more to ponder than before he came!

He rather wished that he had not used the vial so soon. Ah well, so be it. He returned to Cardinal Danski's quarters in the mother Church of Jehosanity in Kefall.

"Will she remarry?" Cardinal Danski asked the moment the two men were alone.

"Most definitely not." He watched the lines on the face of the Cardinal tighten. He added, "However, another possibility has surfaced, a rather unexpected one. Her son, Karpos, wishes for us to name him Emperor."

"What of his mother?" asked a surprised Cardinal Danski.

"He suggested that we kidnap her and send her off to Hieras, of all places. This son is very knowledgeable. What do we know about her son? We will need to move quickly on this." Cardinal Danski nodded and summoned his Mano del Dio Prelate.

The next morning, word came to the Church that Emperor Kreon had died during the night. Would the Church make the necessary funeral arrangements? Pope Christos sent back a reply asking Selene to leave everything in his hands.

During the next couple of days, the reports on Karpos continued to be most promising. He had no vices, unlike those of Kreon, who favored very young men. The Church would have nothing in Karpos' past to keep hidden. For years now, he had been running his fathers' import-export business that

Selene had ran before she became Empress. Although only nineteen, Karpos was known as a keen, shred, and effective business manager, well suited to deal with those issues of the throne. Further, he was young, only nineteen. If the ascended the throne and remained loyal to the Church, they could look forward to a long period of stability in Demokritos, which the Pope desperately wanted. Such would forward his plans for world domination. Once more Cardinal Danski went to his precious records of every Holy Woman of the Eighth Degree in Demokritos, saying a prayer for the thoughtfulness of his predecessor in compiling this massive ledger. He only needed to keep it up to date.

After the funeral, which was well attended because Emperor Kreon had been well liked in spite of his faults and rise to power, Selene expected the Church to make its grand announcement. Instead, the Church had her unveil her memorial to Kreon. "Now is not the best time, Selene. Trust me," the Pope had whispered to her. Thus, Selene again had to bask in the praise the crowds thrust upon her late husband and not herself. She consoled herself with the thought that it is just a matter of time now.

Roxane Thalus was barely eighteen, but miserable. Her father was a wealthy nobleman who had fallen for the lies of the Dorota Elders so long ago. He'd joined their community and saw his wife lose her arms, as well as those of his young three year old daughter. Somehow, he had managed to get out of that mess relatively unscathed, his wealth mostly intact. For the past fourteen years now, he'd done well for himself and his family, which also included two sons who were now twenty and twenty-one. Both were married and on their own. Now only his wife and daughter lived with him in their large estate, that is, if you ignore the many servants required to take care of the two mostly helpless women.

Roxane was daydreaming as she often did of an afternoon. She couldn't remember when, if ever, she had arms. She'd always been this way. Her daydreams were when she was five. She and her brothers raced around the huge estate playing kick the can. Roxane was good at the game, one of the few things she was able to do well. Besides, her two older brothers paid no attention to the fact that she had no arms. They wrestled with her, tickled her, and played with her. Those were the best years of her life, full of life and vigor and most of all fun.

All that changed when she turned ten. "Now it is time to get you transformed into an elegant young woman, Roxane. After all, women like us must look their very best if we are to ever attract the attention of a nice young man." At the time back then, she didn't understand what her mother meant, although now she did. Yes, her mother meant well. After all, what man in his right mind would ever marry a hopeless, helpless woman such as she? None.

Still, that was when the tortures began, Roxane vividly recalled as her daydreams slipped from her, heading towards the present as they often did. Under her mother's direction, the servants put her into a very tightly laced corset, shrinking her waist until she thought she'd be cut in half, if she didn't stop breathing first. Then came the impossible high-heeled Annelise oxfords in which she thought that she was walking on her toes only, which she very nearly was. The large billowing ball gown fitted on top of everything else was hardly noticed. No longer could she run the halls free as a lark. No, now she could barely walk and then only with the greatest of care and difficulty, to say nothing of trying to breathe enough to stay alive.

That was eight years ago. Now eighteen, Roxane was one of those incredibly stunning blondes. Her face was angelic; her blue eyes, enticing; her very long wavy golden locks demanded the attention of all, falling to her waist. Her waist was quite small still, just fourteen inches around, but her bosom was still filling out. Now used to the tall Annelise heels, Roxane was able to walk gracefully. Still, she felt a prisoner in her own home and clothing. She didn't feel attractive, though her two girlfriends claimed this was so. They, too, had no arms, the only teens her parents allowed to be around her for obvious reasons. "Someday, I am going to find a way to get out of here," Roxane confided in her two friends, who giggled and understood. They too wanted desperately to find a boyfriend and get married, though their prospects were slim indeed.

Roxane and her mother were aghast when their doorman announced that Cardinal Danski and Pope Christos were at their door! Her mother was almost beside herself with worry. Did they look their best? Hair done. Oh how she ought to have had their hair done sooner. A million such thoughts flooded the older woman's mind. Roxane, on the other hand, merely wondered what Pope Christos looked like. "Now you see, Roxane, why I insist that you always wear your ball gowns around the house! You never know when someone important will come calling! How do I look?" Roxane didn't have time to answer; the servant led the two men into their drawing room, where the two women were just rising to greet their impressive and most important guests.

"Good afternoon, Most Holy women," Cardinal Danski said humbly, as he gave each woman a welcoming hug. "Allow me to present Pope Christos, the leader of our entire Church of Jehosanity worldwide."

"I am truly honored to meet such Most Holy women," Pope Christos followed the formalities. "I have come to have a little talk with your lovely daughter, Roxane, if I may." Cardinal Danski began chatting with her mother, while Pope Christos asked if there was a more private place where they could talk.

"Follow me, Your Holiness," Roxane said, gliding slowly across the room, hoping that her pace would not offend him. While she now walked gracefully, more like gliding, the tiny steps meant it took forever to cover any distance. She hurried as much as possible, though, and when they entered the sitting room, she was somewhat out of breath from the very tight corset. She sat down on the green divan while Pope Christos pulled up a chair and sat before her. He looked older than she had imagined, perhaps wiser. It was in his eyes, she thought.

"I am here on behalf of a shy young man who is dying to meet you. He is a very eligible bachelor and will take only the very best care of such a Holy Woman as you. He of great financial means, but he is in some very unusual circumstances," Pope Christos found this a bit awkward, since he dare not yet mention the real person or reasons.

"Mom and dad have been very picky about the boys that they allow to date me. None, in fact," Roxane decided to be up front with him. "What unusual circumstances?"

"He needs to marry in short order. That is, needs to marry a Most Holy woman. Trust me, I cannot tell you the reason for this haste, but it is extremely important. I would like you to meet him and see if you could find it in yourself to wed him on such short notice. If so, you may find out the real reason relatively soon. I will say this, such a marriage will be more beneficial to you than you can possibly imagine. Even your parents will gain much by this marriage."

"Will he have me move in with him? I mean if we marry soon," Roxane asked the only thing that really mattered to her. Pope Christos was offering her a way out of the prison of her home! Roxane realized at this moment how desperately she wanted her own life, free from the demands of her mother and father. She doubted that she would ever be free of the corset and heels, but that would be a small thing to endure if she finally had her freedom. She felt like a bird in a bronze cage for the last eight years.

Pope Christos was slightly taken aback by her seemingly strange reply and question. Such was not what he had anticipated, throwing him off his stride. Well then, he knew little about the minds of women, Holy Women especially. Their needs must be so different from his. "Oh absolutely. You would move into his place right away, though your parents would certainly be allowed to come and visit you." From her sudden frown, he realized having them come was not something this beautiful woman desired. Why? He had not the faintest clue.

"Okay, that is perfect. When can I meet this man? I do hope that he is not sickly or an ugly pig."

"Oh let me assure you that he is neither. As of this moment, he is a highly successful businessman. He is a year older than you are, and I believe that you will find him both handsome and most considerate of you and your needs. Shall I send a carriage to pick you up at say six this evening after dinner?" Pope Christos asked.

"Sure. Oh, what should I wear?" Roxane realized that he had not told her where they would be going. Her mother would be insisting that Roxane be properly attired for the affair, whatever it might be.

"My dear Roxane, what you are now wearing will be just perfect," he replied and they returned to her mother and Cardinal Danski. After the two men left, her mother was ecstatic and hovered about her daughter all that afternoon, telling her servants how to brush out every hair on her head or so it seemed to Roxane. Grimly, she endured the afternoon's fuss over her looks.

Promptly at six, the fancy carriage arrived. Although her father tried his best to get the driver to tell him where he was taking his daughter, all he got was she will be most safe and will be returned here in a few hours — totally unsatisfying to him. Still, the Pope and Cardinal were arranging the meeting. At last, he decided that it must somehow be either very holy or very important.

"Wow! Roxane, you are incredibly beautiful!" Karpos exclaimed after Pope Christos introduced the couple here in the Cardinal's private office. He left the two alone to get to know each other.

"Thanks, you are rather cute yourself. Why do you need to get married so soon? Why must she be a Holy Woman? Are you fond of women like us? I'm sure that you could find far more suitable women to date than someone like me. I mean everyone has to do nearly everything for me," Roxane asked. Never having dated before nor had contact with other teens her age, she was not abashed by being so frank and open.

"Let's just say that I will be a man of great power, and in order to so be, I must have a Holy Woman at my side. I would love to tell you more, but now, I cannot. Let's put that all aside for the moment, Roxane. I have only just met you, but I like you already. I do hope that you will not be too upset if you have to leave your home." He said the magic words for her.

"Oh no, no. I have been trying to find a way to get out of there for eight years, Karpos. I'd do almost anything to have my freedom. I will have my freedom if I marry you, right? I mean that I don't want to be told what to do and when to do it all the time. Don't get me wrong, I don't mind following orders, but just not every hour of every day you see."

Karpos looked relieved, she thought. He said, "That's great, Roxane. I promise you that you will have more freedom than you can possibly imagine! I think maybe that it will be the other way around; you will be giving the orders, not taking them any longer. For a flower such as you, I think that is the way it should be. I know what you mean. I've had to take stupid orders from my mother for ten years now. I can't take it any longer either. We are like two peas in a pod, you and I. We both long for our freedom. Perhaps together, united, we both can succeed. I know that unless I marry someone like you, I will never be given my freedom. You are so perfect, so beautiful; I think that I must be dreaming all this up."

"Wow, you too? That's just awful. You know that my folks simply refused to allow any teens with arms to ever come into our home to play with me? I only have two girlfriends, and they only come to visit once a week. I almost never get out of the house either, so I know how awful it must be for you, Karpos. I like you too. Perhaps after we marry we will fall in love with each other, though I don't know anything about such matters myself, only what my two friends tell me. What do you think?"

"Well, I think that if we like each other, then that's a good first step. If we always treat each other with respect and honor, all will work out, don't you think?" he asked, just as unsure about love as she. "I mean I will always treat you with the highest respect and honor, Roxane."

"Oh, I am sure that you will. I can see it in your eyes," she replied, having remembered her brother once saying something like that to her when she was seven. "But are you sure that you will be comfortable with me like I am? I mean, I cannot even hold you or hug you properly," she added.

He grinned, "Not in the least, Roxane. Mom is a Holy Woman too. So you see, I know all about such things. I'm experienced," he bragged. For some reason, he just felt so strongly attracted to this young woman that he was starting to act a bit silly. Now the two began chatting gaily to each other. Time flew by.

The pope knocked on the door and then entered. "My, how time has flown. It has been nearly three hours that you two have been talking. Might I have a word with you alone, Karpos? I believe the cardinal wishes to have a word with you, Most Holy Maiden."

In the next room where they could not be overheard, the pope asked, "Well, Karpos? What do you think? Will she do?"

"Splendid! She is perfect in all ways! She is beautiful and almost a kindred spirit," Karpos replied, full of youthful excitement and anticipation.

In the other room, Cardinal Danski asked, "Well, Most Holy Maiden, what do you think of young Karpos? Do you find him suitable?"

"Oh yes, yes indeed. He is a fine young man. I like him a whole lot, even though we've only just met," Roxane could scarcely restrain her enthusiasm. He nodded and said that he'd be right back. He met the pope and Karpos in the hallway and nodded affirmatively to Pope Christos.

"Okay, son. I suggest that you make your proposal now. If she accepts, then we can tell her more, but not all. Here, it is appropriate to give your fiancé something. Usually, it is a fancy ring, but in her case, it ought to be a necklace. Here, give her this one; it ought to satisfy her and more importantly now, her parents. He took the box and entered the room.

Following the instructions given to him by Pope Christos, Karpos got down on one knee and said, "Roxane, will you marry me and make me the happiest man in the world?"

"Oh! Yes, Karpos, I surely will, but you are making me so incredibly happy that I feel like I might burst!"

"Here, please accept this token of my pledge to you," he added and opened the box for her. Inside was a huge emerald on a gold chain. Both of their eyes opened wide! He'd never seen such a huge gem, neither had she.

Carefully, he placed it around her neck, readjusting the fall of her long wavy hair. "There, you look even more beautiful, Roxane." He leaned over and their lips met for the first time. She nearly fainted from emotion or perhaps from the tight corset. Fortunately, the pope interrupted them, giving her time to control her pounding heart.

"Now that you have accepted, we can shed a little more light on just who Karpos is and why all this secrecy. You see, Roxane, Karpos here is the son of the Empress." Roxane fainted.

A bit later, she awoke with Karpos hovering over her constantly. "I'm sorry, that was such a shock. Is this true?"

"Yes, fair Roxane. I am so sorry that you fainted. Are you sure that you are alright now?"

"Yes, I rather lost my breath there. Now I do understand, Karpos. I just want you to know that I am marrying you because I like you and not because you are the son of the Empress herself." She felt that she just had to say that.

A half hour later, Pope Christos escorted her personally home. It fell upon his shoulders to announce the engagement and marriage of their daughter to Karpos Omela. As he expected, both parents were shocked at the suddenness of it all, but when they learned just who the boy was, they were even more shocked, though they now understood why all the secrecy. That their daughter now wore a fabulously expensive emerald only helped matters.

The next day, Pope Christos went to visit Selene. It was his task to announce the wedding plans of her son to her, hoping to soften the surprise. She must not suspect anything yet. Indeed, Selene was rather surprised. "You mean my son asked you to personally marry them? I guess he got that idea from my marriage to Kreon, though he was only nine at the time. Well, far be it for me to interfere in his life. I do hope that he will be happy with her," Selene responded, after she had recovered her initial shock. She had not even known that Karpos was seeing anyone, much less intended to marry and so soon. The wedding would be in two days. The two chatted for a half hour longer before the pope left, suggesting he had pressing Church matters.

Selene paced her room for a while. Something was gnawing in the back of her mind. How had she missed this vital aspect of her son's life? Well, she had not paid much attention to him at all, not for years, actually. Still, she felt a bit strange about it. Consequently, she called for her coach and headed to the Banca del Dio, saying that she needed to get some funds for her son's wedding presents.

The wedding was attended by many noblemen and their families. Selene went all out to ensure that her son only had the finest of weddings. This much, she felt that she owed him for so neglecting him all these years. I won't bore you with the details. That evening, once the guest had all left and even Selene had retired for the night, the young couple was finally alone in the large palace.

"I cannot believe how huge this place is, Karpos. I just want to run around everywhere!" she twirled around on her toes.

"Well, let's do it! No one is around now, unless we summon them. Oh, can you run in your outfit?" he realized that she was still wearing her billowing white satin wedding gown. "Will you allow me to get you out of your dress? We can run around better that way, I think," he added sheepishly.

"Sure, please do. I cannot see my feet, and I don't want to trip and fall." A few minutes later, she was finally out of the dress and enormous hoop skirt. Her white slip hid her corset and panties, but her expensive black silk hose caught his eyes, along with her white Annelise oxfords.

"How can you walk in those shoes?" he asked, never really having seen his mother's heels up close.

"Only by taking the tiniest of steps. It took me a long time to learn. Mom always made me wear my corset and these heels, even when I go to bed. Not the shoes, mind you, the corset. She says that if I don't wear it always, then my waist will never be small, and I'll look like a fat pig. You don't think I look like a fat pig do you?" she asked.

"Not at all, Roxane! Come on; let's run around for a bit." They began strolling around the halls, but she was unable to run. Actually, she only moved about very slowly, much to her frustration. At last, she began to chat about her favorite game that she used to play with her brothers, kick the can.

"All that fun ended when mom began making me wear these heels," she explained.

"I can take them off if you like," he offered.

"Not much good in that, I'm afraid. I've been wearing them so long now that somehow my feet will not go flat on the floor anymore. Without shoes, I have to walk on my tiptoes anyway, and that is much harder to do without these shoes on. Maybe I should have you wear some like these and then we can play kick the can ourselves. You won't be able to move any faster than I can," she teased him. He picked her up and ran her around the halls anyway, before they headed into his private bedroom. This was one benefit of his living in the old kings and queens quarters. The giant suite of rooms was entirely separate from the rest of the main palace, and the two could do as they pleased here.

Later that night, two men stole into the palace, using the key that Karpos provided Pope Christos. Following the lad's instructions, the pair went directly to Selene's bedroom, where she was sound asleep. The long day had been utterly exhausting for her, and she had simply fallen into her bed, emerald green gown and all. Her servants discussed whether they should wake her and undress her, but decided against it. Selene was soundly asleep, besides they were exhausted too.

One of the men placed a cloth over the sleeping woman's face. Selene woke up and struggled a bit, though she was nearly helpless to prevent the man from holding the smelly cloth over her face. She quickly drifted into a deep sleep. "Damn dress," one man whispered.

"Here, I'll throw her over your shoulder," the other whispered back. Quietly, the two men retraced their steps. A half hour later, they slipped out of the gates, depositing Selene in a carriage. A moment later, the carriage began rolling through the midnight streets of Kefall.

The next morning early, Pope Christos came to the Royal Palace very early. Already Selene's servants were wondering where the Empress was at, for she wasn't in her bedroom or any of her usual locations. "Gather around," Pope Christos requested. A half hour later, he was satisfied that all the palace personnel and aides to the late Emperor and Empress were gathered in the Great Hall.

"I have a vital message from Empress Selene to read to you. I am following her expressed wishes in this matter. Permit me to read her words for you."

I, Empress Selene Deimos, do hereby state this as my final order. Now that my beloved husband has passed on, I feel that I can no longer run our huge country by myself, though I have given it my best these past nine months. At my age, prospects for remarriage are slim. As you know, my son has just married a wonderful Holy Woman of the Eighth Degree and they have my eternal blessings for a long and happy union. I hereby decree this to be my final order for Demokritos. I chose Karpos Omela to be your next Emperor and his new bride, Roxane, will be your new Empress. She will, I am confident and certain, will fill my role as Empress admirably.

I have discussed this with Pope Christos, the leader of my Holy Church of Jehosanity, and have received his blessing and pledge of total support of my decision. I know the Church will fully support Emperor Karpos and Empress Roxane, and I hope that all of you will as well. Give them your full support that Demokritos may continue to be the greatest nation on Tarra.

For my part, I have been given an opportunity to retire to the new Holy Colony for the Most Holy Women of the Eighth Degree. I am off to Hieras Anubis as Pope Christos reads this to you. There I will find the quiet and peace that I deserve after giving so much of myself to our country. May Lord Jehosa bless every one of you, especially my son and his new bride.

Empress Selene Deimos

Roxane let out a squeal of total surprise. Karpos, his hand around her waist, steadied her. He smiled; Pope Christos had worked his magic. He was Emperor, finally free of his mother's constant bickering, nagging, and orders.

Of course, the letter was a total fabrication. Selene never blessed anyone except herself perhaps. The letter from Karpos, giving the details of the palace and where Selene's room was at, along with the key to gain entrance, was not. He had signed it, per the Pope's orders. This document, Pope Christos gave to Cardinal Danski for safekeeping, should the Church ever need leverage over Karpos. However, he doubted that the Church would ever have need to resort to blackmail, not in this case. Still, Pope Christos left nothing to chance. Indeed, this trip to Demokritos had worked out better than he had long planned, immensely better. Karpos would likely rule for the next fifty years, maybe more, ensuring the Church's control over the entire country would continue to grow enormously. Then one day — well, he chose not to get that far ahead of events. Up north, there was a war to conduct, one that would gather all the Greenway and the Sea Princesses into his firm control as well. He had yet to give any consideration to Tashien. First things first.

On January 11, 781, the Pope headed back to Patri and his Royal Yacht. On January 17, he set sail for Megalos. With good winds, he would be home by April 17, just in time to witness the end of the war, if all went well and rapidly. The caravel carrying Selene had sailed a week earlier.

Captain Dante of the Grande Pistola reread the pamphlet that he'd just received from Captain Johns of the Swallowtail, who was just putting in at Patri with a load of ore. Captain Johns brought the latest news from Velona down with him, though it was three months out of date by now. Still, for many sailing the southern oceans, any news was most welcome indeed. Renzo Bartiana's clear and detail descriptions of the Hieras Anubis project were highly upsetting. "The barbarians!" he exclaimed, handing the pamphlet off to his artillery captain.

The guns ship had followed Pope Christos' Royal Yacht from near Megalos down here to Demokritos. Why? Captain Dante called it a hunch. Thus far, it had been a four-month waste of time. But now? After his artillery captain finished, the two men looked at each other and then at the distant silhouette of the Royal Yacht on the horizon. Both ships had left Patri behind and now were out in the open ocean. "Are you thinking what I'm thinking?" the artillery captain asked, a sneaky, sly grin replacing the spat of anger, which had lined his face upon reading Renzo's document.

"Yes indeed. There is the mastermind of this wickedness. Hoist all sails! It's time we overtake yonder yacht!" Captain Dante decided to take the initiative. The Royal Yacht was traveling unescorted with Pope Christos aboard. "We'll take them when there are no other ships around. We want no witnesses."

Slowly that morning, the Grande Pistola began to overtake the slightly slower yacht. With her gun ports still disguised, no one on the yacht would pay the slightest concern for just another merchant caravel plying these southern oceans. Hundreds of caravels traveled these waters, trading with the three countries of the southern continent. Below deck, the gun crews prepared to fire their most important volley of their careers. By now, the artillery captain had read Renzo's paper to his crew and the ships sailors as well. "We'll get the bastard," the gun crew called out. After four months of idleness, the men pitched into action as they had seldom done.

Around one in the afternoon, the Grande Pistola finally drew alongside of the Royal Yacht. "Raise the canvas. Open starboard gun ports. Fire at will!" Captain Dante bellowed his commands. His crew hastily pulled up the lines holding the disguise canvas over the gun ports and then raised the eight gun ports. Almost at once, the gun crews pushed and pulled their eight mighty cannonae out the holes, using their many block and tackles.

On the Royal Yacht, Pope Christos walked the deck. It was summer, and the heat below deck was almost unbearable by day. For hours now, he stared at the endless wave crests on the wide ocean ahead of him. Occasionally, he glanced at the merchant caravel that had been slowly gaining on them and would soon pass them by, probably on its way to some northern port.

Suddenly, his crew began barking all manner of conflicting orders. His captain bellowed, "Hoist all possible sail!" He looked over at the merchant ship and saw eight gun ports open, eight barrels pointed directly at the side of his Royal Yacht!

"Damn, the first mistake that I've made in a half century. The Pope should always travel with an armed escort, in this case, gun ships." The rise of anger quickly abated, replaced with a serene sense of accomplishment. "Demokritos is now under our control for the next fifty years; no more southern worries. Velona will be conquered in a few months. All the Sea Princesses and the Greenway will be Church controlled for the first time in history. Even my Hieras Anubis colony is a perfect model for the future. I am leaving a most holy legacy for my successor. Indeed, I will be one of the most famous, most honored popes in history, second only to Pope Yasi I. Pope Christos will be a legend. I have accomplished so much good in the name of our Lord Jehosa."

Boom! Boom! Boom! Eight cannonae fired. At this close range, all eight struck the Royal Yacht, splintering masts, smashing gaping holes in its hull. The yacht lurched violently to starboard and then rolled back to port. Seawater gushed in through the six large holes. The yacht attempted to roll back to starboard and thus upright, but the sudden weight of the sea held her back. She leaned thirty degrees to port. On deck, sailors clung to whatever was nearby. Pope Christos held on to the railing, remaining on his feet as long as possible, resplendent in his purple robes. Slowly the Royal Yacht continued to roll more to the port. Now men began losing their grips, tumbling down into the ocean. Still, Pope Christos held on, though the ocean waters were now barely five feet from him. At last, the Royal Yacht rolled onto its side, half of its hull already underwater. Pope Christos fell into the sea; his thick, heavy robes absorbed the water, and their heavy weight pulled him under, his hands flailing against the inevitable pull of the ocean.

On January 19, 781, Pope Christos died, as his Royal Yacht sunk at sea some hundred miles north of Demokritos. Only the Grande Pistola witnessed the sinking. News did not reach us in Velona until late April, when the Grande Pistola arrived off Hieras Anubis and Renzo relayed the news to us in Velona. It would be even longer before the Church of Jehosanity realized that their pope had been lost at sea.

Chapter 22 Preludes

Here in Velona, the seeming random bombings continued, though at a slow pace. With so many innocent women, children, and a few men being injured in these terrorist blasts, Gerardo ordered the construction of the world's first Hospital Trauma Center, located in the heart of Velona. Normally, any given doctor had his own office and practice. In a time of crisis such as a bombing, where to take the injured became critically important. Gerardo borrowed the idea from the army, who set up a field tent where those wounded on the battlefield were taken.

On December 6, 780, the Velona Hospital Trauma Center held its grand opening. Essentially a converted warehouse, the hospital could care for as many as five hundred patients at one time. Normally, each doctor in Velona spent one day at the center per month. However, in a crisis time, all doctors were to report there as soon as they could. Ten days later, the hospital got its christening. Another bomb exploded in the markets, killing ten and wounding dozens. The victims were rushed to the hospital, while Cosima and Basilio rushed to the bombsite.

The next day the newspapers carried the findings. Once again, Cosima had found evidence linking the bomber to Vito. Now she and Basilio were considering the distinct possibility that the suicide bombers were being recruited from the Vito immigrant section of town. Their attempts at infiltrating that section of town were thwarted by angry mobs, which encircled those blocks. His police were needed just to keep order and prevent more innocent blood from being spilled. These terrorist attacks were becoming extremely annoying and unsettling to Gerardo and his fledgling government, who were unable to stop them from occurring.

On January 5, 781, another first occurred. Two gun ships from Megalos sailed into the port of Isla la Roca, Velona's prison colony. Located in a stone fortress upon the tiny rock of an island in the middle of the Med Sea some ten mile south of Velona, this facility held our criminals. Obviously, once sent to Isla, there was no possibility of escape, not unless one could swim ten miles in the ocean.

The two gun ships opened fire on the fortress. We now realized their motives: free all our criminals, arm them, and set them against us and our allies. The defenders opened fire with their own cannonae, of which they had ten. The hour-long battle of deafening noise ended with another first for Tarra. This was the first battle in which shore batteries sank attacking gun ships. Both went down, but not before inflicting severe casualties on the defenders. We lost ten men with another fifteen wounded. Gerardo had to send over another replacement garrison force. Yet, the victory was celebrated by all Velona. It was widely reported in the newspaper.

Worse news came as well. Our scouting merchants sailing around the bottom of the Southlands finally brought us the news that we had been dreading. Megalos Centurions were now on the move, heading our way. We got a break, in that they were marching up the long road from Sud, Southlands, heading for New Barq. Obviously, from there, they would strike at Zargarb. Already the news was over a month old — that was the time it took for caravels to bring us the news from way down south. Hastily, Gerardo followed my suggestion and sent word of this to our new allies in Juda Arad, Messiah Bani el Marina. Unbeknownst to us, the Velona Daily Times sent a field reporter along with the caravel and messenger. Thus, Julio Romez became the world's first war correspondent. His accounts of the battle of New Barq filled the newspaper for weeks near the end of February. I also suspect his accounts gave too many others too many bad ideas that were later practiced here in Velona and elsewhere.

During the first week of February, the many messiahs met in Jerilum, Juda Arad, planning their offensive against the Infidels of Megalos, who were marching up from Sud. Messiah Bani spoke often. "Look, this will be a new kind of fighting. No longer will the power of our swords be enough. These Infidels now use the long-gun and cannonae, which kill from extreme distances. Yes, I know that we have some of these long-guns, but not nearly enough. How many, perhaps a thousand at most. Our enemy will have tens of thousands as well as untold numbers of cannonae."

"What then are you proposing, Messiah Bani? Can we not defeat our archenemy?" asked another messiah.

"We must make use of the weakness of the Infidels. Long have we known that the lowly Infidel soldier only follows direct orders from their leaders. Unlike our brave warriors who seize the initiative and only need guidelines, bereft of their leaders, these Infidel soldiers will be useless and ineffective. Thus, we must use our long-guns wisely. We must strike from surprise and take out only their leaders, their officers," Bani explained his bright idea.

"Well, that should be easy. The Infidel officers all ride horses, while their men walk on foot," another messiah joked. Julio Romez wrote in his journal as fast as he could, jotting down the salient facts of this meeting.

"Yes, it is hundreds of miles from where they first cross the river into the Arad at Dakar to New Barq. We should position our long-guns along that route. Shoot from surprise all the leaders you can and then run, run away like the wind across the sands. Do not let them counterattack, do not let even one of our long-guns fall into the hands of the Infidels. When they at last reach New Barq, they must be leaderless. Then we strike and strike hard. I say that it is time that New Barq is captured. Long has this city been under the control and influence of the Infidels. Now it shall be free. New Barq is part of the Arad and must be taken from the hands of the Infidels!" His fiery speech was rewarded with uniform cheering from his fellow messiahs.

Now they set to work preparing their many ambushes. Bani knew that perhaps a dozen leaders at most could be shot during one ambush. One volley and their forces would have to pack up and flee into the sands of the desert. The return fire from so many Infidel long-guns would slaughtered them if they delayed even an instant. Fire and flee became the orders delivered to these men and women. They practiced these tactics for quite some time. All the messiahs realized that failure to flee at once would result in a hail of deadly bullets coming their way.

By the second week in February, the first of the ambush squads were in place, not far from Dakar, where the road veered to the west and a little north, heading straight for New Barq, at the extreme southwestern corner of the Arad. Each squad had twenty-five members with twenty long-guns. Five would hold the horses at the ready concealed and at a close position to the hidden twenty men. Julio Romez begged to be allowed to accompany one of these ambush squads, and finally Bani relented and allowed him to accompany the first of these squads to see action.

On February 16, the action began. Julio reported seeing the first columns of the army from Megalos marching up the long paved road to New Barq. He was with the five who held the horses behind a sand dune and some low shrubs. Using his spyglass, he watched the concealed men and women below, some hundred feet from the road. He spotted seven men riding horses, a hundred men marching along in a tight formation, two cannonae being pulled by several horses, and three wagons bringing up the rear, probably with ammunition and supplies for the many guns. Each soldier carried a long-gun over his shoulder along with a heavy backpack. He could clearly see their rolled bedding at the top of the packs.

Bang! Almost simultaneously twenty gunshots broke the stillness of the desert. Watching through his glasses, he saw all seven men fall from their horses along with one horse and two marching soldiers, which were obvious misses. Chaos erupted among the hundred men, who looked to their leaders for orders. This delay cost them any chance of retaliation. The Arads were now crawling on their bellies back to the safety of the dunes. A minute later, the breathless men and women reached Julio and their horses. Now the sounds of gunfire again broke the silence of the desert. The Infidel soldiers were shooting wildly in all directions, but they had not even seen their attackers and were just firing hoping to draw out more fire so they could kill these unseen assailants. Julio was the last to mount, and he cantered off after the squad.

Pope Christos had lied to the Senate in order to get their permission to send one hundred legions of Megalos Centurions up to the Sea Princes. He claimed that they would be used to garrison the captured Sea Prince sectors. Centurion organization consisted of a legion of one hundred soldiers, which included their captain, four lieutenants, and four sergeants.

Additionally, some were trained to man the cannonae, of which each legion had two. Each ten legions had a Brigade General in charge of that group. One General controlled the ten Brigade Generals.

After ten days of constant ambushing, the legions began arriving in New Barq with only their sergeants in charge, though many legions didn't have all four any more. Messiah Bani's strategy had worked well thus far. While the Infidels had arrived at New Barq, they were essentially leaderless.

Julio's accounts were far more sensational, descriptive, and colorful. They make excellent reading, if one is in to such things. What he had not realized yet was what Messiah Bani and the rest of his army had been doing during these past ten days. The Arad army was forty thousand strong. While some were killed by return gunfire during the ambushes after the initial ones, they had not lost a single long-gun.

As the ambush squads left for their assignments, the remainder of the host headed to New Barq. Messiah Bani's plan was simple. They would enter the city in small numbers during the course of each day, until the whole army was inside the walls of the city. True, the city had long ago outgrown the original walls. Still, if besieged, they could hold up inside, leaving those trapped outside to fend for themselves against an attack. By having his whole army inside with only the ambush squads outside the walls, he hoped for a swift victory when the time came.

Many of his soldiers stayed in several warehouses that Arad supporters had prearranged; others stayed at the various inns. Many simply hid out wherever they could. Now they waited.

Beginning on February 25, the beleaguered and weary Centurions began entering the city, thankful that they had survived all the ambushes. Of course, they headed straight for the main army barracks, which could easily hold all their numbers. The local captain began asking for their leaders and became alarmed with the news of the many ambushes. Each day, he kept looking at the new legions arriving, but saw no leaders! On the last day, the final legion marched in, followed by all those who took part in the ambushes, firing their guns. That was the signal.

As this last legion whirled to face the horde, the captain ordered the barracks emptied. He intended to put down this rebellion from the Arad. That's when Messiah Bani ordered his strike. Forty thousand to a little over ten thousand in close quarters combat with the Centurions still on foot — it became a slaughter in the streets of New Barq! Only about twelve hundred Centurions managed somehow to escape, fleeing off into the Red Desert to the southwest.

Julio's account is unclear at this point. Whether the messiahs were unable to control their soldiers or whether this was part of the overall plan, the accounts don't precisely tell us. By evening, all the many Churches of Jehosanity were in flames. All the residents whose bronze skin suggested that they were from Megalos were murdered. None more brutally than the priests of the wicked Church! Those men were burned at the stake. Julio's colorful account of the sacking of the Churches was widely read here in Velona.

On March 10, 781, New Barq was now back under the control of Juda Arad, for the first time in a very long while. Tens of thousands were killed. Enormous burial pits were dug to handle the carnage. On the positive side, the Arad warriors now had several hundred cannonae and a wealth of long-guns, plus ammunition for all. It was not until early April that the Arad army was able to begin the long ride up toward Zargarb intent on lending a hand there.

Meanwhile in Velona, the beginning of March brought another round of suicide bombings, six more to be precise. As before, they struck at the open markets, where more innocent women and children became victims. Shortly after this, the printing of Julio's narratives began. Newspapers sold like never before. Gerardo believed this widespread dissemination of what took place in New Barq plus the continued bombings was the root cause of Black Monday, though we may never know for sure.

For months, sign up posters for Rimmi's Militia saturated the city. Wherever a poster of Gerardo's asking for volunteers to help fight the Second Crusade was found, beside it was one for Rimmi's Militia as well. On Black Monday the day after the sixth bombing in this latest round, Rimmi's Militia struck.

Okay, call them more of an angry mob than disciplined soldiers; still they were an unstoppable force. Gerardo had already sent the vast majority of his army either to Barcella's front line or to d'Grange's front line. Perhaps a thousand remained in the city as they too geared up for the coming war. Basilio's police force was at half strength, so many of them wanted to go fight for our freedom. He had little choice but to allow them to take a leave of absence. If he hadn't, they would have deserted and gone anyway. Those that remained were hard pressed to maintain security at key facilities and some semblance of order.

At nine on Black Monday, Rimmi worked his militia into a fevered pitch. "How long must we stand by while this vile Church of Jehosanity brings in insane terrorists who blow themselves up just to kill our innocent? How long do we allow these sadists to mutilate our women and girls? Twenty thousand in Hieras Anubis alone. How many more, I ask you? How much longer will we let these wicked priests send money and guns to our neighbors? How much longer will we stand by and do nothing when their evil pawns of the Greenway begin their march to destroy us all?" The crowd yelled and screamed so loudly that Rimmi could not continue for several minutes.

"I say unto you, all of you, I have had enough of the evils of this god-forsaken Church of Jehosanity. Let us show these terrorists that we will not take their reign of terror any longer! Let's show them our justice! Let's show them that they cannot get away with blowing up our wives, our children! Now is the time to strike! Attack the terrorists! Show them no mercy! Those in the Arad know how to do it. Look at New Barq! I say let's burn them out! Burn their damnable churches to the ground. Burn their priests at the stake, just as the messiahs have already shown us the way in New Barq! I say let's rid Velona of these evil terrorists today. Burn them in Hell. Burn all them and then let's burn those in Vito. Let's wipe Vito off the map. Kill all those damnable terrorists, every last man, woman, and child!"

Someone began handing out lit torches and cans of lamp oil. The mob or rather Rimmi's Militia began chanting, "Kill the terrorists! Kill the terrorists!" Ten thousand marched through the streets of Velona moving out from the docks onto the main streets of the city. They headed straight for the mother Church of Jehosanity, whose spires rose higher than even our pride and joy, the Church of the Three Holy Roses.

While the Church of Jehosanity used to have a fair number of followers, after the many bombings, the news that the Cardinals were behind the Greenway war, that the Confessore were mutilating innocent women and girls, they began to doubt their church. Most had stopped going to mass, if only out of fear of reprisals from Rimmi's mobs, who had for weeks now stood around outside these churches, intimidating those who chose to enter.

Rimmi's mob was an unstoppable force. They smashed into the Church of Jehosanity. True, the Mano del Dio members fired their guns and killed a few men, but against the wave of ten thousand violently angry men, such did little but fuel their hatred even further. By the time that Basilio and his beleaguered forces arrived at the church, the mob had moved on. They found the burning bodies of Cardinal Bosto Rems affixed to a stake along with his other priests. The glorious Church of Jehosanity was in total flames. Basilio and the fire workers spent the day making sure that neighboring buildings did not catch fire. The Church was entirely gutted, only a smoke blackened shell of stone remained after the fire finally died out.

Meanwhile across the city, the other smaller Churches of Jehosanity were also attacked, their priest burned at the stake, and the buildings set ablaze. We learned later that large numbers of the mob then mounted up and took their rage out on other towns, which had a Church of Jehosanity. Within a few days, not a single church of theirs remained nor any priest. They had been wiped from the face of Velona. Yet, it did not stop there. Rimmi's Militia then packed up and left Velona, riding across country. At the time, we all breathed a huge sigh of relief. At least they are out of our hair; we had a war about to befall us, which required our full attention.

Later, someone reported to Gerardo what Rimmi had said to the militia just before they left Velona. "We know that all the terrorists come from Vito. I say all those in Vito are terrorists. Kill them all!" Had Gerardo not been preoccupied with the start of the war, he might have used his powers of deduction on this matter.

Gerardo knew from the valuable information gained from Queen Mary Beth that two caravels would be delivering the last batch of long-guns and cannonae to Calgary, just before the war was to begin. Further, the delivery had to be after the ice sheet finally broke up in the spring. The port of Calgary was ice bound for most of the winter season. Hence, Gerardo ordered five of his gun ships to patrol the waters off Fortress d'Grange, easing north into the ice. The objective was to capture of sink these caravels when they appeared. By March 15, the five gun ships finally managed to plow through the ice to just off shore from Calgary. All had expected the caravels to come sailing up the coast of Velona and d'Grange to Calgary. However, the two captains were too smart for that.

Instead, suspecting a possible interception, they sailed around the western side of West Reach and came sailing down to Calgary from the North. Both sides were taken completely by surprise! However, with five gun ships chasing them, the caravel captains wisely surrendered. Two days later, they docked in Velona. Gerardo confiscated their cargos and sent them on their way home. He had a windfall of twenty thousand more long-guns and ten cannonae — all with ammunition supplies as well. These, he put to good use, outfitting the latest wave of volunteers for the Second Crusade.

Chapter 23 The Second Crusade for Religious Freedom

Right on schedule, the Second Crusade for Religious Freedom began. The massive attack came on four fronts simultaneously at dawn on March 21, 781. Unlike the First Crusade in which as Ket Bethany, I played an active role in its fighting, in this Second Crusade, my role was more passive. Stuck in Velona far from all the fighting, I provided guidance and suggestions to Gerardo and Louis, primarily.

King Diget III led the combined forces of half of the Greenway kingdoms in the assault on Fortress d'Grange. They had to smash through there to get to the northern part of the Velona Sector. Simultaneously, Vito's General Franca Mafra led the assault into neighboring Barcella, hoping to get through that sector and attack Velona first. Similarly, Bonilla's General Tito Timus launched his attack against neighboring Pieta. His objective was to conquer Pieta, Solamina, and Zargarb. Likewise, King Ros Williams of Avon led the remainder of the Greenway kingdoms' forces eastward through the Northern Steppes, hoping to avoid fighting the horsemen and invade Zargarb directly. Supposedly, they would be aided by the Centurion legions pushing up from the Southlands. However, the Arad army had just unexpectedly wiped out those legions.

Incredibly rapidly, word spread of the assaults in d'Grange and Barcella via Arsenio's fancy new electrical signaling communications system — the LDCS, the long distance communication system, which sent electrical pulses down a wire beside the rail lines. This fast relay of news right from the front lines all the way back to Gerardo was incredible in its own right. However, it had an entirely unsuspected side effect on me.

At ten that very morning, I received an urgent message from a Mr. Gostina of the Velona Banca del Dio. He needed to see me in my official capacity as Head of World Wide Records and Approvals. Enrico insisted that he accompany me, "After all, Bethany, there's a war on now." He was teasing but I appreciated that he still wanted to be my Protector. We arrived shortly before eleven and Mr. Gostina, a portly man in his fifties, met me at the door. His face was filled with worry lines; even his speech relayed the fact that he was slightly upset.

"How do you do, I am Mr. Gostina of the Vault Department. This is really bad news, isn't it? The war, I mean. I did hope that all we were hearing was mere speculation. Oh dear me. Anyway, if you will follow me, please. This is most urgent and most trying, yes indeed it is most upsetting." I followed him and entered a back stairs, but only after he unlocked the triple locked door. Carefully, he re-locked all three before he led me down the stairs. Again, he unlocked a triple locked door, using a different trio of keys. I stepped into a spacious office.

"My office," he announced, as he re-locked the three locks. On one wall were a large number of securely locked boxes. "These are our public safety boxes, which one may rent for an annual fee. Depending on the size that you need to store your valuables, a client will choose one. They have one of the two keys required to gain access, while I have the other. We guarantee their security, here in the vault. However, that is not why I have asked you to come. No, indeed. This is far more serious, oh yes. If you will follow me, I must show you something. Very few people in the world have ever seen this." He unlocked a triple locked vault and took out another set of keys, then re-locked that vault. He led me to another door, locked in the same manner.

I stepped into another hallway with descending stairs, while he re-locked that door behind us. Again, we descended to an even lower level, carved from bedrock. At the end was yet another door. This one had six locks on it. "I have taken the liberty of retrieving the six keys from their secure locations to save time. Yes, I will replace them in their secure, secret locations when we are finished here." Once more, he began unlocking all these half dozen locks, each one different from the other. At last, he began twirling what looked like a ship's navigation wheel. "This retracts the steel bars, which are set into the bedrock."

He then took a lantern and a lighter, and he entered before me, lighting some dozen wall lanterns. I just stood and stared at the contents of this enormous room. "Here is where the Banca del Dio actually stores the excess deposits from all banks worldwide. As you know, any given bank only keeps a small amount of gold and silver in their vaults. All the excess is sent here. You are looking at the combined wealth of the world, less their spending funds, which is really only a fraction of what is here."

"Now over here are the newly minted Banca coins, gold and silver. That larger section is the various deposits that have been made over the years. When someone like those kings in the Greenway need funds, presumable to pay their soldiers, we melt the old ones down and create these official Banca coins, which are accepted universally. As you know, should a Banca find a need for some additional gold, we ship it to them from here. More often, when a Banca has accumulated funds in excess than what they ordinarily need, they ship that excess here, where it joins this massive pile. Now over there are the various gemstones that have also been accepted as deposits."

"Incredible! I always wondered just where we actually stored all that excess gold and silver," I replied.

"Yes, it is right here beneath our Banca. Only a very few people know about this vault and there are many security features in place, designed to thwart any attempt to steal the gold. As of this moment, there is the equivalent of seven hundred million plus in gold in this vault. Impressive sum. It is about twenty-two thousand tons of the stuff! Now then, the reason for your visit. It is this war."

"You see, we have specially sealed envelopes to be opened only when the criteria written on their outsides are met. This one here, as you can see, is to be opened only when Velona has been attacked by another country, which it has as of nine this morning."

"I duly opened it. I am to contact you and show you this very vault. I am to work with you and accept your guidance for the protection of this gold or its transfer to another safe place, should Velona fall. If in your or my opinion, Velona is about to be conquered, we are ordered to move this gold to a place of safety. I have no idea how we can move twenty-two thousand tons! We would need fleets of caravels. Yet, if Velona should be in danger of being conquered, we must somehow safeguard the world's money supply. Otherwise, the entire economic system of the world would collapse." He wiped the perspiration off his forehead with an embroidered handkerchief.

I replied, "Well, we would need about two thousand caravel runs at least. How many Banca caravels do we have?"

"Ah, now that I do know. Sixty-two, counting those that travel from bank to bank," he replied, thankful that I had asked something that he could answer.

"Okay. I don't believe that Velona is about to be conquered just yet. The war has just begun. However, I do know of a very safe place where all this could be stored. The problem is just how to get this much safely transferred there." I immediately thought of those caverns and tunnels beneath the Appian Way. Few on Tarra even knew that they existed. I wondered how many tons I could lift? Perhaps, if needed, I could get Linda and some others from Dorota to lend me a hand. It would be a bit strange for people to see a massive pile of gold floating out across the open spaces, but if we did it at night, we might succeed. I added, "Okay, I believe that I can deal with its transportation, should the need arise. We should stay in touch as the war progresses. If you believe that the time to evacuate the gold has come, let me know."

"Oh thank you! Thank you! I have no idea how this may be done! Twenty-two thousand tons, oh dear me, I cannot conceive how that may be done. Thank you!" he shook my hand vigorously. Yes, he was that grateful and relieved. "I must admit I was shocked to read that document ordering me to contact you, of all people. Yet, that you can see a way to transport this is a miracle that we may desperately need. Thank you. Thank you."

He then led the way back to his office and then out of the vaults, promising me that he would replace the various keys in their secure locations. I got the impression that I was not supposed to know such information. Once back with Enrico, he asked, "Well? What was all that about?"

"Linda left orders in the event that Velona is ever attacked, I am supposed to move our gold supply if Velona is in danger of falling into enemy hands." I kept it simple; no need for him to know that we were talking about the entire world's reserves of gold, silver, and gems. Once again, I was amazed that Linda had thought of everything before she handed it off to me years ago.

On the low hills around Mont Blanc and southernmost Calgary, two hundred thousand soldiers had massed ready to strike a deathblow to Fortress d'Grange and then Velona. Their encampments stretched all the way to the coast at North Point, an old Santi del Dio port, just across the border from d'Grange. The main road from Calgary to the main city, also called Fortress d'Grange, lay through a U-shaped valley. Into that valley rode the cavalry of King Diget III, King Victor Hammersmith, and King Henry Weatherspoon.

Ranks upon ranks of mounted riders began moving slowly down the road. Teams of horses followed hauling their cannonae. The three kings chose to ride after their cannonae, it being more prudent than being in the very front of their army. All three were convinced victory would be swift and decisive.

His generals insisted that Louis and Bianca remain at least two miles distant from the front lines. Using their spyglasses, they observed their brave men as well as those from Velona as they prepared for the onslaught. "I hope this all works, my love," Louis whispered to her.

"Have faith, your plan is sound," Bianca replied.

When the first batch of cavalry was well inside d'Grange and in the proper position, a general gave the signal. Boom! A distant explosion came from the western slopes. Momentarily, a second one came from the east. The cavalry looked in both directions but saw nothing threatening. If the enemy were firing cannonae, they were too far away to be hit. They rode on. Suddenly, riders began screaming, pointing in both directions. Frantically, the hundreds of cavalry attempted to turn around and gallop back the way they had come. Of course, this only caused massive confusion.

Giant dust clouds appeared closer on both sides. An avalanche of stone swept into these riders, along with an enormous dust cloud. As the dust settled, the three kings saw a mound of stone and rubble, with bits of horses and bodies protruding from the pile, along with twisted barrels of these first cannonae. Dismayed at first, the kings halted their army, attempting to determine what exactly the trap had been.

Several hours later, they sent forth another batch of cavalry, only this time they had the riders spread out all across the valley. All now were forced to bypass the rubble-strewn patch where the paved road had been. They moved further down into d'Grange and their confidence rose once more. Boom!

Once more a pair of explosions echoed in the valley. This time it was not rocks that came down but two massive snow avalanches. A mountain of white greeted the attackers as the haze finally cleared. No trace of the hundreds of cavalry could be seen.

Five more times this surprise action wiped out the vanguard of their army, before they halted for the night. Five thousand men and horses as well as cannonae had been lost, but the three kings were now five miles into d'Grange. During the night, the kings ordered other cavalry to attempt to enter from the remaining two valleys. The first one to the east was very narrow and difficult for wagon passage, while the second one even further to the east was rocky and even narrower.

The next day, similar explosions greeted those attempting the adjacent valleys. So much so that the field generals decided to discontinue along those routes, returning back to the main force. The main force encountered another snow avalanche and then the valley opened up, far too wide for an avalanche to affect those on the road. Now the advance riders encountered something different.

Ahead, they spied small stone blockhouses right out in open spaces. The road wound between them. "What new devilry is this?" one cavalryman riding point called out. As they approached, they quickly found out. Bang! Long-guns began firing upon them from these blockhouses. Every few seconds another shot rang out and another soldier fell from his horse. The cavalry began shooting back, but their bullets ricocheted off the stone walls of the blockhouses.

After a time, the three kings moved in closer to witness this new obstacle. They got to see a number of their cavalry die attempting to charge these strategically placed stone houses. "There must be hundreds of men in there with long-guns," King Victor exclaimed. "So many shots so quickly. It takes minutes to reload."

"How can that be? They are not that large. See, they fire from those small slits. I say that they are few but have many long-guns with them. Let's rush them and take them out," King Diget III ordered. The men watched as a hundred cavalry rushed to take the first of these strange structures. "How can this be? So many shots so quickly?" Only one of the hundred got to within fifty feet of the blockhouse. Bodies lay strewn on the battlefield.

For two days, the kings tried numerous strategies that all led to the destruction of hundreds of men. The blockhouses were strategically placed so that they could provide cover fire for assaults on any one of them. Steadily, they took their heavy toll on the kings' men. On the third day, the kings finally worked out an effective strategy. They pulled up ten cannonae and prepared to bombard the first of the blockhouses. "Hit them with enough cannonae balls and we'll destroy those inside," King Diget III swore.

Louis, Bianca, and his generals had already worked out how one might destroy these blockhouses containing these new MBGs. Cannonae. To counter this threat, Louis had cannonae of his own positioned behind these blockhouses. They were set up on raised stone blocks so that they could fire over the buildings themselves and yet not be easily seen from where the kings' army lay. This worked for a while, since they focused their attention solely on the stone houses.

As the enemy cannonae prepared to fire, Louis' general gave his order to fire. Boom! Ten cannonae fired almost at the same time. Shortly afterwards, the ten balls landed and exploded, sending nails and shrapnel flying in all directions. Many of those men manning the cannonae were killed or wounded.

Now the artillery barrage began in earnest. Shells flew in both directions, raining death explosions. However, this was the signal for the defenders within the blockhouses to evacuate, taking their precious MBGs with them. Using the cover of the artillery barrages with mountains of smoke obscuring the field, the fifty men in each blockhouse raced back down the valley out of reach from the enemy fire. There they put the MBGs into wagons and moved on down the valley, setting up at the next set of blockhouses barely a mile down the road, but around a sharp bend.

Louis knew and had planned for the loss of the ten cannonae. There was no way to evacuate them once the artillery barrages began. Protected in part by the blockhouses in front of them, their losses were drastically less than the opposing gun crews. By the end of that day, Louis' first set of cannonae finally fell silent, but the kings were in no position to do more than advance to the blockhouses, which they found incredibly small on the inside and completely empty. This fact only further confused all three kings.

Bianca and Louis were saddened by the loss of nearly one hundred fifty brave and valiant cannonae gun crewmen. Yet the kings lost twenty times those numbers on this day alone. Not all was going according to plan. Three days into to the battle, they had taken but three miles of d'Grange valleys! The cost in lives was staggering.

Three more similar days followed with nearly identical results. Louis had built four rows of these blockhouses, each about a mile or so from the next. His losses, as expected, were forty cannonae and their crews. Yet by now, the three king's armies had been quartered! However, the valley widened too much for such a strategy, and Louis and the Velona generals switched to a new strategy.

Embolden by the sudden change in the valley, the kings finally felt that they were making progress. They sent out their cavalry in large numbers, spreading out across the valley. Unknown to the enemy, high on the rocky slopes to the west hundreds of Louis' soldiers lay well protected with a supply of pre-loaded long-guns nearby. On the east slopes, equally well protected a strong force of Velona's soldiers waited with a supply of guns at the ready. Behind those in a firing position was another larger batch of soldiers whose job would be to reload the fired weapons.

As the enemy drew withing range, gunfire erupted from high on both slopes. A steady stream convinced the kings that many men must be well hidden on these slopes. While they could use their cannonae to blast them, King Diget III realized that if they kept to the center of the valley, they would be outside the range of the long-guns. They could effectively bypass these soldiers, who would then be unable to do more than retreat deep into the mountains, if that was even possible. They'd effectively be out of the battle.

Now all bunched towards the center of the valley, the lead riders encountered a new and devastating obstacle. Taking a clue from all the bombings in Velona, Louis had his engineers prepare bombs, which would explode if sufficient pressure was placed upon them. These bombs were then placed at random locations here in the central area of the valley. When a horse stepped on one, it detonated. While he really hated to harm so many horses, the army had to be stopped. These random explosions took out several soldiers each. This was now the first use of land bombs anywhere on Tarra. Yes, this war was introducing many firsts for our world, of which I most definitely was not proud. There had been no reasoning with these kings, who were dead set on conquering us.

Four days later and thousands of lives later, the three kings finally reached the end of this ambush zone. However, for days afterwards, explosions continued to plague those troops coming up from behind as well as their supply wagons. Two weeks into the campaign and with the loss of a third of their original soldiers, the kings finally reached the main fork in the road.

The road continued heading south and would eventually enter Velona. The spur road to the west wound down the valleys towards the coast, where the huge city of Fortress d'Grange lay, and its twin fortress towers spiraling skyward. The small bay with its docks lay beyond them. Here, the kings had to make a choice. Having lost so many men, they were ill pressed to split up and go both ways.

"We must bypass the fortress," King Victor said decisively. "We have not enough forces to take it and Velona at the same time."

"True, we can bypass it for now and then return later, once we join forces with Vito," King Henry added.

"We cannot just bypass it!" King Diget III countered. "Think, you fools. If we just leave them, surely after we pass by, their cavalry will ride out and cut off our precious supply wagons! We can't allow that to happen."

He paced around in a tight circle and then spoke suddenly and decisively, "Here's what we do. King Henry, you take ten thousand of your remaining Karka forces and head on down there. For god's sake, don't attack the twin fortresses! Your job is just to keep the d'Grange army pinned down there. From down by the seacoast, there is nothing that they can do to harry us or our supply wagons up here. Just keep them pinned down there. Once we take Velona and join with the Vito army, we will return to you and then crush them utterly."

Unknown to these kings, at Bianca's request, I had left my body back at the estate and had arrived here at the forks. She had asked me to eavesdrop on their plans, if possible. Louis and the generals from Velona had to know precisely what the kings' next move would be. It was critical. Between the two sectors, they had approximately forty thousand soldiers guarding each of the two paths. If the entire army chose to attack d'Grange, then the Velona generals had to move out of their prepared positions and take the risky approach of attacking the rear of this army as it assaulted d'Grange. Conversely, if they chose to bypass d'Grange, somehow Louis had to move the bulk of the forty thousand to assist Velona.

There was a coastal route that Louis' soldiers could follow, which eventually led to another valley system that lead into Velona. From there, they could head on up to the front lines to aid the Velona defenders, but that move would take days, and thus Bianca's request for my assistance. I relayed what I overheard to her, and she, to Louis. I also relayed this to King John of Southway, who was no longer holding up in his castle in Middleton. He wanted revenge for the savage mutilation of his cousin Mary Beth and his sister Ann. I gave him an opportunity.

Now the fighting became far rougher. The Velona generals wanted to make their stand while still here in the mountains of d'Grange. Once the enemy reached the northern edge of the Velona sector, near Alta, the terrain became hilly, and we lost all our major defensive positions. From then on down to Velona, the battle would be even up. We could not protect such a vast expanse of relatively open territory with many towns and villages.

Our forces were positioned high on either side of the valleys where they had a clear line of sight of the enemy cavalry. Our cannonae were also positioned here. Many had done test firings and had the range down pat. Their shells would land in the thick of the enemy forces. Thus began the slaughter of men and horses. For every mile that the enemy took, they lost thousands of men and horses, while we lost hundreds as well. Worse, there was no way to get to the wounded, stranded high on the slopes. Many whose lives could have been saved bled to death for want of aid. Yes, it was a horror filled two weeks. Still, at the end of that time, thirty thousand from d'Grange finally made it to our rear, which greatly aided us.

During that time, King Henry proceeded on down the winding valley road towards the seacoast. Occasionally, these riders spied the ocean and even the tops of the twin fortresses. Still, the remaining defenders continued to ambush the lead riders as often as possible. Their tactics were to strike hard and then retreat further on down the valley, until finally they reached the twin towers and prepared for a long siege. By the time that King Henry sat on his horse and overlooked the twin towers near the entrance of the walled city, he had lost a third of his small force.

However, that was not the worst of his problems. His greatly needed supply wagons were days overdue. Soldiers carried two days' rations with them and those were long gone. His supply wagons ought to have been here yesterday, but failed to arrive. His men grew hungry and irritable. That morning he had sent three riders back up the road to see what was holding up their supply wagons. It was near evening now and they had not returned, which worried him even more. Nothing about this campaign was going according to King Diget's Grand Plan, he mused. In fact, things seemed to be going in favor of the defenders, if that was possible. Still, two hundred thousand to forty thousand in d'Grange and perhaps slightly more than that in Velona — they should be winning decisively. Yet here he was, stomach growling, and they were not winning at all. He also worried about a possible counterstrike from d'Grange. If there were forty thousand down there, he only had seven thousand or so now. He would have to flee in utter disgrace!

At dawn, he rose hungrier than he could ever recall. He used the latrine and listened to the constant gripes from his soldiers. "I'm starving too, so shut up about it!" he yelled angrily back at the soldiers. Just then, an explosion sounded from the rear of his army, spread out along several miles of the road. More explosions, he recognized that sound: cannonae! "What's going on?" he yelled. His aides rushed to him, but were just as confused as he. King Henry ordered a dozen men to ride back there and find out what fool was wasting ammunition. Dozens of cannonae explosions echoed down the valley to his ears. After what seemed an eternity, a couple of riders returned.

"It's King John's army! They are right behind us, firing their cannonae into our troops!"

"Oh dear god!" King Henry exclaimed. His aides looked to him for their orders.

"Damn, here comes the d'Grange army!" someone yelled. King Henry whirled around. His worst fears had manifested themselves! He could see thousands of troops charging out of the twin towers, heading up the road towards his position. While he had perhaps a half hour to prepare, he froze. With King John at his rear and Louis at his front and tall mountains to either side, he was trapped, utterly trapped! There was no way out! He and all his remaining men would be completely slaughtered, if only by cannonae fire!

"What do we do? What do we do now?" an aide screamed, pulling King Henry back into the horrible present.

"Damn! We do the only thing possible. Hoist up white flags! We surrender. Send riders back up the road; spread the word. For heaven's sake, wave white flags if you want to live!" King Henry issued the only possible order. He did not intend to become a dead martyr for King Diget III.

An hour later, King John and Louis, with Bianca at his side, rode up to King Henry, who still held a white flag, waving it before the King and Louis. "I surrender! I surrender!" he called out, facing one direction and then the other.

King John dismounted and drew his sword. Walking up to King Henry, he ordered his men to restrain the king. "Hold his arms out," King John ordered. "King Henry, death is too good for you for what you have done to my cousin Mary Beth. Your Confessore had both her arms cut off! Now she is a helpless woman for the rest of her days!"

"But I didn't know," King Henry pleaded, but he lied. He knew well enough what they were going to do to her. He was promised that she would be taken to Hieras Anubis where she would spend the rest of her days. His lie did not go undetected.

"Lying unto the end, eh. Feel then my judgment upon thee, foul Henry Witherspoon!" King John cried out. With a flash of his blade, he sliced off one of Henry's arms, another flash and his remaining arm was severed. King John was a very strong man with a very sharp blade and an equal sharp vengeance. King Henry screamed and wildly jumped about, blood gushing from what remained of his upper arms. As two field doctors approached to deal with his wounds, King Henry saw his future. Healed, he would be utterly and completely helpless, at the mercy of everyone around him. He made his decision. He dashed to the edge of the nearby cliff and jumped. He fell some fifty feet, smashing into the boulders below. "So be it," King John said solemnly. "At least my cousin is not the coward that her ex-husband is. She is alive and doing well, thanks to Bethany and others. Well met, Louis, Bianca." At last the two monarchs shook hands and began to bring order to the field.

The next day, Louis' ten thousand joined up with King John's forty thousand and together they headed on down the road towards Velona. They would attack the rear of the army, taking King Diget III by complete surprise.

During this same time period, King d'Aine of Ruadan, Highlands, landed his army of twenty thousand on the shores of Westfold, by the coastal village that we had used to escape Westfold last year. In advance, he had sent a message to both King Hugo of Westfold and King James of Blaine that he was going to land an army at their northernmost land and march overland to Brownsville. Why? He was determined to take back Queen d'Aine's kingdom for her, Brownsville. Further, he intended to destroy all priests and Churches of Jehosanity in all of Brownsville! That was the least he could do for Kathleen. During late April, his forces swept through Brownsville doing just that. By the end of April, every church and every priest was destroyed or killed. Queen Kathleen later retook her throne, though he left her five thousand soldiers to protect her and keep order.

What of King Diget III and his offensive? By April 25, having lost another half of his men and with the arrival of King John and Louis at his rear and with no food deliveries for two weeks, he finally admitted defeat and raised the white flag.

Once again, King John attempted to get revenge for his sister, Queen Ann, but King Victor overheard several of King John's men explaining to the others from Velona what he had done to King Henry. King Victor made an instant decision; he pulled his pistol and fired it into his head. No way was he going to become the spectacle that Henry must have been! On the other hand, King Diget III was shipped off to Isla la Roca. The battle for d'Grange and Velona was over here in the north.

On the eastern edge of the Greenway, King Ros of Avon, King James of Urkut, and King Helmut of Redun led their combined army of some hundred fifty thousand across the Elbe River from Melantas into the Northern Steppes. In olden days, the Czar may have just ignored this army as it began following the river down to the Arad and thus Zargarb. However, in recent times, these nomads had finally begun establishing permanent cities. Lying directly in the path of this army were Kelnosky and then Meslokov. Further complicating life for the Czar was the simple fact that Velona and d'Grange had come to his aid when the army from Tashien invaded his lands some twenty years ago. We had completely handled that impossible situation for him, and he felt more than obligated to come to our aid now.

The problem he faced was one of long-guns. The enemy had them, while his valiant cavalry had only a few thousand of these newer weapons. He'd pretty much given up on the one shot handguns, which proved very ineffective years ago. Now facing a multitude of long-guns and cannonae, his brave warriors would be easily slaughtered if they met the enemy head on. In his favor were fifty cannonae acquired over the years. In addition, Zargarb had already sent some twenty thousand troops to aid him. These were positioned north of Kelnosky and were sworn to protect that city. Zargarb promised another twenty thousand once they dealt with the Centurions coming up from the Southlands.

The Czar had only one real option, place the majority of his forces, especially the cannonae, north of Kelnosky with those of Zargarb and use the balance of his forces to cut the enemy's supply lines. The three kings were well aware of the supply problem and arranged for two methods for delivery. The usual wagons would follow in the wake of the army, while small river boats would float down the Elbe River. One or the other ought to get through, they figured.

The Czar had scouts constantly watching the advancing army from the moment they crossed the river into the Steppes. Thus, the defenders had solid information on their enemy's strengths and tactics. Once the supply wagons began crossing several days later, the bands of the Czar's cavalry swept down on them. No supply wagon ever made it to the front lines.

The river boats became more challenging. They were bombarded with hails of arrows, some flaming. Yet, there was little the horsemen could do to stop the boats. Over half of them got past them, bringing much needed food to the army.

By early April, the three kings' army finally reached the opposing army of the Czar and Zargarb. The Zargarb generals, while they had no direct war experience, did have history from which to benefit. Long ago, their predecessors had fought off a vastly superior army from Demokritos. Renzo, in an earlier lifetime, was there at that battle and had made sure that all the details and tactics were written down for posterity. These materials were a mandatory study for anyone from the rank of captain on up to a general. Now they put this to good use.

With the Czar's permission, they chose the battlefield, knowing that the Greenway army would likely be inexperienced in the art of massive warfare. Their one hundred fifty cannonae were positioned in protective bunkers on the tops of three hills, which overlooked the field upon which the enemy would be coming. In the valleys between these, they placed all their thousands of long-gun soldiers, hoping to prevent the enemy from breaking through. The Czar then positioned the bulk of his horsemen several hills further east, ready to attack the flank or rear of the enemy army using their age-old tactics of bows and sabers.

As expected, the three kings led their forces down the path of least resistance, the easiest travel, the center of the valleys. The Zargarb generals were patient and withheld their fire as thousands of the enemy poured into the valley between the three hills. Only when the front lines were almost to the ranks of long-gun defenders did they give the order to fire at will. All the cannonae shots were shrapnel bombs. Each volley into the middle of the enemy swarm contained one hundred fifty of these explosive shells. Combined with the continuous volleys of the long-gun squads, a third of their entire army was lost within the first hour of the battle!

The Zargarb generals had worked out an effective tactic for long-gun utilization. The real problem with them was the two-minute reloading time. That is, once one shoots, two minutes are needed to reload and be ready to fire again. Two minutes against charging cavalry would be devastating. Hence, their new tactic was to have five parallel lines of firing squads. The front row would fire and immediately get down on their knees and begin reloading. The second row behind them would rise and fire their volley, then get down to reload, similarly with the third, fourth, and fifth rows. By the time that the fifth row had finished and began reloading, the first would be ready to fire again, rising up to shoot once more.

The net result of this firing tactic was devastating to the enemy ranks. Between the random cannonae blasts from the tops of the three hills and the nearly continuous long-gun volleys from the two valleys in between the hills, the three kings lost one third of their forces within that first hour and were forced to attempt to withdraw from the battlefield valley.

Those in the rear now trying to reverse course ran straight into the charging thousands of nomad warriors. Having been able to get in close to the enemy's rear, the enemy was unable to wield their long-guns effectively, especially while galloping. The horsemen of the Steppes were masters of shooting their short bows while riding with no hands as well as the use of their sabers. Thousands died there in the rear.

When the three kings discovered what was happening at the rear of their long lines, they took the only option left to them. They gave the order to charge due east and attempt to break out and around these forces guarding the city of Kelnosky. This worked and saved them from a complete rout. Although when they regrouped far to the south and east of Kelnosky, barely half of their original soldiers were with the kings!

Now the defenders faced the more difficult challenge of chasing after the enemy forces. Since the Zargarb generals now knew that river boats were getting past the Czar's forces, they positioned fifty of their cannonae such that they could blow any river boat out of the water. These gun crews were left with the orders to sink any boat that came floating down the river, which they did.

The three kings decided that the enemy would likely have a similar defense around Meslokov in the south. Hence, they countered by moving southeast some hundred miles, moving far out onto the Steppes. Still, the Czar's scouts continued to watch their every move, and there was little the three kings could do about them. All this delayed their advance considerably.

Down south, the Arad warriors finished off New Barq and began riding north to the aid of Zargarb. The remaining Zargarb forces, having learned of the total wipe out of the Centurion army, were now free to assist in the defense of the Steppes. Consequently, their remaining twenty thousand soldiers rode north to the Dragon's Teeth, a set of razor ridges that formed the natural boundary of the Arad and the Steppes. Here, with the protection of the rock formations as cover, they prepared their defenses. By the time that the three kings drew close, the Arad swarm had joined them, bringing the defender's total to nearly sixty thousand, including some two hundred cannonae. The three kings now had barely seventy thousand remaining, and all were extremely low on supplies, especially food. They had hoped to rendezvous with their supply boats where the Elbe River met the Dragon's Teeth, just before entering Zargarb and the Arad.

Not only were their supply boats not there, but also the defenders were present and ready for them. Worse, the remainder of the Czar's army and the other half of the Zargarb army were barely miles behind them. A reasonable commander would have surrendered at this point. The three kings were not reasonable, however. They chose to order their cavalry to smash through the defenders on the Dragon's Teeth.

At first, the hundreds of cannonae fired volley after volley at the charging army. Those bombs exploded left and right. Soldiers and horses dropped out of the battle like flies. Hearing the noise of the cannonae, the Czar and the other Zargarb generals ordered an all-out charge to catch up and join the battle.

Brutality and slaughter. Those were the words that Julio used in his articles that were published in the Velona newspaper in later weeks. When the cannonae stopped firing and the acrid fumes cleared from the battlefield, every last man of the enemy army, kings included, lay dead on the ground. The Czar's men went from man to man, killing any that remained alive. Yes, the allied forces also lost men as well, some three thousand killed and five thousand plus wounded. It took days to bury all the dead soldiers. Julio wrote and wrote in his journal for days, attempting to depict the horrors of modern battles. Eventually, these were published in our newspaper, in the vain hope that it would help prevent future wars.

On the Barcella side, thirty thousand soldiers of Barcella were supported by a like number from Velona. Between them, they had close to six hundred cannonae and two dozen of the new MBGs. Defensively, more than a century ago, Barcella, following the advice of the Santi del Dio, constructed a series of fortresses along their entire border with Vito. Each fortress was independent and commanded a wide field of view and thus battlefield. Roughly twenty miles apart, during peaceful times, cavalry from these garrisons always patrolled the border with Vito. Now they were packed with thousands of troops. No matter where the Vito forces would strike, a fortress would have to be taken or their lines of supply would be cut the moment that they passed by a fortress controlled area of farmlands. Our problem: we had no idea of the size or make up or quality of the Vito army that would assault us, let alone where they would strike.

General Franca Mafra had long studied the defenses of Barcella. He'd made a scale clay model of the border fortresses and now had a good estimate of their strengths and weaknesses. Barcella was not a densely populated sector, a bit on the small side, area-wise, always living in the shadow of its neighbor and protector Velona. He anticipated that Velona would come to the aid of Barcella the moment that his army launched an attack. This, he took into his calculations and plans. It would be foolhardy to strike out down the coastal road and rail line, cutting straight for the city of Barcella. If he did that, the combined forces stationed at all the other border fortresses would surely sweep down behind his army, cutting off supplies or worse.

No, he could not ignore these fortresses. He wanted the coastal road for obvious reasons. Thus, his main strike force would be centered there on the two fortresses that protected the road and now the new rail line. However, he would also send sizable forces to each of the other fortresses and attempt to lay siege to them. Those commanders were under orders not to do more than hold the defenders inside the fortresses. Once he had captured Barcella, those in the fortresses would be forced to surrender.

The Church of Jehosanity had given him two hundred fifty cannonae. Of these, he put five on each of the seven outlying fortresses, just enough to do some wall damage and keep the occupants locked inside. The remainder he divided between the two coastal fortresses that he had to smash. He sent one hundred to the fortress that was five miles north of the road and one hundred fifteen to the one directly beside the road.

He had been steadily growing his army, taking all the young men from every village and conscripting them into his army. With the help of the Church, they were armed with long-guns. Half were on foot, half rode every available horse he could scrounge. He now had sixty thousand or so soldiers ready for the first strike. In Vito, he had hundreds of wagons ready to begin the supply of his army.

When the day came, seven thousand were assigned to the seven northern fortresses, one thousand each, just enough to keep the defenders occupied. The balance he split between the two fortresses that he must take and take quickly. He put twenty-five thousand before each; they were very densely packed. The balance of his troops he had handling the many supply wagons, many of which had to travel long distances from Vito to get to the northernmost Barcella fortress.

As he rode behind the first wave of his assault force along the road leading eventually towards his prize, he felt supremely confident. The suicide bombers that the Church had sent to Velona had surely demoralized them completely. He had wished that they had also bombed Barcella heavily, but the Cardinal refused his suggestion. Why? He had no idea.

The Barcella and Velona generals were waiting and prepared. Instead of holing up within the fortresses, they had their forces spread out across the hills, valleys, and light forests between the two stone monsters. Their hundreds of cannonae were in bunkers to help protect them from enemy fire. Also with them were the MBGs, which would be used to prevent these bunkers from being overrun. Like Zargarb, the long-gun squads were utilizing the same tactic. Five parallel rows of soldiers, heavily supplied with ammunition, waited behind earthen trenches. When they kneeled to reload, the barrier would protect them from most enemy fire.

As the Vito forces drew close to the two fortress towers, General Franca Mafra was taken by surprise. He had not anticipated the defenders would be out in the open. Hence, he ordered an all-out charge. The cavalry rushed to enjoin combat, while the foot soldiers began running. The defender's artillery opened fire and random battlefield explosions began blowing horses and men aside. The general expected this, that's what artillery does. However, once his cavalry and foot soldiers reached the artillery bunkers, they would wipe out the gun crews and then mop up the enemy foot soldiers that were standing in a long line across the fields. Good plan; didn't work.

Much to his dismay and the death of his troops, when the cavalry came within long-gun range, the MBGs and the long-gun squads began firing. "Okay, they get one shot and then my cavalry are on top of them before they can reload. I have them now!" he yelled, supremely pleased. One shot followed the next shot followed the next shot! One line of soldiers disappeared and another line appeared, firing their deadly volley. Closer to the cannonae, which continued to devastate the more distant ranks of his troops, long-guns continued to fire every few seconds. How could there possibly be that many soldiers there? He just couldn't fathom what was happening.

Worse, he had his army packed in so solidly that the artillery fire was far more deadly than it should have been. At last, he ordered a strategic withdrawal from the battlefield; half of his army was gone. Now he ordered the only thing remaining: a charge around the northern fortress, penetrate into Barcella, and worry about supply lines later. He had to pull the defenders out of their prepared positions. This worked; his cavalry rode on past the northern fortress. Now his foot soldiers hastened to follow them.

Sitting along a ridge line five miles from the battlefield, ten thousand Velona cavalry waited patiently. The generals had anticipated that the Vito general might try to bypass the fortresses and had positioned their remaining reinforcements here. As their commanders spotted the cavalry breakthrough, they mounted up and galloped off to intercept them. This time, it was hand-to-hand sword battles from mounted men; all were too close for long-guns. The poorly trained Vito soldiers stood little chance against those from Velona, many of whom were passionately angry with Vito, having lost relatives in the spat of suicide bombings.

Late in the afternoon, General Franca had no choice but to order a full retreat back into Vito to regroup. Only a third of his army remained. He hastily sent recall orders to the other seven thousand troops. During the ensuing few days, those troops returned, but with the combined Barcella and Velona cavalry who had been stationed at those fortresses hot on their tails! The general and his remaining troops took over Vito's westernmost small town of Demira, some five miles from the border. Here the general planned to regroup and try to work out some new strategy. He was very shaken by the viciousness of the defenders artillery and the incredible long-gun power. The general still could not believe what he had seen, so many long-gun shots from almost no soldiers. Did his enemies have some new and terrible weapon?

For ten days, the general waited in Demira for the remainder of his forces to return and regroup. The wagons of supplies were arriving daily. His troops reveled in food and drink, which they now had in gross abundance. During these ten days, the Barcella generals and those of Velona made the decision to follow the Vito army, hoping to encircle them and finish them off completely. Thus, leaving only a skeleton guard at the fortresses, they left the border wide open, as their combined forces moved south to encircle the town of Demira. Pundits have speculated for years what might have happened had they remained at the fortresses.

By the second week in April, the town was entirely surrounded and cut off. All the remaining Vito soldiers were holed up inside. Frightened townsfolk fled in all directions and were allowed to pass through our lines. Then, with their hundreds of cannonae in position, they began shelling the town. Inside, the enemy cannonae tried to fire back, but were relatively ineffective. Positioned at the edges of the town, these batteries were the first casualties of the massive bombardment.

Five days later with the town in near rubble, a shell landed on the general's position, killing him. General Franca Mafra died still wondering how all this could possibly have happened. What new super weapon did Velona and Barcella have?

On the other side, Bonito launched its invasion of Pieta. With only thirty thousand troops, they depended upon the three Greenway kings to bring a mighty army to assist them. Pieta had mustered forty thousand; Solamina, another thirty thousand. Many of these had answered the call for the Second Crusade. Unlike the other battles, this one was very traditional. Both sides lined up their forces and charged into the other.

Outnumbered two to one, Bonilla surrendered on the third day. Both sides lost thousands of men, with thousands more injured or maimed for life. Yet, these Second Crusade volunteers still managed to shout and cheer and hold wild celebrations on their victory.

Chapter 24 Rimmi's Militia

Rimmi screamed to his masses, "We go to wage war on the terrorists! We all know that all the terrorists came from Vito. Vitos are all terrorists. I say kill all those in Vito! Death to Vito! Death to all terrorists! Kill them all! Burn their churches. Kill the terrorists! Kill every one of them! Never again will we allow Vito terrorists to bomb our wives and children! Never. They all must die! Show no mercy! Their terrorists showed no mercy to our defenseless women and little children. No, they did not! Hell no! Show them in Vito no mercy at all. If you don't have the stomach for this, stay behind in Velona. The rest of us who want to stop all these terrorists from maiming and murdering our women and children, follow me! Death to Vito! Death to terrorists. Kill every last one in Vito!"

He had worked the militia up into a frenzy. Men screamed, chanted, and yelled the war cries. Kill the terrorists! Kill everyone in Vito! Show no mercy!

Now armed and ready, Rimmi mounted his horse and his men followed, still yelling wildly and chanting. Off they rode. Rimmi knew that they could not ride down the coastal road through Velona and Barcella. The war was likely being fought there. No, he had it all planned out: how to kill all the terrorists in one sweep. He led his band up the spoke roads of Velona, occasionally following a rim road, until they reached the border of Barcella. Here, they were very nearly at the northern edge of that sector, where very few people lived, mostly shepherds. He raced across the hills, valleys, and gullies, and at last approached the northernmost stone fortress of Barcella, just beyond it lay Vito, home of the terrorists.

The handful of soldiers left to garrison the fortress could do nothing but watch Rimmi's Militia sweep past them. They estimated there were some five thousand men riding hard, chanting, "Kill the terrorists!" They sent a dispatch off to warn the Barcella generals of this, but the notice would not reach them for days.

Rimmi reached the westernmost rim road of Vito. He led his army down it, knowing that eventually they would reach a town. Once they did, they would begin to get their much-desired revenge. Vito terrorists would die, all them, before they could bomb Velona again!

Finally, they reached a village of five hundred. Like a bunch of wild banshees, Rimmi's Militia swarmed into the village yelling and screaming their familiar chants. An hour later, they left the town. Everyone there was dead; the small Church of Jehosanity was in flames. During the next few days, Rimmi split his forces into four parts, so that they could cover more towns. Two went further along the rim road before taking two of the spoke roads southward. Rimmi led his two bands south, and then sent his second band off on the next rim road. Their standing orders were to rendezvous on the outskirts of Vito itself and together eliminate all terrorists in that city!

Word began to spread throughout Vito of the genocide being committed by Rimmi's Militia. I won't repeat what the Barcella and Velona generals said when they heard reports coming in from the outlying towns. They were tied up dealing with the surrender of the Vito army, but they had no choice but to send out several thousand cavalry with orders to stop them by any means possible.

Rimmi's Militia was finally stopped. Attrition took its toll on them, as men fought back in the larger towns. Rimmi and a quarter of his original men made it into Vito and stormed the main Church of Jehosanity there. They set the church ablaze and killed the cardinal and all those within the church complex. However, a Mano del Dio managed to kill Rimmi in the process. The cavalry arrived in time to prevent further massacres and arrested the remaining five hundred men. Ultimately, they were sent to Isla la Roca. Their crime: genocide.

All told, Rimmi's Militia murdered well over ten thousand men, women, and children — the majority was the latter two, since most able bodied men had been forced into Vito's army. Stories of the horrors of the genocide circulated widely around the Sea Princes and into other lands as well.

People argued for decades about it. Vito had sent suicide bombers into Velona, murdering women and children there, so why not return the favor? That was the most common justification for it. Most of us cringed when we heard of the genocide of Rimmi's Militia.

Gerardo accepted the responsibility for Rimmi's actions. "Hey, I ought to have seen it coming and have taken steps to prevent it," he explained to the newspaper reporters and the emissaries from Vito. "After all those terrorist bombings done by suicide bombers from Vito, the seething anger and hatred was quite visible. Naturally, they wanted to fight back and kill the terrorists. Unlike an enemy army, the terrorists do not wear uniforms announcing that they are the terrorists. In their anger and grief, so many men of Velona equated all people living in Vito with the terrorists and struck back. Yes, it is a sad day for the whole world. In my own defense, I was preoccupied with the larger war situation. Still, I ought to have taken some decisive action to prevent Rimmi's Militia from taking the law into their own hands. As a result, I am not asking Vito to make any war reparations at this time. Use your funds to help rebuild the destroyed towns and villages. Use your funds to assist those who were harmed and yet live."

As he finished, I began to clap. Hearing my lone clapping, many others joined me in acknowledging Gerardo and his decisions. He definitely appreciated our moral support.

As far as war reparations are concerned, the six kingdoms and the

Church of Jehosanity were held responsible. Since many of the kingdoms had used up almost all their funds, we made their local church accounts cover their payments. Still, money cannot replace or recompense those whose lives were lost. At least financially, those of us who had to defend ended up not losing vast sums of money.

Chapter 25 Aftermath

Word reached the Church in Urkurt of the King d'Aine's actions in Brownsville. Likewise, the churches in Redun and Karka heard about the slaughter of Brownsville's priests and cardinal, to say nothing of all their magnificent cathedrals having been burned. Hastily, Cardinal Edward Williams sent word of this down to Avon's Cardinal Ames and then sent orders to all his priests in the various towns and cities of Urkut. Satisfied, he packed all his valuables, and accompanied by his two Mano del Dio guards, his Confessore group, and his local priests, he fled Urkut in haste.

They headed down into Redun, hoping there to catch the paved old Centurion road and travel through Brownsville and on into Calgary, where he presumed that they would be safe. The road represented the fastest route to presumed safety. Likewise, the other cardinals took similar measures. By the middle of April, all were at various locations on the Centurion road heading towards Calgary. Yet only Cardinal Cecil Mir of Mont Blanc and his group actually made it into Calgary.

Although King John was down helping to put an end to the war in d'Grange and Velona, he left a sizable force monitoring the Centurion road. Their orders were very specific, and they carried them out with gusto, which is why these groups of religious leaders never made it to the safety of the Church of Jehosanity in Calgary.

When King John began moving north after the war was over, he stopped in Mont Blanc. He quickly discovered that the church leaders had fled to Calgary. He sent a dispatch to King Claghorn demanding the return of these murderous men to face judgment. Unfortunately, Queen Winnie was a Mir and against King John, though now she had to face the fact that they had lost the war. Still her acid tongue convinced her husband, King Claghorn, to deny his request. He replied, "This was supposed to be a Crusade for Religious Freedom. Under that banner, I have granted them sanctuary in Calgary." King John cursed, but knew that he had either to accept this or go to war with King Claghorn.

After some thought, he chose a third route. He sent some of his most trusted men into Calgary, disguised as simple merchants. Their assignment was to keep an eye on the Church and take any opportunity to assassinate both cardinals and any Confessore they could find. Two months later, they returned. Mission accomplished. By the end of the year, only two cardinals remained in all the Greenway. The kingdoms of Westfold and Blaine retained theirs; they had been neutral.

With Brownsville now secure, King d'Aine brought Queen Kathleen home to her castle and put her back on her throne. Of course, now she began to have suitors, for whomever she chose to marry would become king of Brownsville. This time, Kathleen took her time.

King John sent dispatches to Queen Ann and Queen Mary Beth, stating that their kingdoms were now secure and that they could return to their thrones and rule, if they still desired to do so. In the meantime, Gerardo, Louis, and King John appointed provisionary rulers to oversee the other five kingdoms who had lost their rulers. Similarly, Gerardo and Andriano Barcella appointed a provisional ruler for Vito, while Pieta and Solamina did likewise for Bonito.

By mid-May, the soldiers began returning home, and the newspapers carried Juilo's war reports, a new one each day. Velona began celebrating its victory. A party atmosphere lasted for over two weeks. During the middle of all these festivities, a messenger brought King John's letters to the two queens, while shortly after that another messenger brought a notice for the three mischief boys.

Ann, Mary Beth, Luigi, and Pietro were out running laps around the estate when the messenger from King John came. I accepted the package and headed off to interrupt their run. As the four came around the side of the estate, the two boys were attempting to tickle the two women. Suddenly the two turned on the boys and began chasing after them, threatening to tickle them back with their feet and heads. All four were laughing and quite happy. At last I interrupted them.

"Okay, take a break, kids. Ann, Mary Beth, you each has a message from King John," I called out.

"I suppose we had better go read it," Ann tried to stop laughing. Soon, all four panting runners came up to me. "Damn! How am I supposed to open it and read it?" Ann had a flash of helplessness appear again. Mary Beth quickly lost her joviality as well, staring at the package in my hand.

"Oh use your foot," Luigi half teased and half suggested.

"Yeh, use one of yours," Pietro added to Mary Beth.

"Easy for you to say," Ann shot back playfully, but slipped off her shoe and reached up. I stuck it between her toes, but it slipped out as she lowered it. Luigi was about to say something, when Ann gave him a dirty look, "Don't you dare say anything!"

"What? Me? Say something like why don't you sit down and open it?" Luigi teased her back. She couldn't hold back her mirth any longer and broke into a laugh.

Mary Beth struggled mightily and managed to get her message safely on the ground without dropping it. "See, you are more dexterous than your cousin," Pietro teased her. "What's it say?"

"Mind if I open it first, big boy?" she teased him back.

I allowed both women to open their messages by struggling at it with their feet. I hoped that the boys would allow them to do it themselves. This was always the hardest thing for those of us with arms to do — allow those without arms the opportunity to do some action their own way, no matter how awkward it was or how long it took. Their self-respect and independence was very important at this point in their lives. To my surprise, both did not interfere at all. Sitting on the grass holding the paper with their feet, both women read King John's message to them. Both messages were very nearly the same, stating that their kingdoms were now safe for their return. They could have their thrones back, if they so choose.

"Well, Queen Ann, that's a mighty fine offer," Luigi said, though I detected a note of sadness in his voice.

"Yes, Queen Mary Beth, now you can have your throne back," Pietro said in a similar manner. "I know that we can trust King John. If he says it's safe, then it probably is, though Luigi and I are both terribly disappointed that we didn't get a chance to go conquer your countries back for you two."

Queen Ann read the dispatch a second time, before she looked up at Luigi. "Well, it says if I so choose. It is a fine offer, Luigi. However, might I have a second offer?" she winked coyly at him.

"Yes, Pietro. Do I have a second offer to consider besides this one?" Mary Beth grinned.

It took a second for her words to register in Luigi's mind. Suddenly, a big grin appeared and he sat down beside her. "Yes, there is a second offer. Ann, will you marry me?"

Not to be outdone, Pietro dropped to the ground and added, "Second offer, Mary Beth. Will you marry me? Say yes and we can continue enjoying life."

Ann looked at Mary Beth and smiled, "Mary Beth, I have two offers. It is so hard to choose," she teased. Luigi looked pathetic and she relented. "Yes, Luigi, I would love to marry you as long as you do not make me have to be queen of Mont Blanc!"

"I promise," he said, but all other words were cut off by Ann's passionate kiss.

"Same with you, buster, I will marry you, on one condition," Mary Beth said seriously.

"What? I promise anything," Pietro pleaded.

"That you never try to make me be Queen of Karka ever again!" He swore and they embraced.

"Say, now wait a minute, ladies. You were the queens of your kingdoms. Are you sure that you want to throw that away? I mean, don't you have some responsibility to help your kingdoms recover from having been disastrously misled?" I thought that the mischief boys might be taking advantage of these two women and their unique situation.

"Look," Ann said seriously, "I rather married into that position. I wasn't elected or anything like that. Besides, I don't have many body parts to donate to the cause. I don't dare lose any more! I've lived one lifetime as a queen, albeit a rather short one. I've had enough of it. It is a man's world of rulers, not women's. We really don't have much direct control or say, just look pretty, dress nicely, and handle domestic type issues whenever they come up. Run the castle affairs, handle the cooks, and make sure the servants put clean sheets on all the bedding at the proper times. Even if I were to go back, the men would be pressuring me to remarry so that they would have a new king who would really run the affairs of the kingdom. Further, as I am now, I cannot even sign official papers. No, Bethany, I just do not want to go back to that kind of a life again."

She went on, "If I am ever to be even slightly independent again, I have still so very much to relearn how to do. Luigi has shown me that there is so much more to life, so much fun to be had, and so much happiness to experience and to give to others. It may be selfish of me, but right now, I want to be happy. I want to live my life to the fullest that I am able to, while helping others as I best that can and not be so utterly dependent upon everyone around me, especially Luigi."

Ann added, "I hate to have to do this, but Bethany, can you write back to King John and tell him my position? About all that I can do so far is rather scribble my name. I'm sorry to have to put you in such a position. If you don't want to do it, I can beg Luigi to do it for me."

"If you resort to begging me," Luigi teased her, "I will have to tickle you until your face turns blue!" She grinned.

"Okay, Ann. I do understand. I just wanted to make sure that you were rejecting the offer for good reasons. I think that the world would be better off if we women ruled everywhere, and we had our men be subservient to us," I replied half in jest, half-serious.

"Now wait a minute," Pietro interrupted. "You want me to wear the dresses?" Everyone roared with laughter.

Mary Beth then asked, "Bethany, I feel the same way as Ann. This experience has wakened me up to life. Never before have I felt so alive as I have been here, especially around Pietro. Like Ann, I may be being selfish, but I am resolved to be happy for once and truly enjoy my life and those around me. I know that I have so very much to learn how to do by using all these alternate ways, but with Pietro's help and yours and everyone else's, I am going to master it and be able to live a halfway normal life. Until now, I never knew how humiliating it is to be so completely and utterly dependent upon the kindness and assistance of others for nearly everything in daily life. I am determined to somehow rise above it all and be as independent as I once was and then, with Pietro's help, do what I can to assist others in need. Like Ann, Bethany, I must ask you if you will be kind enough to write back to King John for me. I cannot even write my name yet, but I can make an X at the end for you."

"Okay, ladies, consider it done. You both have my blessings on your engagements and on your decisions. I think that I speak for everyone here as well. We are all backing both of you one hundred percent. Now, why don't you gentlemen take your brides-to-be inside and tell all the others of your engagement?" They didn't need to be asked a second time.

"Can I interrupt?" Enrico came up with another pair of messages. "These were just dropped off for you two, Luigi, Pietro. I've already given Nicolo his."

The boys ripped theirs open and read, while Ann and Mary Beth looked over their shoulders. Both were to appear tomorrow morning at ten at Gerardo's office to receive a medal for their invention of the MBGs, which had been pivotal in our recent war.

"But I don't want a medal. I just did my part for the defense," Luigi complained. I ignored his protest and sent them off with Enrico to make their announcements along with their engagements, while I headed to my room to draft the two replies.

At ten, the three mischief boys and the rest of us arrived at Gerardo's office. He smiled and led us all outside, where a huge crowd had gathered. "Ladies and gentlemen, it is with great pride that today I am presenting three of Velona's young men with the first-ever Freedom Medallions for their stellar invention, which greatly aided our ability to successfully defend Velona, d'Grange, and Barcella. Unlike so many of you, they were not on the battlefield. Rather, these men had the foresight to realize how devastating these new long-guns would be in the hands of our enemies. Seeing just how deadly our enemies had become, they put their heads together and invented a powerful counter-weapon, their multi-barreled long-guns or MBGs as we now call them. Their MBGs were put to the test in the defense of Fortress d'Grange and were highly successful in helping stop the charging army. To these three young inventors, we owe our eternal thanks. Without their MBGs, our casualties would have been far, far higher than they were. Their MBGs have drastically lowered the losses of our brave men on the battlefields. It is with great pride and personal honor that I present these Freedom Medallions to Mr. Luigi Angela, Mr. Pietro Bartiana, and Mr. Nicolo Smythe."

One by one, he placed the heavy golden medallions around each of the three young men's necks. Then a band of musicians struck up a lively tune and the large crowd clapped, whistled, and cheered. All three boys basked in the attention, as I suspected the mischief boys would.

Gerardo then took me aside. "Bethany, on June 1, Andriano Barcella, Louis, and I are going to meet with King John up in d'Grange to discuss the official settlement of the war. The new appointees who will be taking control of the six kingdoms will be there as well. Could you possibly come with me to the meeting? I feel strongly that your input may be needed."

"Yes, of course. Train?" I asked. He nodded. My, how we have become so dependent on Dianna's steam trains in so short a time.

Chapter 26 Hieras Anubis

By November, Renzo felt a little more secure down in Hieras Anubis. With the gun ship still anchored just off the bay and with the arrival of four new cannonae and two hundred Velona soldiers, he and Len began to relax a little. For days, they expected another assault from Megalos and the Church of Jehosanity in an attempt to regain their captured city.

Caravels still came to the port. Most dealt with trading goods, but at least four came every month unloading new groups of mutilated women and their children. Most were coming from either Megalos or the Sea Princes, primarily Vito and Bonito. He realized that with the port of Calgary now iced in for the winter, they wouldn't be receiving more from the Greenway at least. Still, the ever increasing numbers of new women continued to put heavier and heavier loads on all the able-bodied men of Hieras, many of whom were now taking responsibility for two additional families besides their own. Renzo certainly held these men in the highest respect, but could do so little to alleviate their monstrous work and care load.

He and Len fully expected another attack. Already a caravel flying the flag of the Church of Jehosanity had sailed past the bay with only a jib flying. Obviously, the captain was surveying very carefully what the situation actually was here in the town. Our gun ship took no action as that caravel made no threatening moves, and several hours later, disappeared heading east by south under full sail.

"Well, assuming two weeks to return to Megalos and allowing for another two weeks to get from Megalos to here, we have a month to prepare for another battle, it seems," Len commented to Renzo.

"Maybe a little longer," Renzo suggested. "They might have to figure out what to do, make preparations, and then load first. Where will they strike and with what and in what numbers?" he asked.

"Good questions. The more that I think about it, maybe they will not try to attack us by sea. There is one gun ship out there, which did sink their other caravel. We are due to get another gun ship here soon. If they are planning to attack us by sea, they ought to bring along at least four gun ships. I know that I sure would. After all, the ground forces cannot land until our gun ships are taken out," Len pointed out.

"Yes, and they will need to bombard our cannonae installation before they can even presume to dock a caravel with soldiers aboard," Renzo added. "Have they got that many gun ships to spare? I wonder if they have already sent their flotilla of gun ships up north for the coming war? They can't be in both places at once."

"Point taken," Len conceded. "Perhaps, they will attack us another way — overland. Look, we came here overland. Why can't they come that way as well? It was a bit tricky landing where we did, west of the small village of West Anu. We really ought to go take a survey of the lands around these settlements and bays. Let's see just how defensible this place is from an overland attack." Both he and Renzo were quite bored and took this as an excellent chance to do a little exploring.

"We've got it covered, dad," Nico teased Renzo, when he told the others about their plans to do a little scouting around. If any trouble came, Kallisto or Ania could easily contact them by telepathy if needed.

Borrowing the two horses of the Elders, the two packed supplies for several days and headed off to West Anu first, where they had originally landed by dingy. After a good survey of that area, both concluded that a major invasion by a large number of troops would be very difficult to execute here. At best, they would have to land by dingy, four to six men at a time. To unload say a thousand troops would take days to get them all ferried ashore, ignoring any kind of reasonable supply line. Then again, perhaps they would not be concerned about supplies, since they could confiscate what they needed from the villagers.

Arcing around the large basin valley of Hieras Anubis proper, the coastal range really was a formidable barrier, except for the valley trail that led up and over the mountains to the savannah, which we had used last lifetime to return the Utu princesses to their homes. Down this trail, an entire army could easily march!

Two days later, they reached the edge of East Anu. Here the coastline was even more treacherous than that west of West Anu. Both concluded that the landing of troops would be even more challenging and difficult here. The coastal terrain was passable, however, but not for cannonae or wagons. Both concluded that the enemy could land sizable forces miles east or west of Hieras Anubis and then march along the coast to the attack. However, they could bring neither their cannonae nor reasonable supplies with them.

"If I was going to invade, I'd come down the valley from the savannah," Len advised Renzo, who agreed with Len's analysis.

"Yes, I think a couple of nighttime guards at each of the two outer villages will be enough. If they see anything, they fire off a shot with their long-guns. That will be the signal that something is wrong," Renzo concluded.

"Good plan, but what about overland across the savannah?" asked Len. "How the devil can we guard and protect against such an assault? Our main cannonae face the ocean. They could drive an entire army down that valley road from the savannah. By the time that we know about it, thousands could be swarming upon us."

"Good point, obviously at this point in time, that is our weak link. I guess we could station some soldiers up on the savannah, but then how would they communicate to us?" Renzo began speculating.

"Only if one of us went with them, but I am leery of sending you or me. We're needed here. Kallisto or Ania perhaps, but then they would be a sitting duck if there was an army from Megalos coming that way," Len pointed out.

"Well, there are some others that we possibly could ask for aid," Ania suggested. The men had returned after their five days of exploration and had briefed everyone, including the two Elders.

"Okay, I give up," Len said, unable to fathom who he had been neglecting. That a Judger may have gotten the better of a Protector rather annoyed him.

She smiled, "The Utu. We made friends with them and did them a great service by returning their princesses to them. If we can find them and if they remember us and if we can work out some arrangements, they could patrol the vast southern savannah and alert us if soldiers are marching or riding our way."

Ania continued, "They might remember me, although I am much older now. If they do, that will very likely help convince them to aid us. They wanted cattle, as I recall. Say, does Stephanos Straton still raise cattle on the Veld close in on the Coastal Range? Back then, he used to ship cows back to Megalos quarterly, using the port of Cape Hope, er that is Hieras Anubis."

"Yes, he still does, but now we buy at least half of the cattle he has. Around the middle of November, he brings another herd down the valley trail where the soldiers meet him and conduct the transaction. Usually, we keep about half and send the other half by caravel to Megalos," Elder Damon answered with a hopeful note. "They ought to be coming in about six days or so."

"Then, we had better get going on this," Ania stated flatly, knowing that Renzo and Len couldn't object. "Renzo, I'll take you with me. Len, you take a batch of soldiers and the funds to pay for the cattle and wait for them at the edge of the savannah. If we are successful, we will meet you there with the Utu, who will take some of the cattle as their payment."

Although there was plenty of additional discussion, her plan prevailed. She and Renzo packed substantial supplies on their horses, while Len and ten soldiers did the same, only they used two packhorses. By noon the next day, Ania and Renzo waved goodbye to Len, who along with the soldiers, began to make a camp there by the entrance to the descending valley, which led down from the coastal range into Hieras Anubis.

Ania and Renzo then nudged each other's memory on the route that we had taken with the wagons carrying the princesses. After five days travel to the northwest, the savannah began to give way to hills with some trees. "This looks sort of familiar," Ania suggested a hopeful note.

"Yes, I think I recall the spread of those trees against the savannah backdrop. We must be getting close," he replied.

As night began to fall, Renzo whispered, "Ania, we are being watched. Ahead and to our right. Careful." They rode a hundred yards further.

Suddenly, two dozen brown-skinned Utu warriors leapt from their hiding places in the tall grass, spears pointing at the two riders. Renzo raised his hands in a sign of peace, as did Ania.

"We came to find the Utu chief and the Utu Princesses. I have been here before, many years ago and helped return your princesses and a lot of cattle," Ania spoke, desperately trying to remember their language. As Renzo recalled, we had a good deal of difficulty speaking to the men and had to use the princesses as translators, because we had only learned the strange language of the Utu princesses. They motioned for us to dismount and we did. Poking at us with their spears, they began to lead us into the nearby trees.

Before long, we heard drums and chanting and knew that we must there. Men with spears surrounded us; they looked at us threateningly. Ania quickly spoke, "Iou, Ada, Iua? She repeated the names of our three favorite princesses who had helped us so unselfishly many years ago in Demokritos. At last, the chief grasped the words and sent two runners off to some large huts. Shortly they returned with twenty of the Utu princesses.

These princesses as a group were just as we remembered them. All wore brass spiraling rings around their necks, creating the illusion of long necks. Each wore a set of lip plates; the top ones were larger than the bottom ones. Renzo and Ania recognized Iou immediately. Yes, she too had aged some twenty years, but her face and eyes were just the same as we remembered. Both Ania and Renzo were very surprised to see the size of her lip plates now. Her top plate was at least sixteen inches in diameter, while her lower plate was about eleven. In spite of having her front teeth, top and bottom, removed, the weight of the plates forced themselves to droop downward at a forty-five degree angle.

"Iou! It is Ania. You look just as alive as when we last brought you and your princesses home with all those cattle! Yes, I know, a miracle has allowed me to get new arms." Iou recognized Ania and came over to her and gave her a loving hug. She touched Ania's arms and squeezed them to see if they were real. Her eyes displayed her smile, though her lips could not. She made some clucking noises and Ida, Iua, and the others whom we had brought back came out to warmly greet Ania and to feel her arms, in disbelief. Seeing that the princesses knew us, the chief grunted, and the men with the spears backed off and returned to their evening meals.

Iou tugged on Ania's arm, leading her into the princess' hut, while Renzo was led over to the men's fires and offered some dinner. Ania chatted with the princesses who wanted to know how the others were. Eventually, Ania began to explain to Iou why she had come, though she kept her words fairly simple, since she'd forgotten much of their unique language, made all the more difficult by their enormous lip plates.

"The bad men have cut off the arms of many, many women down in the town were we docked the boat. Many, many women. We came and killed the bad men who were holding them prisoner. Will be a long time before boats can come to rescue so many, many helpless women. Now we think the bad men will try to attack us from savannah down the valley pass where we came up from the sea." Ania went through this several times until all them grasped what she was saying.

"We came here to ask your chief if he will send out watchers to see if soldiers come onto the savannah and come to valley to attack us. We will pay him with many cows. Can you explain what we want to the chief?" Iou was only too pleased to do so; it meant even more cattle for her. Ania learned that now Iou was their top princess, the leader of all their princesses, primarily because she had the largest lip plates and the most cattle.

After about thirty frustrating minutes, complete with many drawings in the dirt, the chief finally understood our needs. Via Iou he explained his terms for his aid. He wanted five hundred cattle and to give Ania princess status. Apparently, because of her continual assistance to those women who were desperate for help, Ania just had to be given the Utu's highest honor, that of a princess.

"Well, it isn't so bad," Renzo tried to soften the blow to Ania. "Besides, when we get back, perhaps Sandra can work her surgical magic. If not, then there is always the Guardian. He's not let us down yet. Think of this as a temporary honor, Ania."

She had no choice but to agree. The next morning, Renzo headed back to where Len and the soldiers were waiting. His task was to cut out the five hundred head and have them ready for the Utu, who would be along in a couple of days. At the same time, the chief sent out a number of warriors, loaded with supplies for a long trip. These men would be his eyes across the vast savannah. He promised to send word to the soldiers waiting at the valley's edge if any runner spotted any soldiers moving across the savannah. He also said that they would not attack the soldiers unless they came too close to their Utu Nation. Renzo and Ania agreed, telling them about the sticks that shot metal and killed from a long ways away — far better than bows and arrows. They did not want these Utu men being killed by the long-guns!

After seeing Renzo off, Ania was led back into the princess' hut and they began to work on her. At noon, they presented Ania to the chief for formal recognition and approval. Ania now sported a four-inch top lip plate and a slightly smaller lower plate. Her neck was held tightly in the brass spirals, and she could only move her head from side to side at most. She looked just like the other Utu Princesses except she had very small plates for a woman her age. Ania had begged them not to knock out her teeth, explaining that she would do it later when the plates got too big. They granted her this small favor, as they had done to Dita and me so many years ago. Ania noted that they took extreme precautions to make sure everything was sterile and used a salve, which Iou explained was a healing balm. She was given a small pot of it and told to put it on her lips each morning before she put the plates back in. The salve would speed healing.

The next day, after many hugs and farewells, Ania mounted up and rode back to the others, accompanied by a dozen Utu warriors, who came along to protect their newest princess. Five days later, she had to deal with others seeing her new look and was frustrated by her speech difficulties as well as eating and mobility. Once the Utu men left, she carefully unwound the brass spirals, glad to be able to move her neck once more. There was little she could do about the slit lips except to follow Iou's orders with the salve and lip plates. Once home, perhaps this could be undone, she hoped. Meantime, once her lips healed, she stopped wearing the plates and lived with the strange looking lip loops that dangled in front of her mouth.

They waited two more days and a dozen men arrived, herding seven hundred head of cattle. Renzo paid them and they left, but not after staring long at Ania's unusual looks. He then had Len and half of the soldiers drive two hundred on down to Hieras, while the rest waited. The next morning, the Utu warriors arrived so silently that they were not even noticed until they began to move the cattle. Ania spotted them and waved. Broad smiles on their faces, they waved back to their new, revered princess.

"That went well," Renzo commented. "It seems that you are now one of their princesses." Ania gave him a glare that could kill. "Okay, it is just that you can see it in their faces. Come on; let's get back to Hieras. The soldiers will remain here to alert us if the Utu come to warn them. We'll send another six to replace them when we get back. I figure five days of mindless duty up here is more than enough at one time." Ania grinned, but noticed that nothing physical occurred because of the tight lip plates. "Grr," She thought to herself, and couldn't wait to remove them.

Around the middle of December, I relayed to Renzo the new tactics that Gerardo's generals had worked out for the squads of long-gun soldiers. Namely, form them into five lines with only the first line firing first, and then they knelt and began reloading while the second rank rose and fired. Renzo then set to work drilling and training his two hundred soldiers. He discovered that someone had to give the orders so that the continuous action went smoothly. Each day, they practiced and drilled.

Meanwhile, he and Len began working up defensive positions for the cannonae. They had five new ones now and decided to place them at the sides of the basin where they could bombard the incoming soldiers who would be marching down the trail in the valleys from the savannah. They decided to position their long-gun squads squarely in the middle but down range from the cannonae, where a small rise would shield those who were kneeling and reloading their weapons.

Time passed and the new year came. Still no word had come about any invasion, and Renzo began to feel more relaxed. Maybe he and Len were just paranoid about the Megalos church. Perhaps, they had just written it off. Still caravels came with more mutilated women. Their frequency of arrival had not changed at all during their whole occupation, save perhaps an increase some months back. Were they now just dumping their victims onto us? Renzo wondered.

On January 15, he and Len were discussing their situation again. Len said, "Look, if Megalos is going to send soldiers up to the war, which is to start in late March, they are going to have to leave for there pretty soon. If they are transported there by caravel, it will take a whole fleet to do that. If so, they ought to be leaving in another three weeks at most. On the other hand, if they march up the Southlands, they need to get underway in a week or so, I would expect."

"Ah, so if we get by another month without an attack, then we may not be attacked at all?" Renzo said questioningly.

"Be my guess," Len replied. Bang! A lone gunshot sounded in the distance. "Damn! That's the warning shot. I guess they are coming now." The two rushed outside, where many others were not looking around, wondering what was happening. The soldiers knew what that shot meant and began grabbing their weapons and gear. The group began running through the streets of Hieras, heading for their prepared positions at the far end of the valley, several miles distant, just beyond the village of Second Chance. Soon clear of the city, they slowed down and began the long walk. It was several miles to their chosen spot, well clear of any of the homes of the inhabitants. Renzo did not want any collateral damage among these desperate people. They had suffered enough.

By the time that they arrived in the central valley position, a rider came galloping up to them. "The Utu indicated that a large number of soldiers are riding towards us. Impossible to get them to tell us how many, just a bunch. The others are going to wait there a little longer and head back when they can better judge the enemy's numbers."

"We have time, men," Len pointed out. "Get yourselves set up. Then, head back to town and bring up some food supplies and water. We may be here a while."

By evening, our other five soldiers came riding down the valley. Their report was encouraging, at least a little. Around three hundred soldiers with long-guns were riding towards us. They camped for the night at the start of the valley where our soldiers had been camped. Apparently, they would attack us mid-morning.

Ania and Kallisto joined us, bringing some hot supper. "Nico will be along later, once he puts their daughter to bed," Kallisto said to her husband, Len.

Having taken her lip plates out so that she could mostly speak understandably, Ania added, "Kallisto and I will launch balls of fire into their midst. Where should we position ourselves?"

Len and Kallisto took the right flank of our five lines of long-gun squads, while Renzo and Ania took the left flank. "Can you sleep?" Ania whispered.

"Nope, not before a battle. We need to be alert in case they try a nighttime attack," he whispered back. Dawn came as well as breakfast. Surprising them all, two dozen women carried a hot breakfast up to the front lines using their yokes. They wanted to show their appreciation for what these brave Velona soldiers were doing for all of them in Hieras. The soldiers smiled and thanked them repeatedly.

Around ten, we heard the sound of many horses long before we first glimpsed them riding four abreast down the wide valley trail. As they entered the extreme northern edge of the Hieras basin, they halted and surveyed the scene before them. Our lines of soldiers could be plainly seen by these men, but they failed to spot the five cannonae far off to the left and right of their position. Apparently, they figured this would be easy, and they began to gallop towards us, holding their long-guns in one hand. "Lousy way to fire them," Renzo commented. "Okay, steady, wait for my signal." Once the first riders had moved about a quarter mile down the basin, Renzo waved a red flag.

Boom! Boom! The five cannonae began their softening barrages. Explosive shells landed among the charging soldiers. Horses and men went flying. As the first bunch approached the central defensive line, Renzo gave the order to begin firing. Simultaneously, Ania and Kallisto began casting their Druwid balls of fire, as the first rank fired their long-guns. Enemy soldiers dropped like flies, as expected from a single volley of the deadly bullets. What the enemy did not expect was the second rank rising and firing within a few seconds of the first!

They had expected to take some losses, but had anticipated that their remaining riders would overtake and smash through the defensive lines before they could reload their long-guns. Bang. Bang. The second volley dropped more. Then, the third rose and fired. Boom! Boom! The cannonae fired again, raining more death upon the charging enemy ranks. Now the enemy began shooting wildly at the front ranks of the defensive line as the chaos of battle grew.

Horses galloped through the five ranks of our soldiers, some of whom now pivoted and fired at their backs. Ania heard the clash of swords, but continued shooting her spells, even though she could no longer see any actual targets. The accumulated gunpowder smoke and dust from the explosions had obscured the entire battlefield. The cannonae ceased firing. An eerie silence followed; all ears were somewhat deadened to natural sounds. The noise had been deafening.

Groans and moans came faintly to Ania's ears as she tried to hear and see. Slowly the smoke and dust began to drift aside, revealing the bodies strewn over a half-mile long path of the battlefield. She saw Len holding his shoulder, Renzo, likewise. Both were looking around trying to see as well. The central lines had taken the brunt of the casualties on our side. Ania saw the five gun crews racing down from their positions on either side. She heard Len yelling, though his voice sounded faint and distant. "Make sure that they are all dead!" She saw Kallisto moving towards Len and that jarred her back to reality. Ania headed over the bodies to Renzo.

Renzo had taken a saber slice to his right arm. Quickly, Ania wrapped a piece of her shirt around it to stem the blood loss. She looked over at Kallisto, who yelled back, "Gun shot to his shoulder." Again, her voice sounded dim and distant.

"Damn these wars anyway," Ania said.

"What?" Renzo yelled. Ania shook her head.

With some efficiency, Ania and Kallisto began arranging the wounded into a priority lineup. They had some twenty wounded men to handle. Five were dead. They paid no attention to the three hundred soldiers from Megalos, though Ania did see one of their soldiers thrusting his sword into a fallen Megalos man.

"Five dead, twenty wounded," yelled Len to Renzo. "Not bad. Damn, my shoulder hurts like the devil." Kallisto looked up at Len and shook her head. "Make that six dead," Len yelled again to Renzo. Soon, Ania had some of the men create make shift stretchers from their blankets and long-guns. The more severely wounded were carried back into town, while Len and Renzo walked back along with ten others, leaving the rest of their soldiers to deal with the battlefield cleanup.

By nightfall, the two women had worked their magic on the nineteen wounded men, all of whom would recover in time. "You don't have to feed me," Renzo complained to Ania, who was at last spoon feeding him some dinner, compliments of many of the women in Hieras.

She smiled, "Okay, I am just glad my hearing is getting back to normal. I need a long hot bath. So does everyone else, but don't you dare get that wound of yours wet! Bethany will have my hide if anything happens to you." She was partly teasing and partly serious. He grinned and began trying to eat with his left hand, finding it a bit more difficult than he'd imagined and wishing that he had not said anything to Ania.

The next day, both men had their arms in slings. Accompanied by the Elders, they walked back to the battlefield. The soldiers had done a good job, but the burial details were still at it. They had confiscated another two hundred salvageable long-guns, a pile of ammunition, and over a hundred horses, not to mention numerous other smaller items, which could be put to good use. While they were examining the organized pile, a long bell sounded, signaling another arriving caravel.

"Damn, we are totally out of position," Len cursed, as they began to retrace their steps back into Hieras and to the docks, more than three miles distant. By the time that they arrived there, the cannonae crews were leaving their posts and began to report. It seems a caravel from Megalos slowly drifted past the bay and then hastily left the area. "Well, they know that their sneak attack has failed. I wonder what they try next?" he added.

As the weeks past and the end of February approached, caravels continued to bring more victims to Hieras. However, their frequency and the numbers of victims began falling off sharply, much to the pleasure of Renzo. None showed up at all the last week of February. Everyone began to believe the end of the mutilations was at hand. Not quite, another two caravels came during March, but only carried one family each, women with their young children as always.

Now Renzo and Len began complaining, "The war is about to start, and we're stuck down here!" Len griped.

"Damn it. You don't have to remind me. We ought to be back home, but I don't see how we can possible leave," Renzo replied, somewhat disgusted that a permanent solution to the Hieras problem had yet to be found.

That very day, March 10, 781, a caravel from Dorota docked at Hieras Anubis. Five Elders had brought twenty-five women with them. Each one proudly wore a golden medallion around their necks, which read: Givers of the Holy Gift. The Guardian had sent some help! Half of the women were in their forties and armless, while the other half were young women in their late teens or early twenties and their arms were normal. Their job was to deliver therapy session to all those who needed it, which was well over twenty thousand men, women, and children.

The Elders quickly explained what they were going to do, namely follow the same pattern that we had used, that is Dita and I, when we were on Dorota. Train fifty women to deliver the therapy sessions, have them deliver them to each other. Once those were done, those fifty would then tackle fifty more women, giving them the therapy sessions. Meanwhile, those from Dorota would oversee the sessions and train up another batch of fifty women.

Actually, these Givers of the Holy Gift were extremely efficient and very well trained. While we had expected that they would get fifty trained each week, as it turns out, they trained over two hundred. By the middle of April, over three thousand had their traumas fully erased and were off giving others theirs! Ania then estimated that everyone here would be handled by the middle of July! When I heard about this, I was extremely pleased and contacted the Guardian to thank him. Shortly after that, Ania awoke one morning to find her slit lips were fully restored. She could find no trace of a scar. He'd touched her during the night, and she sent him a big thank you.

I relayed the news of the various victories as they occurred, and Renzo and all of Hieras were very relieved to hear of each one. I admit, he was a bit testy about being stuck down there while all the action was going on up north. Still, I know that he was pleased that he had helped make things go right for these badly mistreated people.

For a whole month, no new caravels brought more victims and everyone thought that the end to this diabolical sadism had finally come to an end. That changed when the alarm bell sounded on April 20.

Chapter 27 Selene Omela

Selene slipped in and out of consciousness. It was dark; she was moving. The fuzziness cleared from her mind. She recognized that she was in a carriage. Her stomach tightened; fear slipped its tendrils around her as she remembered fighting off someone. Yes, she was in her bed, a rag over her face. Now she was jostling in some carriage. Slowly, she grasped the fact that she had been kidnaped!

She tried to call out for help but now felt the tight bonds of a cloth gag over her mouth. She bit down on it to try to chew her way out of it. If only she could yell, maybe some of her subjects would come to her rescue. No use, it was too thick. She sat up and strained to see. Yes, there was someone sitting across from her, but who? It was too dark to tell.

Now her waist ached, slowly drowning out her fear. Why had she tried so hard to honor her son at his wedding and worn this most restrictive corset? She knew why. She had wanted to have a fourteen-inch waist to impress her son's bride. That was it. Now she was paying the price; breathing was difficult and her ribs ached. Such constricting pressure. Yet, she still wore her fancy new emerald satin dress with its sixteen-foot hoopskirt. She felt her shoes on her feet. At least, she was still properly dressed. Now she remembered. She had been so exhausted from the wedding that she had just collapsed on her bed and fallen asleep. Perhaps if she had not, she might not be here in this carriage, she thought, but that led her to the awful thought that she would still be here only in her nightgown! At last, she dozed.

The carriage stopped; the lack of motion woke her. Dim light entered the carriage from pulled blinds. Across from her sat a woman of the Church of Jehosanity, a nun she thought. She was awake and looking at her. "Ah, you have awakened. I will remove your gag if you promise not to yell and scream." Selene nodded and the woman leaned over and untied it. "Here, have some water." She held a cup to Selene's lips. Her mouth felt like leather and she drank.

"My name is Alexina and I will be your nurse for this trip. Do you need to use the chamber pot?" Selene desperately did. Shortly after that, a man's hand handed in a basket of food through the door. Selene thought that she saw buildings and the sides of a street. Where was she? Where were they taking her? Why?

The carriage began moving once more, and the nurse opened the basket and helped herself to breakfast, while also feeding Selene. She was a little hungry, but ate little. Her overly tight corset still throbbed at her ribs and hips. She felt full relatively quickly. While the nurse finished her meal, Selene asked, "Where are you taking me? Why have they kidnaped me? Do you know that I am the Empress? Someone will pay for this with their life," she added a bit defiantly.

"We know that you used to be the Empress Selene. Pope Christos has appointed your son and his new bride to be our new Emperor and Empress. You are being taken to a special colony for women such as yourself, where you will learn how to take care of your own needs, to feed yourself, get dressed yourself, and such. They tell me that you might even be able to learn to write, though I honestly don't see how. It is called Hieras Anubis. This will be a long journey, at least three months, maybe more. So sit back and relax, Selene. If you cause trouble, they will gag you or worse, put you back to sleep."

"Are you telling me that Pope Christos ordered this done to me?" Selene asked, completely shocked. In the back of her mind, she had sensed something might happen, which is why she had visited the Banca del Dio recently.

"Yes, His Holiness spoke to me about it — the very pope himself! He wants you to have the best second chance for a rewarding life. That's what he said. Hieras Anubis will give you that second chance," the matronly nun replied, obviously awed by the personal visit of Pope Christos.

"Don't I get a say in where I am to go? I don't want to go to this place. I want to go back to my own home and run my business. Look, I have money. I will pay you and these men anything. Just let me go, please," Selene began to beg.

"I'm sorry, but we cannot do that. Pope's orders. Now sit back and relax; we'll be in Patri in no time."

Selene was shocked. This woman would not take money to set her free. Maybe the men would. During the next few days, she took every opportunity to convince the hand that brought them their food baskets to set her free in return for quite a lot of gold. Her pleas were ignored. Selene quickly realized that they intended to put her on a caravel. Patri was a very large port city. Once on an ocean going ship, she would have no chance of escape or being set free. She tried all manner of begging and pleading and bribing during those few days, all to no avail. Her heart sank as she began to hear sea gulls and smell the scent of the ocean.

"Sorry that we have to do this, but we cannot afford to have any scenes here at the docks," Alexina explained as she put that weird smelling rag over Selene's face. Once more, she tried to stop the nun, but soon drifted into a deep sleep. She didn't see the men carrying her body wrapped in a blanket onto the caravel and taken below deck into a cabin. The nurse followed behind them.

Selene awoke to the gentle rocking of the ship. She heard various odd creaking sounds of the heavy timbers of the caravel as it slid through the ocean's waters. She opened her eyes and found herself lying on a small bed inside a small cabin. The nurse was sitting beside her bed, dabbing at her forehead with a wet rag. At least that felt good, Selene thought. "There now, awake again. I'm sorry that we had to do that to you again. But no matter, we are now at sea. The captain says that we will make Hieras Anubis sometime in April. So you just lie there and enjoy the three month ocean trip. I am in the next cabin. If you need something, just holler. I will leave you now." The nurse rose and left the cabin, closing the door behind her. Selene's heart sank as she saw the doorknob. Even if she had wanted to leave this cabin, she could not possibly open the door. At last, grief overwhelmed her, and she began to cry softly to herself.

Depression set in. Pope Christos himself betrayed her! What had she done to deserve his betrayal? Selene had an eidetic memory, and she began looking back over her life to see what she had done that would have caused His Holiness to betray her. The only thing that she saw was her refusal to remarry. Indeed, as she looked back over the pope's reactions to that, Selene realized that was what sparked her trip to the Banca. No matter how she looked at things, this was a male dominated world when it came to rulers. True, Demokritos had had sole female Empresses in the past, but like Selene, she had not lasted very long either. "He just could not have a woman running the country," Selene said bitterly to herself.

With nothing to look at but the small cabin walls for three months, Selene found herself looking at her near photographic memories of her life. She saw how full of life she had been as a little girl, how she had excelled in her father's business, and how happy she had been during those years when she had her arms. As she looked over the memories of her first marriage to Omela, she realized that it was her own urge to gain more power that had caused her to desire to become a Holy Woman of the Eighth Degree. Her husband didn't really care much what she did as long as she kept his business afloat. She grinned as she recalled the chaos that she'd found his business was in when she had stepped in to help him out.

Yes, she had gained more power, vastly so, now that she reflected upon the events of her life. She may have lost her arms, but she gained vast power and influence, especially because of her close association with the Church of Jehosanity. That had enabled her to remarry and become the Empress. "In a man's world, I did what I had to do to gain power, wealth, and fame," she defended her actions to the walls of her cabin.

As the days dragged on, she began to see what she had given up to gain all that wealth and power. It hit her like a rock! In her current circumstances, she was now totally helpless and utterly dependent upon this nurse for everything! Worse, she'd worn these Annelise outfits all her adult life as part of her overall package for success in a man's world. Her heels were extreme, seven inches high; she could barely walk on smooth surfaces and then only by taking the tiniest of steps. It was far worse if she removed her heels. Her legs had somehow changed, and she could not put her feet flat on the floor and had to tip toe around when barefoot, terribly awkward, and tiring to say the least. She had no choice but to continue wearing these extreme heels. Her aching waist she had put up with all her life. Even when she slept, she wore them, and all for a tiny waist that men would notice and admire, aiding her in obtaining what she desired. Now she could not live without wearing it all the time! When she did take it off to bathe, she could barely sit up on her own in the tub! She was dependent on others carefully handling her body when her corset was removed. For years now, she knew that she had no choice but to continue wearing these constricting, tight corsets as well as the impossibly tall high heels.

Combined with her lack of arms, Selene was almost constrained into a no-motion, no-action type of life style. She sat and talked, but that was about all. She now realized just how miserable she really was. She'd given all that up and now had lost everything that she'd given that all up for!

Worse, she now saw memories of her little boy, Karpos. At last, Selene also saw that she had given up motherhood as well. She'd paid almost no attention whatsoever to the raising of her own son. No wonder he had no qualms about usurping her throne! There was no mother-son bond between them at all. Now she was forty and would likely never get a chance to redo that. She explained to her walls, "I never did like to cook, dust, and keep house. I hated just doing wifely things. Even raising a son was not something that I had any connection to — I wonder why?" In the ensuing days, she could not find an answer to that.

As the weeks dragged on, she began to think about the future. She had money, if only she could get to a Banca del Dio. She could start over. Perhaps in Velona. Yes, there she could begin a new company and rebuild her power base once more. "It's what I do best," she discussed with her walls. "I am an astute businesswoman. It shouldn't be too hard to find a way from this Hieras place to Velona. Heck, it must be right next door, if it takes three months to get there from home."

April 20, Alexina brought Selene her lunch. "Well, the captain says that we've arrived, nearly so. They're gliding into the docks. In an hour, you will be in your new home and can finally start learning how to care for yourself. I suggest that you start with a bath." Selene looked a mess, three months in the same clothes! Never had she ever felt so grimy, so filthy. The nurse had not once even given her a sponge bath. Still, Selene felt relaxed; she could start over and that was what mattered. All this talk of caring for herself was poppycock. Everyone knows that one needs arms to dress yourself, to brush out your hair, to give yourself a bath, and even to eat.

Unceremoniously, a strong man entered her room and lifted her up, billowing dress and all. He threw her over his shoulder and climbed up the steps. Selene started to protest, but then thought better of it as she saw how steep the stairs were, completely unmanageable in her heels and dress. Maybe if she still had her arms, she thought. On deck, she could see a small crowd of people standing on the docks. Soldiers, well perhaps this disgrace could be somehow borne. The man carried her across the narrow gangplank. Again, Selene was thankful for this as well; she'd never have negotiated that narrow board. At last, he sat her down on the wooden docks. "Last one to come, I'm told," he called out to the people watching. "She's all yours." What did he mean by that, she wondered. Selene took as deep a breath as she could and began to move slowly towards these people, wondering what they must think of her and how she could find passage to Velona.

By the time that she reached the crowd, the caravel had already begun its slow slide back out into the bay. She turned to see it go and noticed what had to be a gun ship not too far out at sea. Its sails were down. Although curious, she moved on and saw that the many soldiers had begun to head off in many directions. Several men and women, obviously not soldiers, remained and were at least smiling at her. She took this as a hopeful sign.

"Hello. I am Selene Omela, the Empress of Demokritos, er make that betrayed empress now. I have been kidnaped by Pope Christos' men and brought here. I would like to somehow get to Velona, please." There, she had been quite up front with them.

"Welcome to Hieras Anubis, Selene. I am Elder Cadmus, and this is Elder Damon. We are the original founders of this city, and we have also been betrayed by the late Pope Christos. These are our saviors from Velona. Mr. Renzo Bartiana and his son Marco and his wife, Rosina, and their adopted daughter Carmela." Selene noticed that their three year old little girl had no arms like herself. "Mr. Len Bartiana and his wife, Kallisto. Mrs. Ania West Po."

Ania spoke up, "Well, this is a pleasant surprise, Selene. We expected more women who had just undergone the surgical removal of their arms. This is the Church of Jehosanity's dumping ground for their mutilated women and even a few men. Originally, it was to be a perfect society colony, similar to what used to be on Dorota. Only now, we know that it was simply a ploy to get all the armless women off Megalos and elsewhere. After that, anyone who spoke out against the Church of governments had their arms cut off and were sent here as well. The original population has grown from the initial eight thousand or so to now well over twenty-three thousand, the vast majority are armless, as yourself."

"In spite of it all, the Elders and the original Dorota women had worked their magic once more. You will find that here the women and few men have learned Alternate Ways to accomplish the normal actions of life, Selene. You will find them very independent indeed. However, as the Elders point out, it does take a new person at least four years to master all these Alternate Ways of caring for themselves."

Ania continued, "Normally with new arrivals, we set them up with a willing family, where they can live and be assisted with life and begin the slow learning process. However, since you are the first royalty and are not just recovering from your surgery, I'd be honored if you would consent to stay with us and allow us to help you get settled in. Also, Dorota has learned of our plight here and has sent twenty-five of their very special Givers of the Holy Gift here to help erase the traumas suffered by nearly everyone here. I will see that you also receive this very precious gift as soon as possible."

Selene realized at once that Ania, and perhaps the others too, were treating her differently. Her first thought was, well they should, since I am the empress. However, she realized that her position was long gone, that she was wholly at their mercy. "Thank you. It has been very hard for me to adjust. For three months all I could do was sit on my bed. I never was allowed out of that small cabin. As you know, I have always had servants to attend to my needs. Now I find myself without them and am most desperate for your kind offer. Is there a Banca del Dio here? If so, I can pay you for my keep. I do have substantial funds. Can we get a boat to Velona one day?"

"Come on; time enough for all that," Ania grinned. Who didn't want to leave here?

"Let's get you bathed and into some clean clothes and fed, if you are hungry. We have lots to discuss, Selene," Kallisto added, motioning for her to follow them as they headed back to their place, the ex-governor's mansion. Selene moved exceedingly slowly, and Kallisto quickly realized why, quietly slipping her arm around Selene's waist, steadying her. "Why don't the rest of you go on ahead and get a nice hot bath ready for us?" Ania nodded. She too realized why Selene was moving so slowly, though Rosina had not yet guessed.

As they slowly walked along, Selene noticed that the townsfolk had come out of their homes. She saw hundreds of armless women going about their lives. Many were carrying market produce in a pair of baskets attached to a wooden yoke. She saw kids playing in the streets; many young girls were running around with the boys, only they, like she, had no arms as well. Everywhere she looked, she saw more of the same. She was startled to see a couple of armless men using yokes to carry loads as well. Ania's description of these people began to sink home into her mind.

"All these people — they are victims of the Church of Jehosanity too?" she asked.

"Yes, except for a few who came originally from Dorota," Kallisto answered. "Criminal, don't you think?"

"Very much so. Say, she hinted that Pope Christos was somehow dead?"

"Yes, one of our Velona gun ships sunk his Royal Yacht when he was sailing back from Demokritos. Everyone here cheered when they heard the news, but honestly, it does nothing to alleviate what has been done to them. At least the traumatic emotional scars are now being healed. Yet, they will have to live, as you have, without their arms for the rest of their lives. I kind of wish the pope had been captured and had his arms removed," Kallisto added, slightly testy. Selene grinned; she liked that thought.

For the rest of that day, Selene constantly was taken by complete surprise at every turn. Inside the fancy mansion, the many women who were attending her needs were as armless as she was. Yet, they helped bathe her, washed out her hair, and even fed her. Several actually cooked their evening meal. How? Selene had no idea at all. She was just shocked to see these women actually doing all these things.

However, Ania and Kallisto had to help in several ways. Renzo, Len, Kallisto, and Ania all guessed right about Selene's physical condition, and the two women lent a hand and verified it. After peeling off the many layers of her filthy satin dress, they found that Selene was wearing a very tight corset and had a very tiny waist. She was also wearing the impossibly high Annelise oxfords. This all four had guessed would be the case as well as the consequences, which if so, would make Selene unique among the other women here.

After removing her heels, Kallisto asked Selene if she could walk around a bit. "It is terribly hard, but okay," Selene replied and attempted to walk some on her tiptoes. After sitting again, the two examined her feet closely. It was obvious that she could not get her feet to go flat on the floor. She had no choice at all but to walk on her tiptoes. This would make it vastly more difficult for her to learn the Alternate Ways because she would have to be wearing these heels, which someone would have to tie and untie for her. All the other women wore slip on shoes, which they could slide on and off at will, whenever they needed their toes and feet for some action. Selene could not.

They also discovered just how weak her waist and back muscles were. Once the corset was removed, Selene had extreme difficulty holding her body in any position. It was as if her waist had somehow turned to rubber. Great care had to be exercised when handling her body this way. By the time that Selene was bathed and her long hair washed, dried, and brushed out, the other women here in the mansion also realized that Selene was going to have far more problems learning the Alternate Ways. For example, with the corset on, Selene could not get her foot even close to her mouth to feed herself the way these women did. Perhaps if she limbered up she could get it closer, but being unable to bend would cause problems far beyond just feeding herself. Ania now realized that she was quite right in intervening on Selene's behalf, insisting that she come live with them, instead of another willing family.

Once bathed, they had no choice but to lace Selene back into her corset. "Oh, this one is so tight and it is so hard to breathe, but now I can at least move around. I am almost useless without it. How strange," she replied. They also put her Annelise heels back on her feet as well. At least she could walk this way, albeit slowly compared to everyone else.

"I'm afraid that there are no fancy ball gowns anywhere in Hieras,

Selene. At least these simple cotton dresses are easy to put on and take off," Ania explained. "Plus they are cool. It gets hot around here in the summer, I'm told."

"Thanks, I feel like a new woman. I so needed that bath. Thank you all. Though it is a simple dress, it will have to do, won't it? At least until we can get to Velona," Selene replied.

While the women began cooking their supper, Ania and Kallisto sat with Selene and the three began chatting about what had been going on around Hieras. Selene was appalled at the two attempts to retake the city and with the vast numbers of mutilated women, girls, and men. She then told them about herself as well. By the time that dinner was served, Selene now knew what the true situation was here in Hieras Anubis. That she had been the sole ruler of Demokritos for almost a year and Empress for many years helped her grasp rapidly the actual scene.

Selene was amazed that the armless wife of Elder Damos, Eirene, had the task of feeding her with her feet. Yet, everyone took this as perfectly normal. Even the three year old Carmela was doing a halfway decent job of using a spoon with her right foot. "Don't worry, Selene, we will work with you and see if there is any way you can be able to do some things for yourself. It will take time," Eirene explained, as she saw Selene staring at her with an amazed look in her eyes.

Selene watched the women as they went about the cleanup activities. Using their yokes, the women gathered up the dirty dishes and carried them to the low sinks. True, those with arms also lent a hand, but she marveled at how well these women performed such duties. A spark of envy rose in her heart. These women were so like her and yet so very different. Then, it struck her! These women were very independent, while she was completely dependent on others.

"I have to learn to be independent once again!" Selene suddenly declared aloud.

Ania grinned, "Of course, Selene, it will just take you somewhat longer. We will all put our heads together to work out Alternate Ways that you can do. Patience and practice." Selene thanked her.

Once the dishes were done, Renzo and Len sat down with a pot of tea and began discussing once more just what could realistically be done here. Selene became quite curious and joined them. Len was saying, "Look, for the last few months, fewer and fewer women have been dumped off here. Do you suppose that that man was right? That Selene is the last one? That they will stop sending them here now?"

"Perhaps so, since the war is over and they lost," Renzo replied. "If so, are you thinking what I'm thinking?"

"Time to really figure out what to do with these people," Len replied. "I sure wish that we could just somehow move them all to where they want to go."

Elder Damon joined them, "You know, I've been talking to a lot of our people. After what's been happening here, none of us can ever feel safe while we are here in Hieras. I think that somehow we had all better move. But where can we go?"

"How can you go? That's a better question, Elder Damon," Len pointed out. "Even if you found a satisfactory place, think about how many caravels that it would take to move all of your people!"

Damon ran his hands through his head. He knew very well the answer to that. It seemed an impossible task.

Selene broke in on their conversation. "I know where you can get fifty caravels." The men suddenly turned to stare at her.

"Where? How?" asked Len.

"Well, let's see, the nurse told me that it is around late April. You would have to act within a couple of weeks, I think," Selene replied, looking at some of her mental images of several documents that she had signed over a year ago. Well, not signed personally; she'd had her assistant sign them for her.

"What do you mean, Selene?" Renzo asked.

"I said that I was the sole ruler of Demokritos, didn't I? Well, I signed an order for fifty new caravels to be built and ready for delivery by May 15 this year."

"Yes, but those would be down in Demokritos. That's three month's sailing time," Len pointed out.

"Oh no. You see, we've pretty much used up all the easily available big trees in building our vast fleets. These are being built somewhere up north at a place called San Palo. It is someplace along the western coast of someplace called Southlands. I am weak on my geography this far north," Selene answered quietly.

"Wow! We're on the bottom west central coast of the Southlands, Selene. San Palo is on around the hump and part way up, probably five hundred miles from here," Len exclaimed.

"Yes, but those are Demokritos ships," Renzo pointed out this salient detail.

"I bought them to give to the seven kingdoms to appease their desires for a way to increase the income of their individual kingdoms. If you can get there before they set sail, you can offer them gold to ferry everyone from here to somewhere else. They will be quite happy to do so for gold, since that is their primary goal, to make money for the seven kingdoms of Demokritos," Selene pointed out. "If you will guarantee my passage aboard one of them at some point so I can get to someplace like Velona, I will pay for the ships, that is, if I can ever find a Banca del Dio somewhere."

She had another idea, "Say as yet, they will not likely have heard about my having been dethroned. If you mention my name, they will think that I am still their Empress. You ought to have no trouble at all setting up this business deal, but you had better act quickly, before they all set sail for Demokritos."

"Selene, I could kiss you!" Renzo exclaimed. "You are the answers to our prayers!"

"Careful old boy. If Bethany finds out, she'll tan your hide," Len teased him. Renzo kissed her on her forehead anyway and she grinned. She began to see a way out of this place and into civilization once more.

"If someone will write for me, I will dictate the proper document," Selene said. Ania and Kallisto took charge of that department, while Renzo contacted me with the news.

I took it to Gerardo right away. He was in his room here at our estate, working late as usual. Soon, however, the West Po's were planning to return to their own homes. They were waiting for Chief Inspector Basilio to declare officially that it was safe to do so. He had not done so yet, preferring to be certain before giving his word.

"Well, yes, Bethany, I have been giving it some thought, though I admit, it has been on the back burner so to speak. Something has to be done with those unfortunate victims. We cannot let them stay down there. Hieras is too close to Megalos. I fear that once we pull our forces out of there, Megalos will zoom in and take them over once more. I won't let that happen," Gerardo explained, sliding the papers that he had been working on aside. Suggestions?" he asked.

"How about bringing them here to Velona?" I tossed out. "Once they are here, if some want to return to their own countries, we can arrange that, but in relative safety."

"I think that is wise. Yet, they have such unique needs — you know, twenty some thousand of them," Gerardo countered.

"Well, why not add on a new subdivision just for them?"

"Brilliant. All new construction, opening up a new section, adding more jobs and income, perfect. I think that it ought to be on the eastern outskirts, beyond out wealthier section here, don't you think? That way, the initial crime rates will be lower than if they settle on any other side, especially the western edge, near the poorer sections of town," he suggested. We talked a little longer, and then I made contact with Renzo and told him the idea.

Renzo interrupted the group. "Say, Bethany and Gerardo have worked it all out."

Selene looked confused, "Where's Bethany? Gerardo?"

"Oh, my wife and the monarch of Velona. We use telepathy to chat," Renzo explained. He began to outline our idea of creating a new subdivision on the eastern side of Velona, one that had fishing boat access to the Med Sea, although no direct port for caravels. They could use the main huge docks like everyone else.

The Elders liked the idea, especially when they learned that Gerardo planned to use war retribution to help fund the construction project. I Mind Linked us all together so that we could work out the details more rapidly. Selene was awestruck with this miracle — this Mind Link telepathy. They needed about six thousand small homes, but Damon suggested that they be duplexes because so many men were also helping support a second family who had no male head of the household any longer. This would make it easier for those men and their wives to help the less fortunate woman and her children survive. Selene was appalled at the idea that there were so many armless women with children here and no husband to help or provide for them. Slowly, Selene began to see the real tragedy here.

Six caravel trips to and from Velona would be required minimally just to transport the people. Another three trips would be needed to move their possessions and livestock. With the basic needs worked out, Selene was able to better draft the letter, asking for ten trips to and from Velona, with an option for an additional two. She suggested a payment of five hundred thousand gold for the operation, which would yield a profit of ten thousand gold for each caravel captain. This would be pure profit for them and a great way to get started on the right foot for the kingdoms.

Renzo and Ania decided that they would deliver the message and handle the negotiations. Selene added, "If they balk, you can offer them more, up to say a million in gold, but sometime I will need to get to a Banca del Dio."

"No need, Selene," Renzo replied. "My wife, Bethany, she works at the master Banca del Dio in Velona. She will have the transfer waiting for the captains the moment they land in Velona with the first load." Selene was even more impressed and very certain now that she had to get to Velona!

They returned in the gun ship two weeks later with a signed contract. The ships would arrive in one week, ready to ferry the first batch to their new homes. Gerardo sent out his engineers to lay out the new subdivision and construction began a few days later. The first of these new duplexes would be ready when the caravels arrived in just over a month. Gerardo knew that it would be a race against time to get the homes built in time for the new arrivals, but with the staggered times and enough workers, he was determined to make it work out.

He also decided this was an excellent opportunity to put the older vessels of Vito and Bonito to work. Those Sea Prince sectors had been so completely left out of modern commerce for so long; hence, this would give them paying fares and help rebuild their shipping economy. Thus, he used more war reparations to pay fifty of their ships to ferry the livestock and household furnishings from Hieras Anubis to Velona. As a result, many in Vito and Bonito began to see this as the dawn of a new age for their sectors.

During the two weeks that Renzo and Ania were gone, Kallisto saw to it that Selene received her therapy sessions. The results were amazing as expected. "But I have total recall of everything in my life," Selene began to protest.

Kallisto, who was running her sessions, replied, "That is one very precious gift that you have, Selene. Highly useful and valuable, right?" Selene agreed. "Now take a look at when you got your surgery done."

"Well, I am walking into the doctor's office there in Kefall. I remember that I was feeling nervous about it. Then, I am lying in bed and my shoulders ached. A nurse gave me a drink of water," Selene replied.

"Now what happened in between those two points in time?" Kallisto asked.

"Well I suppose that they did my surgery, but I don't have any memories of it. I must have been unconscious, you see."

"Okay, close your eyes and let's return to that time where you were nervous at the doctor's office," Kallisto coached her. Slowly, bits of the incident began to appear, more and more with each recounting. Then, Selene screamed! She'd hit the actual underlying pain of the surgery! From there on, things became clearer to Selene; more and more graphical images became visible until she'd seen the whole operation, filling in the gaps between her two original memories.

Although Kallisto had removed all traces of the trauma, Selene was not cheerful about it. "Honestly, I had to do it. I needed to do it so I could get more power and control, so I didn't have much choice." Kallisto kept asking her if there was something that had happened earlier in time.

Eventually, Selene said, "Well, I do have these strange images here." They were off and running once more. "I see a man, yes, a businessman. Successful, yes, fine suit. Oh, he has a wife. She's a Woman of the Eighth Degree too. Oh, he is not being very nice to her. He tells her to take care of her own damn needs and not to bother him with it. 'You did it, now live with it,' he says to her. 'I'm the businessman. I have the power and control in this family. You do what I say from now on, you pathetic, helpless thing.' That is not a very nice thing to say and do to one of us. Well, he never actually hits her, just verbal and emotional abuse. He certainly is not appreciating her special sacrifice for him."

On their third pass through it, Selene suddenly opened her eyes wide. "I was him! That was me. I was the successful businessman. My wife did it just to get me to pay more attention to her; she was trying to control me by suddenly being utterly helpless. It didn't work, and it backfired on her. Oh! I felt awful about what I'd done to her, especially when she died so young. I felt terribly guilty about how I had mistreated her. She was just trying to gain a little attention and control over me and my affections. No wonder this life I felt that I just had to do this myself. I knew that it would get me power and control, which it did somehow. Wait, I have lived before? Oh my god. I have. What am I? Who am I? This is so incredible, Kallisto. Suddenly, I have all these memories of that whole lifetime as a businessman." Selene began laughing, and Kallisto ended the therapy session, satisfied that she'd gotten the root consideration out of the way.

After that session, Selene's personality changed remarkably. Some said that she became more human, more sensitive to the needs of others, and more understanding. She took an interest in all the women who were like herself. With Kallisto's arm around her waist for support, she began walking the streets of Hieras, stopping to chat with the other women and girls. It was an amazing transformation, but rather commonplace around Hieras these days. So many women were now getting their therapy sessions with miraculous results.

Selene now really wanted to learn the Alternate Ways of these women. Kallisto and later Ania promised to figure out how to perhaps undo some of Selene's physical limitations that the other women did not have. "Once we get back to Velona, we will devote all our time and efforts to helping you, Selene. It's just down here, we are severely limited in what we have access to, such as other types of heels and such. Still, we can work on getting your legs more limber."

We had all expected to see Selene off on the first wave of caravels bound for Velona, but she surprised us all. "I will go on the last boat trip. I want to see all these women safely off first. They deserve it far more than I do. I can't possibly take a seat from one of them. Their suffering and situations are just horrible; mine isn't."

Towards the end of October, Selene, assisted by the supporting arms of Kallisto, finally walked off the gangplank onto the docks of Velona. I, of course, rushed to hug Renzo, followed by the swarm of everyone else thronging our long gone loved ones.

Chapter 28 Mystery Solved

On June 1, 781, Messiah Bani el Marina and his wife, Tamina, arrived at our gates once more, back from the Arad. Of course, Gerardo insisted on holding a banquet in their honor, and I think that it pleased them to receive such a warm recognition for their part in the Second Crusade. However, it was now time that I honored my part of the bargain with them. They wanted to see or acquire the actual original Holy Gospels written by the ten disciples of the Great Messiah, Jes Amir. They also wanted at least to see the remains of his wife, the Blessed Holy Mother. Why? I had no idea; suspicions, yes, facts, no.

Since many were involved in dealing with the aftereffects of the war, I decide to keep this trip simple. There shouldn't be any real trouble or threats in Mont Blanc, since the Church of Jehosanity had been pretty well wiped out there by King John. I asked my son Nico to come with me; he was now fifteen and begging for some action. We four took the train to Fortress d'Grange, where Louis insisted that Bianca and their son Leroy, who was now seventeen, accompany us on this search mission. He also provided us with large carriage, and eagerly the two teens just had to be the drivers, jostling each other to see who drove first. Leroy won because it was his dad's carriage, and he was two years older. Ah, teens! Bani, Tamina, Bianca, and I rode inside and watched the countryside roll by.

Signs of the war were everywhere, especially so once we hit the main north south road that led on up to the major fork, where one road led to Calgary, one led on into Southway, and one veered to the right to Mont Blanc. Workers were still removing the stone rubble and clearing the valley roadway. A few times, we had to take a wide detour around sections, which were completely blocked from the avalanches. Under normal conditions, we could have made Mont Blanc in one long day's travel. This trip, we were forced to stop and spend the night at a North Point inn. On June 4, we finally got our first view of Mont Blanc.

Brown limestone walls rose high from the rocky, whitish dome peak that was Mont Blanc. Memories from my distant past came back to me as I compared the then and now in my mind. What struck me most was its size. How the city had grown! Now four times the size of the initial walls, the city was teeming with life, though women and children predominated. So many of their young men had died in the war. Yes, life would be hard on these people, but such is a result of wars. Leaders never anticipate losing a war; they never consider the terrible price that their families must endure once it is over.

As we entered the outskirts of the city, we spotted several charred Churches of Jehosanity and as we at last approached the gatehouse of the walled part of the city, we could see the towering fire-blackened shell of their main cathedral. Of course, Bani and Tamina cheered at these sights. To these from the Arad, the Church of Jehosanity represented a total and complete perversion of their religious beliefs of Lord Jehosa. I may have been unique in that I was their Blessed Holy Mother, Bethany Madelyn Amir, wife of Jes and mother of his children. I had been with him throughout his life and was present at all his sermons, along with his ten disciples. I really did know just how badly the Church of Jehosanity had perverted Jes' teachings. Yet, I dare not talk of this among those who did not have strong reality on their previous lifetimes. Such would be "unbelievable" to those who only believed that this was their only life.

"So few men," Messiah Bani commented as we rode through the crowded streets of Mont Blanc. Only one older man stood guard at the gatehouse and he allowed us through after only asking our names. The fortress towers rose high above the manor house. I remembered my Druwid days, when I visited here and stayed in these towers. Fond memories indeed. At the manor house, we disembarked and were met by the new provisional governor, Tom Weston. An older man of fifty, Tom had been the steward of the towers, making sure that they ran smoothly. Now King John had appointed him to oversee the kingdom until free elections for a new king could be held.

We introduced ourselves and he had us come in for tea. After exchanging the usual pleasantries, I got to the point of our visit. "We are looking for the original copies of the Holy Gospels written by the ten disciples of the Great Messiah. I know that at one time in the distant past, the Santi del Dio used to store their valuable items here in the caves behind the towers. By chance are they still here?"

"Well, Mrs. Bartiana, I have been steward here for nearly forty years. I've seen nothing like that. We've donated most of the valuable items that the Santi acquired to the Laird Foundation for the Arts. I guess that's been close to fifty years ago, at least that's what I have heard. You are welcome to go check on the caverns, if you like. We store our long-term food supplies there now. Also, it used to be the king's armory, but they took nearly everything with them when they went off to war."

"Thanks. We'll look around. Say, are there any Churches of the Blessed Holy Mother still around Mont Blanc or the general area?" I asked, figuring the Church of Jehosanity may have wiped them out.

"Well, that is a peculiar question. The cardinal did his best to outlaw that church here in Mont Blanc, but what with all the cathedrals around and so many folks who belonged to it, he didn't totally succeed. There is one on First Street just beyond the walls. The rest in our city have sort of disappeared. However, if you care to visit some of the other towns in the kingdom, I'm sure you'll find many more of them. The cardinal's big influence, you see, was only here in Mont Blanc itself," Tom explained.

After finishing our tea, we headed for the caverns behind the two stone fortress towers. One of the reasons for choosing this location back then was for easy access to the limestone caverns, which so dot this Langdoc region. As I entered, memories of Rea Helios and her art collection and all of her father's inventions that we had rescued from Megalos returned to me, rather overlapping the present view of the caverns. We found grain storage bins and what had been a large armory. I also recalled how they had set up secret doors, masked by Druwid illusions. Bianca and I set to work seeing if we could find those. No luck, they had been removed, and the space reused for general storage. After a couple hours, we gave up trying and headed for the only remaining Church of the Blessed Holy Mother here in Mont Blanc.

This cathedral was huge and very gothic in nature. As we entered the holy place, I sensed a strong presence of some kind of energy field, though I could not place it. We spotted the fleur-de-lis motifs in the many stained glass windows, the symbol of the old Santi and the original worshipers. I also spotted many of the circles with the six pointed stars in them; they also figured prominently in the many tapestries, paintings, and ceiling frescoes. While lacking the golden splendor of the Megalos style churches, this church seemed more attuned to the worshipers and Lord Jehosa. At least that is my own personal opinion. It seemed appropriate that we bow and pray before searching around, if the pastor would allow such.

Presently, a woman entered from a side door. "May I help you? I am the pastor of our Church of the Blessed Holy Mother. Pastor Carol Beltson."

"I am Bethany Bartiana, my son Nico, Bianca d'Grange and her son, Leroy. These are our guests from Juda Arad, Messiah Bani el Marina and his wife, Tamina."

"My! It has been so very long since we have had true visitors from the Holy Land here in our church. Welcome indeed, messiah," she replied, her face becoming animated and a little flushed. "We are doing our very best to uphold the faith in the Blessed Holy Mother, the wife of the Great Messiah and mother of all true kings and queens of Tarra. It has been hard. The blasphemous Church of Jehosanity has all but destroyed our churches here in Mont Blanc itself. They killed my husband, Tom, who was the pastor of our church and head of the Council of Priests. I took over upon his death because those who remained feared for their lives too. I figured that they would not assassinate a woman. Guess I was right. It is so good to have true believers in our church once again."

Bani and Tamina bowed and I said, "I am so sorry about your husband. It is good that the Church of Jehosanity has been put back into its place here and in Velona. Perhaps now, your church can thrive once more. You know, some of us are descended from the Blessed Holy Mother. Last year, the Church of Jehosanity discovered the secret cache of our birth records kept in Nuadilan's mother Church of the Blessed Holy Mother. They murdered the sister who looked after those records, tortured her into

279

revealing the secret location."

Carol gasped so I knew that this was news to her, and I continued, "We attempted to find out what they did with them and why, but so far we have had no luck. Perhaps they have been lost or misplaced when all these cardinals were killed or run out of their churches."

"Oh, this is terrible news. Just terrible. So many lives are now at risk. I will spread the word to the other pastors and descendants here in the Greenway. Still, we may be all right. You see, Tom had our records, which were stored here, moved when the talk of war escalated. He didn't want to take any chances of this church being burned down, as they did with our other ones here in Mont Blanc. Unfortunately, I do not know their new location. I can only give you the clue that Tom gave to me: Our Holy Symbol. Now that the war is ended, I am sure that whoever is now watching over those precious ledgers will send word to those who need to know."

She went on, "If you are one of the rightful kings and queens, you best take extreme care. While I've heard that the Church of Jehosanity was burned down in Velona, you can be sure their Mano del Dio assassins are still everywhere! One of them even came into our church here."

"Wow. What did the assassin want?" I asked, becoming curious.

"To see if we really did have the Holy Remains of King Diget I in our vaults below the chapel here. Tom had no choice but to show him; he held a gun to Tom's head."

"Incredible. May we see his tomb? I've heard many wonderful things about King Diget I," I asked. I had an urge to see where my son, Tegid, was actually buried. I had no idea whatever happened to either of those boys, Tegid or Taliesin.

"It would be a great honor for me to show you; please, it is this way." She led us to a back stairs. As we descended, I noticed that Bani was keenly interested. I could see his line of thought. If they had the remains of King Diget I, perhaps they also had the Blessed Holy Mother's remains as well, since it had been King Diget I who had found them and set up the fake tomb in Nuadilan.

She had to light a half dozen lanterns for us. The vault smelled musty. A layer of dust covered nearly everything. A number of crypts held former priests of the church. However, four tombs stood prominently in the center. On the top of each was a life-sized carving of the occupant. "Here lie the remains of King Diget I and his lovely wife Lina." I looked at the stone carving. It had to be his likeness; his right hand was missing. I knew that he'd lost it in his youthful pursuit of battles and fame as a fighter. After that, he wised up and became a good king.

I noticed the other two. Tears came to my eyes. Here was the final resting place of my other son, Bard Tal, or Taliesin, and his wife, Lia Inez. I knew it was here because the carving showed a woman who had no arms, just as I remembered her. So many rich memories flooded my mind that I could not speak for several minutes.

"Bard Tal was perhaps the most famous bard in the world," Pastor Carol explained, thinking that perhaps we did not know who he was. Bianca nicely covered for me, asking her about him.

I whispered to Nico, "These are your great-great-great-great-great uncles." Of course, everyone else overheard this.

"Wow! Really? Incredible mom," Nico was a bit awed by this revelation. So were Pastor Carol and our two friends from the Arad.

"You have a powerful lineage, Mrs. Bartiana. These two here are the great-grandsons of the Blessed Holy Mother and the Great Messiah!" Carol explained, very much impressed with our lineage.

Bani decided this was an opportune time. "We, the original faithful followers of the Great Messiah and his wife, were nearly wiped out in the destruction of the Arad centuries ago. Now we are strong once more. It is our goal to wipe out this false Church of Jehosanity, wipe it from the face of Tarra! Yet, we need to reveal the original Holy Gospels that his disciples wrote, and we know that the actual remains of the Blessed Holy Mother were found by King Diget I here. Our Holy Quest is to find both of these, that we may then use them to destroy this evil, wicked church. Perhaps Pastor Carol, you know something of these that might help us locate them?"

Her face fell, and I knew that she did not. Perhaps her husband had known, but he was assassinated before he could pass that along to her. She said sadly, "Yes, we know that King Diget I did go on a Holy Quest to recover the remains of our Blessed Holy Mother. They are kept in her original church in Nuadilan, West Reach, and the very church that she founded and preached at for so many years before her death. As far as the Holy Gospels, I only know of the copies that are in the Laird Foundation Library in Velona. Perhaps you have seen them?"

"Yes, we have seen the copies of the originals. They are kept in a very secure vault. Yet, they are but copies. We must see and pray over the true originals written by the hands of the disciples themselves," Bani replied, no longer so excited.

"Perhaps you should visit some of our other cathedrals in our kingdom. Some other pastor might be able to assist you," Pastor Carol offered her best lead. We thanked her and left.

Back at our carriage, Bianca said, "Well, it's not been a total loss. We now know where Tegid and Taliesin are entombed."

"Nico, Leroy, go see if you can find us a good map of the kingdom of Mont Blanc, please," I asked. I needed to think.

We stayed at an inn but found the innkeeper rather unfriendly to us. He'd been a supporter of the king and church and had now lost both. We chose not to discuss things until we were up in our rooms. I spread out the map on the floor and studied it.

"So many towns," Nico pointed out. "Le'Ours, Middleton, Dion,

Drillon, Reims."

What did I remember about King Diget I? Somehow, he was the clue to this whole thing. Then, I remembered when I was a little girl, Lizzy Ann, Alan had told me that King Diget I was building many new towns and cathedrals. He showed me a map, which had the then current towns marked on it and asked me to show him where these new towns would be built. "Okay, Lizzy Ann. Here's your puzzle for today." I remember hearing him challenging me with those very words. I remembered working it out, drawing a circle and a bunch of lines. Well, if I could figure it out back then, I could figure it out now. I stared at the map and then went for a pencil. Soon, I began drawing over the map.

"What are you doing, mom? There are no roads where you have drawn that circle," Nico asked. I didn't answer yet. A half hour later, I had it worked out. They had added the new towns and cathedrals just where I had told Alan that they would be built!

"Look, if you look only at the lines that I have drawn here, what do you see?" I asked.

Bani gasped, "It's the symbol of the Blessed Holy Mother!" Now everyone saw the circle with the inverted two triangles inscribed within it, forming a six-pointed star. Six towns or cathedrals lay on the circle. On the northern top of the circle was Tolous. Going clockwise from there were Diget, Drillon, Middleton, Mont Blanc, and Reims. These formed the six points of the star. On the line between Tolous and Mont Blanc lay La Cross just south of Tolous and Kunigunde. Both were also on lies radiating from Reims. From Reims to Diget lay La Cross and Fons. On the line from Reims to Middleton lay Kunigunde and Le'Ours. On the lie from Mont Blanc to Drillon lay Le'Ours and then Dion. On the line from Middleton to Diget lay Dion and then Colombe just below Diget. On the line from Drillon to Tolous lay Colombe and then Fons.

Everyone began talking at once, pointing out how incredible this all was. King Diget I must have had some terrific engineers back then to lay this out so absolutely perfectly. After a bit, Nico said, "Hey mom, you missed one. There's this Sante de Mere town." Indeed, right smack in the very center of the circle and stars lay this additional town. A winding road from Colombe led to it. Two even longer winding roads led to it from La Cross and Fons.

We only had a dozen more towns and cathedrals to check out. It seemed a doable trip; each town was around ten to twenty miles apart, depending on the connecting roads. The next day, we headed out of Mont Blanc towards Le'Ours. Now we got a good look at the Langdoc region. Limestone rocks and hills dotted the landscape, rising towards the distant Appian Way mountain range. We spotted shepherds with their flocks wandering in search of the sparse grasses. Occasionally, we spotted vineyards, nicely tended. This was picturesque landscape, but sparsely populated for a good reason; few crops would grow here.

That afternoon, we rolled into Le'Ours and discovered a quaint town cradled on a high hilltop, which commanded a good view of the northern valleys around it. Home to several thousand people, Le'Ours had only one church steeple and we headed for it. Here was another gothic cathedral of the Blessed Holy Mother, beautiful in its simple grandeur.

As we stepped inside, I once more felt that peculiar energy flow emanating from within the huge space. It was decorated almost identically to the church in Mont Blanc. Here we met Father Amos and asked if we could tour his magnificent church. As expected, he was more than willing to share the beauty of his prized cathedral, especially so when he learned of the messiah's identity. However, we learned nothing more about the secret location of the Amir birth records, the remains of the Blessed Holy Mother, or the original copies of the ten Gospels.

I suspected that Father Amos knew more than he was saying, but try as I might, I could not get anything more out of him than that we should follow the Holy Path, whatever that meant. We stayed at a local inn that evening and mulled over his cryptic message.

"Maybe he means that we need to travel to all these cathedrals," Nico suggested. "Maybe we should visit them in some kind of order." While that sounded plausible, no one had any idea what that order might be.

The next day, we drove on down the winding road to Dion, again getting there mid-afternoon. Dion had five thousand inhabitants and as expected another duplicate Church of the Blessed Holy Mother. We went directly to the church and went inside the main chapel. Its layout was almost the same as the other two churches. Once more, I felt some strange energy emanating from within the chapel. Father Samuel, an elderly man, greeted us, and we asked for a tour of his church. Although we pretty much said the same things that we had said to Pastor Carol, Father Samuel had little to offer in the way of aid, save he repeated what Father Amos had said. "Follow the Holy Path." We could not get him to explain this any further.

At the inn that night, we asked around to see if any locals might shed more light on what was meant by a Holy Path. None had any real ideas or if they did, they didn't tell us. However, I did notice several men who were sitting in a back corner watching us. They didn't seem threatening, but still I didn't like eyes staring at my back.

The next day, we had little choice but to continue towards Drillon. This easternmost town had a population of closer to eight thousand and a beautiful gothic cathedral as well. Once more, we headed straight for it. Once inside, we found it nearly identical to the others, with two exceptions. One, it was around twenty-five percent larger than the others were, and two, it had numerous tapestries depicting some of the exploits of King Diget I. We got no further information from its pastor. Okay, he did tell us to follow the Holy Path. Grrr.

At the inn, we again spent time chatting with the locals, but once more found out nothing about a Holy Path. However, Bianca pointed out that the same two men who had been spying on us last night were here at this inn. Again, I felt their stares on me. I tried to ignore them.

The following day, we decided to head back northwestward to Colombe. The road to the next town on the outer circle, Diget, was very long and circuitous, perhaps taking more than a day by carriage. We estimated that we could make Colombe by nightfall, which we did, barely. It was dark when we arrived, and we took rooms at an inn once more. After dumping our stuff in our rooms, we headed down to grab some supper. This time, Bianca was alert for strangers keeping an eye on us.

"Don't turn around, Bethany, but those same two men who have been spying on us the last two nights just walked into the inn!" Bianca whispered to me. "We should confront them," she suggested.

After we ate, I grew tired of feeling their stares on my back. "Okay, Bianca, let's go see who they are and why they are following us." I was a little annoyed. She and I walked up to them. Both men pretended to be more interested in talking about the weather and sipping their pints.

"Okay, who are you two and why are you following us and watching us?" I asked.

"We live around here," one of the men replied. From his accent, I knew that was true; he had a deep Greenway brogue, reminiscent of the Highlanders of West Reach. "You are strangers, are you not? Velona and the Arad, if I am not mistaken. Better we ask what are you doing in our country? Why are you visiting our sacred churches?"

He attempted to twist things around, trying to pump information from me. I lied, "Now that the war is over, we are taking our Arad friends on a tour of some of the Blessed Holy Mother churches of the Greenway. You didn't answer my questions. Why are you following us?"

"We are not following you. It is just a coincidence that you happen to be staying at the same inns as we. After all, there are not that many inns where travelers can stay in these remote Langdoc towns. We couldn't help overhearing you were asking everyone about a Holy Path. Why?"

"None of your business." I turned to go, figuring that I was wasting my time with these men. They were not about to reveal anything useful.

"Some things are better left alone," the man replied. We retired for the night, leaving the two men to their pints.

"That was a veiled threat," Bianca whispered to me when we got to our rooms. "We should teach them a lesson in manners."

"Ah forget it. Let's see if they keep on following us," I advised. Yes, I was growing more and more frustrated with this whole business, but I was enjoying seeing the magnificent churches.

The road to Sante de Mere was both long and winding around and about the limestone peaks. I call them peaks, but they were more like very tall, rounded hills, sparse with vegetation. The road was not well traveled, and unlike the previous days, we passed and saw no one on the road. We did see an occasional vineyard and shepherd. Near sunset, we spied our objective, a small town sitting atop the tallest peak around here for miles. At dusk, we finally rode into the town.

At the edge of the village of about a thousand people, a large sign read: Sante de Mere. We rolled past it and began looking for an inn. There was only one, Les Bains. We entered the quaint establishment, and it seemed as if we had taken a step back in time. Oil lanterns provided the only light. The tables and chairs looked to be a hundred years old, though sturdy and simple. Homey was how Bianca described it. I felt as if we were entering someone's dining room. Five older men were sitting near the bar sipping red wine and smoking pipes. Their conversation ceased the instant that we filed inside.

A middle aged man with a limp and a white apron came around the bar towards us. "Welcome strangers to Les Bains. I am Charles Montbolo. Dinner? Rooms? Baths? What will it be?" His friendly voice was disarming and charming, Bianca thought.

"How about all three?" she replied. "There are six of us. I do hope that you have room enough."

He grinned, while the five older men muttered something undistinguishable. I got the impression that they were not pleased to see us; perhaps we were interrupting their evening social hour or something.

"A gold and two silvers, please," Charles replied, "in advance, if you don't mind."

I grinned and dug out the coins from my pouch and handed them to him. He grinned and replied, "Stairs there. There are only three rooms, so take your pick. None are locked. Why don't you take your things up first? I'll have your supper waiting for you. After that, why, Lilly will show you to the baths. We are rather famous for our baths, you see. Only public bath in Sante de Mere."

We got our things, while Nico and Leroy dealt with the horses and joined us. Bianca and I took one room, our sons, another, and our Arad couple, the third. "This is like someone's home," Bianca suggested as we dumped our bag onto the single bed. "Sure is homey and quaint. Hope the food is good. I could sure use a bath."

When we returned, once again the five older men ceased their talking and eyed us. Lilly came out carrying a large tray. She was a kindly older woman, slightly portly, not particularly pretty, but very friendly. We soon discovered that she was an excellent cook. "Hope you don't mind mutton chops, taters, and meal bread. Mince pudding for desert. This is all there is, so don't go asking for seconds. If we had known that you would be dropping by, why, I would have cooked more. If you will be staying longer, let us know. We don't want to waste any food around here. Too expensive, if you know what I mean. Oh, there's plenty of the house specialty red wine. Locally made in fact." We thanked her and promised to give her plenty of warning if we would be staying longer.

"Oh, this is the best lamb chops I've ever had!" Bianca exclaimed. "Melts in your mouth." Her comment brought some affirmative grunts from some of the older men, who continued to watch us.

At last, one of the old codgers finally was brave enough to ask, "You're not from around these parts."

Sipping the delicious, light sweet wine, I answered, "No, my son and I are from Velona. Those two are from d'Grange. They are from Juda Arad. We are here visiting the wonderful Churches of the Blessed Holy Mother. We've seen several magnificent cathedrals so far. We are all very glad that the wicked Church of Jehosanity has been kicked out of Mont Blanc." I figured these old fellows were more likely to be against that church than for it, primarily because of their age. I was right.

"Now you don't say! Well, yes, it is a shame that it took a war to get rid of them. Finally, they are gone. Good riddance, I says. Darts, young man?" he asked Nico.

"Sure," Nico replied, pleased to have been asked. The four other older gentlemen chuckled. After a few minutes, I saw why. The old man, who we learned was called Franco, was the local dart-tossing expert. He skunked Nico, and then Leroy tried it, losing almost as badly. All five men were now warming up to us and chuckling at the frustrated young lads.

Grinning evilly, Bianca said, "Boys, why don't you let a real woman show you how darts are played?"

"Mom!" Leroy protested and sat down, embarrassed. The five men chuckled.

"Ladies toss first," Franco suggested.

"Are you sure that you want me to go first?" Bianca said demurely. He insisted. "Okay, here goes. The objective is to get all the darts in that tiny spot in the center, right?" she asked. I held my head in my hands. She was putting them on! After more chuckles, he told her that was correct. Bianca then tossed all five darts rapid fire. All five stuck solidly in the very center. Three of the men, who chose the wrong time to sip their wine, choked and spewed wine out their noses.

"Okay, your turn, Franco. I seem to have gotten them all in the center."

Nico's mouth fell open, while Leroy groaned, "Mom! How did you do that?" Leroy was thankful that he'd said nothing before now.

Franco had two in the center before admitting defeat. "What say we move a little further back? Make it a bit harder?" Bianca suggested.

"What did you have in mind, ma'am?" Franco asked, rubbing his head, completely baffled at her incredibly lucky toss.

"Golly, this room is awfully small. Okay, how about from way over here?" She had walked to the far wall, as far as one could get from the dartboard. Lilly had come out to check on our meal, and Charles quickly told her that Bianca had just beaten old Franco.

"She's tossing from there?" she said bewildered. Once more, Bianca let the five darts fly in rapid succession.

"Oh darn, I'm out of practice, Franco. I only got three in the center circle," Bianca teased them. The other two had just barely missed the center. Nico about fainted, while Leroy just stared at the dart board.

This warmed the five old men up to us. Soon we were all chatting. "Where did you ever learn to toss darts like that?" Franco asked.

"From my dad and a little from my mom, but mostly dad," Bianca replied. I knew that she meant Renzo — well actually, Dita. Soon Messiah Bani tried it and managed to get one in the center. Nico and Leroy had the good sense to stay seated the rest of the evening.

After we finished our wine, Lilly led us through a side door. Now we understood the name of this inn, Les Bains — the baths. Fully half of the entire main floor was devoted to a huge bathhouse. You had your choice of tubs or a large pool. We chose the pool because we could all bathe at once. Lilly had soap and towels laid out for us. She explained that the mineral waters came up from the ground nice and warm all year round. Their inn was relatively famous for their bath. Some claimed the mineral waters could actually heal the sick. An hour later, completely relaxed, pink skinned, and warm, we headed to our rooms and slept the sleep of babes!

The next day, we walked over to the small Church of the Blessed Holy Mother. Unlike the others that we had visited, this one was small and relatively humble. There was no fancy gothic architecture here. Rather this one was plain limestone block. Its many stained glass windows were exquisitely done and we saw the familiar motifs of the circle with its inscribed six-pointed star and many fleur-de-lis. We stepped inside, and I was reminded of my own first church that we built in Nuadilan centuries ago. That original wooden structure was later redone in stone. I suddenly felt like I was back in those olden days as Bethany Madelyn Amir. I half expected to see my daughter Sarah come walking out of a door!

This time, the energy radiating from this church was perhaps twice as strong as the others had been! It made one feel holy, if one can say such. A door opened and an elderly priest walked into this main chapel. "Good morning. Services are at ten on Saturdays. Evening masses are at seven. I am Father Ben Brockhurst."

We introduced ourselves, and I explained our mission, that we were looking for the ledgers of birth records, for the actual tomb of the Blessed Holy Mother, and the original Holy Gospels. As I finished up, the door opened, and the two men who had been spying on us at the last three inns walked inside, nodding to Father Ben.

"These folk have come to see the Holy Ledgers, the tomb, and the

Gospels," Father Ben said to the two men. Apparently, he knew both of them.

The one who had done the talking the other night stepped up to us, while the other remained by the door, as if guarding it. "What do you know of the Holy Ledger? What is its importance to you? Why do you seek such a thing?" he asked in a firm manner.

Before I could answer, Messiah Bani replied. "I am Messiah Bani el Marin. I am of the ancient Qaam Sect, the true believers of the Great Messiah and Bethany Madelyn Amir, the Blessed Holy Mother. We have come seeking the truth and knowledge of those who are Lord Jehosa's rightful kings and queens of Tarra, not these imposters who have been ousted."

"I am Bethany Bartiana, daughter of Luisa Angela, daughter of Fredio Brandy, son of Lilly Sue Benito, daughter of Sarah Amber Benito, daughter of Lilly Ann Penton, daughter of Sarah Elizabeth Amir, daughter of Jes and Bethany Amir." I spouted my precise lineage, hoping somehow to impress this man into divulging more information.

"Our original records were kept at the church in Nuadilan. Later, they were kept at the church in Velona. However, last year, the Mano del Dio tortured the sister who kept the records in Nuadilan. They killed her and stole the records. Fortunately, others in the past made copied of the originals, so the records in Velona are pretty complete all the way back. Part of my mission is to warn the keeper of the records here in the Greenway to be alert for the Mano del Dio, who may well attempt to steal them."

"I see. I believe that can be arranged," the man said. "What about the rest of your request?" Damn, this man was not divulging anything!

"Okay, we were called in by that very church in Nuadilan to investigate the supposed theft of the remains of the Blessed Holy Mother. We went there and conducted our investigation only to prove conclusively that King Diget I did not in fact entomb the remains in the sarcophagus that he had carven for that purpose. The tomb was and always has been empty. Thus, we presume that King Diget I reconsidered and put her remains in another location. We know that he had a duplicate sarcophagus made only a week after he ordered the original. We know he had the second one shipped over to the mainland from West Reach. Since King Diget I lived here in the Greenway and was obviously a devout follower of the Blessed Holy Mother, we conclude that somewhere around here lie her remains. Particularly so, because of the Holy Alignment of the cathedrals of this area." I quickly outlined the towns forming the circle and those that formed the crossing of the six lines that made the two triangles.

"Until recently, I was not aware that this town existed. Yet, it lies in the very center of that architectural Holy Symbol." Suddenly, I realized the name of this town: Sante de Mere was a conjunction of two dialects. It meant Holy Mother. "We are standing in this church here at the center, the

Holy Mother. What better place to hold the remains of our Blessed Holy Mother?" I rested my case. Now I was certain that her remains lay somewhere within or under this very church! King Diget I's mystery was solved as far as I was concerned. He'd realized that her remains would never be safe over in West Reach. He brought them here and placed them in the very center of her holiest of shrines, the dozen cathedrals that he built in her honor, this one being the thirteenth, but somehow very different.

"Yes! Bethany! Her Holy Remains *must* lie here!" Messiah Bani exclaimed, following my reasoning.

The man stared long at me before answering, "Perhaps that can be arranged. What of the third request?"

I let Bani answer that one, since it was he who was insisting on finding the original copies. "We Qaam, the eternally faithful of Lord Jehosa and his son and his Holy Wife, have embarked on a Holy Mission to destroy once and for all time this vile and wicked perversion, this Church of Jehosanity. To do so, we need the original Holy Gospels written by the hands of the ten Holy Disciples of the Great Messiah. We must see the originals."

The man asked, "Have you not seen the copies in the vaults of the Laird Foundation Library? Those were authentic reproductions made soon after the Santi del Dio found them in the desert of Arad."

"Yes, but they are copies. We must see the originals. We must show them to the world if we are to expose these evil, wicked men," Bani tried to explain.

"Perhaps they may be seen," the man replied, again completely non-committal. Just who was this man?

"If you will finish your visit to this Holy Church and return to your inn, I will see what can be done and meet with you in a day or two. I can promise you no more," he added, again far too non-committal for my liking. I knew that the tomb must be here, probably somewhere below us. More than likely, so were the Gospels and the Holy Ledgers. He was resolute, and we had little choice but to do as he said. Father Ben held a brief prayer service for us all and we left the little church.

We walked slowly back towards the inn. With nothing else to do, we all decided to stroll around the village. The day was warm and pleasant, plenty of sunshine. Children were playing in the streets, and we visited their local farmer's market. Munching on some early pears, we continued our stroll. Bianca and I spotted a quaint shop and decided to go shopping, while the boys, quite bored, decided to go back to the inn and drink wine and shoot darts. Bani and Tamina went for a stroll on their own.

"Look at these quilts, mom," Bianca gushed her enthusiasm. The shop had a dozen of the most incredible handmade quilts that we'd ever seen. Gay colors predominated. The shopkeeper told us that several village ladies made these and sold them to him from time to time. One was called a single wedding ring, another the double wedding ring, and a third was the windmill. The workmanship was first rate and the quilting stitches, tiny and even. Bianca and I bought the entire dozen! The shopkeeper was extraordinarily pleased with this sale; he made a tidy profit in just one day. I suspected that he had just sold a year's worth of quilts. Yes, we had a bit trouble carrying all twelve quilts back to the inn.

As evening came, the five older men returned and dined with us. Unfortunately, the boys had already consumed too much wine and headed off to bed right after eating another superb meal by Lilly. Bianca played some darts with the men and we chatted a while before turning in for the night.

The next morning was time for services, and Franco and Lilly invited us to join everyone in the village for the morning services. We joined them and walked to the lovely church. Nearly everyone in the whole village was there, packing the pews. Pastor Ben held a service remarkably similar to those that I had given over a century ago as the Blessed Holy Mother. Evidently, my sermons had been passed down from pastor to pastor all these years. It was refreshing to hear these people learning about the Seven Aspects of Life. If everyone lived by those ideas, the world would be a better place. After the service ended, we wandered out along with the many other villagers, all chatting away.

The man who had promised to get back to us slipped quietly to my side from seemingly nowhere. "We will come and get you this evening at seven. Be ready." He veered off into another direction before I could reply.

Come seven, we were more than ready. Bani and Tamina were very excited; finally their quest may be realized, at least in part. I did not see anyone just handing over the remains or the Gospels. The man entered the inn and motioned to me. We six headed out after him. The sun was setting behind the western low mountains. He said nothing as we walked back to the church.

Once we entered, we saw eight other men were there along with Father Ben. After he shut the door, our man said, "If you wish to proceed, we must blindfold you and lead you to what you seek. Do you so consent?" We did, of course. Though Bianca and I could see without our eyes, we kept quiet about this. We were led into a side room and then through a secret stone door that had been previously slid open to one side, revealing a long set of descending stairs. The men held onto us and made sure that we negotiated the stairs without mishap. Then we walked down a long tunnel until at last we entered a large room. Two dozen lanterns provided good illumination. Our blindfolds were removed.

"On that table are the Holy Ledgers, while on the other table are the ten Holy Gospels. If you wish to handle either, we must insist that you wear the protective gloves you see there. The other that you seek lies yonder."

While Bani and Tamina rushed to see the Gospels, we four headed for the large sarcophagus. It was precisely identical to the one we'd seen back in Nuadilan, only for our benefit, they had slid the cover open, revealing a collection of bones and a skull. They had carefully arranged them to resemble the way they were in my original body. I smiled; it was the right remains. The Grey Creature had smashed in my head with his hand-held device and the skull reflected that damage. So my son had really gone off searching for my dead body. What was strange is that so many people now worshiped these silly bones, for that was all that they were, just bones.

Next, I looked over the Holy Ledgers. To my amazement, I saw that this set also contained nearly everything that we had written in ours back in Velona! They also contained a copy of everything that had been kept in Nuadilan. I felt somewhat better about all this. At least, there was still one complete record of all these births, though I still didn't think that all this fuss was worth much.

I noticed that both Bani and Tamina had tears in their eyes; emotions overcame them completely, even more so when they bent over the remains. Both prayed for quite some time over the sarcophagus. The Gospels looked much as I had remembered them, perhaps a bit more yellowed with age.

Finally, the man spoke. "You must forgive our extreme secrecy, Mrs. Bartiana, Nico. I am called George le Mont. I am the leader of the GMSB, a secret organization founded by King Diget I, shortly after his return from West Reach, when he brought these Holy Remains back with him. We are the Gardes de la Mère Sainte Bénie. We are the protectors of the Blessed Holy Mother and their children, the rightful kings and queens of Tarra."

He elaborated, "Yes, we have made periodic trips in secret to both Nuadilan and Velona to copy your records. Ours here are the complete records of all the Holy Children. Well, unless there have been some additional entries within the last few months. We will continue our constant vigilance and duty to all your heirs and never allow these records to fall into the hands of our enemies, the Church of Jehosanity."

"Yes, King Diget I realized that these remains could not be well protected in Nuadilan and so he brought them here in secret. Few on Tarra know of their location. No one other than you has ever worked out their location here in Sante de Mere. I bow to your great wisdom, Mrs. Bartiana." I smiled.

He continued, "I am afraid that for security reasons, we cannot allow you to see where this room is located. I can say, as you probably have guessed, that we brought the Holy Ledger and the Gospels here from their secret and secure hiding places, and will return them once you have left this evening."

"Know this, Mrs. Bartiana and Nico, that the GMSB is a large organization and a very secret one. Few even know of our existence; we wish to remain anonymous, for obvious reasons. I am their Maître Grand. You will not know the name of any other member of our organization. Yet, we will know of you and keep watch over you. We are the protectors of the Holy Line."

"Yes, but," Messiah Bani interrupted, "we, the faithful Qaam, could use these — the Blessed Holy Mother's remains and these original Gospels — we could use these to bring down the evil, wicked Church of Jehosanity! Without them, we cannot do this. Please, you must help us destroy his church!"

"Messiah Bani, as noble and worthy as your goal is, I am afraid that now is *not* the time for these to be revealed unto the world. You have the copies in the Laird Library; use them, for they are an exact copy, though not in the same hand as the originals. They are word for word the same. Use them," George le Mont suggested. "Now is not the time for these to be revealed unto the world."

"But why?" he pleaded.

I intervened. "Because these Gospels have been published in several languages already and widely dispersed. Yet, nothing has come of their existence. They have not changed people's minds about the distorted and perverted versions that the Church of Jehosanity distribute. Secondly, the Mano del Dio would love to get their hands on this list of heirs. Long ago, they began assassinating us and very nearly did wipe out the entire line. We cannot risk the lives of so many just now. Look, the suicide bombers nearly wiped out all of us in Velona. No, the risk is too great at this time. As far as her remains go, the Church can just claim that they are anyone's bones in that sarcophagus. It will be difficult to prove otherwise to the world. Perhaps one day the engineers will have invented a way actually to date these remains and prove that they come from 603 and even perhaps who she was. Just now, the time is not right for these to be revealed. They would no longer be safe from the long arm of the Church of Jehosanity."

George nodded humbly to me, "You are worthy of our love and respect. We too were greatly saddened by the bombers who killed so many of the West Po's over whom we were watching. I hate to say this, but we did not see that one coming and failed utterly to protect them. Since then, we are more determined than ever to maintain these items in secret for that day in the future when it will be time for them to be revealed." I knew what he meant. Bani and Tamina also realized the wisdom of what I said, and at last accepted the fact that their Holy Quest was at an end. They had seen the actual remains, prayed over them, seen and read a bit from the original Holy Gospels, and seen the ancient documents, which defined the Holy Lineage from their Great Messiah and his wife. With this, they would be content. Few had ever seen even this much.

"Now it is time that you return to your inn and your lives," George suggested. Again, blindfolded, we were led up and out into the main chapel before the blindfolds were removed.

I took George aside for a private word. "I didn't know that your group was looking after us. Do you know about the Forze Segrete?"

"Yes we do. Linda d'Grange did well to establish them worldwide. Our Maître Grand at that time suggested that idea to her."

"Might I ask the name of your Maître Grand who suggested it to Linda?" I asked.

"You may. It was Chaucer d'Grange, her husband. She never did know that Chaucer was our Maître Grand or that our organization existed. Our first Maître Grand was none other than Lia Inez Amir, the wife of the Bard Tal as he is known in your land." I smiled broadly. I knew her well, and yet I had not known that she had been a part of this organization or that she was its first leader. Amazing what I had not known back then!

"George, you do not know what these simple facts mean to me! Incredible, just incredible. Thank you." I gave him a hug and finally got a blush out of him.

"Though we may never meet again, Mrs. Bartiana, it has been my greatest honor to have met you and shown you what we all are guarding until the Day of Revelation is at hand! Again, I am utterly amazed that you discovered this place and us. No one since King Diget I has ever done so on their own."

I don't know why I did what I did next; perhaps it was just the spur of the moment thing. "George, are you aware that we are all immortal spiritual beings that inhabit for a time these fleshly bodies?" He nodded that he did, though I had no way of knowing for sure. "Well, I have had many bodies here on Tarra. King Diget I and Taliesin were my sons back then and before that Jes Amir was my husband. So it is very hard to hide too much from me. Eventually, I find out, though I must admit that in this case, my children did a terrific job keeping this one from me. I had no idea of your existence all these many, many years. I compliment you and all those in your organization for a job very, very well done. If you ever need anything, let me know. Again, please share this with those that you trust. Thank you, George le Mont, if that is actually your name." I grinned and he, though terribly awed and nearly white as a ghost, grinned sheepishly back at me. Who calls themselves George the Mount, eh?

Satisfied and a bit humbled, we walked back to the inn. The next day, we decided to take the long, winding road north to La Cross and then down to Kunigunde and on into Mont Blanc. That way we could visit two more of these magnificent cathedrals. We really didn't want to backtrack the way that we had come.

During the ride, I asked Bani what he would do next. "We are committed to the complete destruction of the Church of Jehosanity. I had thought by revealing the true Gospels and the Blessed Holy Mother's remains that they would convince those who have been duped into believing in this church to forsake it. Now I see that will not be enough. As you have said, the actual Holy Gospels have been available in several languages and has done nothing to stop them, not even in Velona. Rather, we have seen that it is deeds that stop the Church of Jehosanity, so that must now be the road we Qaam must follow if we are to achieve a Holy Victory."

I didn't ask him what precisely he meant by this. When we returned to d'Grange, Louis arranged passage for the two back to New Barq. I stayed on a few more days before Nico and I returned home. Once there, I held a large group meeting for all of us who were of the Amir line and explained all we had discovered. I didn't want the knowledge to die with me. With everyone knowing about the tomb, the ledgers, the Gospels, especially the GMSB, that is, the Gardes de la Mère Sainte Bénie, and their Maître Grand, this George le Mont, surely this time the knowledge would not be lost.

Chapter 29 Long Loose Ends

With the messiah and his wife on their way home and with the war reparations well underway, there was little that I needed to do as we entered July 781. While I looked forward to Renzo's return, that would not be for months yet. All this ancient history revelations had my mind focused on such memories. Thus, it wasn't a surprise when Dianna dropped by one night to chat privately with me.

"When you and Bianca were bringing Ann back through those secret caverns and tunnels beneath the Appian Way, she said that she found stairs and tunnels going upwards and a room full of alien stuff," Dianna began. At once, I knew where this was headed. As our resident alien artifact engineer for so many lifetimes now, she just had to get into that room!

"Okay, okay, I can take a hint. We should go check it out, right, Dianna?" I interrupted her.

"Well, now seems like a very good time to do that. I mean, the war is over and things are getting back to normal. Soon we will have to help out all the Hieras folks, so now is a good time, don't you think?" she asked, though almost begging me.

"Okay, let's do it. I'll contact Bianca and see if she is free to join us," I agreed and suggested. Dianna was greatly relieved! Arturo wanted to come along just to see what we had indirectly discovered. Besides, on our last trip, he was good at the tunnel navigation. I insisted that we limit our party to just the four of us. The fewer who knew about this the better. Besides, there shouldn't be any trouble at all. A short trip over the Paese de Dio and into the tunnels — not much chance of anything going wrong.

Since we intended to bring as much back with us as we could, Dianna decided that we should bring along four packhorses. Driving a wagon across those grasslands would leave too conspicuous a trail. I still intended to limit knowledge of this secret passage under the impassable Appian Way. On July 7, we four set out from Alta, where we stopped to pick up Bianca at their ranch home. She had gotten the supplies for us as well as all the horses we needed from their ever-growing herd.

After four easy going days along the green grasslands of the Paese, we four felt totally at peace with the world, contented just to be alive and admiring this God's Country. Late that fourth day, we spied the black cavern entrance and spent the night just inside, making our preparations for the exploration.

Sitting around our last campfire inside the protection of the cavern walls, Bianca explained, "Well, it is about one third the total distance through the tunnels from here, two-thirds from the other side where we began last time. Two days walking and we should be there. I am not sure if we can take the horses up, though. If the stairs or whatever it was is too steep, we might have to leave them here."

"We can't leave them alone in the dark," Arturo pointed out. "If we must leave them behind, perhaps it will be best if I remain with them. If you run into troubles, I guess you can somehow lead me up to yourselves. I hate missing out on all the exploring, but we just cannot leave the horses alone in the dark." I agreed, though I hated for Arturo to miss out on the discoveries, if we made any.

For two days, we four led our eight horses through the pitch-black darkness of the cool tunnels. While we each kept our blue light spells constantly activated, we only used our lanterns sparsely and only at meal times. Late that second day, Bianca took us off to the left at a spur junction. We camped in another large chamber that night, one that we had never been in before. There was no horse dung on the floor, either fresh or ancient.

The next morning, we began our ascent from this cavern. While the way was steep, the horses managed well. The passage twisted and turned, but ever wound its way upwards. Compared to the easy walking we'd done thus far, this incessant climbing wore all of us out, even with our frequent breaks. Sleeping that night was problematical. Just try to sleep on a stone floor that is sharply rising upwards. So far, we could not possibly have gotten lost. There were no side passages. It was as if someone had very carefully carved this passage upwards for some purpose.

A bit grumpy, we headed upwards the next day, and towards evening, if evening you can call it here in this eternally black tunnel, we finally came to the side chamber that Bianca had discovered during her explorations to find our way through the tunnels when we were rescuing Queen Ann.

"Oh my god!" exclaimed an out of breath Dianna. "Get out the lanterns!" We had entered a level chamber some hundreds of feet in diameter, though it was not circular, but rather irregular. We had come across the Grey Creature's workshop, laboratory, or storage facility, which one was rather hard to determine at a glance.

Dianna took charge immediately. "Light all lanterns. We must be systematically thorough about this. We have a treasure trove here. Take these coils of wires. See, they are not only flexible, like the fancy communication lines of Arsenio's, but also they are covered or coated with some kind of rubber like substance. Thus, as you can see here from this end, they can support two parallel metal lines spaced very closely together. I bet Arsenio will have a grand time with these wires!"

We lit our dozen lanterns and soon had the room well lighted. All four of us began our thorough search of this place. Dust lay on top of everything, probably more than a century's worth of dust. Hence, we had not the slightest worry that a Grey Creature would disturb us in our search. I came across what I thought was the best find, another cache of their blaster weapons. These dozen would nicely compliment the seven that we now had in our possession. Already, these devices had saved lives, Dianna's most recently.

Arturo found a cache of gold bullion, but Bianca found what Dianna later called the Comm Stone. Not really a stone per se, it was a large disk, three feet in diameter. Concentric rings around it contained writing, letters to be exact. What got Dianna's instant attention away from some unknown machines was Bianca's comment, "Hey, I can read this; here's our alphabet."

All three of us stopped everything and began looking over her shoulders. "Hey, that is the Megalos alphabet," I pointed out, "and that of Tashien too." Two of the middle rings contained their letters.

"Yes, they correspond exactly!" Dianna exclaimed, highly excited about this discovery. "Look, there is the Dorota alphabet and that of the Greenway. Yet, these outermost two rings — I've seen those letters before! Where?"

"Sort of reminds me of the writing we saw on all those mantis creatures' things," I noted curiously.

"Grey Creatures! Bethany, this outer ring has the Grey Creatures' corresponding letters on it. I have studied them extensively. And you are right, this second one looks an awfully lot like those we found on the mantis documents! With this, I ought to be able to decipher so many of those things that we recovered from the alien sights! Eureka, this is the find of the century! Whoopee!"

She added, "We must bring back anything with writing on it!"

Bianca teased her, "Oh, you mean this thing?" She pointed to a wall-sized machine of some kind, which had writing below a number of control nobs. Dianna just gave her and exasperated look! Our searching and examinations ended only when we were just too tired to continue. Arturo had long ago ceased looking and had fixed us up some dinner, if it was that time.

The next day, Bianca and I decided to see where else this climbing tunnel may lead. Dianna didn't want to leave her precious finds and Arturo volunteered to stay behind with her and begin loading the packhorses. She and I took one packhorse with us and headed on up the climbing tunnel. About a quarter mile on up, we felt a cold blast of air on our faces and soon saw daylight ahead. "I wonder where we are?" she said.

"Oh wow! This is utterly incredible!" Bianca exclaimed. We had stepped out of the tunnel's entrance and stood on a relatively flat area perhaps two hundred feet wide. We were at the very top of one of the mountains of the Appian Way. We looked down upon the granite mountains below, with the thin strip of the Paese de Dio clearly visible as well as the rough gorges and trees of Barcella off in the distance. What a spectacular view. Perhaps we were the first two humans to have ever had this particular view!

I then looked forward along this relatively flat space and very nearly fell over! Images flashed in my mind, almost obscuring the present view. There was Jes fighting one of those Grey Creatures! He had wounded it in its leg and was going in for the kill. There was Alabaster Benjamin Crowley, the founder of the Druwids, heading in to help him. I was Mind Linked to Alabaster and saw the images that were now replaying in my mind.

"Bethany! What's wrong? You are white as a sheet!" Bianca, I discovered, was holding on to me. "You almost fell there."

"I know this place," I managed to say and simply Mind Linked her to me and replayed those ancient memories once more.

"Wow! So this is where it happened! Say, where's the rest of the mountaintop over there? She asked. Indeed, we should have been looking at the peak with its pole tower that used to entrap spiritual beings and which had entrapped both Jes and Alabaster. Both were gone. We walked across the open, windswept area towards where the peak ought to have been.

"Hey, look at this," Bianca pointed out. There on the ground was a skull and a pile of bones; they looked human in size. Near its finger bones lay a rusted sword. "Is this what's left of Jes' body?" she asked more curious than anything else.

"Well, I'll be! You are right; it's lying right where he fell, right where I saw his body get clobbered by the second Grey Creature that he didn't see! Those are the remains of the Great Messiah all right." We moved over to where the peak had been. All that was left was a fine powder dust, most of which had long ago blown off the peak. Pockets of the dust remained here and there.

"Well, in that battle between the mantis and the Grey Creatures, we saw and heard a great explosion up here. I bet the mantis disintegrated their installation here," I theorized. "Did a good job of it; there's nothing left at all but dust!"

"I sure hope that mankind never gets their hands on that kind of a weapon!" Bianca declared. "Well, now what? We should have the others come up to see the view. Do you think we ought to recover those remains of Jes? Perhaps have them buried beside Bethany's?"

I smiled, "Somehow, I like that idea, dear. Let's." I sent word to have the other two join us. They were mesmerized by the view, just as we had been. All four of us then picked up the bones and stored them in a large sack, before heading back into the tunnel again. Although it was summertime below, up here on the very top of the Appian Way, it was still a bit chilly.

We spent another day searching and loading our four packhorses with what Dianna most greatly desired to bring back with us. She found a cache of what she called writings. Those filled one whole packhorse. We brought back the blasters, of course, and the coils of wire. Arturo suggested that we leave the ton of gold behind. "Hey, only we know about it. There's something like thirty-two thousand gold here; think of it as a secret stash.

Who knows, someday you might need some gold and it is here waiting for you. Besides, we cannot pack a ton out on these horses."

Two days later, we were back at the tunnel, which led upwards from the tunnel that traversed the base of the mountains. A week later, we arrived at Louis and Bianca's ranch, just at the start of the Paese de Dio. Louis had come to meet us, curious about what we found. He was pleased that I gave two of the blasters permanently to him and his wife. "Now you both cannot be shot by bullets," I explained.

"Or blown up by a bomb, as I nearly was," Dianna explained, as she showed them both how to operate them and to recharge them. "Just be very careful of this setting here. When you activate it this way, it disintegrates everything before it out to about twenty-five feet. Makes about a three foot hole in solid rock, for example."

Over a warm dinner, Louis asked, "Dianna, do you really think that you will learn useful things from all those writings the aliens left behind?" We'd showed him the Comm Stone.

'I don't know. I sure hope it is not their grocery shopping lists, though," she replied. We all laughed. How ironic it would be to have this amazing translation disk only to learn what they needed from the store!

The next day, Louis accompanied us to Alta, where we put Dianna and all the many sacks onto the train headed for the city of Velona. The rest of us headed up into d'Grange to resupply. Bianca, Arturo, and I planned to take the bones back to the church in Sante de Mere before returning to our homes.

Once more, we three set off for Mont Blanc and the unique towns with their Blessed Holy Mother cathedrals. We took Bianca's carriage, and all three of us spent most of the trip riding topside with Arturo, watching the countryside go by and taking turns driving the horses. We had a very pleasant trip back to Sante de Mere.

Entering the church, I once more felt its unique energy flows. Father Ben was genuinely surprised to see us enter his church. "My, what brings you back to our Holy Church so soon?" he asked.

"I have brought something for you and the guardians. Please have George le Mont come here and meet with us. I'll explain it to you both then. For now, let's say that it is perhaps equal in importance to she whom you care for below." I teased him, but I didn't know what these people's reactions to having the remains of the Great Messiah here might be.

Two days later, George appeared at our inn, just as mysteriously as before. One minute we were playing darts with the older gentlemen and the next moment, there stood George. "Ah, there you are," I said slightly surprised. "Let's go to the church, please."

"I didn't think that I would see you again, Bethany. I admit, I am a bit surprised. Father Ben says that you have something for us?" he attempted to get me to elaborate as we walked over to the church.

"I can be as tight lipped as you," I teased him. "You will just have to wait until we are together with Father Ben." He gave me a quizzical look and then smiled.

Once in the safety of the cathedral and with no one else present save we five, I presented them with the sack of bones. "Inside are the remains of the Great Messiah himself, Jes Amir. I know these are his remains. They can be no other's. I will not say where we found them, only that they are his, as I witnessed the death of his human body. He was not crucified on a cross by the Centurions. He devised that hoax so he could escape the destruction of the Arad, since so many there would not believe that he was offering spiritual freedom. They wanted freedom from the Centurions, went to war to gain it, and lost utterly. He and we fled to West Reach."

"I was hoping that you might consider entombing them beside my bones below. If not, would you please guard them? One day, someone may be able to use them to prove that they are really his remains, as well as those of Bethany Madelyn's. They may also be then able to prove the direct lineage of all their descendants, though at this time, I do not know how that may be done. As you have said, George, 'Now is not the time.'" He grinned.

Both men were extremely excited about these remains. "Do you realize that these remains, if proven to be those of Jes, would totally destroy the Church of Jehosanity's claim that Jes was not human?" George asked.

"Yes, they certainly would do that. That church has invented more lies about Jes than he and I could ever have imagined. Yet, one day, we may be able to put an end to that church and their lies. We do not have a soul; we are souls. Ah well, don't get me going on religion," I teased. All grinned.

A week later, we arrived back home. Gerardo insisted on Dianna's being the chief engineer on the new subdivision for the Hieras people. With her approval, I decided to begin work with the Comm Stone. All the many items that we had discovered over the centuries were now stored in the basement secure vault of the Laird Foundation Library.

My first action was to go through all these many items and group them into three sections, one for each of the known aliens. The Grey Creatures had left us with around ten actual documents, if such is the right word. If an object had extensive writing on it, I called it a document for want of any better description. In contrast, the mantis creatures had left us volumes, over fifty of those! We had about a dozen from the Doll Creatures of Tashien. After spending one day reorganizing this stuff, I began to decipher what seemed to be the titles of each of these "documents." As I suspected, some were operational manuals. We now had an actual operation manual for our many blasters! Well, I at least translated the title of that document and set that one aside for extensive study.

After a week, I had the titles of all these documents translated and arranged in groups, with the most promising to be done first. I then held a conference with my extended group and had them go over the list of titles. As expected, Dianna and Arsenio greatly desired to have those, which most likely held engineering secrets, translated first. One whole evening accompanied by five pots of tea finally led to a finalized order of translation. I had now a total of one hundred documents to translate. Some were very long; others relatively short. I ignored the lengths. We based our decisions on their titles alone.

The top five documents that we picked were entitled: Field Manual for the Operation and Maintenance of the Argo5000 (that was our blaster and a Grey Creature document), Design and Construction of an Optimum Prison (a mantis document), Prison Maintenance (a Grey Creature document), Electronic Circuitry Design (a Grey Creature document), Schedule of Maintenance (a mantis document).

With the help of the blaster document, Dianna was able to resurrect five of the old blasters, which no longer were operational, bringing our total to twenty-four of these devices. Many of us felt that these gave us an edge in survival, especially if any of these aliens should reappear here.

I must insert a strong caution here. Although I had translated the documents into our Velona dialect, that alone did not guarantee any real understanding of their contents. For example, many of the documents referred to a distance measurement of a dulcet. In fact, all three aliens used this unit. Exactly how big is a dulcet? I had no clue except that it must be a very huge distance, as it referred to distances between star systems.

Yes, Arsenio and Dianna-Enyo were able to gain valuable clues and ideas from the engineering manuals. In time, I suspected they would create even more marvelous inventions as a result. However, as I began unraveling the other three documents, I became more and more fascinated by our "history."

All three of these aliens belonged to a loose group of star systems often referred to as Federation 19. I gathered that all three were more or less enemies of each other. However, all three civilizations suffered from similar problems. All had "criminals" with which to deal, that was understandable. What I also found incredible was their hatred for their artists, musicians, mathematicians, great thinkers, and creative engineers. Apparently, these three civilizations depended upon things remaining at some status quo at all times. Artists and great thinkers posed an enormous risk to these three civilizations in that they represented change.

While you and I appreciate all the benefits that positive change can bring to civilizations, apparently within Federation 19 such positive change was on par with criminal activities, close to treason! As a result, these people had to be handled and removed from their societies. The problem that they faced was simple. Merely killing the person's physical body did nothing more than slightly delay the threat that person posed to their societies. That is, the person would quickly pick up another "baby body" — a new mantis,

Grey Creature, or Doll body — and soon be back fighting for their desired change.

All three societies had been doing this for an extended period, how long was unknown, a "fleething," whatever that represented. The results were dismal. Those whose bodies had been slain often came back with an intense hatred and anger, which only made things worse for those societies as time rolled on. They had to come up with another way of solving their problem. Apparently, the Doll Creatures proposed taking the person, the being, and dumping him or her off in some remote part of the universe, far from the Federation 19. For a time, this seemed to be the answer, until those so dumped began reappearing back in the Federation causing even more problems.

The mantis came up with a better answer: build a penal colony on some remote planet and imprison the undesirables there. In an unprecedented period of cooperation among these enemies, they proposed to share a common penal colony, Tarra. They could not, however, seem to agree on the optimum method of imprisoning a spiritual being there. All three took advantage of a long running project of the mantis creatures: the development of sophisticated mammalian bodies on Tarra.

Apparently, they conducted their experiments at a place on Tarra called Chichulain. At this time, we do not know where this place may be located. My suspicions tend toward the mostly unexplored continent, in which Wanakan lies, far to the west of our dog bone continent. Each of the three took a batch of the latest model of mammalian bodies and devised their own best ideas for imprisoning a spiritual being inside them. All three agreed on one aspect: when a physical body died, the spiritual being's memories had to be scrambled. Over time, this incessant scrambling of a person's memories would all but guarantee that they would never be able to find their way back to Federation 19, even if they somehow escaped the mammalian prisons.

The Doll Creatures used electronics to bombard continuously the beings who were imprisoned in these mammalian bodies. According to their documents, this forced the spiritual being to remain firmly inside the body and kept their emotional tone very low. All this we had witnessed firsthand in Tashien a few years back. It had been diabolically effective at nearly destroying the spiritual beings!

The Grey Creature's approach involved disguising themselves as one of us, and fomenting unrest, conflicts, and wars. This then occupied the minds of the prisoners sufficiently. Again, we had long witnessed the effects of their meddling in the Sea Prince sectors.

The mantis engineers continued their experiments. Having produced an excellent prison, they continued their prison experiments. That is, they worked on the improvement of their mammalian bodies, unwilling or unable to use electronic methods and unable to disguise themselves and merge into the mammalian population as the Grey Creatures did.

Apparently, their experiments on the Isle of Right and Dorota looked very promising, according to their documents. A civilization without crime and in which every spiritual being was kept busy at the business of bare survival of the species was their objective. That way, there would be no need of prison wardens or extensive jailors to watch over the civilization, unlike what the Doll and Grey Creatures had to do. What I found distressing was the hint that, as I was translating this document, somewhere their genetic engineers were working on genetic modifications!

I discussed this with Sandra, our resident Healer. Neither of us knew what the word genetic meant exactly. Modifications sounded ominous to us both. She said, "Well, Dianna was planning to spend this lifetime working on learning more about our physical bodies, but she got sidetracked onto these more critical mechanical inventions."

"Well, we don't need more Doctor Yi's experimenting," I added, recalling the horrors of my last lifetime and his surgical experiments on Dita and me.

"So true," Sandra added. "You might give Arturo a word. He's into the breeding of plants. He might be able to give you some insight."

I found him out tending our many flower and shrubs, which he had been handling with loving care for nearly a half century. "Ah yes, you see Bethany, each plant carries with its seeds the blueprint of itself. When the seed germinates, it produces a new plant modeled upon its parents. Now, if you stress the parents into some new form, the offspring inherit it. You see these beautiful pink roses? Well, I crossed the red and white ones, forcing a new color into existence. Now each time I plant the offspring of these, pink roses continue to appear. Only rarely does a new plant revert back to its ancestral white or red color," he explained his lengthy research project to me in relatively simple terms.

"What amazes me, Bethany, is that this tiny little seed carries the entire genetic blueprint of the whole rosebush in it. Whatever that blueprint may be, it must be incredibly tiny in size. So referring to your mantis situation, perhaps a similar thing occurs with humans. When a new baby is formed, it carries along with it the merged characteristics of both parents. That's why you look so much like your mother."

He continued, "I do believe that what the mantis document is suggesting — this continued genetic experimentation on us — may be something that we do not want to have happen to our bodies of the future. I haven't seen anything good come from the mantis controlled areas of Tarra. I think that you ought to be a bit worried about it."

I chuckled, "I am worried. I guess it shows. Yet, what can I do about it? That's what I've been asking myself."

"And what did you answer yourself?" Arturo teased me. His grin escalated into a sweeping smile that shone from his eyes.

"I wish I had an answer. It seems that the aliens are always two steps ahead of our knowledge," I replied. I gave him a hug and headed to make a cup of tea and to think.

"Here, try some of this new recipe," Sandra sat down beside me as I fixed my tea. "I call it pumpkin bread. It's a bread really, but with a lot of pumpkin mixed in with it. Try a piece," she suggested.

"Wow, delicious! Brilliant, 'nother one, please," I wolfed that slice down. Before I stopped, I'd eaten a quarter of the loaf. "Oops," I said with half an apologetic look on my face.

Sandra laughed, "See, I told you it was good. Now, how did it go with Arturo?" She sat down and helped herself to some tea as well. I told her what we'd discussed.

"You know, I ought to send you around to Doctor Gasparo Flavio. He's been doing some interesting research," Sandra suggested and wrote down his address. It was 1010 Hampton Way, about ten blocks further west of our place and near the edge of the city. I decided to take a stroll; the day was sunny and quite pleasant.

His residence was both his clinic and his research facility. On his gate, a plain sign read Doctor Flavio. I walked inside, following the signs for his clinic. "Hi, I'm nurse Adelina. How can we help you?" a young blonde woman asked as I walked into the main room beyond the front doors.

I introduced myself and asked if I could chat with the doctor. "Sure, he's got no patients right now. He's back in his research lab. If you will follow me." She led me down a hall, passing several rooms where he dealt with patients. He'd converted half of the first floor room into his research laboratory.

As we entered, he was peering into a metal tube, intently studying something. Doctor Gasparo was probably forty with short blonde hair and pale blue eyes that many women would just die to have themselves. He looked up as we entered, "Patient?" he asked his nurse.

I introduced myself and the nurse left us alone. "Ah, Sandra's daughter. Yes, I know your mother, excellent healer, indeed yes. How may I help you? Would you like to see my latest discovery?"

"Sure. What have you found?" I asked, thinking this was a good way to break the ice.

"Here, have a look through my tiny-scope. It magnifies tiny things so that we can see them." I looked and saw all manner of moving things, for want of a better term. "You see them? Those are living cells from my body." This was fascinating. With a little encouragement, Doctor Gasparo began showing me slides of all manner of things.

"Now here I have isolated what caused so many folks to get ill from moldy bread," he became more and more animated as he proudly showed off some of his findings. "These are germs here which cause our bodies to get ill. Now I am working on finding a way to kill them. You see, every organism has some antagonist. If I am successful, then we can treat patients who take ill and cure them rapidly, perhaps even invent a way to prevent them from taking ill in the first place. These germs are on our hands, and, if one does not wash them before eating, they get into our bodies through the digestive track. Oh, yes, over here is my drawing of our digestive system."

He took me over to a life-sized precise drawing of a human body's internal organs. Now we were off discussing entirely different aspects. Gradually, I began to realize that Gasparo was probably the most advanced researcher in Velona. When I told him so and that I was most impressed with his work, he replied, "Well, yes, I suppose that I am at that. I have been at it for twenty years now, ever since my wife died."

"I'm sorry. How did it happen?" I gave him polite sympathy.

"We were married only a year when she took ill with cholera. After she passed away, I swore on her grave to find out what caused her illness and to find a cure. Well, I've done that. One of those tiny bacteria, more like a wiggle worm, is the cause, and I have found a treatment that cures it. Water, salt, sugar, and baking soda mixed with fruit juices must be given in large volumes. I've treated a dozen cases with my concoction and all recovered nicely. I've been at it ever since, using all the funds that I earn from my patients. If only I had more funds, there is so much more to be learned," he lamented.

"No matter, I have put in my bid to examine all the people who will be arriving from somewhere down south, Hieras something or other. Gerardo will be paying me a hundred gold to give each person a checkup. He wants to make sure that they are all healthy, you see. That will help fund my research another couple of months," he explained.

This mention of funds finally reminded me of why I had come. Doctor Gasparo was one of those fellows with whom one can easily be entertained by his enthusiasm for his work. "Say, what do you know about genetics? My father-in-law has done extensive work on roses. His new varieties retain their genetic blueprint, as he calls it, from their parents, though he has seen some reversion back to their original colors."

"Ah yes, I find this absolutely a fascinating area, Mrs. Bartiana, just fascinating. Do you realize that a human body begins as a single cell? Well actually, it begins with a round thing from a woman and a wiggly thing from a male. These join and form a single living cell. It then grows and multiplies and after nine months, a baby is born fully functional and alive. Amazing, that genetic blueprint must somehow be stored in that single cell. Of course, you can now see why some children look so similar to one or the other of their parents. I just wish that I had more funds to investigate all this further. Why, there is so much to investigate about our human bodies, I could spend several whole lifetimes at it." He chatted merrily away.

Okay, I admit that I was extremely impressed with the man and what he'd discovered. "Doctor Gasparo, I would like to fund your entire research projects, all them. How much gold do you need on a yearly basis to do everything?" I asked.

"What? All? Oh my!" he sat down rapidly; his legs became a bit weak.

"Yes, your research is extremely valuable and highly needed in our world. I have funds just sitting around in the Banca. Why not put them to good use?" I explained. "Of course, the knowledge you gain must be shared with the world."

"Oh my. Dear me, of course, yes it must be shared. This is all so sudden. Perhaps a thousand a year would suffice," he finally answered my question.

"Suppose that you had ten thousand a year? Could you not get larger facilities and hire additional researchers and learn more far more quickly?" I suggested. Yes, I was trying to find a way to get more known about genetics, before the mantis might return and experiment on us once more. I didn't tell him my ulterior motive, however. I would not have been believed.

He fainted. Thankfully, he was sitting down. After reviving him, we talked at length about it. In the end, he insisted that we name this new research facility the Bethany Bartiana Medical Research Foundation. I agreed to fund fully all the research, as long as I received periodic reports on their discoveries and that everything was to be shared with the world at large.

Since all the new construction was going on just ten blocks further to the west where the new duplexes were being built to house those from Hieras Anubis, Gerardo decided this was a good location for the new research building. He simply added one additional large building to the mix. Of course, I covered its construction costs.

The new facility was finished just as the last of the duplexes was finished around the end of October 781. Doctor Gasparo moved into the new huge complex the day that Renzo arrived on the last of the caravels from Hieras Anubis.

When they arrived, we took Selene for a royal tour of Velona, the city, before bringing her to our home. To say that she was impressed with our city would be an understatement. Selene met our whole group, including the two ex-queens, with whom she felt a strong bond immediately. Since Ania and Kallisto had promised to work with her to see how she might be able to learn Alternate Ways, given her severe limitations, we took her in to live with us for a while.

However, per Gerardo's orders, everyone coming from Hieras Anubis needed to have a medical checkup, including Renzo. We took Selene to visit Doctor Gasparo the next day. "Ah, my very last patients," he said with a smile. "Once I have checked up on you, then I can begin my research once more."

"So how are all the folks from Hieras?" I asked him.

"Splendid, considering their awful circumstances. Just fine. All wounds have healed, no signs of infections. They are all perfectly healthy. Still, I believe Gerardo was wise in having them all examined. It would only take one ill person to infect a larger population, you see. It's these little germ things," he explained.

He began his last examination. Selene was the last one that he needed to check out. "Oh dear, you are different from the others," he said with a worried tone.

"How so, Doctor Gasparo? I feel perfectly fine," Selene replied, growing slightly worried.

"Oh, I don't mean to imply that you are ill. Far from it, my lovely woman. You are in perfect health, well mostly. I do wish that you were not forcing your waist to be so small. I can see that you have been wearing those overly high Annelise heels for a very long time. What I meant, Selene, is that unlike the other women whom I have examined, I believe that you will have a vastly more difficult time learning to do things for yourself with your feet."

"Well, now I understand. Yes, I totally agree, but Ania says she might be able to help me overcome these difficulties," Selene replied, her cheery disposition returning.

"Ah, Selene, I am certain that these two physical limitations can be undone. If you can stay here at my Foundation for some time, there is some physical therapy that I can do which should undo both. Please, it will not be any bother, and I am sure that I can handle your needs, unless you would rather stay with Ania or Bethany. Perhaps one of them could stay here with you, as an alternative. How long it will be is the unknown, you see," Doctor Gasparo attempted to explain. "I am prepared to begin at once."

Selene decided to try his therapy and moved temporarily into his new home adjoining the foundation building. After removing her shoes, he began stretching her leg and calf muscles. He worked on her legs for over an hour before giving her a break.

"Oh, you don't have to stop, doctor! That felt fabulous. No one has ever massaged my legs so well," Selene both complimented him and thanked him. Next, he worked on her stomach and back muscles. By the time he finished, Selene's body was more relaxed than it ever had been in her life.

"Now I know that it is awkward for you to go around without wearing your heels, but let's see if you can manage it," he explained. "If you can, your muscles will take far less time to stretch back to where they ought to be."

Selene agreed, but asked, "What about my corset? Shouldn't we tighten it back up? It is awfully loose."

"No, it is tight enough to provide support and yet loose enough to work your various muscle groups. Now then, we need to give your body a bit of a rest. Would you like to see some of my research?" he asked, wondering what Selene might be interested in doing during the necessary relaxation time periods.

"You mentioned this germ thing earlier. What is that all about?" she asked. Doctor Gasparo was off and running now. He began explaining and showing her his collection of slides in his tiny-scope. Selene was fascinated with this.

"You mean those wiggling things are what cause cholera?" she asked.

"Yes, this was my very first research project. You see my young wife died from cholera and I promised her that I would find a cure," he explained.

Sometime later, Selene commented, "Say, Doctor Gasparo, this slide here, number one hundred fifteen, it has the same thing on it as your slide twenty."

"What? There must be an error. Let me see!" He compared the two and was astounded. "By golly, Selene, you are absolutely right! I have a duplicate here and didn't even notice it. How were you able to spot that?"

"I've an eidetic memory, doctor. I never forget anything that I see or hear," she replied.

"Now that would be exceptionally useful in my medical research!" he complimented her.

A month later, Selene's feet finally rested flat on the floor, and she didn't need to wear a corset for support any longer. Now she could begin to learn the Alternate Ways from the many grateful women who lived in this suburb with them. True, she worked diligently at it for over three years before she gained her full independence, but something else far more important than all this occurred. Three things, as a matter of fact.

First, Selene finally discovered love. She and Gasparo became passionately in love with each other long before that first month ended, and they married around the first of the year.

Second, Selene cancelled her plans to open up a new import-export business. Instead, she became Doctor Gasparo's right hand woman. She discovered that she was keenly interested in his work, was good at record keeping, which he was not, and the two of them made an excellent team. She also donated some of her own private funds to help support the foundation, along with mine. The result is that within a year, they had a dozen full time doctors working on various projects under the supervision of these two.

Third, Selene became pregnant! While they both thought that this would not be likely, since she was forty, she defied logic. Late the next summer, she gave birth to their daughter, Annetta. Both doted over their newborn, happy as larks.

I was secretly very pleased with all of this. Now we had real breakthroughs in medicine occurring nearly every month. I saw us as catching up to the mantis and their experiments on human bodies. The more knowledge that we gained in this area the better. Already, thanks to Dianna-Enyo and Arsenio, we had numerous new mechanical inventions and breakthroughs. Now at last, we were catching up in the medical arena.

Things looked very promising indeed. Once more, Renzo and I

relaxed and simply enjoyed life and our grandchildren as they began arriving.
The End.

Other Books by Vic Broquard

Without Warning (fantasy)

The Trident Series: (fantasy)
    Volume 1 The Trident and the Book
    Volume 2 The Trident and the Scepter
    Volume 3 The Trident and the Resurrection

The Adventures of Elizabeth Stanton Series: (science fiction)
    Volume 1 The Evolution of the Path
    Volume 2 The Great Messiah
    Volume 3 Of Kings and Queens and Troubadours
    Volume 4 Chaos in the Aftermath
    Volume 5 Power Plays
    Volume 6 Age of Exploration
    Volume 7 Abducted
    Volume 8 The Emperor and Empress
    Volume 9 A Job Worth Doing
    Volume 10 Degradation
    Volume 11 The Second Crusade
    Volume 12 When Worlds Collide
    Volume 13 Dark Ages

The Lindsey Barron Series: (fantasy)
    Volume 1 The Rod of the Apocalypse
    Volume 2 The Board of Governors
    Volume 3 The Crown of Moses
    Volume 4 Dominus for President
    Volume 5 The National Health Care Program
    Volume 6 States Justice
    Volume 7 Cross and Double-cross

Zoran Chronicles Series: (fantasy)
    Volume 1 A Dragon in Our Town
    Volume 2 Dragons, Power, Courts, and War

Planet of the Orange-red Sun Series: (science fiction)
    Volume 1 When Kingdoms Fall
    Volume 2 Dark Ages
    Volume 3 Age of the Towers
    Volume 4 Difficillis Exitus
    Volume 5 Age of the Lords
    Volume 6 The Renegade Tower

The Return of the Wizards: Twelve Companions – The Making of Wizards (fantasy)

www.ingramcontent.com/pod-product-compliance
Lightning Source LLC
Chambersburg PA
CBHW080731250626
47170CB00011B/2897